BOOKS BY MARGARET ATWOOD

FICTION
The Edible Woman (1969)
Surfacing (1972)
Lady Oracle (1976)
Dancing Girls (1977)
Life Before Man (1979)
Bodily Harm (1981)
Murder in the Dark (1983)
Bluebeard's Egg (1983)
The Handmaid's Tale (1985)
Cat's Eye (1988)
Wilderness Tips (1991)
Good Bones (1992)
The Robber Bride (1993)
Alias Grace (1996)
The Blind Assassin (2000)
*Good Bones and
Simple Murders* (2001)
Oryx and Crake (2003)
The Penelopiad (2005)
The Tent (2006)
Moral Disorder (2006)
The Year of the Flood (2009)
MaddAddam (2013)
Stone Mattress (2014)
The Heart Goes Last (2015)
Hag-Seed (2016)

FOR CHILDREN
Up in the Tree (1978)
Anna's Pet
(with Joyce Barkhouse) (1980)
For the Birds (1990)
*Princess Prunella and
the Purple Peanut* (1995)
*Rude Ramsay and
the Roaring Radishes* (2003)
*Bashful Bob and Doleful
Dorinda* (2004)
Wandering Wenda (2011)

NON-FICTION
*Survival: A Thematic Guide to
Canadian Literature* (1972)
Days of the Rebels 1815–1840 (1977)
Second Words (1982)
*Strange Things: The Malevolent North
in Canadian Literature* (1996)
*Negotiating with the Dead: A Writer
on Writing* (2002), republished as
On Writers and Writing (2014)
*Moving Targets: Writing with Intent,
1982–2004* (2004)
*Payback: Debt and the Shadow Side of
Wealth* (2008)
*In Other Worlds: SF and the Human
Imagination* (2011)

POETRY
Double Persephone (1961)
The Circle Game (1966)
The Animals in That Country (1968)
*The Journals of Susanna
Moodie* (1970)
Procedures for Underground (1970)
Power Politics (1971)
You Are Happy (1974)
Selected Poems (1976)
Two-Headed Poems (1978)
True Stories (1981)
Interlunar (1984)
*Selected Poems II: Poems Selected
and New 1976–1986* (1986)
Morning in the Burned House (1995)
The Door (2007)

ALIAS GRACE

MARGARET ATWOOD

EMBLEM

McClelland & Stewart

Library and Archives Canada Cataloguing in Publication
data available upon request

ISBN 978-0-7352-5339-1
eBook ISBN 978-1-55199-486-4

The drawing on page 13 is reproduced from *The Trials of James McDermott and
Grace Marks . . . for the murder of Thomas Kinnear. . . .* Toronto, 1843
(Courtesy, Metropolitan Toronto Reference Library).

The excerpt on page 532 is from "The Poems of Our Climate" by Wallace Stevens
from *The Collected Poems of Wallace Stevens.* Copyright © 1942 by Wallace Stevens and
renewed 1970 by Holly Stevens. Reprinted by permission of Alfred A. Knopf Inc.

Cover Image: Sabrina Lantos, courtesy of Halfire Entertainment

Printed and bound in the United States of America

McClelland & Stewart,
a division of Random House of Canada Limited,
a Penguin Random House Company

www.penguinrandomhouse.ca

4 5   17 18 19 20 21

Penguin
Random House
EMBLEM EDITIONS

For Graeme and Jess

Whatever may have happened through these years,
God knows I speak truth, saying that you lie.

– William Morris,
"The Defence of Guenevere."

I have no Tribunal.

– Emily Dickinson,
Letters.

I cannot tell you what the light is, but I can tell you what it is not. . . . What is the motive of the light? What is the light?

– Eugene Marais,
The Soul of the White Ant.

CONTENTS

Alias Grace

I.

JAGGED EDGE

At the time of my visit, there were only forty women in the Penitentiary. This speaks much for the superior moral training of the feebler sex. My chief object in visiting their department was to look at the celebrated murderess, Grace Marks, of whom I had heard a great deal, not only from the public papers, but from the gentleman who defended her upon her trial, and whose able pleading saved her from the gallows, on which her wretched accomplice closed his guilty career.

– Susanna Moodie,
Life in the Clearings, 1853.

Come, see
real flowers
of this painful world.

– Bashō.

1.

Out of the gravel there are peonies growing. They come up through the loose grey pebbles, their buds testing the air like snails' eyes, then swelling and opening, huge dark-red flowers all shining and glossy like satin. Then they burst and fall to the ground.

In the one instant before they come apart they are like the peonies in the front garden at Mr. Kinnear's, that first day, only those were white. Nancy was cutting them. She wore a pale dress with pink rosebuds and a triple-flounced skirt, and a straw bonnet that hid her face. She carried a flat basket, to put the flowers in; she bent from the hips like a lady, holding her waist straight. When she heard us and turned to look, she put her hand up to her throat as if startled.

I tuck my head down while I walk, keeping step with the rest, eyes lowered, silently two by two around the yard, inside the square made by the high stone walls. My hands are clasped in front of me; they're chapped, the knuckles reddened. I can't remember a time when they were not like that. The toes of my shoes go in and out under the hem of my skirt, blue and white, blue and white, crunching on the pathway. These shoes fit me better than any I've ever had before.

It's 1851. I'll be twenty-four years old next birthday. I've been shut up in here since the age of sixteen. I am a model prisoner, and give no trouble. That's what the Governor's wife says, I have over-heard her saying it. I'm skilled at overhearing. If I am good enough and quiet enough, perhaps after all they will let me go; but it's not easy being quiet and good, it's like hanging on to the edge of a bridge when you've already fallen over; you don't seem to be moving, just dangling there, and yet it is taking all your strength.

I watch the peonies out of the corners of my eyes. I know they shouldn't be here: it's April, and peonies don't bloom in April. There are three more now, right in front of me, growing out of the path itself. Furtively I reach out my hand to touch one. It has a dry feel, and I realize it's made of cloth.

Then up ahead I see Nancy, on her knees, with her hair fallen over and the blood running down into her eyes. Around her neck is a white cotton kerchief printed with blue flowers, love-in-a-mist, it's mine. She's lifting up her face, she's holding out her hands to me for mercy; in her ears are the little gold earrings I used to envy, but I no longer begrudge them, Nancy can keep them, because this time it will all be different, this time I will run to help, I will lift her up and wipe away the blood with my skirt, I will tear a bandage from my petticoat and none of it will have happened. Mr. Kinnear will come home in the afternoon, he will ride up the driveway and McDermott will take the horse, and Mr. Kinnear will go into the parlour and I will make him some coffee, and Nancy will take it in to him on a tray the way she likes to do, and he will say What good coffee; and at night the fireflies will come out in the orchard, and there will be music, by lamplight. Jamie Walsh. The boy with the flute.

I am almost up to Nancy, to where she's kneeling. But I do not break step, I do not run, I keep on walking two by two; and then Nancy smiles, only the mouth, her eyes are hidden by the blood and hair, and then she scatters into patches of colour, a drift of red cloth petals across the stones.

I put my hands over my eyes because it's dark suddenly, and a man is standing there with a candle, blocking the stairs that go up; and the cellar walls are all around me, and I know I will never get out.

This is what I told Dr. Jordan, when we came to that part of the story.

II.

ROCKY ROAD

On Tuesday, about 10 minutes past 12 o'clock, at the new Gaol in this City, James McDermot, the murderer of Mr. Kinnear underwent the extreme sentence of the law. There was an immense concourse of men, women and children anxiously waiting to witness the last struggle of a sinful fellow-being. What kinds of feelings those women can possess who flocked from far and near through mud and rain to be present at the horrid spectacle, we cannot divine. We venture to say they were not very *delicate* or *refined*. The wretched criminal displayed the same coolness and intrepidity at the awful moment that has marked his conduct ever since his arrest.

– *Toronto Mirror*,
November 23rd, 1843.

Offence	Punishment
Laughing and talking	6 lashes; cat-o'-nine-tails
Talking in wash-house	6 lashes; rawhide
Threatening to knock convict's brains out	24 lashes; cat-o'-nine-tails
Talking to Keepers on matters not related to their work	6 lashes; cat-o'-nine-tails
Finding fault with rations when required by guards to sit down	6 lashes; rawhide, and bread and water
Staring about and inattentive at breakfast table	Bread and water
Leaving work and going to privy when other convict there	36 hours in dark cell, and bread and water

– Punishment Book,
Kingston Penitentiary, 1843.

Grace Marks alias Mary Whitney   *James McDermott*
As they appeared at the Court House.   *Accused of Murdering*
       Mr. Thos. Kinnear & Nancy Montgomery.

2.

THE MURDERS OF THOMAS KINNEAR, ESQ.
AND OF HIS HOUSEKEEPER NANCY MONTGOMERY
AT RICHMOND HILL
AND THE TRIALS OF GRACE MARKS
AND JAMES McDERMOTT
AND THE HANGING OF JAMES McDERMOTT
AT THE NEW GAOL IN TORONTO, NOVEMBER 21st, 1843.

> Grace Marks she was a serving maid,
> Her age was sixteen years,
> McDermott was the stable hand,
> They worked at Thomas Kinnear's.
>
> Now Thomas Kinnear was a gentleman,
> And a life of ease led he,
> And he did love his housekeeper,
> Called Nancy Montgomery.

O Nancy dear, do not despair,
To town I now must go,
To bring some money home for you,
From the Bank in Toronto.

O Nancy's no well-born lady,
O Nancy she is no queen,
And yet she goes in satin and silk,
The finest was ever seen.

O Nancy's no well-born lady,
Yet she treats me like a slave,
She works me so hard from dawn to dark,
She'll work me into my grave.

Now Grace, she loved good Thomas Kinnear,
McDermott he loved Grace,
And 'twas these loves as I do tell
That brought them to disgrace.

O Grace, please be my own true love,
O no it cannot be,
Unless you kill for my dear sake,
Nancy Montgomery.

He struck a blow all with his axe,
On the head of Nancy fair,
He dragged her to the cellar door
And threw her down the stairs.

O spare my life McDermott,
O spare my life, said she,

O spare my life, Grace Marks she said,
And I'll give you my dresses three.

O 'tis not for my own sake,
Nor yet my babe unborn,
But for my true love, Thomas Kinnear,
I'd live to see the morn.

McDermott held her by the hair,
And Grace Marks by the head,
And these two monstrous criminals,
They strangled her till dead.

What have I done, my soul is lost,
And for my life I fear!
Then to save ourselves, when he returns,
We must murder Thomas Kinnear.

O no, O no, I beg not so,
I plead for his life full sore!
No he must die, for you have sworn
You'd be my paramour.

Now Thomas Kinnear came riding home,
And on the kitchen floor
McDermott shot him through the heart
And he weltered in his gore.

The peddler came up to the house,
Will you buy a dress of me;
O go away Mr. Peddler,
I've dresses enough for three.

The butcher came up to the house,
He came there every week;
O go away Mr. Butcher,
We've got enough fresh meat!

They robbed Kinnear of his silver,
They robbed him of his gold,
They stole his horse and wagon,
And to Toronto they rode.

All in the middle of the night,
To Toronto they did flee,
Then across the Lake to the United States,
Thinking they would scape free.

She took McDermott by the hand,
As bold as bold could be,
And stopped at the Lewiston Hotel,
Under the name of Mary Whitney.

The corpses were found in the cellar,
Her face it was all black,
And she was under the washtub,
And he was laid out on his back.

Then Bailiff Kingsmill in pursuit,
A Charter he did take,
Which sailed as fast as it could go
To Lewiston, across the Lake.

They had not been in bed six hours,
Six hours or maybe more,

When to the Lewiston Hotel he came,
And knocked upon the door.

O who is there, said Grace so fair,
What business have you with me?
O you have murdered good Thomas Kinnear,
And Nancy Montgomery.

Grace Marks she stood up in the dock,
And she denied it all.
I did not see her strangled,
I did not hear him fall.

He forced me to accompany him,
He said if I did tell,
That with one shot of his trusty gun,
He'd send me straight to H_ll.

McDermott stood up in the dock,
I did not do it alone,
But for the sake of her person fair,
Grace Marks, she led me on.

Young Jamie Walsh stood up in court,
The truth he swore to tell;
O Grace is wearing Nancy's dress,
And Nancy's bonnet as well!

McDermott by the neck they hanged,
Upon the Gallows high,
And Grace in Prison drear they cast,
Where she must pine and sigh.

They hanged him for an hour or two,
Then took down the body,
And cut it into pieces
At the University.

From Nancy's grave there grew a rose,
And from Thomas Kinnear's a vine,
They grew so high they intertwined,
And thus these two were joined.

But all her weary life Grace Marks
Must in Prison locked up be,
Because of her foul sin and crime,
In the Kingston Penitentiary.

But if Grace Marks repent at last,
And for her sins atone,
Then when she comes to die, she'll stand
At her Redeemer's throne.

At her Redeemer's throne she'll stand,
And she'll be cured of woe,
And He her bloodied hands will wash,
And she'll be white as snow.

And she will be as white as snow,
And into Heaven will pass,
And she will dwell in Paradise,
In Paradise at last.

III.

PUSS IN THE CORNER

She is a middle-sized woman, with a slight graceful figure. There is an air of hopeless melancholy in her face which is very painful to contemplate. Her complexion is fair, and must, before the touch of hopeless sorrow paled it, have been very brilliant. Her eyes are a bright blue, her hair auburn, and her face would be rather handsome were it not for the long curved chin, which gives, as it always does to most persons who have this facial defect, a cunning, cruel expression.

Grace Marks glances at you with a sidelong, stealthy look; her eye never meets yours, and after a furtive regard, it invariably bends its gaze upon the ground. She looks like a person rather above her humble station. . . .

– Susanna Moodie,
Life in the Clearings, 1853.

The captive raised her face; it was as soft and mild
As sculptured marble saint; or slumbering unweaned child;
It was so soft and mild, it was so sweet and fair,
Pain could not trace a line, or grief a shadow there!

The captive raised her hand and pressed it to her brow;
"I have been struck," she said, "and I am suffering now;
Yet these are little worth, your bolts and irons strong:
And, were they forged in steel, they could not hold me long."

– Emily Brontë,
"The Prisoner," 1845.

3 .

1859.

I am sitting on the purple velvet settee in the Governor's parlour, the Governor's wife's parlour; it has always been the Governor's wife's parlour although it is not always the same wife, as they change them around according to the politics. I have my hands folded in my lap the proper way although I have no gloves. The gloves I would wish to have would be smooth and white, and would fit without a wrinkle.

I am often in this parlour, clearing away the tea things and dusting the small tables and the long mirror with the frame of grapes and leaves around it, and the pianoforte; and the tall clock that came from Europe, with the orange-gold sun and the silver moon, that go in and out according to the time of day and the week of the month. I like the clock best of anything in the parlour, although it measures time and I have too much of that on my hands already.

But I have never sat down on the settee before, as it is for the guests. Mrs. Alderman Parkinson said a lady must never sit in a chair a gentleman has just vacated, though she would not say why; but Mary Whitney said, Because, you silly goose, it's still warm from his bum; which was a coarse thing to say. So I cannot sit here without thinking of the ladylike bums that have sat on this very settee, all delicate and white, like wobbly soft-boiled eggs.

The visitors wear afternoon dresses with rows of buttons up their fronts, and stiff wire crinolines beneath. It's a wonder they can sit down at all, and when they walk, nothing touches their legs under the billowing skirts, except their shifts and stockings. They are like swans, drifting along on unseen feet; or else like the jellyfish in the waters of the rocky harbour near our house, when I was little, before I ever made the long sad journey across the ocean. They were bell-shaped and ruffled, gracefully waving and lovely under the sea; but if they washed up on the beach and dried out in the sun there was nothing left of them. And that is what the ladies are like: mostly water.

There were no wire crinolines when I was first brought here. They were horsehair then, as the wire ones were not thought of. I have looked at them hanging in the wardrobes, when I go in to tidy and empty the slops. They are like birdcages; but what is being caged in? Legs, the legs of ladies; legs penned in so they cannot get out and go rubbing up against the gentlemen's trousers. The Governor's wife never says legs, although the newspapers said legs when they were talking about Nancy, with her dead legs sticking out from under the washtub.

It isn't only the jellyfish ladies that come. On Tuesdays we have the Woman Question, and the emancipation of this or that, with reform-minded persons of both sexes; and on Thursdays the Spiritualist Circle, for tea and conversing with the dead, which is a comfort to the Governor's wife because of her departed infant son. But mainly it is the ladies. They sit sipping from the thin cups, and the Governor's wife rings a little china bell. She does not like being the Governor's wife, she would prefer the Governor to be the governor of something other than a prison. The Governor had good-enough friends to get him made the Governor, but not for anything else.

So here she is, and she must make the most of her social position and accomplishments, and although an object of fear, like a spider, and of charity as well, I am also one of the accomplishments. I come into the room and curtsy and move about, mouth straight, head bent, and I pick up the cups or set them down, depending; and they stare without appearing to, out from under their bonnets.

The reason they want to see me is that I am a celebrated murderess. Or that is what has been written down. When I first saw it I was surprised, because they say Celebrated Singer and Celebrated Poetess and Celebrated Spiritualist and Celebrated Actress, but what is there to celebrate about murder? All the same, *Murderess* is a strong word to have attached to you. It has a smell to it, that word – musky and oppressive, like dead flowers in a vase. Sometimes at night I whisper it over to myself: *Murderess, Murderess.* It rustles, like a taffeta skirt across the floor.

Murderer is merely brutal. It's like a hammer, or a lump of metal. I would rather be a murderess than a murderer, if those are the only choices.

Sometimes when I am dusting the mirror with the grapes I look at myself in it, although I know it is vanity. In the afternoon light of the parlour my skin is a pale mauve, like a faded bruise, and my teeth are greenish. I think of all the things that have been written about me – that I am an inhuman female demon, that I am an innocent victim of a blackguard forced against my will and in danger of my own life, that I was too ignorant to know how to act and that to hang me would be judicial murder, that I am fond of animals, that I am very handsome with a brilliant complexion, that I have blue eyes, that I have green eyes, that I have auburn and also brown hair, that I am tall and also not above the average height, that I am well and decently dressed, that I robbed a dead woman to appear so, that I am brisk and smart about my work, that I am of a sullen disposition with a quarrelsome temper, that I have the appearance of a person rather above my humble station, that I am a good girl with a pliable nature and no harm is told of me, that I am cunning and devious, that I am soft in the head and little better than an idiot. And I wonder, how can I be all of these different things at once?

It was my own lawyer, Mr. Kenneth MacKenzie, Esq., who told them I was next door to an idiot. I was angry with him over that, but he said it was by far my best chance and I should not appear to be too intelligent. He said he would plead my case to the utmost of his ability, because whatever the truth of the matter I was little more than a child at the time, and he supposed it came down to free will and whether or not one held with it. He was a kind gentleman although I could not make head nor tail of much of what he said, but it must have been good pleading. The newspapers wrote that he performed heroically against overwhelming odds. Though I don't know why they called it pleading, as he was not pleading but trying to make all of the witnesses appear immoral or malicious, or else mistaken.

I wonder if he ever believed a word I said.

When I have gone out of the room with the tray, the ladies look at the Governor's wife's scrapbook. Oh imagine, I feel quite faint, they say, and You let that woman walk around loose in your house, you must have nerves of iron, my own would never stand it. Oh well one must get used to such things in our situation, we are virtually prisoners ourselves you know, although one must feel pity for these poor benighted creatures, and after all she was trained as a servant, and it's as well to keep them employed, she is a wonderful seamstress, quite deft and accomplished, she is a great help in that way especially with the girls' frocks, she has an eye for trimmings, and under happier circumstances she could have made an excellent milliner's assistant.

Although naturally she can be here only during the day, I would not have her in the house at night. You are aware that she has spent time in the Lunatic Asylum in Toronto, seven or eight years ago it was, and although she appears to be perfectly recovered you never know when they may get carried away again, sometimes she talks to herself and sings out loud in a most peculiar manner. One cannot take chances, the keepers conduct her back in the evenings and lock her up properly, otherwise I wouldn't be able to sleep a wink. Oh I don't blame you, there is only so far one can go in Christian charity, a leopard cannot change its spots and no one could say you have not done your duty and shown a proper feeling.

The Governor's wife's scrapbook is kept on the round table with the silk shawl covering it, branches like vines intertwined, with flowers and red fruit and blue birds, it is really one large tree and if you stare at it long enough the vines begin to twist as if a wind is blowing them. It was sent from India by her eldest daughter who is married to a missionary, which is not a thing I would care to do myself. You would be sure to die early, if not from the rioting natives as at Cawnpore with horrid outrages committed on the persons of respectable gentlewomen, and a mercy they were all slaughtered and put out of their misery, for only think of the shame; then from the malaria, which turns you entirely yellow, and you expire in raving fits; in any case before you could turn around, there you would be, buried under a palm tree in a foreign clime. I have seen pictures of them in the book of Eastern engravings the Governor's wife takes out when she wishes to shed a tear.

On the same round table is the stack of Godey's Ladies' Books with the fashions that come up from the States, and also the Keepsake Albums of the two younger daughters. Miss Lydia tells me I am a romantic figure; but then, the two of them are so young they hardly know what they are saying. Sometimes they pry and tease; they say, Grace, why don't you ever smile or laugh, we never see you smiling, and I say I suppose Miss I have gotten out of the way of it, my face won't bend in that direction any more. But if I laughed out loud I might not be able to stop; and also it would spoil their romantic notion of me. Romantic people are not supposed to laugh, I know that much from looking at the pictures.

The daughters put all kinds of things into their albums, little scraps of cloth from their dresses, little snippets of ribbon, pictures cut from magazines – the Ruins of Ancient Rome, the Picturesque Monasteries of the French Alps, Old London Bridge, Niagara Falls in summer and in winter, which is a thing I would like to see as all say it is very impressive, and portraits of Lady This and Lord That from England. And their friends write things in their graceful handwriting, *To Dearest Lydia from your Eternal Friend, Clara Richards; To Dearest Marianne In Memory of Our Splendid Picnic on the Shores of Bluest Lake Ontario.* And also poems:

> As round about the sturdy Oak
> Entwines the loving Ivy Vine,
> My Faith so true, I pledge to You,
> 'Twill evermore be none but Thine, Your Faithful Laura.

Or else:

> Although from you I far must roam,
> Do not be broken hearted,
> We two who in the Soul are One
> Are never truly parted. Your Lucy.

This young lady was shortly afterwards drowned in the Lake when her ship went down in a gale, and nothing was ever found but her box with her initials done in silver nails; it was still locked, so although damp, nothing spilt out, and Miss Lydia was given a scarf out of it as a keepsake.

When I am dead and in my grave
And all my bones are rotten,
When this you see, remember me,
Lest I should be forgotten.

That one is signed, *I will always be with you in Spirit, Your loving 'Nancy,' Hannah Edmonds*, and I must say the first time I saw that, it gave me a fright, although of course it was a different Nancy. Still, the rotten bones. They would be, by now. Her face was all black by the time they found her, there must have been a dreadful smell. It was so hot then, it was July, still she went off surprisingly soon, you'd think she would have kept longer in the dairy, it is usually cool down there. I am certainly glad I was not present, as it would have been very distressing.

I don't know why they are all so eager to be remembered. What good will it do them? There are some things that should be forgotten by everyone, and never spoken of again.

The Governor's wife's scrapbook is quite different. Of course she is a grown woman and not a young girl, so although she is just as fond of remembering, what she wants to remember is not violets or a picnic. No Dearest and Love and Beauty, no Eternal Friends, none of those things for her; what it has instead is all the famous criminals in it – the ones that have been hanged, or else brought here to be penitent, because this is a Penitentiary and you are supposed to repent while in it, and you will do better if you say you have done so, whether you have anything to repent of or not.

The Governor's wife cuts these crimes out of the newspapers and pastes them in; she will even write away for old newspapers with crimes that were done before her time. It is her collection, she is a lady and they are all collecting things these days, and so she must collect something, and she does this instead of pulling up ferns or pressing flowers, and in any case she likes to horrify her acquaintances.

So I have read what they put in about me. She showed the scrapbook to me herself, I suppose she wanted to see what I would do; but I've learnt how to keep my face still, I made my eyes wide and flat, like an owl's in torchlight, and I said I had repented in bitter tears, and was now a changed person, and would she wish me to remove the tea things now; but I've looked in there since, many times, when I've been in the parlour by myself.

A lot of it is lies. They said in the newspaper that I was illiterate, but I could read some even then. I was taught early by my mother, before she got too tired for it, and I did my sampler with leftover thread, A is for Apple, B is for Bee; and also Mary Whitney used to read with me, at Mrs. Alderman Parkinson's, when we were doing the mending; and I've learnt a lot more since being here, as they teach you on purpose. They want you to be able to read the Bible, and also tracts, as religion and thrashing are the only remedies for a depraved nature and our immortal souls must be considered. It is shocking how many crimes the Bible contains. The Governor's wife should cut them all out and paste them into her scrapbook.

They did say some true things. They said I had a good character; and that was so, because nobody had ever taken advantage of me, although they tried. But they called James McDermott my paramour. They wrote it down, right in the newspaper. I think it is disgusting to write such things down.

That is what really interests them – the gentlemen and the ladies both. They don't care if I killed anyone, I could have cut dozens of throats, it's only what they admire in a soldier, they'd scarcely blink. No: was I really a paramour, is their chief concern, and they don't even know themselves whether they want the answer to be no or yes.

I'm not looking at the scrapbook now, because they may come in at any moment. I sit with my rough hands folded, eyes down, staring at the flowers in the Turkey carpet. Or they are supposed to be flowers. They have petals the shape of the diamonds on a playing card; like the cards spread out on the table at Mr. Kinnear's, after the gentlemen had been playing the night before. Hard and angular. But red, a deep thick red. Thick strangled tongues.

It's not the ladies expected today, it's a doctor. He's writing a book; the Governor's wife likes to know people who are writing books, books with forward-looking aims, it shows that she is a liberal-minded person with advanced views, and science is making such progress, and what with modern inventions and the Crystal Palace and world knowledge assembled, who knows where we will all be in a hundred years.

Where there's a doctor it's always a bad sign. Even when they are not doing the killing themselves it means a death is close, and in that way they are like ravens or crows. But this doctor will not hurt me, the Governor's wife promised it. All he wants is to measure my head. He is measuring the heads of all the criminals in the Penitentiary, to see if he can tell from the bumps on their skulls what sort of criminals they are, whether they are pickpockets or swindlers or embezzlers or criminal lunatics or murderers, she did not say Like you, Grace. And then they could lock those people up before they had a chance to commit any crimes, and think how that would improve the world.

After James McDermott was hanged they made a plaster cast of his head. I read that in the scrapbook too. I suppose that's what they wanted it for – to improve the world.

Also his body was dissected. When I first read that I did not know what *dissected* was, but I found it out soon enough. It was done by the doctors. They cut him into pieces like a pig to be salted down, he might as well have been bacon as far as they were concerned. His body that I listened to breathing, and the heart beating, the knife slicing through it – I can't bear to think of it.

I wonder what they did with his shirt. Was it one of the four sold to him by Jeremiah the peddler? It should have been three, or else five, as odd numbers are luckier. Jeremiah always wished me luck, but he did not wish any to James McDermott.

I did not see the hanging. They hanged him in front of the jail in Toronto, and You should have been there Grace, say the keepers, it would have been a lesson to you. I've pictured it many times, poor James standing with his hands tied and his neck bare, while they put the hood over his head like a kitten to be drowned. At least he had a priest with him, he was not all alone. If it had not been for Grace Marks, he told them, none of it would have happened.

It was raining, and a huge crowd standing in the mud, some of them come from miles away. If my own death sentence had not been commuted at the last minute, they would have watched me hang with the same greedy pleasure. There were many women and ladies there; everyone wanted to stare, they wanted to breathe death in like fine perfume, and when I read of it I thought, If this is a lesson to me, what is it I am supposed to be learning?

I can hear their footsteps now, and I stand up quickly and brush my apron smooth. Then there's the voice of a strange man, This is most kind of you Ma'am, and the Governor's wife saying I am so happy to be of help, and he says again, Most kind.

Then he comes through the doorway, big stomach, black coat, tight waistcoat, silver buttons, precisely tied stock, I am only looking up as far as the chin, and he says This will not take long but I'd appreciate it Ma'am if you'd remain in the room, one must not only be virtuous, one must give the appearance of virtue. He laughs as if it is a joke, and I can hear in his voice that he is afraid of me. A woman like me is always a temptation, if possible to arrange it unobserved; as whatever we may say about it later, we will not be believed.

And then I see his hand, a hand like a glove, a glove stuffed with raw meat, his hand plunging into the open mouth of his leather bag. It comes out glinting, and I know I have seen a hand like that before; and then I lift my head and stare him straight in the eye, and my heart clenches and kicks out inside me, and then I begin to scream.

Because it's the same doctor, the same one, the very same black-coated doctor with his bagful of shining knives.

4 .

I was brought round with a glass of cold water dashed in the face, but continued screaming, although the doctor was no longer in sight; so was restrained by two kitchen maids and the gardener's boy, who sat on my legs. The Governor's wife had sent for the Matron from the Penitentiary, who arrived with two of the keepers; and she gave me a brisk slap across the face, at which I stopped. It was not the same doctor in any case, it only looked like him. The same cold and greedy look, and the hate.

It's the only way with the hysterics, you may be sure Ma'am, said the Matron, we have had a great deal of experience with that kind of a fit, this one used to be prone to them but we never indulged her, we worked to correct it and we thought she had given it up, it might be her old trouble coming back, for despite what they said about it up there at Toronto she was a raving lunatic that time seven years ago, and you are lucky there was no scissors nor sharp things lying about.

Then the keepers half-dragged me back to the main prison building, and locked me into this room, until I was myself again is what they said, even though I told them I was better now that the doctor was no longer there with his knives. I said I had a fear of doctors, that was all; of being cut open by them, as some might have a fear of snakes; but they said, That's enough of your tricks Grace, you just wanted the attention, he was not going to cut you open, he had no knives at all, it was only a callipers you saw, to measure the heads with. You've given the Governor's wife a real fright now but it serves her right, she's been spoiling you too much for your own good, she's made quite a pet out of you hasn't she, our company is hardly good enough for you any more. Well so much the worse, you will have to endure it because now you will have a different sort of attention for a time. Until they have decided what is to be done with you.

This room has only a little window high up with bars on the inside, and a straw-filled mattress. There's a crust of bread on a tin plate, and a stone crock of water, and a wooden bucket with nothing in it which is there for a chamber pot. I was put in a room like this before they sent me away to the Asylum. I told them I wasn't mad, that I wasn't the one, but they wouldn't listen.

They wouldn't know mad when they saw it in any case, because a good portion of the women in the Asylum were no madder than the Queen of England. Many were sane enough when sober, as their madness came out of a bottle, which is a kind I knew very well. One of them was in there to get away from her husband, who beat her black and blue, he was the mad one but nobody would lock him up; and another said she went mad in the autumns, as she had no house and it was warm in the Asylum, and if she didn't do a fair job of running mad she would freeze to death; but then in the spring she would become sane again because it was good weather and she could go off and tramp in the woods and fish, and as she was part Red Indian she was handy at such things. I would like to do that myself if I knew how, and if not afraid of the bears.

But some were not pretending. One poor Irishwoman had all her family dead, half of them of starving in the great famine and the other half of the cholera on the boat coming over; and she would wander about calling their names. I am glad I left Ireland before that time, as the sufferings she told of were dreadful, and the corpses piled everywhere with none to bury them. Another woman had killed her child, and it followed her around everywhere, tugging at her skirt; and sometimes she would pick it up and hug and kiss it, and at other times she would shriek at it, and hit it away with her hands. I was afraid of that one.

Another was very religious, always praying and singing, and when she found out what they said I had done, she would plague me whenever she could. Down on your knees, she would say, Thou shalt not kill, but there is always God's grace for sinners, repent, repent while there is yet time or damnation awaits. She was just like a preacher in church, and once she tried to baptize me with soup, thin soup it was and with cabbage in it, and she poured a spoonful of it over my head. When I complained of it, the Matron gave me a dry look with her mouth all tight and straight across like a box lid, and she said, Well Grace perhaps you should listen to her, I have never heard of you doing any true repenting, much though your hard heart stands in need of it; and then I was suddenly very angry and I screamed, I did nothing, I did nothing! It was her, it was her fault!

Who do you mean, Grace, she said, compose yourself or it's the cold baths and the strait-waistcoat for you, and she gave the other matron a glance: There. What did I tell you. Mad as a snake.

The matrons at the Asylum were all fat and strong, with big thick arms and chins that went straight down into their necks and prim white collars, and their hair twisted up like faded rope. You have to be strong to be a matron there in case some madwoman jumps on your back and starts to tear out your hair, but none of it improved their tempers any. Sometimes they would provoke us, especially right before the visitors were to come. They wanted to show how dangerous we were, but also how well they could control us, as it made them appear more valuable and skilled.

So I stopped telling them anything. Not Dr. Bannerling, who would come into the room when I was tied up in the dark with mufflers on my hands, Keep still I am here to examine you, it is no use lying to me. Nor the other doctors who would visit there, Oh indeed, what a fascinating case, as if I was a two-headed calf. At last I stopped talking altogether, except very civilly when spoken to, Yes Ma'am No Ma'am, Yes and No Sir. And then I was sent back to the Penitentiary, after they had all met together in their black coats, Ahem, aha, in my opinion, and My respected colleague, Sir I beg to differ. Of course they could not admit for an instant that they had been mistaken when they first put me in.

People dressed in a certain kind of clothing are never wrong. Also they never fart. What Mary Whitney used to say was, If there's farting in a room where they are, you may be sure you done it yourself. And even if you never did, you better not say so or it's all Damn your insolence, and a boot in the backside and out on the street with you.

She often had a crude way of speaking. She said *You done* and not *You did*. No one had taught her otherwise. I used to speak that way as well, but I have learnt better manners in prison.

I sit down on the straw mattress. It makes a sound like shushing. Like water on the shore. I shift from side to side, to listen to it. I could close my eyes and think I'm by the sea, on a dry day without much wind. Outside the window far away there's someone chopping wood, the axe coming down, the unseen flash and then the dull sound, but how do I know it's even wood?

It's chilly in this room. I have no shawl, I hug my arms around myself because who else is there to do it? When I was younger I used to think that if I could hug myself tight enough I could make myself smaller, because there was never enough room for me, at home or anywhere, but if I was smaller then I would fit in.

My hair is coming out from under my cap. Red hair of an ogre. A wild beast, the newspaper said. A monster. When they come with my dinner I will put the slop bucket over my head and hide behind the door, and that will give them a fright. If they want a monster so badly they ought to be provided with one.

I never do such things, however. I only consider them. If I did them, they would be sure I had gone mad again. *Gone mad* is what they say, and sometimes *Run mad*, as if mad is a direction, like west; as if mad is a different house you could step into, or a separate country entirely. But when you go mad you don't go any other place, you stay where you are. And somebody else comes in.

I don't want to be left by myself in this room. The walls are too empty, there are no pictures on them nor curtains on the little high-up window, nothing to look at and so you look at the wall, and after you do that for a time, there are pictures on it after all, and red flowers growing.

I think I sleep.

It's morning now, but which one? The second or the third. There's fresh light outside the window, that's what woke me. I struggle upright, pinch myself and blink my eyes, and get up stiff-limbed from the rustling mattress. Then I sing a song, just to hear a voice and keep myself company:

Holy, holy, holy, Lord God Almighty,
Early in the morning our song shall rise to thee,
Holy, holy, holy, merciful and mighty,
God in three persons, Blessed Trinity.

They can hardly object if it's a hymn. A hymn to the morning. I have always been fond of sunrise.

Then I drink the last of the water; then I walk around the room; then I lift my petticoats and piss in the bucket. A few more hours and it will reek in here like a cesspool.

Sleeping in your clothes makes you tired. The clothes are crumpled, and also your body underneath them. I feel as if I've been rolled into a bundle and thrown on the floor.

I wish I had a clean apron.

Nobody comes. I'm being left to reflect on my sins and misdemeanours, and one does that best in solitude, or such is our expert and considered opinion, Grace, after long experience with these matters. In solitary confinement, and sometimes in the dark. There are prisons where they keep you in there for years, without a glimpse of a tree or horse or human face. Some say it refines the complexion.

I've been shut up alone before. Incorrigible, said Dr. Bannerling, a devious dissembler. Remain quiet, I am here to examine your cerebral configuration, and first I shall measure your heartbeat and respiration, but I knew what he was up to. Take your hand off my tit, you filthy bastard, Mary Whitney would have said, but all I could say was Oh no, oh no, and no way to twist and turn, not how they'd fixed me, trussed up to the chair with the sleeves crossed over in front and tied behind; so nothing to do but sink my teeth into his fingers, and then over we went, backwards onto the floor, yowling together like two cats in a sack. He tasted of raw sausages and damp woollen underclothes. He'd of been much better for a good scalding, and then put in the sun to bleach.

No supper last night or the night before that, nothing except the bread, not even a bit of cabbage; well that is to be expected. Starvation is calming to the nerves. Today it will be more bread and water, as meat is exciting to criminals and maniacs, they get the smell of it in their nostrils just like wolves and then you have only yourself to blame. But yesterday's water is all gone and I'm very thirsty, I am dying of thirst, my mouth tastes bruised, my tongue is swelling. That's what happens to castaways, I've read about them in legal trials, lost at sea and drinking each other's blood. They draw straws for it. Cannibal atrocities pasted into the scrapbook. I'm sure I would never do such a thing, however hungry.

Have they forgotten I'm in here? They'll have to bring more food, or at least more water, or else I will starve, I will shrivel, my skin will dry out, all yellow like old linen; I will turn into a skeleton, I will be found months, years, centuries from now, and they will say Who is this, she must have slipped our mind, Well sweep all those bones and rubbish into the corner, but save the buttons, no sense in having them go to waste, there's no help for it now.

Once you start feeling sorry for yourself they've got you where they want you. Then they send for the Chaplain.

Oh come to my arms, poor wandering soul. There is more joy in Heaven over the one lost lamb. Ease your troubled mind. Kneel at my feet. Wring your hands in anguish. Describe how conscience tortures you day and night, and how the eyes of your victims follow you around the room, burning like red-hot coals. Shed tears of remorse. Confess, confess. Let me forgive and pity. Let me get up a Petition for you. Tell me all.

And then what did he do? Oh shocking. And then what?

The left hand or the right?

How far up, exactly?

Show me where.

Possibly I hear a whispering. Now there's an eye, looking in at me through the slit cut in the door. I can't see it but I know it's there. Then a knocking.

And I think, Who could that be? The Matron? The Warden, come to give me a scolding? But it can't be any of them, because nobody here does you the courtesy of knocking, they look at you through the little slit and then they just walk in. Always knock first, said Mary Whitney. Then wait until they give you leave. You never know what they may be up to, and half of it's nothing they want you to see, they could have their fingers up their nose or some other place, as even a gentlewoman feels the need to scratch where it itches, and if you see a pair of heels sticking out from under the bed it's best to take no notice. They may be silk purses in the daytime, but they're all sows' ears at night.

Mary was a person of democratic views.

The knock again. As if I have a choice.

I push my hair back under my cap, and get up off the straw mattress and smooth down my dress and apron, and then I move as far back into the corner of the room as I can, and then I say, quite firmly because it's as well to keep hold of your dignity if at all possible,

Please come in.

5 .

The door opens and a man enters. He's a young man, my own age or a little older, which is young for a man although not for a woman, as at my age a woman is an old maid but a man is not an old bachelor until he's fifty, and even then there's still hope for the ladies, as Mary Whitney used to say. He's tall, with long legs and arms, but not what the Governor's daughters would call handsome; they incline to the languid ones in the magazines, very elegant and butter wouldn't melt in their mouths, with narrow feet in pointed boots. This man has a briskness about him which is not fashionable, and also rather large feet, although he is a gentleman, or next door to it. I don't think he is English, and so it is hard to tell.

His hair is brown, and wavy by nature – unruly it might be called, as if he can't make it lie flat by brushing. His coat is good, a good cut; but not new, as there are shiny patches on the elbows. He has a tartan vest, tartan has been popular ever since the Queen took up with Scotland and built a castle there, full of deer's heads or so they say; but now I see it isn't real tartan, only checked. Yellow and brown. He has a gold watch-chain, so although rumpled and untended, he is not poor.

He doesn't have the side-whiskers, as they have begun to wear them now; I don't much like them myself, give me a moustache or a beard, or else nothing at all. James McDermott and Mr. Kinnear were both clean-shaven, and Jamie Walsh too, not that he had anything much to shave; except that Mr. Kinnear had a moustache. When I used to empty his shaving basin in the mornings, I would take some of the wet soap – he used a good soap, from London – and I would rub it on my skin, on the skin of my wrists, and then I would have the smell of it with me all day, at least until it was time to scrub the floors.

The young man closes the door behind him. He doesn't lock it, but someone else locks it from the outside. We are locked into this room together.

Good morning, Grace, he says. I understand that you are afraid of doctors. I must tell you right away that I myself am a doctor. My name is Dr. Jordan, Dr. Simon Jordan.

I look at him quickly, then look down. I say, Is the other doctor coming back?

The one that frightened you? he says. No, he is not.

I say, Then I suppose you are here to measure my head.

I would not dream of it, he says, smiling; but still, he glances at my head with a measuring look. However I have my cap on, so there's nothing he can see. Now that he has spoken I think he must be an American. He has white teeth and is not missing any of them, at least at the front, and his face is quite long and bony. I like his smile, although it is higher on one side than the other, which gives him the air of joking.

I look at his hands. They are empty. There's nothing at all in them. No rings on his fingers. Do you have a bag with knives in it? I say. A leather satchel.

No, he says, I am not the usual kind of doctor. I do no cutting open. Are you afraid of me, Grace?

I can't say that I am afraid of him yet. It's too early to tell; too early to tell what he wants. No one comes to see me here unless they want something.

I would like him to say what kind of a doctor he is if he's not the usual kind, but instead he says, I am from Massachusetts. Or that is where I was born. I have travelled a good deal since then. I have been going to and fro in the earth, and walking up and down in it. And he looks at me, to see if I understand.

I know it is the Book of Job, before Job gets the boils and running sores, and the whirlwinds. It's what Satan says to God. He must mean that he has come to test me, although he's too late for that, as God has done a great deal of testing of me already, and you would think he would be tired of it by now.

But I don't say this. I look at him stupidly. I have a good stupid look which I have practised.

I say, Have you been to France? That is where all the fashions come from.

I see I have disappointed him. Yes, he says. And to England, and also to Italy, and to Germany and Switzerland as well.

It is very odd to be standing in a locked room in the Penitentiary, speaking with a strange man about France and Italy and Germany. A travelling man. He must be a wanderer, like Jeremiah the peddler. But Jeremiah travelled to earn his bread, and these other sorts of men are rich enough already. They go on voyages because they are curious. They amble around the world and stare at things, they sail across the ocean as if there's nothing to it at all, and if it goes ill with them in one place they simply pick up and move along to another.

But now it's my turn to say something. I say, I don't know how you manage, Sir, amongst all the foreigners, you never know what they are saying. When the poor things first come here they gabble away like geese, although the children can soon speak well enough.

This is true, as children of any kind are very quick to learn.

He smiles, and then he does a strange thing. He puts his left hand into his pocket and pulls out an apple. He walks over to me slowly, holding the apple out in front of him like someone holding out a bone to a dangerous dog, in order to win it over.

This is for you, he says.

I am so thirsty the apple looks to me like a big round drop of water, cool and red. I could drink it down in one gulp. I hesitate; but then I think, There's nothing bad in an apple, and so I take it. I haven't had an apple of my own for a long time. This apple must be from last autumn, kept in a barrel in the cellar, but it seems fresh enough.

I am not a dog, I say to him.

Most people would ask me what I mean by saying that, but he laughs. His laugh is just one breath, Hah, as if he's found a thing he has lost; and he says, No, Grace, I can see you are not a dog.

What is he thinking? I stand holding the apple in both hands. It feels precious, like a heavy treasure. I lift it up and smell it. It has such an odour of outdoors on it I want to cry.

Aren't you going to eat it, he says.

No, not yet, I say.

Why not, he says.

Because then it would be gone, I say.

The truth is I don't want him watching me while I eat. I don't want him to see my hunger. If you have a need and they find it out, they will use it against you. The best way is to stop from wanting anything.

He gives his one laugh. Can you tell me what it is, he says.

I look at him, then look away. An apple, I say. He must think I am simple; or else it's a trick of some sort; or else he is mad and that is why they locked the door – they've locked me into this room with a madman. But men who are dressed in clothes like his cannot be mad, especially the gold watch-chain – his relatives or else his keepers would have it off him in a trice if so.

He smiles his lopsided smile. What does Apple make you think of? he says.

I beg your pardon, Sir, I say. I do not understand you.

It must be a riddle. I think of Mary Whitney, and the apple peelings we threw over our shoulders that night, to see who we would marry. But I will not tell him that.

I think you understand well enough, he says.

My sampler, I say.

Now it is his turn to know nothing. Your what? he says.

My sampler that I stitched as a child, I say. A is for Apple, B is for Bee.

Oh yes, he says. But what else?

I give my stupid look. Apple pie, I say.

Ah, he says. Something you eat.

Well I should hope you would, Sir, I say. That's what an apple pie is for.

And is there any kind of apple you should not eat? he says.

A rotten one, I suppose, I say.

He's playing a guessing game, like Dr. Bannerling at the Asylum. There is always a right answer, which is right because it is the one they want, and you can tell by their faces whether you have guessed what it is; although with Dr. Bannerling all of the answers were wrong. Or perhaps he is a Doctor of Divinity; they are the other ones prone to this kind of questioning. I have had enough of them to last me for a long while.

The apple of the Tree of Knowledge, is what he means. Good and evil. Any child could guess it. But I will not oblige.

I go back to my stupid look. Are you a preacher? I say.

No, he says, I am not a preacher. I am a doctor who works not with bodies, but with minds. Diseases of the mind and brain, and the nerves.

I put my hands with the apple behind my back. I do not trust him at all. No, I say. I won't go back there. Not to the Asylum. Flesh and blood cannot stand it.

Don't be afraid, he says. You aren't mad, really, are you Grace?

No Sir I am not, I say.

Then there is no reason for you to go back to the Asylum, is there?

They don't listen to reason there, Sir, I say.

Well that is what I am here for, he says. I am here to listen to reason. But if I am to listen to you, you will have to talk to me.

I see what he's after. He is a collector. He thinks all he has to do is give me an apple, and then he can collect me. Perhaps he is from a newspaper. Or else he is a travelling man, making a tour. They come in and they stare, and when they look at you, you feel as small as an ant, and they pick you up between finger and thumb and turn you around. And then they set you down and go away.

You won't believe me, Sir, I say. Anyway it's all been decided, the trial is long over and done with and what I say will not change anything. You should ask the lawyers and the judges, and the newspaper men, they seem to know my story better than I do myself. In any case I can't remember, I can remember other things but I have lost that part of my memory entirely. They must have told you that.

I would like to help you, Grace, he says.

That is how they get in through the door. Help is what they offer but gratitude is what they want, they roll around in it like cats in the catnip. He wishes to go home and say to himself, I stuck in my thumb and pulled out the plum, what a good boy am I. But I will not be anybody's plum. I say nothing.

If you will try to talk, he continues, I will try to listen. My interest is purely scientific. It is not only the murders that should concern us. He's using a kind voice, kind on the surface but with other desires hidden beneath it.

Perhaps I will tell you lies, I say.

He doesn't say, Grace what a wicked suggestion, you have a sinful imagination. He says, Perhaps you will. Perhaps you will tell lies without meaning to, and perhaps you will also tell them deliberately. Perhaps you are a liar.

I look at him. There are those who have said I am one, I say.

We will just have to take that chance, he says.

I look down at the floor. Will they take me back to the Asylum? I say. Or will they put me in solitary confinement, with nothing to eat but bread?

He says, I give you my word that as long as you continue to talk with me, and do not lose control of yourself and become violent, you shall remain as you were. I have the Governor's promise.

I look at him. I look away. I look at him again. I hold the apple in my two hands. He waits.

Finally I lift the apple up and press it to my forehead.

IV.

YOUNG MAN'S FANCY

Among these raving maniacs I recognised the singular face of Grace Marks – no longer sad and despairing, but lighted up with the fire of insanity, and glowing with a hideous and fiend-like merriment. On perceiving that strangers were observing her, she fled shrieking away like a phantom into one of the side rooms. It appears that even in the wildest bursts of her terrible malady, she is continually haunted by a memory of the past. Unhappy girl! When will the long horror of her punishment and remorse be over? When will she sit at the feet of Jesus, clothed with the unsullied garments of his righteousness, the stain of blood washed from her hand, and her soul redeemed, and pardoned, and in her right mind? . . .

Let us hope that all her previous guilt may be attributed to the incipient workings of this frightful malady.

– Susanna Moodie,
Life in the Clearings, 1853.

It is of the greatest regret that we do not have the knowledge whereby we might cure these unfortunate afflicted. A surgeon can cut open an abdomen and display the spleen. Muscles can be cut out and shown to young students. The human psyche cannot be dissected nor the brain's workings put out on the table to display.

When a child, I have played games with a blindfold obscuring my vision. Now I am like that child. Blindfolded, groping my way, not knowing where I am going, or if I am in the proper direction. Someday, someone will remove that blindfold.

> – Dr. Joseph Workman,
> Medical Superintendent,
> Provincial Lunatic Asylum, Toronto;
> Letter to "Henry," a young and troubled
> enquirer, 1866.

One need not be a Chamber – to be Haunted –
One need not be a House –
The Brain has Corridors – surpassing –
Material Place –
. . .

Ourself behind ourself, concealed –
Should startle most –
Assassin hid in our Apartment
Be Horror's least. . . .

> – Emily Dickinson, c. 1863.

6.

To Dr. Simon Jordan, M.D., Laburnum House, Loomisville, Massachusetts, The United States of America; from Dr. Joseph Workman, Medical Superintendent, The Provincial Lunatic Asylum, Toronto, Canada West.

April 15th, 1859.

Dear Dr. Jordan:

I beg to acknowledge receipt of your letter of 2nd Inst. and to thank you for the Letter of Introduction from my esteemed colleague, Dr. Binswanger of Switzerland; the establishment of whose new Clinic I have followed with great interest. Permit me to say, that as an acquaintance of Dr. Binswanger, you would be most welcome to inspect the Institution of which I am the Superintendent, at any time. I would be most pleased to show you over the premises myself, and to explain our methods to you.

As you intend to establish an institution of your own, I should emphasize that sanitation and good drainage are of the first importance, as it is of no use to attempt to minister to a mind diseased, whilst the body is afflicted by infections. This side of things is too often neglected. At the time of my advent here, we had many Cholera outbreaks, perforating Dysentries, intractable Diarrhoeas, and the whole deadly Typhoid family, which were plaguing the Asylum. In the course of my investigations as to their source, I discovered a large and exceedingly noxious cesspool underlying every part of the cellars, in some places the consistency of a strong infusion of black tea, and in others like viscid soft soap, which was undrained due to the failure of the builders to connect the drains to the main sewer; in addition to which, the water supply for both drinking and washing was drawn through an intake pipe from the lake, in a stagnant bay, close by the pipe through which the main sewer discharged its putrid flow. It is no wonder that the inmates often complained that their drinking water tasted of a substance which few among them had ever experienced any great longing to consume!

The inmates here are pretty evenly divided as to sex; as to symptoms, there is a great variety. Religious fanaticism I find to be fully as prolific an exciting cause of insanity as intemperance – but I am inclined to believe that neither religion nor intemperance will induce insanity in a truly sound mind – I think there is always a predisposing cause which renders the individual liable to the malady, when exposed to any disturbing agency, whether mental or physical.

However, for information regarding the chief object of your enquiry, I regret that you must seek elsewhere. The female prisoner, Grace Marks, whose crime was murder, was returned to the Penitentiary at Kingston in August of 1853, after a stay of fifteen months. As I myself was appointed only some three weeks prior to her departure, I had little chance of making a thorough study of her case. I have therefore referred your letter to Dr. Samuel Bannerling, who attended her under my predecessor. As to the degree of insanity by which she was primarily affected, I am unable to speak. It was my impression that for a considerable time past she had been sufficiently sane to warrant her removal from the Asylum. I strongly recommended that in her discipline, gentle treatment should be adopted; and I believe she presently spends a part of each day as a servant in the Governor's family. She had, towards the latter end of her stay, conducted herself with much propriety; whilst by her industry and general kindness towards the patients, she was found a profitable and useful inmate of the house. She suffers occasionally under nervous excitement, and a painful overaction of the heart.

One of the chief problems facing the superintendent of a publicly funded institution such as this, is the tendency on the part of prison authorities to refer to us many troublesome criminals, among them atrocious murderers, burglars and thieves, who do not belong among the innocent and uncontaminated insane, simply to have them out of the prison. It is impossible that a building constructed with a proper reference to the comfort and the recovery of the insane, can be a place of confinement for criminal lunatics; and certainly much less so for criminal impostors; and I am strongly inclined to suspect that the latter class are more numerous than may generally be supposed. Besides the evil consequences inevitably resulting to the patients from the commingling of innocent with criminal lunatics, there is reason to apprehend a deteriorating influence on the tempers and habits of the Keepers and Officers of the Asylum, unfitting them for the humane and proper treatment of the former.

But as you propose to establish a private institution, you will, I trust, incur fewer difficulties of this nature, and will suffer less from the irritating political interference that frequently prevents their rectification; and in this, as in general matters, I wish you every success in your endeavours. Enterprises such as yours are unfortunately much required at present, both in our own country and in yours, as, due to the increased anxieties of modern life and the consequent stresses upon the nerves, the rate of construction can scarcely keep pace with the numbers of applicants; and I beg to proffer any small assistance, which it may lie within my power to bestow.

Yours very truly,

Joseph Workman, M.D.

❧

From Mrs. William P. Jordan, Laburnum House, Loomisville, Massachusetts, The United States of America; to Dr. Simon Jordan, care of Major C. D. Humphrey, Lower Union Street, Kingston, Canada West.

April 29th, 1859.

My Dearest Son:

Your long-awaited note containing your present address and the instructions for the Rheumatism Salve arrived today. It was a joy to see your dear handwriting again, even so little of it, and it is good of you to take an interest in your poor Mother's failing constitution.

I take this opportunity to write you a few lines, while enclosing the letter which arrived here for you the day after your departure. Your recent visit to us was all too brief – when may we expect to see you among your family and friends once more? So much travelling cannot be salutary, either for your peace of mind, or for your health. I long for the day when you choose to settle down among us, and to establish yourself properly, in a manner fitting to you.

I could not help but observe, that the enclosed letter is from the Lunatic Asylum in Toronto. I suppose you intend to visit it, although surely you must have seen every such establishment in the world by now and cannot possibly benefit from seeing another. Your description of those in France and England, and even of the one in Switzerland, which is so much cleaner, filled me with horror. We must all pray to have our sanity preserved; but I have grave doubts concerning your future prospects, should your proposed course of action be pursued. You must forgive me for saying, dear Son, that I have never been able to understand the interest you take in such things. No one in the Family has ever concerned himself with Lunatics before, although your Grandfather was a Quaker clergyman. It is commendable to wish to relieve human suffering, but surely the insane, like idiots and cripples, owe their state to Almighty Providence, and one should not attempt to reverse decisions which are certainly just, although inscrutable to us.

In addition, I cannot believe a private Asylum could possibly be made to pay, as the relatives of Lunatics are notoriously neglectful once the afflicted person has been put away, and wish to hear or see nothing more of them; and this neglect extends to the settlement of their bills; and then there is the cost of food and fuel, and of the persons who must be put in charge of them. There are so many considerations to attend to, and surely the daily consorting with the insane would be far from conducive to a tranquil existence. You must think too of your future wife and children, who ought not to be placed in such close proximity to a pack of dangerous madmen.

I know it is not my place to determine your path in life, but I strongly urge that a manufactury would be far preferable, and although the textile mills are not what they were, due to the mismanagement of the politicians, who abuse the public trust unmercifully and become worse with every passing year; yet there are many other opportunities at present, and some men have done very well at them, as you hear of new fortunes being made every day; and I am sure you have as much energy and sagacity as they. There is talk of a new Sewing Machine for use in the home, which would do exceedingly well if it might be cheaply produced; for every woman would wish to own such an item, which would save many hours of monotonous toil and unceasing drudgery, and would also be of great assistance to the poor seamstresses. Could you not invest the small inheritance remaining to you after the sale of your poor Father's business, in some such admirable but dependable venture? I am certain that a Sewing Machine would relieve as much human suffering as a hundred Lunatic Asylums, and possibly a good deal more.

Of course you have always been an idealist, and filled with optimistic dreams; but reality must at some time obtrude, and you are now turned thirty.

I say these things, not from any wish to meddle or interfere, but out of a Mother's anxious care for the future of her only and beloved Son. I do so hope to see you well-established before I die – it would have been your dear Father's wish, as well – you know I live only for your welfare.

My health took a turn for the worse after your departure – your presence always has an improving effect upon my spirits. I was coughing so much yesterday that my faithful Maureen could scarcely get me up the stairs – she is almost as old and feeble as I am, and we must have looked like two old witches hobbling up a hill. Despite the concoctions I am dosed with several times a day, brewed by my good Samantha in the kitchen – which taste as vile as all medicines ought to, and which she swears cured her own Mother – I continue much the same; although I was well enough today to receive as usual in the parlour. I had several visitors, who had heard of my indisposition, among them Mrs. Henry Cartwright, who has a good heart although not always a very polished manner, as is often the case with those whose fortunes have been of recent acquisition; but that will come in time. Accompanying her was her daughter Faith, whom you will recall as an awkward girl of thirteen, but who is now grown up and recently returned from Boston, where she was staying with her Aunt, to broaden her education. She has turned out a charming young woman, everything one might wish for, and displayed a courtesy and gentle kindness many would admire, and which is worth so much more than flamboyant good looks. They brought with them a basket of delicacies – I am thoroughly spoiled by dear Mrs. Cartwright – for which I expressed much gratitude, although I could barely taste anything, as I have no appetite at present.

It is a sad thing to be an invalid, and I pray every night that you may be spared, and will take care not to overtire yourself with too much study and nervous strain, and with staying up all night by lamplight, ruining your eyes and puzzling your brain to pieces, and to wear wool next the skin until the warm weather is fully here. Our first lettuces have appeared, and the apple tree is budded; I suppose where you are it is still covered with snow. I do not think that Kingston, being so far north and on the lakeshore, can be at all good for the lungs, as it must be very chill and damp. Are your rooms well-heated? I do hope you are eating strengthening food, and that they have a good butcher there.

I send you all my love, dear Son, and Maureen and Samantha beg to be remembered to you; and all of us await the news, which we hope will come very soon, of your next Visit to us, until which I remain as always,

Your very loving,

Mother.

❧

From Dr. Simon Jordan, care of Major C. D. Humphrey, Lower Union Street, Kingston, Canada West; to Dr. Edward Murchie, Dorchester, Massachusetts, The United States of America.

May 1st, 1859.

My dear Edward:

I was sorry not to have been able to make a visit to Dorchester, to see how you are getting on, now that you have hung your shingle up, and have been busy ministering to the local halt and the blind, while I have been gypsying about Europe, seeking how to cast out devils; which, between us, I have not learned the secret of as yet; but as you may suppose, the time between my arrival at Loomisville, and my departure from it, was much taken up with preparations, and the afternoons were perforce consecrated to my mother. But upon my return, we must arrange to meet, and to lift a glass or two together "for auld lang syne"; and to talk over past adventures, and current prospects.

After a moderately smooth journey across the Lake, I have arrived safely at my destination. I have not yet met my correspondent and, as it were, employer, the Reverend Verringer, as he is away on a visit to Toronto, and so I still have that pleasure to anticipate; although if his letters to me are any indication, he suffers like many clergymen from a punishable lack of wit and a desire to treat us all as straying sheep, of which he is to be the shepherd. However, it is to him – and to the good Dr. Binswanger, who proposed me to him as the best man for the purpose on the western side of the Atlantic – for the price, which is not high, the Methodists being notoriously frugal – that I owe this splendid opportunity; an opportunity which I hope to be able to exploit in the interests of the advancement of knowledge, the mind and its workings being still, despite considerable progress, a *terra incognita*.

As to my situation – Kingston is not a very prepossessing town, as it was burned to the ground some two decades ago and has been rebuilt with charmless dispatch. The new buildings are of stone or brick, which will, one hopes, make them less prone to conflagrations. The Penitentiary itself is in the style of a Greek temple, and they are very proud of it here; though which pagan god is intended to be worshipped therein, I have yet to discover.

I have secured rooms in the residence of a Major C. D. Humphrey, which although not luxurious, will be commodious enough for my purposes. I fear however that my landlord is a dipsomaniac; on the two occasions upon which I have encountered him, he was having difficulty putting on his gloves, or else taking them off, he seemed uncertain which; and gave me a red-eyed glare, as if to demand what the Devil I was doing in his house. I predict that he will end as an inhabitant of the private Asylum I still dream of establishing; although I must curb my propensity to view each new acquaintance as a future paying inmate. It is remarkable how frequently military men, when retired on half-pay, go to the bad; it is as if, having become habituated to strong excitements and violent emotions, they must duplicate them in civilian life. However, my arrangements were made, not with the Major – who would doubtless not have been able to recall having made them – but with his long-suffering wife.

I take my meals – with the exception of the breakfasts, which have thus far been even more deplorable than the breakfasts we shared as medical students in London – at a squalid inn located in the vicinity, where every meal is a burnt offering, and nothing is thought the worse for the addition of a little dirt and grime, and a seasoning of insects. That I remain here despite these travesties of the culinary art, I trust you will recognize as a measure of my true devotion to the cause of science.

As for society, I must report that there are pretty girls here as elsewhere, albeit dressed in the Paris fashions of three years ago, which is to say the New York fashions of two. Despite the reforming tendencies of the country's present government, the town abounds both in disgruntled Tories, and also in petty provincial snobberies; and I anticipate that your bearish and carelessly dressed, and what is more to the purpose, your Yankee democrat friend, will be viewed with some suspicion by its more partisan inhabitants.

Nonetheless, the Governor – at the urging of Reverend Verringer, I suppose – has gone out of his way to be accommodating, and has arranged to have Grace Marks placed at my disposal for several hours every afternoon. She appears to act in the household as a sort of unpaid servant, though whether this service is viewed by her as a favour or a penance, I have yet to ascertain; nor will it be an easy task, as the gentle Grace, having been hardened in the fire now for some fifteen years, will be a very hard nut to crack. Enquiries such as mine are ineffective, unless the trust of the subject may be gained; but judging from my knowledge of penal institutions, I suspect Grace has had scant reason to trust anyone at all for a very long period of time.

I have had only one opportunity thus far of viewing the object of my investigations, and so it is too soon to convey my impressions. Let me say only that I am hopeful; and, as you have so kindly expressed a desire to have news of my progress, I will take pains to keep you informed of it; and until then, I remain, my dear Edward,

Your old friend and erstwhile companion,

Simon.

7.

Simon sits at his writing table, gnawing the end of his pen and looking out the window at the grey and choppy waters of Lake Ontario. Across the bay is Wolfe Island, named after the famous poetic general, he supposes. It's a view he does not admire – it is so relentlessly horizontal – but visual monotony can sometimes be conducive to thought.

A gust of rain patters against the windowpane; low tattered clouds are scudding above the lake. The lake itself heaves and surges; waves are pulled in against the shore, recoil, are pulled in again; and the willow trees below him toss themselves like heads of long green hair, and bend and thrash. Something pale blows past: it looks like a woman's white scarf or veil, but then he sees it is only a gull, fighting the wind. The mindless turmoil of Nature, he thinks; Tennyson's teeth and claws.

He feels none of the jaunty hopefulness he has just expressed. Instead he is uneasy, and more than a little dispirited. His reason for being here seems precarious; but it's his best chance at the moment. When he entered upon his medical studies, it was out of a young man's perversity. His father was a wealthy mill owner then, and fully expected Simon to take over the business in time; and Simon himself expected the same thing. First, however, he would rebel a little; he would slip the traces, travel, study, test himself in the world, and also in the world of science and medicine, which had always appealed to him. Then he would return home with a hobby-horse to ride, and the comfortable assurance that he need not ride it for money. Most of the best scientists, he knows, have private incomes, which allows them the possibility of disinterested research.

He hadn't expected the collapse of his father, and also of his father's textile mills – which came first he's never been sure. Instead of an amusing row down a quiet stream, he's been overtaken by a catastrophe at sea, and has been left clinging to a broken spar. In other words he has been thrown back on his own resources; which was what, during his adolescent arguments with his father, he claimed to most desire.

The mills were sold, and the imposing house of his childhood, with its large staff of domestics – the chambermaids, the kitchen maids, the parlour maids, that ever-changing chorus of smiling girls or women with names like Alice and Effie, who cosseted and also dominated his childhood and youth, and whom he thinks of as having somehow been sold along with the house. They smelled like strawberries and salt; they had long rippling hair, when it was down, or one of them did; it was Effie, perhaps. As for his inheritance, it's smaller than his mother thinks, and much of the income from it goes to her. She sees herself as living in reduced circumstances, which is true, considering what they have been reduced from. She believes she is making sacrifices for Simon, and he doesn't want to disillusion her. His father was self-made, but his mother was constructed by others, and such edifices are notoriously fragile.

Thus the private asylum is far beyond his reach at present. In order to raise the money for it he would have to be able to offer something novel, some new discovery or cure, in a field that is already crowded and also very contentious. Perhaps, when he has established his name, he will be able to sell shares in it. But without losing control: he must be free, absolutely free, to follow his own methods, once he has decided exactly what they are to be. He will write a prospectus: large and cheerful rooms, proper ventilation and drainage, and extensive grounds, with a river flowing through them, as the sound of water is soothing to the nerves. He'll draw the line at machinery and fads, however: no electrical devices, nothing with magnets. It's true that the American public is unduly impressed by such notions – they favour cures that can be had by pulling a lever or pressing a button – but Simon has no belief in their efficacy. Despite the temptation, he must refuse to compromise his integrity.

It's all a pipe dream at present. But he has to have a project of some sort, to wave in front of his mother. She needs to believe that he's working towards some goal or other, however much she may disapprove of it. Of course he could always marry money, as she herself did. She traded her family name and connections for a heap of coin fresh from the mint, and she is more than willing to arrange something of the sort for him: the horse-trading that's becoming increasingly common between impoverished European aristocrats and upstart American millionaires is not unknown, on a much smaller scale, in Loomisville, Massachusetts. He thinks of the prominent front teeth and duck-like neck of Miss Faith Cartwright, and shivers.

He consults his watch: his breakfast is late again. He takes it in his rooms, where it arrives every morning, carried in on a wooden tray by Dora, his landlady's maid-of-all-work. She sets the tray with a thump and a rattle on the small table at the far end of the sitting room, where, once she has gone, he seats himself to devour it, or whatever parts of it he guesses to be edible. He has adopted the habit of writing before breakfast at the other and larger table so he may be seen bent over his work, and will not have to look at her.

Dora is stout and pudding-faced, with a small downturned mouth like that of a disappointed baby. Her large black eyebrows meet over her nose, giving her a permanent scowl that expresses a sense of disapproving outrage. It's obvious that she detests being a maid-of-all-work; he wonders if there is anything else she might prefer. He has tried imagining her as a prostitute – he often plays this private mental game with various women he encounters – but he can't picture any man actually paying for her services. It would be like paying to be run over by a wagon, and would be, like that experience, a distinct threat to the health. Dora is a hefty creature, and could snap a man's spine in two with her thighs, which Simon envisions as greyish, like boiled sausages, and stubbled like a singed turkey; and enormous, each one as large as a piglet.

Dora returns his lack of esteem. She appears to feel that he has rented these rooms with the sole object of causing trouble for her. She fricassees his handkerchiefs and overstarches his shirts, and loses the buttons from them, which she no doubt pulls off routinely. He's even suspected her of burning his toast and overcooking his egg on purpose. After plumping down his tray, she bellows, "Here's your food," as if calling a hog; then she stumps out, closing the door behind her just one note short of a slam.

Simon has been spoiled by European servants, who are born knowing their places; he has not yet reaccustomed himself to the resentful demonstrations of equality so frequently practised on this side of the ocean. Except in the South, of course; but he does not go there.

There are better lodgings than these to be had in Kingston, but he doesn't wish to pay for them. These are suitable enough for the short time he intends to stay. Also there are no other lodgers, and he values his privacy, and the quiet in which to think. The house is a stone one, and chilly and damp; but by temperament – it must be the old New Englander in him – Simon feels a certain contempt for material self-indulgence; and as a medical student he became habituated to a monkish austerity, and to working long hours under difficult conditions.

He turns again to his desk. *Dearest Mother*, he begins. *Thank you for your long and informative letter. I am very well, and making considerable headway here, in my study of nervous and cerebral diseases among the criminal element, which, if the key to them may be found, would go a long way towards alleviating . . .*

He can't go on; he feels too fraudulent. But he has to write something, or she will assume he has drowned, or died suddenly of consumption, or been waylaid by thieves. The weather is always a good subject; but he can't write about the weather on an empty stomach.

From the drawer of his desk he takes out a small pamphlet that dates from the time of the murders, and which was sent to him by Reverend Verringer. It contains the confessions of Grace Marks and James McDermott, as well as an abridged version of the trial. At the front is an engraved portrait of Grace, which could easily pass for the heroine of a sentimental novel; she'd been just sixteen at the time, but the woman pictured looks a good five years older. Her shoulders are swathed in a tippet; the brim of a bonnet encircles her head like a dark aureole. The nose is straight, the mouth dainty, the expression conventionally soulful – the vapid pensiveness of a Magdalene, with the large eyes gazing at nothing.

Beside this is a matching engraving of James McDermott, shown in the overblown collar of those days, with his hair in a forward-swept arrangement reminiscent of Napoleon's, and meant to suggest tempestuousness. He is scowling in a brooding, Byronic way; the artist must have admired him.

Beneath the double portrait is written, in copperplate: *Grace Marks, alias Mary Whitney; James McDermott. As they appeared at the Court House. Accused of Murdering Mr. Thos. Kinnear & Nancy Montgomery.* The whole thing bears a disturbing resemblance to a wedding invitation; or it would, without the pictures.

Preparing himself for his first interview with Grace, Simon had disregarded this portrait entirely. She must be quite different by now, he'd thought; more dishevelled; less self-contained; more like a suppliant; quite possibly insane. He was conducted to her temporary cell by a keeper, who'd locked him in with her, after warning him that she was stronger than she looked and could give a man a devilish bite, and advising him to call for help if she became violent.

As soon as he saw her, he knew that this wouldn't happen. The morning light fell slantingly in through the small window high up on the wall, illuminating the corner where she stood. It was an image almost mediaeval in its plain lines, its angular clarity: a nun in a cloister, a maiden in a towered dungeon, awaiting the next day's burning at the stake, or else the last-minute champion come to rescue her. The cornered woman; the penitential dress falling straight down, concealing feet that were surely bare; the straw mattress on the floor; the timorous hunch of the shoulders; the arms hugged close to the thin body, the long wisps of auburn hair escaping from what appeared at first glance to be a chaplet of white flowers – and especially the eyes, enormous in the pale face and dilated with fear, or with mute pleading – all was as it should be. He'd seen many hysterics at the Salpêtrière in Paris who'd looked very much like this.

He approached her with a calm and smiling face, presenting an image of goodwill – which was a true image, after all, because goodwill was what he felt. It was important to convince such patients that you, at least, did not believe them to be mad, since they never believed it themselves.

But then Grace stepped forward, out of the light, and the woman he'd seen the instant before was suddenly no longer there. Instead there was a different woman – straighter, taller, more self-possessed, wearing the conventional dress of the Penitentiary, with a striped blue and white skirt beneath which were two feet, not naked at all but enclosed in ordinary shoes. There was even less escaped hair than he'd thought: most of it was tucked up under a white cap.

Her eyes were unusually large, it was true, but they were far from insane. Instead they were frankly assessing him. It was as if she were contemplating the subject of some unexplained experiment; as if it were he, and not she, who was under scrutiny.

Remembering the scene, Simon winces. I was indulging myself, he thinks. Imagination and fancy. I must stick to observation, I must proceed with caution. A valid experiment must have verifiable results. I must resist melodrama, and an overheated brain.

There's a scuffling outside the door, then a thumping. It must be his breakfast. He turns his back, and can feel his neck retracting down into his collar like a turtle's into its shell. "Come in," he calls, and the door flies open.

"Here's your food," bawls Dora. The tray bumps down; she marches out, and the door bangs shut behind her. Simon has a fleeting and unbidden image of her, strung up by the ankles in a butcher-shop window, with cloves stuck into her and a rind on her like a sugared ham. The association of ideas is truly remarkable, he thinks, once one begins to observe its operations in one's own mind. Dora – Pig – Ham, for instance. In order to get from the first term to the third, the second term is essential; though from the first to the second, and from the second to the third, is no great leap.

He must make a note of it: *Middle term essential*. Perhaps a maniac is simply one for whom these associative tricks of the brain cross the line that separates the literal from the merely fanciful, as may happen under the influence of fevers, and of somnambulistic trances, and of certain drugs. But what is the mechanism? For there must be one. Is the clue to be found in the nerves, or in the brain itself? To produce insanity, what must first be damaged, and how?

His breakfast must be getting cold, if Dora has not deliberately chilled it in advance. He levers himself out of his chair, disentangling his long legs, stretches himself and yawns, and goes over to the other table, the one with the tray on it. Yesterday his egg was like india-rubber; he'd mentioned it to his landlady, the wan Mrs. Humphrey, and she must have admonished Dora, because today the egg is so undercooked as to be scarcely jellied, with a blueish tinge to it like an eyeball.

Curse the woman, he thinks. Sullen, brutish, vengeful; a mind that exists at a sub-rational level, yet cunning, slippery and evasive. There's no way to corner her. She's a greased pig.

A piece of toast cracks like slate between his teeth. *Dearest Mother*, he composes in his head. *The weather here is very good; the snow is almost gone, spring is in the air, the sun is warming the lake, and already the vigorous green tips of –*

Of what? He has never known much about flowers.

8 .

I am sitting in the sewing room, at the head of the stairs in the Governor's wife's house, in the usual chair at the usual table with the sewing things in the basket as usual, except for the scissors. They insist on removing those from within my reach, so if I want to cut a thread or trim a seam I have to ask Dr. Jordan, who takes them out of his vest pocket and returns them to it when I have finished. He says he does not feel any such rigmarole is necessary, as he considers me to be entirely harmless and in control of myself. He appears to be a trusting man.

Although sometimes I just bite the thread off with my teeth.

Dr. Jordan has told them that what he wishes is an atmosphere of relaxation and calm, it is more conducive to his purposes whatever they may be, and so he recommended that I was to be kept in the same daily routine as much as possible. I continue to sleep in my allotted cell, and I wear the same clothing and eat the same breakfast, in silence if you can call it silence, forty women, most of them in here for nothing worse than stealing, who sit chewing their bread with their mouths open and slurping their tea in order to make a noise of some sort even if not speech, with an edifying Bible passage read out loud.

You can have your own thoughts then, but if you laugh you must pretend you are coughing or choking; choking is better, if choking they hit you on the back, but if coughing they have the doctor. A hunk of bread, a mug of weak tea, meat at dinner but not much of it, because overfeeding on rich foods stimulates the criminal organs of the brain, or so say the doctors, and the guards and keepers then repeat it to us. In that case, why are their own criminal organs not more stimulated, as they eat meat and chickens and bacon and eggs and cheese, and as much as they can get. That is why they are so fat. It is my opinion that they sometimes take what is intended for us, which would not surprise me in the least, as it is dog eat dog around here and they are the bigger dogs.

After breakfast I am brought over to the Governor's mansion as usual, by two of the keepers who are men and not above making a joke amongst themselves when out of hearing of the higher authorities. Well Grace says the one, I see you have a new sweetheart, a doctor no less, has he gone down on his knees yet or have you lifted your own up for him, he'd better keep a sharp eye out or you'll have him flat on his back. Yes says the other, flat on his back in the cellar with his boots off and a bullet through his heart. Then they laugh; they consider this very comical.

I try to think of what Mary Whitney would say, and sometimes I can say it. If you really thought that of me you should hold your dirty tongues, I said to them, or one dark night I'll have them out of your mouths roots and all, I won't need a knife, I'll just take hold with my teeth and pull, and not only that I'll thank you to keep your filthy screw's hands to yourself.

Now can't you take a bit of fun, I'd welcome it if I was you says the one, we're the only men that's ever going to lay a hand on you for the rest of your life, you're shut up in there like a nun, come now, confess you're longing for a tumble, you was ready enough with that runty little James McDermott before they stretched his crooked neck for him, the murdering bastard, and That's the way Grace, says the other, up on your high horse, just like a spotless maiden, no legs on you at all, you're as pure as an angel you are, in a pig's ear as if you'd never seen the inside of a man's bedroom in the tavern in Lewiston, we heard about that, putting on your stays and stockings you was when you was nabbed, but I'm glad to see there's still a touch of the old hellfire left, they ain't worked it out of you yet. I like a bit of spirit in a woman, says the one, Or a whole bottleful says the other, gin leads to sin, God bless it, there's nothing like a little fuel to make the fire burn. Drunker the better says the one, and out stone cold is the best, then you don't have to listen to them, there's nothing worse than a squalling whore. Were you noisy Grace, says the other, Did you squeal and moan, did you wiggle underneath that swarthy little rat, looking at me to see what I'll say. Sometimes I say I won't have that kind of talk, which makes them laugh heartily; but as a rule I say nothing.

And that is the way we pass the time, out to the prison gateway, Who goes there oh it's only you, Good day Grace, got your two young men with you have you, tied to your apron strings, a wink and a nod and then along the street, each holding fast to an arm, they don't need to do that but they like it, they lean in on me closer and closer until I am squeezed between them, through the mud, over the puddles, around the piles of horse dung, past the trees in bloom in the fenced yards, their tassels, their flowers like pale yellow-green caterpillars dangling, and the dogs barking and the carriages and wagons passing, splashing through the water in the road, and the people staring because it's obvious where we have come from, they can tell by my clothing, until we go up the long drive with herbaceous borders and around to the servants' entrance, and Here she is all safe and sound, she tried to escape didn't you Grace, tried to give us the slip, she's a cunning one for all her big blue eyes, well better luck next time my girl, you should've hitched up your petticoats higher and shown a clean pair of heels and some ankle while you was at it, says the one. Oh no, higher still, says the other, hoisted them up around your neck, you should've gone off like a ship in full sail, arse to the wind, we would've been smitten by your dazzling charms, knocked on the head like lambs at slaughter, struck by lightning we would've been, you would've got clean away. They grin at each other and laugh, they have been showing off. They have been talking to each other all this time, and not to me.

They are a low class of person.

I do not have the run of the house as before. The Governor's wife is still frightened of me; she's afraid I will have another fit, and she doesn't want any of her best teacups broken; you would think she never heard anyone scream before. So I do not dust these days, or carry in the tea tray or empty the chamber pots or make up the beds. Instead I am set to work in the back kitchen, cleaning the pots and pans in the scullery, or else I work in the laundry. I do not mind that so much as I always liked doing the laundry, it is hard work and roughens the hands, but I like the clean smell afterwards.

I help the regular laundress, old Clarrie, who is part coloured and used to be a slave once, before they did away with it here. She is not afraid of me, she doesn't mind me or care what I may have done, even if I killed a gentleman; she only nods, as if to say, So that's one less of them. She says I am a steady worker and pull my share and don't waste the soap, and I know the treatment of fine linen, I have the way of it, and also how to get out the stains, even from the blonde lace, which is not easy to come by; and a good clear starcher too, and can be trusted not to burn the things in ironing, and that is enough for her.

At noon we go into the kitchen and Cook gives us what is left over, from the larder; at the very least some bread and cheese and meat broth but usually something more, as Clarrie is a favourite of hers and is known to have a temper if crossed, and the Governor's wife swears by her, especially for laces and ruffles, and says she is a treasure and has no equal, and would be annoyed to lose her, so she is not stinted; and because I am with her neither am I.

It's better food than I'd get on the inside of the walls. Yesterday we had the chicken carcass and all that was on it. There we sat at the table like two foxes in the henhouse gnawing the bones. They make such a fuss about the scissors upstairs, but the whole kitchen is bristling with knives and skewers all over like a porcupine, I could slip one into my apron pocket as easy as rolling off a log, but of course they never even think about that. Out of sight out of mind is their motto, and below stairs is like below ground as far as they are concerned, and little do they know that the servants carry away more out the back door with a spoon than the master can bring in the front door with a shovel; the trick of it is to do it little by little. One small knife would never be missed, and the best place to hide it would be in my hair, under my cap, well pinned in, as it would be a nasty surprise if it fell out at the wrong time.

We cut up the chicken carcass with one of the knives, and Clarrie ate the two little oysters off the bottom, near the stomach you might say, she likes to get those if they are left, and she being the senior has first choice. We did not say much to each other but we grinned, because eating this chicken was so good. I ate the fat off the back and the skin, I sucked the rib bones, then I licked my fingers like a cat; and after we were done, Clarrie had a quick smoke of her pipe on the step, and then it was back to work. Miss Lydia and Miss Marianne between them dirty a lot of washing, although much of it is not what I would call dirty at all; I believe they try things on in the morning and change their minds, and then take the things off and drop them carelessly on the floor and step on them, and then into the wash they must go.

After the hours have gone by and the sun on the clock upstairs has moved around to the middle of the afternoon, Dr. Jordan arrives at the front door. I listen for the knocking and the ringing and the clatter of the maid's footsteps, and then I am taken up the back stairs, my hands washed as white as snow with the soap from the laundry and my fingers all wrinkled from the hot water like someone newly drowned, but red and rough all the same, and then it is time to sew.

Dr. Jordan sits down in the chair across from me; he has a notebook which he puts on the table. He always brings something with him; the first day it was a dried flower of some sort, blue it was, the second day a winter pear, the third an onion, you never know what he will bring, although he inclines to the fruits and vegetables; and at the beginning of each talk he asks me what I think about this thing he has brought, and I say something about it just to keep him happy, and he writes it down. The door must be kept open at all times because there cannot be even a suspicion, no impropriety behind closed doors; how comical if they only knew what goes on every day during my walk here. Miss Lydia and Miss Marianne pass by on the stairs and peep in, they want to have a look at the Doctor, they are as curious as birds. Oh I believe I left my thimble in here, Good day Grace, I hope you are feeling yourself again, Do excuse us please Dr. Jordan, we do not mean to disturb you. They give him ravishing smiles, the word has gone around that he is unmarried and with money of his own, although I do not think either of them would settle for a Yankee doctor if they could get something better; however they like to practise their charms and attractions on him. But after he has smiled at them with his uneven smile, he frowns. He doesn't pay much attention to them, they are only silly young girls and not the reason he is here.

I am the reason. So he does not wish our talk to be interrupted.

On the first two days there was not much talk to interrupt. I kept my head down, I did not look at him, I worked away at my quilt blocks, for the quilt I am making for the Governor's wife, there are only five blocks left to be finished. I watched my needle go in and out, although I believe I could sew in my sleep, I've been doing it since I was four years old, small stitches as if made by mice. You need to start very young to be able to do that, otherwise you can never get the hang of it. The main colours are a double-pink print with a branch and flower in the lighter pink, and an indigo with white doves and grapes.

Or else I looked over the top of Dr. Jordan's head, at the wall behind him. There's a framed picture there, flowers in a vase, fruits in a bowl, in cross-stitch, done by the Governor's wife, clumsily too as the apples and peaches look square and hard, as if they're carved out of wood. Not one of her best efforts, which must be why she's hung it in here and not in a spare bedchamber. I could do better myself with my eyes closed.

It was difficult to begin talking. I had not talked very much for the past fifteen years, not really talking the way I once talked with Mary Whitney, and Jeremiah the peddler, and with Jamie Walsh too before he became so treacherous towards me; and in a way I had forgotten how. I told Dr. Jordan that I did not know what he wanted me to say. He said it wasn't what he wanted me to say, but what I wanted to say myself, that was of interest to him. I said I had no wants of that kind, as it was not my place to want to say anything.

Now Grace, he said, you must do better than that, we made a bargain.

Yes Sir, I said. But I cannot think of anything.

Then let us discuss the weather, he said; you must have some observations to make on it, since that is the way everyone else begins.

I smiled at that, but I was just as shy. I was not used to having my opinions asked, even about the weather and especially by a man with a notebook. The only men of that kind I ever encountered were Mr. Kenneth MacKenzie, Esq., the lawyer, and I was afraid of him; and those in the courtroom at the trial, and in the jail; and they were from the newspapers, and made up lies about me.

Since I could not talk at first, Dr. Jordan talked himself. He told me about how they were building railroads everywhere now, and how they laid down the tracks, and how the engines worked, with the boiler and the steam. This had the effect of setting me more at my ease, and I said I would like to ride in a railway train like that; and he said that perhaps someday I would. I said I did not think so, being sentenced to be here for life, but then you never can tell what time will have in store for you.

Then he told me about the town where he lives, which is called Loomisville, in the United States of America, and he said it was a mill town although not as prosperous as before the cheap cloth from India came in. He said his father once owned a mill, and the girls who worked in it came from the country, and were kept very tidy and lived in boarding houses provided, with respectable and sober landladies and no drink allowed and sometimes a parlour piano, and only twelve hours of work per day and Sunday mornings off for church; and by the moist and reminiscing look in his eye, I would not be surprised to learn that he once had a sweetheart among them.

Then he said these girls were taught to read, and had their own magazine which they published, with literary offerings. And I said what did he mean by literary offerings, and he said they wrote stories and poems which they put into it, and I said under their own names? He said yes, which I said was bold of them, and didn't it scare away the young men, as who would want a wife like that, writing things down for everyone to see, and made-up things at that, and I would never be so brazen. And he smiled, and said it did not appear to trouble the young men, as the girls saved up their wages for their dowries, and a dowry was always acceptable. And I said that at least after they got married, they would be too busy to make up any more stories, because of all the children.

Then I was sad, as I remembered that I would never be married now, or have any babies of my own; though there can be too much of a good thing you could say, and I would not like to have nine or ten and then die of it, as happens to many. But still it is a regret.

When you are sad it is best to change the subject. I asked if he had a mother living, and he said yes, although her health was not good; and I said that he was fortunate to have a mother living, as mine was not. And then I changed the subject again, and said I was very fond of horses, and he told me about his horse Bess, that he had as a boy. And after a time, I don't know how it was, but little by little I found I could talk to him more easily, and think up things to say.

And that is how we go on. He asks a question, and I say an answer, and he writes it down. In the courtroom, every word that came out of my mouth was as if burnt into the paper they were writing it on, and once I said a thing I knew I could never get the words back; only they were the wrong words, because whatever I said would be twisted around, even if it was the plain truth in the first place. And it was the same with Dr. Bannerling at the Asylum. But now I feel as if everything I say is right. As long as I say something, anything at all, Dr. Jordan smiles and writes it down, and tells me I am doing well.

While he writes, I feel as if he is drawing me; or not drawing me, drawing on me – drawing on my skin – not with the pencil he is using, but with an old-fashioned goose pen, and not with the quill end but with the feather end. As if hundreds of butterflies have settled all over my face, and are softly opening and closing their wings.

But underneath that is another feeling, a feeling of being wide-eyed awake and watchful. It's like being wakened suddenly in the middle of the night, by a hand over your face, and you sit up with your heart going fast, and no one is there. And underneath that is another feeling still, a feeling like being torn open; not like a body of flesh, it is not painful as such, but like a peach; and not even torn open, but too ripe and splitting open of its own accord.

And inside the peach there's a stone.

9.

From Dr. Samuel Bannerling, M.D., The Maples, Front Street,
Toronto, Canada West; to Dr. Simon Jordan, M.D., care of Mrs.
William P. Jordan, Laburnum House, Loomisville, Massachusetts,
The United States of America. Redirected, care of Major C. D.
Humphrey, Lower Union Street, Kingston, Canada West.

April 20th, 1859.

Dear Dr. Jordan:

I am in receipt of your request to Dr. Workman of April 2nd, concerning the convict Grace Marks, and of a note from him asking that I supply you with any further information at my disposal.

I must inform you at once that Dr. Workman and I have not always seen eye to eye. In my estimation – and I was at the Asylum for more years than he has yet been there – his policies of leniency have led him to undertake a fool's errand, namely the transforming of sows' ears into silk purses. Most who suffer from the more severe nervous and cerebral disorders cannot be cured, but merely controlled; for which purposes, physical restraint and correction, a restricted diet, and cupping and bleeding to reduce excessive animal spirits, have in the past proven efficacious enough. Although Dr. Workman claims to have obtained positive results in several cases previously considered hopeless, these supposed cures will no doubt in time prove to have been superficial and temporary. The taint of insanity is in the blood, and cannot be removed with a little soft soap and flannel.

Dr. Workman had the opportunity of examining Grace Marks for a few weeks only, whereas I had her under my care for over a year; and therefore his opinions on the subject of her character cannot be worth a great deal. He was, however, perspicacious enough to discover one pertinent fact – namely that, as a lunatic, Grace Marks was a sham – a view previously arrived at by myself, although the authorities of that time refused to act upon it. Continuous observation of her, and of her contrived antics, led me to deduce that she was not in fact insane, as she pretended, but was attempting to pull the wool over my eyes in a studied and flagrant manner. To speak plainly, her madness was a fraud and an imposture, adopted by her in order that she might indulge herself and be indulged, the strict regimen of the Penitentiary, where she had been placed as a just punishment for her atrocious crimes, not having been to her liking.

She is an accomplished actress and a most practised liar. While among us, she amused herself with a number of supposed fits, hallucinations, caperings, warblings and the like, nothing being lacking to the impersonation but Ophelia's wildflowers entwined in her hair; but she did well enough without them, as she managed to deceive, not only the worthy Mrs. Moodie, who like many high-minded females of her type, is inclined to believe any piece of theatrical twaddle served up to her, provided it is pathetic enough, and whose inaccurate and hysterical account of the whole sad affair you have no doubt read; but also several of my own colleagues, this latter being an outstanding example of the old rule of thumb, that when a handsome woman walks in through the door, good judgment flies out through the window.

Should you nonetheless decide to examine Grace Marks at her current place of abode, be pleased to consider yourself amply warned. Many older and wiser heads have been enmeshed in her toils, and you would do well to stop your ears with wax, as Ulysses made his sailors do, to escape the Sirens. She is as devoid of morals as she is of scruples, and will use any unwitting tool that comes to hand.

I should alert you also to the possibility that, once having involved yourself in her case, you will be besieged by a crowd of well-meaning but feeble-minded persons of both sexes, as well as clergymen, who have busied themselves on her behalf. They pester the Government with petitions for her release, and will attempt in the name of charity to waylay and conscript you. I have had repeatedly to beat them away from my door, whilst informing them that Grace Marks has been incarcerated for a very good reason, namely the vicious acts which she has committed, and which were inspired by her degenerate character and morbid imagination. To let her loose upon an unsuspecting public would be irresponsible to the last degree, as it would merely afford her the opportunity of gratifying her bloodthirsty tastes.

I am confident that, should you choose to explore the matter further, you will arrive at the same conclusions as have already been arrived at, by,

Your obedient servant,

(Dr.) Samuel Bannerling, M.D.

1 0 .

This morning Simon is to meet with Reverend Verringer. He's not looking forward to it: the man has studied in England, and is bound to give himself airs. There is no fool like an educated fool, and Simon will have to trot out his own European credentials, and flourish his erudition, and justify himself. It will be a trying interview, and Simon will be tempted to start drawling, and saying *I reckon*, and acting the British Colonial version of the wooden-nutmeg-peddling Yankee, just to annoy. He must restrain himself, however; too much depends on his good behaviour. He keeps forgetting he is no longer rich, and therefore no longer entirely his own man.

He stands in front of his looking glass, attempting to tie his stock. He hates cravats and stocks, and wishes them at the Devil; he resents his trousers as well, and all stiff and proper clothing generally. Why does civilized man see fit to torture his body by cramming it into the strait-jacket of gentlemanly dress? Perhaps it is a mortification of the flesh, like a hair shirt. Men ought to be born in little woollen suits which would grow with them over the years, thus avoiding the whole business of tailors, with their endless fussing and snobberies.

At least he isn't a woman, and thus not obliged to wear corsets, and to deform himself with tight lacing. For the widely held view that women are weak-spined and jelly-like by nature, and would slump to the floor like melted cheese if not roped in, he has nothing but contempt. While a medical student, he dissected a good many women – from the labouring classes, naturally – and their spines and musculature were on the average no feebler than those of men, although many suffered from rickets.

He's wrestled his stock into the semblance of a bow. It's lopsided, but the best he can do; he can no longer afford a valet. He brushes down his unruly hair, which rebounds instantly. Then he takes up his topcoat, and on second thought his umbrella. There's a weak sunlight making its way in through the windows, but it's too much to hope that it won't rain. Kingston in the spring is a watery place.

He makes his way stealthily down the front stairs, but not stealthily enough: his landlady has taken to waylaying him on some trivial matter or another, and she glides out from the parlour now, in her faded black silk and lace collar, clutching her customary handkerchief in one thin hand, as if tears are never far off. She was obviously a beauty not so long ago, and could still be one if she would take the trouble to be so, and if the centre parting in her fair hair were not quite so severe. Her face is heart-shaped, her skin milky, her eyes large and compelling; but although her waist is slender, there is something metallic about it, as if she is using a short length of stove-pipe instead of stays. Today she wears her habitual expression of strained anxiety; she smells of violets, and also of camphor – she is doubtless prone to headaches – and of something else he can't quite place. A hot dry smell. A white linen sheet being ironed?

As a rule, Simon avoids her type of attenuated and quietly distraught female, although doctors attract such women like magnets.

Still, there's a severe and unadorned elegance about her – like a Quaker meeting house – which has its appeal; an appeal which, for him, is aesthetic only. One does not make love to a minor religious edifice.

"Dr. Jordan," she says. "I wanted to ask you . . ." She hesitates. Simon smiles, prompting her to get on with it. "Your egg this morning – was it satisfactory? This time I cooked it myself."

Simon lies. To do otherwise would be unpardonably rude. "Delicious, thank you," he says. In reality the egg had the consistency of the excised tumour a fellow medical student once slipped into his pocket for a joke – both hard and spongy at the same time. It takes a perverse talent to maltreat an egg so completely.

"I am so glad," she says. "It is so difficult to get good help. You are going out?"

The fact is so obvious that Simon merely inclines his head.

"There is another letter for you," she says. "The servant mislaid it, but I have found it again. I have placed it on the hall table." She says this tremulously, as if any letter for Simon must be tragic in content. Her lips are full, but fragile, like a rose on the verge of collapse.

Simon thanks her, says goodbye, picks up his letter – it's from his mother – and leaves. He doesn't wish to encourage long conversations with Mrs. Humphrey. She's lonely – as well she might be, married to the sodden and straying Major – and loneliness in a woman is like hunger in a dog. He has no wish to be the recipient of dolorous afternoon confidences, behind drawn curtains, in the parlour.

Nonetheless she's an interesting study. Her idea of herself, for instance, is much more exalted than her present circumstances warrant. Surely there was a governess in her childhood: the set of her shoulders proclaims it. So fastidious and stern was she when he was arranging for the rooms, that he'd found it embarrassing to ask whether washing was included. Her manner had implied that she was not in the habit of discussing the state of men's personal items with them, such painful matters being best left to the servants.

She'd made it clear, although indirectly, that it was much against her will that she'd been forced to let lodgings. This was the first time she'd done so; it was due to an encumbrance which would surely prove temporary. Moreover, she was very particular – *A gentleman of quiet habits, if willing to take meals elsewhere*, her notice had read. When, after an inspection of the rooms, Simon had said he wished to take them, she'd hesitated, and then asked for two months' rent in advance.

Simon had seen the other lodgings on offer, which were either too expensive for him or much dirtier, so he'd agreed. He'd had the sum with him in ready cash. He'd noted with interest the blend of reluctance and eagerness she'd displayed, and the nervous flush this conflict had brought to her cheeks. The subject was distasteful to her, almost indecent; she hadn't wanted to touch his money in a naked state, and would have preferred it to be enclosed in an envelope; yet she'd had to restrain herself from snatching at it.

It was much the same attitude – the coyness about fiscal exchange, the pretence that it hadn't really taken place, the underlying avidity – that characterized the better class of French whore, although the whores were less gauche about it. Simon doesn't consider himself an authority in this area, but he would have failed in his duty to his vocation if he'd refused to profit by the opportunities Europe afforded – opportunities which were by no means so available, nor so various, in New England. To heal humanity one must know it, and one cannot know it from a distance; one must rub elbows with it, so to speak. He considers it the duty of those in his profession to probe life's uttermost depths, and although he has not probed very many of them as yet, he has at least made a beginning. He'd taken, of course, all proper precautions against disease.

Outside the house he encounters the Major, who stares at him as if through a dense fog. His eyes are pink, his stock is askew, and he is missing a glove. Simon tries to imagine what sort of debauch he's been on, and how long it has lasted. There must be a certain freedom in not having a good name to lose. He nods, and lifts his hat. The Major looks affronted.

Simon sets out to walk to Reverend Verringer's residence, which is on Sydenham Street. He hasn't hired a carriage or even a horse; the expense would not be not justified, as Kingston is not a large place. The streets are muddy and cluttered with horse dung, but he has good boots.

The door of Reverend Verringer's impressive manse is opened by an elderly female with a face like a pine plank; the Reverend is unmarried, and has need of an irreproachable housekeeper. Simon is ushered into the library. It is so self-consciously the right sort of library that he has an urge to set fire to it.

Reverend Verringer rises from a leather-covered wing chair, and offers him a hand to shake. Although his hair and his skin are equally thin and pallid, his handshake is surprisingly firm; and despite his unfortunately small and pouting mouth – like a tadpole's, thinks Simon – his Roman nose indicates a strong character, his high-domed forehead a developed intellect, and his somewhat bulging eyes are bright and keen. He cannot be over thirty-five; he must be well connected, thinks Simon, to have risen so fast in the Methodist establishment, and to have procured such an affluent congregation. Considering the books, he must have money of his own. Simon's father used to have books like that.

"I am glad you could come, Dr. Jordan," he says; his voice is less affected than Simon has feared. "It is kind of you to oblige us. Your time must be valuable indeed." They sit, and coffee appears, brought in by the slab-faced housekeeper on a tray which is plain in design, but nonetheless of silver. A Methodist tray: not flamboyant, but quietly affirmative of its own worth.

"It is a matter of great professional interest to me," says Simon. "It is not often that such a case presents itself, with so many intriguing features." He speaks as if he personally has treated hundreds of cases. The thing is to look interested, but not too eager, as if the favour is being conferred by him. He hopes he's not blushing.

"A report from you would be a considerable help to our Committee," says Reverend Verringer, "should such a report favour the theory of innocence. We would attach it to our Petition; Government authorities are much more inclined nowadays to take expert opinion into consideration. Of course," he adds, with a shrewd glance, "you will be paid the sum agreed on, no matter what your conclusions."

"I fully understand," says Simon with what he hopes is an urbane smile. "You studied in England, I think?"

"I began the pursuit of my vocation as a member of the Established Church," says Reverend Verringer, "but then had a crisis of conscience. Surely the light of God's word and grace is available to those outside the Church of England, and through more direct means than the Liturgy."

"I would certainly hope so," says Simon politely.

"The eminent Reverend Egerton Ryerson, of Toronto, followed much the same course. He is a leader in the crusade for free schooling, and for the abolition of alcoholic beverages. You have heard of him, naturally."

Simon has not; he emits an ambiguous h'm, which he hopes will pass for agreement.

"You yourself are . . . ?"

Simon dodges. "My father's family was Quaker," he says. "For many years. My mother is a Unitarian."

"Ah yes," says Reverend Verringer. "Of course, everything is so different in the United States." There is a pause, while they both consider this. "But you do believe in the immortality of the soul?"

This is the trick question; this is the trap that might put paid to his chances. "Oh yes, of course," says Simon. "It is not to be doubted."

Verringer seems relieved. "So many scientific men are casting doubts. Leave the body to the doctors, I say, and the soul to God. Render unto Caesar, you might say."

"Of course, of course."

"Dr. Binswanger spoke very highly of you. I had the pleasure of meeting him while travelling on the Continent – Switzerland is of great interest to me, for historical reasons – and I talked with him of his work; and therefore it was natural for me to consult him, when seeking an authority on this side of the Atlantic. An authority" – he hesitates – "who would be within our means. He said you are well up on cerebral diseases and nervous afflictions, and that in matters concerning amnesia you are on your way to becoming a leading expert. He claims you are one of the up-and-coming men."

"It is kind of him to say so," Simon murmurs. "It is a baffling area. But I have published two or three little papers."

"Let us hope that, at the conclusion of your investigations, you will be able to add to their number, and to shed light on a puzzling obscurity; for which society will give you due recognition, I am sure. Especially in such a famous case."

Simon notes to himself that, although tadpole-mouthed, Reverend Verringer is no fool. Certainly he has a sharp nose for other men's ambitions. Could it be that his switch from the Church of England to the Methodists had coincided with the falling political star of the former in this country, and the rising one of the latter?

"You have read the accounts I sent you?"

Simon nods. "I can see your dilemma," he says. "It is difficult to know what to believe. Grace appears to have told one story at the inquest, another one at the trial, and, after her death sentence had been commuted, yet a third. In all three, however, she denied ever having laid a finger on Nancy Montgomery. But then, some years later, we have Mrs. Moodie's account, which amounts to a confession by Grace, of having actually done the deed; and this story is in accordance with James McDermott's dying words, just before he was hanged. Since her return from the Asylum, however, you say she denies it."

Reverend Verringer sips at his coffee. "She denies the *memory* of it," he says.

"Ah yes. The memory of it," says Simon. "A proper distinction."

"She could well have been convinced by others that she had done something of which she is innocent," says Reverend Verringer. "It has happened before. The so-called confession in the Penitentiary, of which Mrs. Moodie has given such a colourful description, took place after several years of incarceration, and during the long regime of Warden Smith. The man was notoriously corrupt, and most unfit for his position. He was accused of behaviour of the most shocking and brutal kind; his son, for instance, was permitted to use the convicts for target practice, and on one occasion actually put out an eye. There was talk of his abusing the female prisoners also, in ways you may well imagine, and I am afraid there is no doubt about it; a full enquiry was held. It is to Grace Marks' mistreatment at his hands that I attribute her interlude of insanity."

"There are some who deny that she was in fact insane," says Simon.

Reverend Verringer smiles. "You have heard from Dr. Bannerling, I suppose. He has been against her from the beginning. We on the Committee have appealed to him – a favourable report from him would have been invaluable to our cause – but he is intransigent. A Tory, of course, of the deepest dye – he would have all the poor lunatics chained up in straw, if he had his way; and all hanged who look sideways. I am sorry to say that I consider him to have been a part of the same corrupt system that was responsible for the appointment of a coarse and profane man such as Warden Smith. I understand that there were irregularities at the Asylum as well – so much so that Grace Marks, upon her return from it, was suspected of being in a delicate condition. Happily these rumours were unfounded; but how craven – how callous! – to attempt to take advantage of those who are not in control of themselves! I have spent much time in prayer with Grace Marks, attempting to heal the wounds caused to her by these unfaithful and blameworthy betrayers of the public trust."

"Deplorable," says Simon. It might be considered prurient to ask for more details.

A sudden and illuminating thought strikes him – Reverend Verringer is in love with Grace Marks! Hence his indignation, his fervour, his assiduousness, his laborious petitions and committees; and above all, his desire to believe her innocent. Does he wish to winkle her out of jail, vindicated as a spotless innocent, and then marry her himself? She's still a good-looking woman, and would no doubt be touchingly grateful to her rescuer. Abjectly grateful; abject gratitude in a wife being, no doubt, a prime commodity on Verringer's spiritual exchange.

"Fortunately there was a change of government," says Reverend Verringer. "But even so, we do not wish to proceed with our present Petition, until we know ourselves to be on absolutely firm ground; which is why we have taken the step of calling upon you. I must tell you frankly that not all the members of our Committee were in favour of it, but I succeeded in convincing them of the need for an informed and objective viewpoint. A diagnosis of latent insanity at the time of the murders, for instance – however, the utmost caution and rectitude must be observed. There is still a widespread feeling against Grace Marks; and this is a most partisan country. The Tories appear to have confused Grace with the Irish Question, although she is a Protestant; and to consider the murder of a single Tory gentleman – however worthy the gentleman, and however regrettable the murder – to be the same thing as the insurrection of an entire race."

"Every country is plagued by factionalism," says Simon tactfully.

"Even apart from that," says Reverend Verringer, "we are caught between the notion of a possibly innocent woman, whom many believe to be guilty, and a possibly guilty woman, whom some believe to be innocent. We would not want the opponents of reform to be given an opportunity of crowing over us. But, as our Lord says, 'The truth shall make you free.'"

"The truth may well turn out to be stranger than we think," says Simon. "It may be that much of what we are accustomed to describe as evil, and evil freely chosen, is instead an illness due to some lesion of the nervous system, and that the Devil himself is simply a malformation of the cerebrum."

Reverend Verringer smiles. "Oh, I doubt it will go so far as that," he says. "No matter what science may accomplish in the future, the Devil will always be at large. I believe you have been invited to the Governor's house on Sunday afternoon?"

"I have had that honour," says Simon politely. He has been intending to make his excuses.

"I look forward to seeing you there," says Reverend Verringer. "I myself arranged the invitation for you. The Governor's excellent wife is an invaluable member of our Committee."

11.

At the Governor's residence, Simon is directed to the parlour, which is almost large enough to be called a drawing room. All possible surfaces of it are upholstered; the colours are those of the inside of the body – the maroon of kidneys, the reddish purple of hearts, the opaque blue of veins, the ivory of teeth and bones. He imagines the sensation it would produce if he were to announce this *aperçu* out loud.

He is greeted by the Governor's wife. She is a handsome woman of forty-five or so, of an obvious respectability, but dressed in the hectic manner of the provinces, where the ladies appear to feel that if one row of lace and ruching is good, three must be better. She has the alarmed, slightly pop-eyed look that signals either an overly nervous disposition or a disease of the thyroid.

"I am so glad you could honour us," she says. She tells him that the Governor is regrettably away on business, but that she herself is deeply interested in the work he is doing; she has such a respect for modern science, and especially for modern medicine; such a number of advances have been made. Especially the ether, which has spared so much distress. She fixes him with a deep and meaningful gaze, and Simon sighs inwardly. He is familiar with that expression: she is about to make him an unsolicited gift of her symptoms.

When he first received his medical degree, he was unprepared for the effect it would have on women; women of the better classes, married ladies especially, with blameless reputations. They seemed drawn to him as if he possessed some priceless but infernal treasure. Their interest was innocent enough – they had no intention of sacrificing their virtue to him – yet they longed to entice him into shadowy corners, to converse with him in lowered voices, to confide in him – timorously, and with quavers, because he also inspired fear. What was the secret of his allure? The face he saw in the mirror, which was neither ugly nor handsome, could scarcely account for it.

After a time he thought he knew. It was knowledge they craved; yet they could not admit to craving it, because it was forbidden knowledge – knowledge with a lurid glare to it; knowledge gained through a descent into the pit. He has been where they could never go, seen what they could never see; he has opened up women's bodies, and peered inside. In his hand, which has just raised their own hands towards his lips, he may once have held a beating female heart.

Thus he is one of the dark trio – the doctor, the judge, the executioner – and shares with them the powers of life and death. To be rendered unconscious; to lie exposed, without shame, at the mercy of others; to be touched, incised, plundered, remade – this is what they are thinking of when they look at him, with their widening eyes and slightly parted lips.

"I suffer so terribly," the Governor's wife's voice begins. Coyly, as if displaying an ankle, she relates a symptom – agitated breathing, a constriction around the ribs – with a hint of more and richer ones to follow. She has a pain – well, she doesn't like to say exactly where. Whatever could be the cause of it?

Simon smiles, and says he is no longer practising general medicine.

After a momentary thwarted frown, the Governor's wife smiles too, and says she would like him to meet Mrs. Quennell, the celebrated Spiritualist and advocate of an enlarged sphere for women, and the leading light of our Tuesday discussion circle, as well as of the spiritual Thursdays; such an accomplished person, and so widely travelled, in Boston and elsewhere. Mrs. Quennell, in her huge crinoline-supported skirt, resembles a lavender-coloured Bavarian cream; her head appears to be topped with a small grey poodle. In her turn she presents Simon to Dr. Jerome DuPont, of New York, who is visiting just now, and who has promised to give a demonstration of his remarkable powers. He is well known, says Mrs. Quennell, and has stayed with Royalty in England. Or not exactly Royalty; but aristocratic families, all the same.

"Remarkable powers?" says Simon politely. He would like to know what they are. Possibly the fellow claims to levitate, or personifies a dead Indian, or produces spirit rappings, like the celebrated Fox sisters. Spiritualism is the craze of the middle classes, the women especially; they gather in darkened rooms and play at table-tilting the way their grandmothers played at whist, or they emit voluminous automatic writings, dictated to them by Mozart or Shakespeare; in which case being dead, thinks Simon, has a remarkably debilitating effect on one's prose style. If these people were not so well-to-do, their behaviour would get them committed. Worse, they populate their drawing rooms with fakirs and mountebanks, all of them swathed in the grubby vestments of a self-proclaimed quasi-holiness, and the rules of society dictate that one must be polite to them.

Dr. Jerome DuPont has the deep liquid eyes and intense gaze of a professional charlatan; but he smiles ruefully, and gives a dismissive shrug. "Not very remarkable, I'm afraid," he says. He has a trace of a foreign accent. "Such things are merely another language; if one speaks it, one takes it simply for granted. It is others who find it remarkable."

"You converse with the dead?" asks Simon, his mouth twitching.

Dr. DuPont smiles. "Not I," he says. "I am what you might call a medical practitioner. Or an investigative scientist, like yourself. I am a trained Neuro-hypnotist, of the school of James Braid."

"I have heard of him," says Simon. "A Scotsman, isn't he? A noted authority on clubfoot and strabismus, I believe. But surely professional medicine does not recognize these other claims of his. Is not this Neuro-hypnotism simply the reanimated corpse of Mesmer's discredited Animal Magnetism?"

"Mesmer posited a magnetic fluid encircling the body, which was certainly erroneous," says Dr. DuPont. "Braid's procedures involve the nervous system alone. I might add that those who dispute his methods have not tried them. They are more accepted in France, where the doctors are less prone to craven orthodoxies. They are more useful in hysterical cases, than in others, of course; they cannot do much for a broken leg. But in cases of amnesia" – he gives a faint smile – "they have frequently produced astounding, and, I may say, very rapid results."

Simon feels at a disadvantage, and changes the subject. "DuPont – is it a French name?"

"The family was French Protestant," says Dr. DuPont. "But only on the father's side. He was an amateur of chemistry. I myself am an American. I have visited France professionally, of course."

"Perhaps Dr. Jordan would like to make one of our party," says Mrs. Quennell, breaking in. "On our spiritual Thursdays. Our dear Governor's wife finds them such a comfort, to know that her little one, now on the other side, is so well and happy. I am sure Dr. Jordan is a sceptic – but we always welcome sceptics!" The tiny bright eyes beneath the doggy coiffure twinkle roguishly at him.

"Not a sceptic," says Simon, "only a medical doctor." He has no intention of being lured into some compromising and preposterous rigmarole. He wonders what Verringer is thinking of, to include such a woman on his Committee. But evidently she is wealthy.

"Physician, heal thyself," says Dr. DuPont. He seems to be making a joke.

"Where do you stand on the Abolitionist question, Dr. Jordan?" says Mrs. Quennell. Now the woman is turning intellectual, and will insist on a belligerent discussion of politics, and will doubtless order him to abolish slavery in the South at once. Simon finds it tiresome to be constantly accused, in his individual person, of all the sins of his country, and especially by these Britishers, who seem to think that a conscience recently discovered excuses them for not having had any conscience at all at an earlier period. On what was their present wealth founded, but on the slave trade; and where would their great mill towns be without Southern cotton?

"My grandfather was a Quaker," he says. "As a boy, I was taught never to open cupboard doors, in case some poor fugitive might be concealed within. He always felt that to put his own safety at risk was worth a good deal more than barking at others from behind the protection of a fence."

"Stone walls do not a prison make," says Mrs. Quennell gaily.

"But all scientists must keep an open mind," says Dr. DuPont. He appears to be back in their previous conversation.

"I am sure Dr. Jordan's mind is as open as a book," says Mrs. Quennell. "You are looking into our Grace, we are told. From the spiritual point of view."

Simon can see that if he tries to explain the difference between the spirit, in her sense of the word, and the unconscious mind, in his, he will get hopelessly tangled; so he merely smiles and nods.

"What approach are you taking?" says Dr. DuPont. "To restore her vanished memory."

"I have begun," says Simon, "with a method based on suggestion, and the association of ideas. I am attempting, gently and by degrees, to re-establish the chain of thought, which was broken, perhaps, by the shock of the violent events in which she was involved."

"Ah," says Dr. DuPont, with a superior smile. "Slow but steady wins the race!" Simon would like to kick him.

"We are sure she is innocent," says Mrs. Quennell. "All of us on the Committee! We are convinced of it! Reverend Verringer is getting up a Petition. It is not the first, but we are in hopes that this time we will be successful. 'Once more unto the breach' is our motto." She gives a girlish wiggle. "Do say you are on our side!"

"If at first you don't succeed," says Dr. DuPont solemnly.

"I have not drawn any conclusions, as yet," says Simon. "In any case, I am less interested in her guilt or innocence, than in . . ."

"Than in the mechanisms at work," says Dr. DuPont.

"That is not quite how I would put it," says Simon.

"It is not the tune played by the musical box, but the little cogs and wheels within it, that concern you."

"And you?" says Simon, who is beginning to find Dr. DuPont more interesting.

"Ah," says DuPont. "For me it is not even the box, with its pretty pictures on the outside. For me, it is only the music. The music is played by a physical object; and yet the music is not that object. As Scripture says, 'The wind bloweth where it listeth.'"

"St. John," says Mrs. Quennell. "'That which is born of the Spirit is spirit.'"

"'And that which is born of the flesh is flesh,'" says DuPont. The two of them peer at him with an air of gentle but unanswerable triumph, and Simon feels as if he is suffocating under a mattress.

"Dr. Jordan," says a soft voice at his elbow. It is Miss Lydia, one of the Governor's wife's two daughters. "Mama sent me to ask if you have yet seen her scrapbook."

Simon inwardly blesses his hostess, and says he has not had that pleasure. The prospect of murky engravings of the beauty spots of Europe, their borders decorated with paper fern fronds, is not usually alluring to him, but at the moment it beckons like an escape. He smiles and nods, and is led away.

Miss Lydia places him on a tongue-coloured settee, then fetches a heavy book from the adjacent table and arranges herself beside him. "She thought you might find it of interest, because of whatever it is you are doing with Grace."

"Oh?" says Simon.

"It has got all of the famous murders in it," Miss Lydia explains. "My mother cuts them out and pastes them in, and the hangings, too."

"Does she indeed?" asks Simon. The woman must be a ghoul as well as a hypochondriac.

"It helps her to make up her mind, as to which among the prisoners may be worthy objects of charity," says Miss Lydia. "Here is Grace." She opens the book across their knees and leans in his direction, gravely instructive. "I take an interest in her; she has remarkable abilities."

"Like Dr. DuPont?" Simon says.

Miss Lydia stares. "Oh, no. I do not go in for any of that. I would never let myself be hypnotized, it is so immodest! I mean that Grace has remarkable abilities as a dressmaker."

There is a subdued recklessness about her, thinks Simon; when she smiles, both bottom and top teeth show. But at least she is healthy-minded, unlike the mother. A healthy young animal. Simon is conscious of her white throat, encircled with a modest ribbon ornamented with a rosebud, as befits an unmarried girl. Through layers of delicate fabric, her arm presses against his. He is not an insensible block, and although Miss Lydia's character, like that of all such girls, must be unformed and childish, she has a very small waist. A cloud of scent rises from her, lily of the valley, enveloping him in olfactory gauze.

But Miss Lydia must be unconscious of the effect she is producing on him, being necessarily ignorant of the nature of such effects. He crosses his legs.

"Here is the execution," says Miss Lydia. "Of James McDermott. It was in several of the newspapers. This one is *The Examiner*."

Simon reads:

What a morbid appetite for such sights, must exist in society, when so large an assemblage, in the present state of our roads, had collected, to witness the dying agony, of an unfortunate but criminal fellow being! Can it be supposed that public morals are improved, or the tendency to the commission of flagrant crimes repressed, by such public sights as these.

"I am inclined to agree," says Simon.

"I would have attended it if I had been there," says Miss Lydia. "Wouldn't you?"

Simon is taken aback by such directness. He disapproves of public executions, which are unhealthily exciting and produce bloodthirsty fancies in the weaker-minded part of the population. But he knows himself; and, given the opportunity, his curiosity would have overcome his scruples. "In my professional capacity, perhaps," he says cautiously. "But I wouldn't have allowed my sister to attend, supposing I had one."

Miss Lydia widens her eyes. "But why not?" she says.

"Women should not attend such grisly spectacles," he says. "They pose a danger to their refined natures." He's conscious of sounding pompous.

In the course of his travels, he's encountered many women who could scarcely be accused of refined natures. He has seen madwomen tearing off their clothes and displaying their naked bodies; he has seen prostitutes of the lowest sort do the same. He's seen women drunk and swearing, struggling together like wrestlers, pulling the hair from each other's heads. The streets of Paris and London swarm with them; he's known them to make away with their own infants, and to sell their young daughters to wealthy men who hope that by raping children they will avoid disease. So he is under no illusions as to the innate refinement of women; but all the more reason to safeguard the purity of those still pure. In such a cause, hypocrisy is surely justified: one must present what ought to be true as if it really is.

"Do you think I have a refined nature?" says Miss Lydia.

"I am certain of it," says Simon. He wonders if that is her thigh he can feel against his, or only part of her dress.

"I am sometimes not so sure," says Miss Lydia. "There are people who say that Miss Florence Nightingale does not have a refined nature, or she would not have been able to witness such degrading spectacles without impairing her health. But she is a heroine."

"There is no doubt of that," says Simon.

He suspects she's flirting with him. It's far from disagreeable, but, perversely, it makes him think of his mother. How many acceptable young girls has she trailed discreetly before him, like feathered fishing lures? She arranges them, always, next to a vase of white flowers. Their morals have been irreproachable, their manners candid as spring water; their minds have been presented to him as unbaked pieces of dough which it would be his prerogative to mould and form. As one season's crop of girls proceeds into engagement and marriage, younger ones keep sprouting up, like tulips in May. They are now so young in relation to Simon that he has trouble conversing with them; it's like talking to a basketful of kittens.

But his mother has always confused youth with malleability. What she really wants is a daughter-in-law who can be moulded, not by Simon, but by herself; and so the girls continue to be floated past him, and he continues to turn away indifferently, and to be gently accused by his mother of laziness and ingratitude. He rebukes himself for it – he's a sad dog and a cold fish – and takes care to thank his mother for her pains, and to reassure her: he will marry eventually, but he isn't ready for it yet. First he must pursue his researches; he must accomplish something of value, discover something of note; he has his name to make.

He already has a name, she sighs reproachfully; a perfectly good name, which he seems determined to exterminate by refusing to pass it on. At this point she always coughs a little, to signify that his was a difficult birth, which almost killed her, and fatally weakened her lungs – a medically implausible effect which, during his boyhood, used to reduce him to a jelly of guilt. If he would only produce a son, she continues – having, of course, married first – she would die happy. He teases her by saying that in that case it would be sinful of him to marry at all, since to do so would amount to matricide; and he adds – to soften the acerbity – that he can do much better without a wife than without a mother, and especially such a perfect mother as herself; at which she gives him a sharp look which tells him she knows several tricks worth two of that, and is not deceived. He's too clever for his own good, she says; he needn't think he can get round her by flattery. But she's mollified.

Sometimes he's tempted to succumb. He could choose one of her proffered young ladies, the richest one. His daily life would be orderly, his breakfasts would be edible, his children would be respectful. The act of procreation would be undergone unseen, prudently veiled in white cotton – she, dutiful but properly averse, he within his rights – but need never be mentioned. His home would have all the modern comforts, and he himself would be sheltered in velvet. There are worse fates.

"Do you think that Grace has one?" says Miss Lydia. "A refined nature. I am sure she did not do the murders; although she is sorry for not having told anyone about them, afterwards. James McDermott must have been lying about her. But they say she was his paramour. Is it true?"

Simon feels himself blushing. If she's flirting, she isn't conscious of it. She is too innocent to understand her lack of innocence. "I couldn't say," he murmurs.

"Perhaps she was abducted," says Miss Lydia dreamily. "In books, women are always being abducted. But I have not personally known anyone that was. Have you?"

Simon says he has never had such an experience.

"They cut off his head," says Miss Lydia in a lower voice. "McDermott's. They have it in a bottle, at the University in Toronto."

"Surely not," says Simon, disconcerted afresh. "The skull may have been preserved, but surely not the entire head!"

"Like a big pickle," says Miss Lydia with satisfaction. "Oh, look, Mama wants me to go and talk to Reverend Verringer. I would rather talk to you – he is so pedagogical. She thinks he is good for my moral improvement."

Reverend Verringer has indeed just come into the room, and is smiling at Simon with annoying benevolence, as if Simon is his protégé. Or perhaps he is smiling at Lydia.

Simon watches Lydia as she glides across the room; she has that oiled walk they cultivate. Left to himself on the settee, he finds himself thinking of Grace, as he sees her every weekday, seated opposite him in the sewing room. In her portrait she looks older than she was, but now she looks younger. Her complexion is pale, the skin smooth and unwrinkled and remarkably fine in texture, perhaps because she's been kept indoors; or it may be the sparse prison diet. She's thinner now, less full in the face; and whereas the picture shows a pretty woman, she is now more than pretty. Or other than pretty. The line of her cheek has a marble, a classic, simplicity; to look at her is to believe that suffering does indeed purify.

But in the closeness of the sewing room, Simon can smell her as well as look at her. He tries to pay no attention, but her scent is a distracting undercurrent. She smells like smoke; smoke, and laundry soap, and the salt from her skin; and she smells of the skin itself, with its undertone of dampness, fullness, ripeness – what? Ferns and mushrooms; fruits crushed and fermenting. He wonders how often the female prisoners are allowed to bathe. Although her hair is braided and coiled up under her cap, it too gives off an odour, a strong musky odour of scalp. He is in the presence of a female animal; something fox-like and alert. He senses an answering alertness along his own skin, a sensation as of bristles lifting. Sometimes he feels as if he's walking on quicksand.

Every day he has set some small object in front of her, and has asked her to tell him what it causes her to imagine. This week he's attempted various root vegetables, hoping for a connection that will lead downwards: Beet – Root Cellar – Corpses, for instance; or even Turnip – Underground – Grave. According to his theories, the right object ought to evoke a chain of disturbing associations in her; although so far she's treated his offerings simply at their face value, and all he's got out of her has been a series of cookery methods.

On Friday he tried a more direct approach. "You may be perfectly frank with me, Grace," he had said. "You need hold nothing back."

"I have no reason not to be frank with you, Sir," she said. "A lady might conceal things, as she has her reputation to lose; but I am beyond that."

"What do you mean, Grace?" he said.

"Only, I was never a lady, Sir, and I've already lost whatever reputation I ever had. I can say anything I like; or if I don't wish to, I needn't say anything at all."

"You don't care about my good opinion of you, Grace?"

She gave him a quick sharp look, then continued her stitching. "I have already been judged, Sir. Whatever you may think of me, it's all the same."

"Judged rightly, Grace?" He could not resist asking.

"Rightly or wrongly does not matter," she said. "People want a guilty person. If there has been a crime, they want to know who did it. They don't like not knowing."

"Then you have given up hope?"

"Hope of what, Sir?" she asked mildly.

Simon felt foolish, as if he'd committed a breach of etiquette. "Well – hope of being set free."

"Now why would they want to do that, Sir?" she said. "A murderess is not an everyday thing. As for my hopes, I save that for smaller matters. I live in hopes of having a better breakfast tomorrow than I had today." She smiled a little. "They said at the time that they were making an example of me. That's why it was the death sentence, and then the life sentence."

But what does an example do, afterwards? thought Simon. Her story is over. The main story, that is; the thing that has defined her. How is she supposed to fill in the rest of the time? "Do you not feel you have been treated unjustly?" he said.

"I don't know what you mean, Sir." She was threading the needle now; she wet the end of the thread in her mouth, to make it easier, and this gesture seemed to him all at once both completely natural and unbearably intimate. He felt as if he was watching her undress, through a chink in the wall; as if she was washing herself with her tongue, like a cat.

V.

BROKEN DISHES

My name is Grace Marks, and I am the daughter of John Marks, who lives in the Township of Toronto, he is a Stonemason by trade; we came to this country from the North of Ireland about three years ago; I have four sisters and four brothers, one sister and one brother older than I am; I was 16 years old last July. I have lived servant during the three years I have been in Canada at various places. . . .

– Voluntary Confession of Grace Marks,
to Mr. George Walton, in the Gaol,
on the 17th of November, 1843,
Star and Transcript, Toronto.

. . . All the seventeen years,
Not once did a suspicion visit me
How very different a lot is mine
From any other woman's in the world.
The reason must be, 'twas by step and step
It got to grow so terrible and strange:
These strange woes stole on tiptoe, as it were,
Into my neighbourhood and privacy,
Sat down where I sat, laid them where I lay;
And I was found familiarized with fear,
When friends broke in, held up a torch and cried
"Why, you Pompilia, in the cavern thus,

"How came that arm of yours about a wolf?
"And the soft length, – lies in and out your feet
"And laps you round the knee, – a snake it is!"
And so on.

– Robert Browning,
The Ring and the Book, 1869.

1 2 .

This is the ninth day I have sat with Dr. Jordan in this room. The days haven't been all in a row, as there are the Sundays, and on some other days he did not come. I used to count from my birthdays, and then I counted from my first day in this country, and then from Mary Whitney's last day on earth, and after that from the day in July when the worst things happened, and after that I counted from my first day in prison. But now I am counting from the first day I spent in the sewing room with Dr. Jordan, because you can't always count from the same thing, it gets too tedious and the time stretches out longer and longer, and you can scarcely bear it.

Dr. Jordan sits across from me. He smells of shaving soap, the English kind, and of ears; and of the leather of his boots. It is a reassuring smell and I always look forward to it, men that wash being preferable in this respect to those that do not. What he has put on the table today is a potato, but he has not yet asked me about it, so it is just sitting there between us. I don't know what he expects me to say about it, except that I have peeled a good many of them in my time, and eaten them too, a fresh new potato is a joy with a little butter and salt, and parsley if available, and even the big old ones can bake up very beautiful; but they are nothing to have a long conversation about. Some potatoes look like babies' faces, or else like animals, and I once saw one that looked like a cat. But this one looks just like a potato, no more and no less. Sometimes I think that Dr. Jordan is a little off in the head. But I would rather talk with him about potatoes, if that is what he fancies, than not talk to him at all.

He has a different cravat on today, it is red with blue spots or blue with red spots, a little bit loud for my taste but I cannot look at him steady enough to tell. I need the scissors and so I ask for them, and then he wants me to begin talking, so I say, Today I will finish the last block for this quilt, after this the blocks will all be sewn together and it will be quilted, it is meant for one of the Governor's young ladies. It is a Log Cabin.

A Log Cabin quilt is a thing every young woman should have before marriage, as it means the home; and there is always a red square at the centre, which means the hearth fire. Mary Whitney told me that. But I don't say this, as I don't think it will interest him, being too common. Though no more common than a potato.

And he says, What will you sew after this? And I say, I don't know, I suppose I will be told, they don't use me for the quilting, only for the blocks because it is such fine work, and the Governor's wife said I was thrown away on the plain sewing such as they do at the Penitentiary, the postbags and uniforms and so forth; but in any case the quilting is in the evening, and it is a party, and I am not invited to parties.

And he says, If you could make a quilt all for yourself, which pattern would you make?

Well there is no doubt about that, I know the answer. It would be a Tree of Paradise like the one in the quilt chest at Mrs. Alderman Parkinson's, I used to get it out on the pretence of seeing if it needed mending, just to admire it, it was a lovely thing, made all of triangles, dark for the leaves and light for the apples, the work very fine, the stitches almost as small as I can do myself, only on mine I would make the border different. Hers is a Wild Goose Chase border, but mine would be an intertwined border, one light colour, one dark, the vine border they call it, vines twisted together like the vines on the mirror in the parlour. It would be a great deal of work and would take a long time, but if it were mine and just for me to have, I would be willing to do it.

But what I say to him is different. I say, I don't know, Sir. Perhaps it would be a Job's Tears, or a Tree of Paradise, or a Snake Fence; or else an Old Maid's Puzzle, because I am an old maid, wouldn't you say, Sir, and I have certainly been very puzzled. I said this last thing to be mischievous. I did not give him a straight answer, because saying what you really want out loud brings bad luck, and then the good thing will never happen. It might not happen anyway, but just to make sure, you should be careful about saying what you want or even wanting anything, as you may be punished for it. This is what happened to Mary Whitney.

He writes down the names of the quilts. He says, Trees of Paradise, or Tree?

Tree, Sir, I say. You can have a quilt with more than one of them on it, I have seen four with their tops pointed into the middle, but it is still called Tree.

Why is that, do you suppose, Grace? he says. Sometimes he is like a child, he is always asking why.

Because that is the name of the pattern, Sir, I say. There is also the Tree of Life, but that is a different pattern. You can also have a Tree of Temptation, and there is the Pine Tree, that is very nice as well.

He writes that down. Then he picks up the potato and looks at it. He says, Is it not wonderful that such a thing grows under the ground, you might say it is growing in its sleep, out of sight in the darkness, hidden from view.

Well, I don't know where he expects a potato to grow, I have never seen them dangling about on the bushes. I say nothing, and he says, What else is underground, Grace?

There would be the beets, I say. And the carrots are the same way, Sir, I say. It is their nature.

He seems disappointed in this answer, and does not write it down. He looks at me and thinks. Then he says, Have you had any dreams, Grace?

And I say, What do you mean, Sir?

I think he means do I dream of the future, do I have any plans for what I may do in my life, and I think it is a cruel question; seeing as I am in here until I die, I do not have many bright prospects to think about. Or perhaps he means do I daydream, do I have fancies about some man or other, like a young girl, and that notion is just as cruel if not more so; and I say, a little angry and reproachful, What would I be doing with dreams, it is not very kind of you to ask.

And he says, No, I see you mistake my meaning. What I am asking is, do you have dreams when you are asleep at night?

I say, a little tartly because it is more of his gentleman's nonsense and also I am still angry, Everybody does, Sir, or I suppose they do.

Yes, Grace, but do you? he says. He has not noticed my tone or else he has chosen not to notice it. I can say anything to him and he would not be put out or shocked, or even very surprised, he would only write it down. I suppose he is interested in my dreams because a dream can mean something, or so it says in the Bible, such as Pharaoh and the fat kine and the lean kine, and Jacob with the angels going up and down the ladder. There is a quilt called after that, it is the Jacob's Ladder.

I do, Sir, I say.

He says, What did you dream last night?

I dreamt that I was standing at the door of the kitchen at Mr. Kinnear's. It was the summer kitchen; I had just been scrubbing the floor, I know that because my skirts were still tucked up and my feet were bare and wet, and I had not yet put my clogs back on. A man was there, just outside on the step, he was a peddler of some sort, like Jeremiah the peddler who I once bought the buttons from, for my new dress, and McDermott bought the four shirts.

But this was not Jeremiah, it was a different man. He had his pack open and the things spread out on the ground, the ribbons and buttons and combs and pieces of cloth, very bright they were in the dream, silks and cashmere shawls and cotton prints gleaming in the sun, because it was broad daylight and full summer.

I felt he was someone I had once known, but he kept his face turned away so I could not see who it was. I could sense that he was looking down, looking at my bare legs, bare from the knee and none too clean from scrubbing the floor, but a leg is a leg, dirty or clean, and I did not pull down my skirts. I thought, Let him look, poor man, there's nothing like that where he's come from. He must have been a foreigner of some sort, he'd walked a long way, and he had a darkish and a starved look to him, or so I thought in the dream.

But then he wasn't looking any more, he was trying to sell me something. He had a thing of mine and I needed it back, but I had no money so I could not buy it from him. We will trade then, he said, we will bargain. Come, what will you give me, he said in a teasing way.

What he had was one of my hands. I could see it now, it was white and shrivelled up, he was dangling it by its wrist like a glove. But then I looked down at my own hands, and I saw that there were two of them, on their wrists, coming out of the sleeves as usual, and I knew that this third hand must belong to some other woman. She was bound to come around looking for it, and if I had it in my possession she would say I had stolen it; but I did not want it any more, because it must have been cut off. And sure enough, there was the blood now, dripping and thick like syrup; but I was not horrified by it at all, as I would have been by real blood if awake; instead I was anxious about something else. Behind me I could hear the music of a flute, and this made me very nervous.

Go away, I said to the peddler man, you must go away right now. But he kept his head turned aside and would not move, and I suspected he might be laughing at me.

And what I thought was: It will get on the clean floor.

I say, I can't remember, Sir. I can't remember what I dreamt last night. It was something confusing. And he writes that down.

I have little enough of my own, no belongings, no possessions, no privacy to speak of, and I need to keep something for myself; and in any case, what use would he have for my dreams, after all?

Then he says, Well, there is more than one way to skin a cat.

I find that an odd choice of words, and I say, I am not a cat, Sir.

And he says, Oh I remember, nor are you a dog, and he smiles. He says, The question is, Grace, what are you? Fish or flesh or good red herring?

And I say, I beg your pardon, Sir?

I do not take well to being called a fish, I would leave the room except that I don't dare to.

And he says, Let us begin at the beginning.

And I say, The beginning of what, Sir?

And he says, The beginning of your life.

I was born, Sir, like anyone else, I say, still annoyed with him.

I have your Confession here, he says, let me read you what you said in it.

That is not really my Confession, I say, it was only what the lawyer told me to say, and things made up by the men from the newspapers, you might as well believe the rubbishy broadsheet they were peddling about, as that. The first time I set eyes on a newspaper man I thought, Well then, does your mother know you're out? He was almost as young as I was, he had no business writing for the papers as he was barely old enough to shave. They were all like that, wet behind the ears, and would not know the truth if they fell over it. They said I was eighteen or nineteen or not more than twenty, when I was only just turned sixteen, and they couldn't even get the names right, they spelled Jamie Walsh's name three different ways, Walsh, Welch, Walch, and McDermott's too, with a Mc and a Mac, and one t and two, and they wrote down Nancy's name as Ann, she was never called that in her life, so how could you expect them to get anything else right? They will make up any old thing to suit themselves.

Grace, he says then, who is Mary Whitney?

I give him a quick look. Mary Whitney, Sir? Now where would you get such a name as that? I say.

It is written underneath your portrait, he says. At the front of your Confession. *Grace Marks, Alias Mary Whitney.*

Oh yes, I say. It is not a good likeness of me.

And Mary Whitney? he says.

Oh, that was just the name I gave, Sir, at the tavern in Lewiston when James McDermott was running away with me. He said I should not give my own name, in case they came looking for us. He was gripping my arm very tight at the time, as I recall. To make sure I would do as he told me.

And did you give any name that came into your head? he says.

Oh no, Sir, I say. Mary Whitney was once a particular friend of mine. She was dead by that time, Sir, and I did not think she would mind it if I used her name. She sometimes lent me her clothing, too.

I stop for a minute, thinking of the right way to explain it.

She was always kind to me, I say; and without her, it would have been a different story entirely.

1 3.

There is a little verse I remember from a child:

> Needles and pins, needles and pins,
> When a man marries his trouble begins.

It doesn't say when a woman's trouble begins. Perhaps mine began when I was born, for as they say, Sir, you cannot choose your own parents, and of my own free will I would not have chosen the ones God gave me.

What it says at the beginning of my Confession is true enough. I did indeed come from the North of Ireland; though I thought it very unjust when they wrote down that *both of the accused were from Ireland by their own admission*. That made it sound like a crime, and I don't know that being from Ireland is a crime; although I have often seen it treated as such. But of course our family were Protestants, and that is different.

What I remember is a small rocky harbour by the sea, the land green and grey in colour, with not much in the way of trees; and for that reason I was quite frightened when I first saw large trees of the kind they have here, as I did not see how any tree could be that tall. I don't recall the place very well, as I was a child when I left it; only in scraps, like a plate that's been broken. There are always some pieces that would seem to belong to another plate altogether; and then there are the empty spaces, where you cannot fit anything in.

We lived in a cottage with a leaky roof and two small rooms, on the edge of a village near a town that I did not name for the newspapers, as my Aunt Pauline might still be living and I would not wish to bring disgrace upon her. She always thought well of me, although I heard her telling my mother what could be expected of me really, with so few prospects and with a father like that. She thought my mother had married beneath her; she said it was the way in our family, and she supposed I would end up the same; but to me she said that I should strive against it, and set a high price on myself, and not take up with the first Hail-fellow-well-met that should happen along, the way my mother had, without looking into his family or background, and that I should be wary of strangers. At the age of eight I did not have much idea of what she was talking about, although it was good advice all the same. My mother said Aunt Pauline meant kindly but had standards, which were all very well for those that could afford them.

Aunt Pauline and her husband, who was my Uncle Roy, a slope-shouldered and outspoken man, kept a shop in the nearby town; along with general goods they sold dress materials and pieces of lace, and some linens from Belfast, and they did well enough. My mother was Aunt Pauline's younger sister, and prettier than Aunt Pauline, who had a complexion like sandpaper and was all bone, with knuckles on her as big as chickens' knees; but my mother had long auburn hair, it was her I got it from, and round blue eyes like a doll, and before her marriage she had lived with Aunt Pauline and Uncle Roy and helped them with the shop.

My mother and Aunt Pauline were a dead clergyman's daughters – a Methodist, he was – and it was said their father had done something unexpected with the church money, and after that could not get a position; and when he died they were penniless, and were turned out to fend for themselves. But both had an education, and could embroider and play the piano; so that Aunt Pauline felt she too had married beneath her, as keeping a shop was not how a lady should live; but Uncle Roy was a well-meaning man although unpolished, and respected her, and that counted for something; and every time she looked into her linen closet, or counted over her two sets of dishes, one for everyday and one real china for best, she blessed her lucky stars and was thankful, because a woman could do worse; and what she meant was that my mother had.

I don't think she said such things to hurt my mother's feelings, although it had that effect, and she would cry afterwards. She'd begun life under Aunt Pauline's thumb and continued the same way, only my father's thumb was added to it. Aunt Pauline was always telling her to stand up to my father, and my father would tell her to stand up to Aunt Pauline, and between the two of them they squashed her flat. She was a timid creature, hesitating and weak and delicate, which used to anger me. I wanted her to be stronger, so I would not have to be so strong myself.

As for my father, he was not even Irish. He was an Englishman from the north of it, and why he had come to Ireland was never clear, as most who were inclined to travel went in the other direction. Aunt Pauline said he must have been in some trouble in England, and had come across to get himself out of the way in a hurry. Marks may not even have been his real name, she said; it should have been Mark, for the Mark of Cain, as he had a murderous look about him. But she only said that later, when things had gone so wrong.

At first, said my mother, he seemed a well-enough young man, and steady, and even Aunt Pauline had to admit that he was handsome, being tall and yellow-haired and having kept most of his teeth; and at the time they married, he had money in his pocket, as well as good prospects, for he was indeed a stone-mason, as the newspapers wrote down. Even so, Aunt Pauline said my mother would not have married him unless she'd had to, and it was covered up, although there was talk of my eldest sister Martha being very large for a seventh-month child; and that came from my mother's being too obliging, and too many young women were caught in that fashion; and she was only telling me this so I would not do the same. She said my mother was very fortunate in that my father did agree to marry her, she would give him that, as most would have been on the next boat out of Belfast when they heard the news, leaving her high and dry on the shore, and what could Aunt Pauline have done for her then, as she had her own reputation and the shop to consider.

So my mother and my father each felt trapped by the other.

I do not believe my father was a bad man to begin with; but he was easily led astray, and circumstances were against him. Being an Englishman, he was none too welcome even among the Protestants, as they were not fond of outsiders. Also he claimed my uncle said he'd tricked my mother into marriage so he could have a fine time, living at ease and dipping into their money from the shop; which was true in part, as they could not refuse him because of my mother and the children.

I learnt all this at an early age. The doors in our house were none too thick, and I was a little pitcher with big ears, and my father's voice was loud when drunk; and once he would get going, he did not notice who might be standing just around the corner or outside the window, as quiet as a mouse.

One thing he said was that his children were too many in number, and would have been even for a richer man. As they wrote in the papers, there ended by being nine of us, nine living that is. They did not put in the dead ones, which were three, not counting the baby that was lost before being born, and never had a name. My mother and Aunt Pauline called it the lost baby, and when I was little I wondered where it had been lost, because I thought it was lost the way you would lose a penny; and if it had been lost, then perhaps it might someday be found.

The other three dead ones were buried in the churchyard. Although my mother prayed more and more, we went to church less and less, because she said she was not going to have her poor tattery children paraded in front of everyone like scarecrows, with no shoes. It was only a parish church but despite her feeble nature she had her pride, and being a clergyman's daughter she knew what was decent in a church. She did so long to be decent again, and for us to be decent as well. But it is very hard, Sir, to be decent, without proper clothes.

I used to go to the churchyard though. The church was only the size of a cowshed, and the churchyard mostly overgrown. Our village was once larger, but many had moved away, to Belfast to the mills, or across the ocean; and often there was no one left from a family to tend the graves. The graveyard was one of the places I would take the younger children when my mother said I was to get them out of the house; so we would go and look at the three dead ones, and the other graves as well. Some were very old, and had gravestones with the heads of angels on them, though they looked more like flat cakes with two staring eyes, and a wing coming out on either side where the ears should have been. I did not see how a head could fly around without a body attached; and also I did not see how a person could be in Heaven, and in the churchyard too; but all agreed that it was so.

Our three dead children did not have stones but only wooden crosses. They must be all overgrown by now.

When I reached the age of nine, my older sister Martha left to go into service, and so all the work that Martha used to do around the house was now on me; and then two years after that, my brother

Robert went to sea on a merchant ship, and was never heard from again; but as we ourselves moved away shortly thereafter, even if he had sent word it would not have reached us.

Then there were five little ones and myself remaining at home, with another on the way. I cannot remember my mother when she wasn't in what they call a delicate condition; although there is nothing delicate about it that I can see. They also call it an unhappy condition, and that is closer to the truth – an unhappy condition followed by a happy event, although the event is by no means always happy.

Our father by this time was fed up with it. He would say, What are you bringing another brat into this world for, haven't you had enough of that by now, but no you can't stop, another mouth to feed, as if he himself had nothing to do with it at all. When I was quite young, six or seven, I put my hand on my mother's belly, which was all round and tight, and I said What is in there, another mouth to feed, and my mother smiled sadly and said Yes I fear so, and I had a picture of an enormous mouth, on a head like the flying angel heads on the gravestones, but with teeth and all, eating away at my mother from the inside, and I began to cry because I thought it would kill her.

Our father used to go away, even as far as Belfast, to work for the builders that had hired him; and then when the job was over he would come home for a few days, and then be out seeking another piece of work. When he was home he would go to the tavern, to get away from the squalling. He said a man could not hear himself think in all that racket, and he had to look about him, with such a large family, and how he was to keep their bodies and souls together was beyond him. But most of the looking about he did was at the bottom of a glass, and there were always those willing to help him look; but when he was drunk he would become angry and begin cursing the Irish, and abusing them as a pack of low useless thieving scoundrels, and there would be a fight. But he had a strong arm, and soon not many friends left, as although they were happy enough to drink with him they did not want to be at the wrong end of his fist when the time came for it. And so he would drink by himself, more and more, and as the drink got stronger the nights got longer, and he began to miss jobs of work in the daytime.

And so he got a reputation for not being reliable, and the jobs of work became few and far between. It was worse when he was home than when he was not, as by this time he was not confining his rages to the tavern. He would say he did not know why God had saddled him with such a litter, the world did not need any more of us, we should all have been drowned like kittens in a sack, and then the younger ones would be frightened. So I would take the four that were old enough to walk that far, and we would hold hands in a row, and go to the graveyard and pick weeds, or down to the harbour, and scramble among the rocks on the shore and poke at stranded jellyfish with sticks, or look in the tide pools for whatever we could find.

Or we would go out on the little dock where the fishing boats tied up. We were not supposed to go there because our mother feared we might slip over and drown, but I would lead the children there anyway, because the fishermen would sometimes give us a fish, a nice herring or a mackerel, and any sort of food was badly needed at home; sometimes we did not know what we were going to eat from one day to the next. We were forbidden by our mother to beg, and we would not, or not in so many words; but five ragged little children with hungry eyes is a hard sight to resist, or it was in our village then. And so we would get our fish more often than not, and go off home with it as proud as if we had caught it ourselves.

I will confess to having a wicked thought, when I had the young ones all lined up on the dock, with their little bare legs dangling down. I thought, I might just push one or two of them over, and then there would not be so many to feed, nor so many clothes to wash. For by this time I was the one who had to do most of the washing. But it was only a thought, put into my head by the Devil, no doubt. Or more likely by my father, for at that age I was still trying to please him.

After a time he got into doubtful company, and was seen about with some Orangemen of bad reputation, and there was a house burnt down twenty miles away, of a Protestant gentleman that had taken the side of the Catholics, and another one found with his head bashed in. There were words about it between my mother and father, and he said how the Devil did she expect him to turn a penny, and the least she could do was to keep it a secret, not that you could ever trust a woman as far as you could throw her, as they'd betray any man as soon as look at him, and Hell was too good for the lot. And when I asked my mother what the secret was, she brought out the Bible, and said I must swear on it to keep the secret too, and that God would punish me if I broke such a sacred promise; which terrified me very much, as I was in danger of letting it out unawares, because I had no idea at all of what it was. And being punished by God must be a terrible thing, as he was so much larger than my father; and after that I was always very careful about keeping the secrets of others, no matter what they might be.

For a time there was money, but things did not improve, and words came to blows, although my poor mother did little enough to provoke them; and when my Aunt Pauline came to visit, my mother would whisper to her, and show the bruises on her arms, and cry, and say He was not always this way; and Aunt Pauline would say, But look at him now, he's nothing more than a boot with a hole in it, the more you pour in at the top, the more it runs out at the bottom, it's a shame and a disgrace.

My Uncle Roy came with her in their one-horse gig, bringing some eggs from their hens and a slab of bacon, for our own hens and pig were long gone; and they sat in the front room, which was hung about with drying clothes, because no sooner would you get your wash done and spread out on a sunny day in that climate, than it would cloud over and begin to drizzle; and Uncle Roy, who was a very plain-spoken man, said he didn't know a man who could turn good money into horse piss faster than my father could. And Aunt Pauline made him say Pardon me, because of the language; though my mother had heard much worse than that, as when our father was drinking he had a mouth on him as foul as a running sewer.

By now it was no longer the little money our father brought into the house that was keeping us alive. Instead it was my mother and her shirt sewing, at which I helped her, and my younger sister Katey too; and it was Aunt Pauline who got her the work, and brought it and took it away again, which must have been an expense to her because of the horse, and the extra time and trouble. But she would always bring some food with her, for although we had our little potato patch and our own cabbages, it was by no means enough; and she would bring leftover pieces of cloth from the shop, out of which our own clothes were made, such as they were.

Our father was long since past asking where such things came from. In those days, Sir, it was a matter of pride for a man to support his own family, whatever he might think of that family itself; and my mother, although weak-spirited, was too wise a woman to tell him anything about it. And the other person who did not know as much about it as there was to know was Uncle Roy, although he must have guessed it, and seen that certain items vanished from his own house, only to reappear in ours. But my Aunt Pauline was a strong-minded woman.

The new baby came, and there was more washing for me to do, as was always the case with a baby, and our mother was ill for a longer time than usual; and I had to get the dinners, as well as the breakfasts, which I had been doing already; and our father said we should just knock the new baby on the head and shove it into a hole in the cabbage patch, as it would be a good deal happier under the sod than above it. And then he said it made him hungry just to look at it, it would look very nice on a platter with roast potatoes all round and an apple in its mouth. And then he said why were we all staring at him.

At this time a surprising thing happened. Aunt Pauline had despaired of ever having children, and so had regarded all of us as her own; but now there were signs that she was in the family way. And she was very happy about it, and my mother was happy for her. But Uncle Roy said to Aunt Pauline that there had to be a change, as he could not go on supporting our family now, with his own to think of, and some other plan would have to be made. Aunt Pauline said we could not be left to starve, no matter how bad my father might be, as her sister was her own flesh and blood and the children were innocent; and Uncle Roy said who ever said anything about starving, what he had in mind was emigration. Many were doing it, and there was free land to be had in the Canadas, and what my father needed was to wipe the slate clean. Stone-masons were in great demand over there because of all the building and works that were going forward, and he had it on good authority that soon there would be many railway stations to be constructed; and an industrious man could do well for himself.

Aunt Pauline said that was all very well, but who would pay for the passages? And Uncle Roy said he had some put by and would reach very deep into his pocket, and it would be enough to pay not only for our passages but for the food we would need on the journey; and he had his eye on a man who would arrange everything, for a fee. He had it all planned out before he brought it up for discussion, my

Uncle Roy being a man who liked to have his ducks lined up in a row before shooting them.

And so it was decided, and my Aunt Pauline came specially in her gig despite her condition, to repeat all of this to my mother, and my mother said she would have to talk to my father and obtain his agreement, but this was only for show. Beggars cannot be choosers, and they did not have any other road open to them; and as well, there had been some strange men about the village, talking about the house that was burnt and the man that was killed, and asking questions; and after that my father was in a hurry to get himself out of the way.

So he put a good front on it, and said it was a new start in life, and it was generous of my Uncle Roy, and he would regard the passage money as a loan and would pay it back as soon as he began to prosper; and Uncle Roy pretended to believe him. He had no wish to humiliate my father, only to see the last of him. As for his generosity, I suppose he thought it would be best to bite the bullet and pay out one large sum of money, rather than to be bled to death over the years penny by penny; and in his shoes I would have done the same.

And so all was set in motion. It was decided that we would sail at the end of April, as that way we would arrive in the Canadas at the beginning of summer, and have the warm weather while we got ourselves well settled. Much planning went on between Aunt Pauline and my mother, and a good deal of sorting and packing; and both tried to be cheerful, but both were downhearted. After all they were sisters, and had been through thick and thin, and they knew that once the ship set sail it was not likely they would ever see each other again in this life.

My Aunt Pauline brought a good linen sheet, only a little flawed, from the shop; and a thick warm shawl, as she'd heard it was cold on the other side of the ocean; and a little wicker hamper, and inside it, packed in straw, a china teapot, and two cups and saucers, with roses on them. And my mother thanked her very much, and said how good she had been to her always, and that she would treasure the teapot forever, in remembrance of her.

And there was a great deal of quiet weeping.

14.

We went up to Belfast in a cart hired by my uncle, which was a long journey and very jolting, but it did not rain much. Belfast was a large and stony city, the biggest place I had ever been in, and clattering with wagons and carriages. It had some grand buildings, but also many poor people, who worked in the linen mills day and night. The gas lamps were lit as we arrived in the evening, which were the first I ever saw; and they were just like moonlight, only greener in colour.

We slept at an inn which was so thick with fleas you would have thought it was a dog kennel; and we took all of the boxes into the room with us so as not to be robbed of our earthly goods. I didn't have the chance to see much more, as in the morning we had to get on board the ship at once, and so I hustled the children along. They did not understand where we were going, and to tell you the truth, Sir, I don't believe any of us did.

The ship was lying alongside the dock; it was a heavy hulking brute that had come across from Liverpool, and later I was told that it brought logs of wood eastward from the Canadas, and emigrants westward the other way, and both were viewed in much the same light, as cargo to be ferried. The people were already going aboard with all their bundles and boxes, and some of the women were wailing a good deal; but I did not do so, as I did not see the use of it, and our father was looking grim and in need of silence, and not in any mood to spare the back of his hand.

The ship was rocking to and fro with the swell, and I did not trust it at all. The younger children were excited, the boys in particular, but my heart sank within me because I had never been on a ship, not even the small fishing boats in our harbour, and I knew we were to sail across the ocean, out of sight of land, and if we were to be in a shipwreck or fall overboard, not one of us could swim.

I saw three crows sitting in a row on the crossbeam of the mast, and my mother saw them too, and she said it was bad luck, for three crows in a row meant a death. I was surprised at her saying this, as she was not a superstitious woman; but I suppose she was melancholy, for as I have noticed, those who are depressed in spirits are more likely to consider bad omens. But I was badly frightened by it, although I did not show it because of the young children: if they saw me taking on, they would do so as well, and there was enough noise and tumult already.

Our father put on a brave appearance and strode ahead up the gangplank, carrying the largest bundle of clothing and bedding, and gazing around him as if he knew all about it and was not afraid; but our mother came up very sadly, with her shawl drawn around her, shedding furtive tears, and she wrung her hands and said to me, Oh what has driven us to this, and as we stepped on board the ship she said, My foot will never touch land again. And I said, Mother, why do you say that? And she said, I feel it in my bones.

And so it turned out.

Our father paid to have our larger boxes carried aboard and stowed away; it was a shame to waste the money but it was the only way to do it, as he could not carry all the things on by himself, as the porters were coarse and importunate, and would have hindered him. The deck was very crowded, with many comings and goings, and the men shouting to us to get out of their way. The boxes we would not need on board were taken to a special room, which was to be kept locked to prevent thievery, and the store of food which we had brought with us for the voyage had its own place too; but the blankets and sheets went below into our beds; and our mother insisted on keeping Aunt Pauline's teapot with her, as she did not want to let it out of her sight; and she tied the wicker hamper to the upright post of the bed with a piece of twine.

Where we were to sleep was below the deck, down a greasy ladder into what they called the hold, which was built all through with beds. Hard rough wooden slabs they were, poorly nailed together and six feet long and six feet wide, with two persons to each, and three or four if children; and two layers of them, one on top of the other, with scarcely the room to squeeze in between. When you were in the bottom bed there was no space to sit up fully, as if you tried it you banged your head on the bed above; and if you were in the top one you stood more chance of tumbling out, and farther to fall if you did. It was everyone together, crammed in like herrings in a box, and no windows or any way of letting in the air, except the hatchways that led down. Already the air was close enough, but nothing like how it got later on. We had to snatch our beds and put our things on them at once, there was such a shove and scramble, and I did not want us to be separated, with the children alone and frightened in a strange place at night.

We set sail at noon, when all was stowed aboard. Once they had raised the gangplank and there was no way back to land, we were summoned by bell for an address from the Captain, who was leathery-skinned and a Scot from the south. He told us we must obey the rules of the ship, and that there must be no cooking fires made, as all our food would be cooked by the ship's cook if brought promptly at the bell; and no smoking of pipes, especially below decks, as it could lead to fires, and those who could not do without tobacco could always chew and spit. And there was to be no washing of clothes, except on the days when the weather was right, and he would be the judge of that; for if it was too blustery we would lose our possessions overboard, and if it rained the hold would be full of wet steamy cloth at night, and he gave us his word for it that this was not a thing we would enjoy.

Also there was to be no bringing of bedding up on deck to air it without permission, and all were to obey the orders of himself and the First Mate, and any of the other officers, as the ship's safety depended on it; and in case of breach of discipline we would have to be locked up in a cubby-hole, so he hoped no one would be tempted to try his patience. Furthermore, he said, drunkenness would not be tolerated, as it led to falling down; we could get as drunk as a lord once ashore, but not on his ship; and for our own safety we were not allowed up on deck at night, as then we might be lost overboard. His sailors were not to be interfered with in their duties, nor bribed for favours; and he had eyes in the back of his head, and would know it immediately if attempted. As his men could testify, he ran a tight ship, and on the open seas the Captain's word was law.

In case of illness there was a doctor on board, but most could expect to feel unwell until they got their sea legs, and the doctor was not to be pestered with trifles such as a little seasickness; and if all went well we would be on land again in six or eight weeks' time. In conclusion, he wished to say that every ship afloat had a rat or two aboard, and this was a sign of luck because it was the rats who knew first when a ship was fated to sink, so he did not want to be bothered about it, should some well-bred lady happen to catch sight of one. He supposed none of us had ever seen a rat before – at this there was laughter – but in case we were curious, he had one fresh killed, and very appetizing too should we be hungry. There was more laughter, as it was a joke he was telling, to set us more at ease.

When the laughter had stopped he said that to sum it up, his ship was not Buckingham Palace, and we were not the Queen of France, and like everything else in this life you got what you paid for. And he wished us a pleasant voyage. Then he retired to his cabin, and left us to sort ourselves out as best we could. In his heart he most likely wished us all at the bottom of the sea, so long as he could keep the money for our transport. But at least he seemed to know what he was about, and that made me feel easier. I needn't tell you that many of his instructions were not followed, especially as to the smoking and drinking; but those indulging had to be sly about it.

At first things did not go too badly. The clouds thinned and there was fitful sunlight, and I stayed on deck and watched them tacking the boat out of the harbour, and as long as we were in the shelter of the land I did not mind the motion. But as soon as we were out upon the Irish Sea and they ran up more of the sails, I began to feel strange and sick, and soon lost my breakfast into the scuppers, holding a little one by each hand who was doing the same. I was by no means alone, as many others were lined up like pigs at a trough. Our mother was prostrated, and our father was sicker than I was, so neither of them was any use with the children. It was fortunate we had eaten no dinner, or things would have been much worse with us. The sailors were ready for this, having seen it before, and they hauled up many buckets of salt water to wash all away.

After a while I was better; it may have been the fresh sea air, or that I was getting accustomed to the rolling and heaving of the ship, and also, if you'll excuse me for putting it this way, Sir, there was nothing left to be sick with; and as long as I was above on the deck I did not feel so ill. There was no question of any supper for our family, as all were too indisposed; but a sailor told me that if we could drink some water and nibble on a piece of ship's biscuit it would be better for us; and as we had laid in a supply of biscuit on my uncle's instructions, we did this as best we could.

Thus things were a little improved until nightfall, and then we had to go below, when they became much worse. As I have said, all the passengers were stuffed in together, with no walls between, and most as sick as dogs; and so not only could you hear the retchings and groanings of your neighbours, which made you sick just to listen to them, but hardly any air got in, and so the hold became fouler and fouler and the stench was enough to turn your stomach inside out.

And if you'll forgive me for mentioning this, Sir, there were no proper ways to relieve yourself. There were buckets provided, but in plain view of all, or they would have been if there had been any light; but as it was, there were gropings in the dark, and curses, and buckets being overturned by mistake, and even if the bucket remained upright, what didn't go into it went onto the floor. Happily it was none too solid a floor, so at least some went below into the bilge. It did make me reflect, Sir, that there are times when women with their skirts are better off than men with their trousers, for at least we carry around with us a sort of natural tent, whereas the poor men had to stagger about with their trousers down around their ankles. But as I say, there was not much light.

What with the pitching and surging of the ship, and the creaking it made, and the sloshing of the waves, and the noise and the stink, and the rats running to and fro as bold as lords and ladies, it was like being a suffering soul in Hell. I thought of Jonah in the belly of the whale, but at least he only had to stay there three days, and we had eight weeks of it ahead of us; and he was in the belly all by himself, and did not have to listen to the moaning and vomiting of others.

After several days it did improve, as the seasickness of many sub-sided; but the air was always foul at night, and there were always noises. Less retching, to be sure, but more coughing and snores; and also a good deal of crying and praying, which can be understood under the circumstances.

But I did not mean to offend your sensibilities, Sir. The ship was after all only a sort of slum in motion, though without the gin shops; and I hear they have got better ships now.

Perhaps you would like to open the window.

There was one good effect of all the suffering. The passengers were Catholic and Protestant mixed, with some English and Scots come over from Liverpool thrown into the bargain; and if in a state of health, they would have squabbled and fought, as there is no love lost. But there is nothing like a strong bout of seasickness to remove the desire for a scrap; and those who would cheerfully have cut each other's throats on land, were often to be seen holding each other's heads over the scuppers, like the tenderest of mothers; and I have sometimes noted the same thing in prison, as necessity does make strange bedfellows. A sea voyage and a prison may be God's reminder to us that we are all flesh, and that all flesh is grass, and all flesh is weak. Or so I choose to believe.

After several days I had my sea legs, and so I could fetch and carry up and down the ladder to the deck, and see about the meals. Each family supplied its own food, which was brought to the ship's cook and put into a net bag, and plunged into a cauldron of boiling water and boiled along with the meals of the others; and so you got not only your own dinner, but a taste of what the others were eating as well. Salt pork we had, and salt beef; we had some onions and potatoes, though not many of these because of the weight; and dried peas, and a cabbage which was soon gone, as I felt we should eat it before it wilted. The oatmeal we had could not be boiled in the main cauldron, but was mixed up with hot water and left to steep, and the tea as well. And we had biscuit, as I said before.

My Aunt Pauline had given my mother three lemons, worth their weight in gold, as she said it was well known they were good against the scurvy; and these I carefully preserved in case of need. All in all we had enough to keep strength in our bodies, which was more than some, who had spent their main money for the passage; and we had a little to spare, or so I felt, since our parents were not in a condition to eat their share of the food. So I gave several biscuits to our next neighbour, who was an elderly woman by the name of Mrs. Phelan, and she thanked me very much and said God bless you. She was a Catholic, and travelling with her daughter's two children, who had been left behind when the family emigrated; and now she was taking them to Montreal, as her son-in-law had paid their passage; and I helped her with the children, and later I was glad I did so. Bread cast upon the waters comes back to you tenfold, as I am sure you have often heard, Sir.

And when we were told we might do a washing, as the weather was fair, with a good drying wind – it was much needed by then, because of all the sickness – I did a coverlet of hers as well as our own things. It was not much of a washing, as all we could use were the buckets of sea water provided, but at least it got off the worst of the mess, although the things smelled of salt after.

A week and a half out we were overtaken by a ferocious gale, and the ship was tossed around like a cork in a tub, and the praying and shrieking became ferocious. There was no question of cooking anything, and at night it was impossible to sleep, as you would be rolled out of your bed unless you held on, and the Captain sent the First Mate to tell us to stay calm, as it was merely an ordinary gale and nothing to become worked up over, and also it was blowing us in the direction we wanted to go. But water was coming down the hatchways, and so they closed them; and we were all shut up in the pitch darkness with even less air than we had before, and I thought we would all be smothered. But the Captain must have known this, because the hatches were opened from time to time. Those near them became very wet, however; it was their turn to pay for the better supply of air they had enjoyed until then.

The gale blew itself out after two days, and there was a general thanksgiving service held for the Protestants, and there was a priest on board who said a Mass for the Catholics; and it was impossible to avoid attending both, in a manner of speaking, due to the cramped conditions; but nobody objected to it, for as I have said, the two sorts tolerated each other better than they did on land. I myself had become very friendly with old Mrs. Phelan; and she was brisker on her feet by this time than my own mother, who continued weak.

After the gale it grew colder. We began to meet fog, and then icebergs, which were said to be more numerous than usual for the season; and we went more slowly for fear of running into them; for the sailors said that the biggest part of them was under the water, and invisible, and it was lucky there was not a high wind, or we might be driven onto one, and the boat crushed; but I was never tired of looking at them. Great mountains of ice they were, with peaks and turrets, white and sparkling when the sun lit on them, with blue lights in the centres of them; and I thought, this must be what the walls of Heaven are made of, only not so cold.

But it was amongst the icebergs that our mother fell gravely ill. She had been in her bed most of the time because of the seasickness, and had not eaten anything except biscuit and water, and a little gruel made from oatmeal. Our father had not been much better, and if you had measured by the size of the groans, he was worse; and things were in a sorry state, as during the storm we had not been able to do any washing or airing of the bedding. So I did not notice at first what a bad turn my mother had taken. But she said she had such a violent headache she could scarcely see, and I brought wet cloths and laid them on her forehead; and I saw she had a fever. Then she began to complain that her stomach hurt very much, and I felt it. There was a hard swelling, and I thought it was another little mouth to feed, although I did not know how it could have come on so quickly.

So I told old Mrs. Phelan, who'd told me she'd delivered sixteen babies, nine of her own included; and she came at once, and felt the thing, poking and prodding, and my mother screamed; and Mrs. Phelan said I ought to send for the ship's doctor. I did not like to, because the Captain said he should not be pestered over trifles; but Mrs. Phelan said this was no trifle, and no baby neither.

I asked our father, but he said I should do whatever the Devil I liked, as he was too sick to have any thoughts about it; so at last I did send. But the doctor did not come, and my poor mother was getting worse by the hour. By this time she could scarcely speak, and what she did say made no sense at all.

Mrs. Phelan said it was a shame, and they would treat a cow better, and she said the best way to get the doctor was to say it might be the typhus, or else the cholera, as there was nothing on earth they were more afraid of, on board a ship. And so I did say that, and the doctor came straight away.

But he was of no more use – if you'll excuse me, Sir – than tits on a rooster, as Mary Whitney liked to say, because after taking my mother's pulse and feeling her forehead, and asking questions to which there were no answers, all he could tell us was that she did not have cholera, which I knew already, having made it up myself. As to what she did have, he couldn't say; it was most likely a tumour, or a cyst, or else a burst appendix; and he would give her something for the pain. And he did do that; I think it was laudanum, and a great dose of it, because my mother soon became quiet, which was no doubt his object. He said we must just hope she would pull through the crisis; but there was no way of telling what it was, without cutting her open, and that would kill her for certain.

I asked if she might be carried up on deck, for the air, but he said it would be a mistake to move her. And then he went away as quickly as possible, while remarking to no one in particular that the air was so foul down here he was half choked. And that was another thing I knew already.

My mother died that night. I wish I could tell you that she had visions of angels at the last, and made us a fine deathbed speech, as in books; but if she did have any visions she kept them to herself, for she did not say a word, about them or anything else. I fell asleep, though I had meant to wake and watch, and when I woke up in the morning she was dead as a mackerel, with her eyes open and fixed. And Mrs. Phelan put her arm around me, and folded me in her shawl, and gave me a drink from a little bottle of spirits she had by her for medicine; and said it would do me good to cry, and at least the poor thing was out of her sufferings, and in Heaven now with the blessed saints, even though she was a Protestant.

Mrs. Phelan also said that we had not opened the window to let out the soul, as was the custom; but perhaps it would not be counted against my poor mother, as there were no windows in the bottom of the ship and therefore none to be opened. And I had never heard of a custom like that.

I did not cry. I felt as if it was me and not my mother that had died; and I sat as if paralyzed, and did not know what to do next. But Mrs. Phelan said we could not leave her lying there, and did I have a white sheet for her to be buried in. And then I began to worry terribly, because all we had was the three sheets. There were two old ones that had been worn through and then cut in two and turned, and also the one new sheet given to us by Aunt Pauline; and I did not know which to use. It seemed like disrespect to use an old one, but if I used the new one it would go to waste as far as the living were concerned; and all my grief became concentrated, so to speak, on the matter of the sheets. And finally I asked myself what my mother would prefer, and since she'd always placed herself second best in life, I decided on the old one; and at least it was more or less clean.

The Captain having been notified, two sailors came to carry my mother up onto the deck; and Mrs. Phelan came up with me, and we arranged her, with her eyes closed and her pretty hair down, because Mrs. Phelan said a body should not be buried with the hair knotted. I left her in the same clothes she had on, except for the shoes. I kept back the shoes, and her shawl as well, which she would have no need of. She looked pale and delicate, like a spring flower, and the children stood around crying; and I had each one of them kiss her on the forehead, which I wouldn't have done if I thought she'd died of anything catching. And one of the sailors, who was an expert at such things, tucked the sheet around her very neatly, and sewed it up tight, with a length of old iron chain at the feet, to make her sink. I had forgotten to cut off a lock of her hair to keep, as I should have done; but I was too confused to remember it.

As soon as the sheet was over her face I had the notion that it was not really my mother under there, it was some other woman; or that my mother had changed, and if I was to take away the sheet now, she would be someone else entirely. It must have been the shock of it that put such things into my head.

Fortunately there was a clergyman on board, who was making the crossing in one of the cabins, the same that had done the thanksgiving service after the gale; and he read a short prayer, and my father managed to totter up the ladder from the hold, and he stood there with his head bowed, looking rumpled and unshaven, but at least he was there. And then with the icebergs floating around us and the fog rolling in, my poor mother was tipped into the sea. I hadn't thought about where she was going until this moment, and there was something dreadful about it, to picture her floating down in a white sheet amongst all the staring fish. It was worse than being put into the earth, because if a person is in the earth at least you know where they are.

And then all was over, so quickly, and the next day went on as before, only without my mother.

That night I took one of the lemons and cut it up, and made each of the children eat a piece of it, and I ate a piece of it myself. It was so sour that you felt it must be doing you good. It was the only thing I could think of, to do.

And now I have only one more thing to tell you about this voyage. When we were still becalmed, and in the thickest of the fog, the wicker basket with Aunt Pauline's teapot fell off onto the floor, and the teapot broke. Now, that basket had stayed where it was all during the storm, through the tumbling and the pitching and tossing; and it had been tied to the bedpost.

Mrs. Phelan said that no doubt it had come untied when someone was trying to steal it, but they'd stopped when in danger of being seen, and it wouldn't have been the first thing to change hands in that way. But this is not what I thought. I thought it was my mother's spirit, trapped in the bottom of the ship because we could not open a window, and angry at me because of the second-best sheet. And now she would be caught in there for ever and ever, down below in the hold like a moth in a bottle, sailing back and forth across the hideous dark ocean, with the emigrants going one way and the logs of wood the other. And that made me very unhappy.

You see what queer ideas a person can get. But I was only a young girl at the time, and very ignorant.

1 5 .

It was fortunate that we were not becalmed any longer, or else our food and water would have run out; but a wind sprang up and the fog cleared, and they said we had passed Newfoundland safely, although I never got a glimpse of it and was not sure whether it was a city or a country; and soon we were in the St. Lawrence River, although it was a good while before there was any land. And when we did see it, on the north side of the ship, it was all rocks and trees, and looked dark and forbidding, and not fit for human habitation at all; and there were clouds of birds that screamed like lost souls, and I hoped that we would not be compelled to live in such a place.

But after a time there were farms and houses visible on the shore, and the land had the appearance of being more placid, or tamer as you might say. We were required to stop at an island and to undergo an inspection for cholera, as many before us had brought it into the country on the ships; but as the dead people on our ship had died of other things – four besides my mother, two from consumption and one from apoplexy, and one jumped overboard – we were allowed to proceed. I did have the chance to give the children a good scrubbing-off in the river water, although it was very cold – at least their faces and arms, which they were very much in need of.

The next day we saw the city of Quebec, on a steep cliff over-looking the river. The houses were of stone, and there were peddlers and hawkers at the dock in the harbour, selling their wares, and I was able to buy some fresh onions from one of them. She spoke nothing but French, but we conducted the business with our fingers; and I believe she made me a better price because of the children and their thin little faces. We were so thirsty for these onions that we ate them raw, like apples, which gave us wind afterwards, but I have never known an onion to taste so good.

Some of the passengers got off the ship at Quebec, to take their chances there, but we continued on.

I cannot think of anything else I need mention about the rest of the journey. It was more travelling and most of it uncomfortable, some-times overland to avoid the rapids, and then in another ship on Lake Ontario, which was more like a sea than a lake. There were hordes of small biting flies, and mosquitoes as big as mice; and the children were in danger of scratching themselves to death. Our father was in a bleak and melancholy mood, and often said that he did not know how he would manage, with our mother dead. At these times it was best to say nothing.

At last we reached Toronto, which was where they said the free land could be obtained. The city was not in a good situation, being flat and damp; it was raining that day, and there were many wagons and men hurrying, and quantities of mud, except for the main streets which were paved. The rain was soft and warm, and the air had a thick and swampy feel to it, like oil clinging to the skin, which I was later to learn was usual for that season of the year, and produc-tive of many fevers and summer illnesses. There was some gas light-ing but not as grand as Belfast.

The people appeared to be very mixed as to the kinds of them, with many Scots and some Irish, and of course the English, and many Americans, and a few French; and Red Indians, although they had no feathers; and some Germans; with skins of all hues, which was very new to me; and you never could tell what sort of speech you were going to hear. There were many taverns, and much drunkenness around the harbour, because of the sailors, and altogether it was just like the Tower of Babel.

But we did not see much of the town that first day, as we needed to get a roof over our heads with as little expense as possible. Our father had struck up acquaintance with a man from the ship, who was able to give us some information; and so he left us with a mug of cider amongst us, crammed with our boxes into one room of a tavern which was filthier than a pig wallow, and went off to make further enquiries.

He came back in the morning and told us he had found lodgings, and so we went there. They were east of the harbour, off Lot Street, at the back of a house which had seen better days. The landlady's name was Mrs. Burt, a respectable widow of a seafaring man, or so she told us, and quite stout and red in the face, with a smell like that of a smoked eel; and some years older than my father. She lived in the front part of the house, which was badly in need of a coat of paint, and we lived in the two rooms in the back part, which was more like an outbuilding. There was no cellar under it, and I was glad it wasn't winter, as the wind would have blown right through it. The floors were of wide boards, set too close to the ground, and beetles and other small creatures would make their way up through the cracks between them, worse after a rain, and one morning I found a live worm.

The rooms were not let furnished, but Mrs. Burt lent us two bedsteads with corn-shuck mattresses, until my father should get on his feet again, she said, after the sad blow he had suffered. For water we had a pump outside in the yard; as for cooking, we had the use of an iron stove that was in the passageway between the two parts of the house. It was not really a cookstove, it was meant for heating, but I did the best I could with it, and after a time of struggle I learnt its ways, and could force it to boil a kettle. It was the first iron stove I ever had to deal with, so as you may imagine there were some anxious moments, not to mention the smoke. But the fuel for it was plentiful, as the whole country was covered with trees, which they were doing their best to chop down and clear away. Also there were scraps of board left over from all the building which was being done, and you could have the board-ends from the workmen for a smile and the trouble of carrying them off.

But to tell you the truth, Sir, there was not much to cook, as our father said he needed to save the little money we had, so he could set himself up properly once he'd had a chance to look around him; and so at first we lived mostly on porridge. But Mrs. Burt had a goat in a shed at the back of her yard, and gave us fresh milk from it, and as it was now late June, some onions from her kitchen garden in return for having us hoe the weeds for her, and there were plenty of those; and when she was making bread she would make an extra loaf for us.

She said she was sorry for us because our mother had died. She had no children of her own, her only one having died of the cholera at the same time as her dear departed husband, and she missed the sound of little feet, or so she told our father. She would gaze at us wistfully and call us poor motherless lambs or little angels, though we were ragged enough and none too clean either. I believe she had the idea of making a match with my father; he was putting forth his best qualities, and taking some care with himself; and such a man, so recently bereaved and with so many children, must have seemed to Mrs. Burt like a fruit ready to fall from the tree.

She used to have him into the front part of the house to console him; she said that none knew better than a widow like herself, what it was to lose a spouse, it knocked a body down, and such were in need of a true and sympathizing friend, one who could share in his sorrows; and she let on that she was just the one for the job; and she may have been right about that, as there were no others applying for it.

As for our father, he took the hint and played up, and went around like a man half-stunned, with a handkerchief always at the ready; and he said his heart had been torn alive out of his body, and whatever was he going to do without his beloved helpmeet by his side, now in Heaven, having been too good for this earth, and all these innocent little mouths to feed. I used to listen to him going on in Mrs. Burt's parlour, the wall between the two parts of the house being none too thick, and if you put a tumbler to a wall and your ear against the other end of it, you can hear even better. We did have three tumblers, as Mrs. Burt had lent them to us, and I tried them all in turn, and soon picked out the best one for the purpose.

I'd found it hard enough when our mother died, but attempted to keep myself together through it all, and to put my shoulder to the wheel; and to hear my father snivelling away in that fashion was enough to turn the stomach. I believe it was only then that I truly began to hate him, especially considering how he had treated our mother in life, no better than if she had been a rag for cleaning his boots. And I knew – although Mrs. Burt did not – that it was all put on, and that he was working on her feelings because he was behind in the rent, having taken the money for it to the nearest tavern; and then he sold my mother's china cups with the roses, and although I begged for the broken teapot he sold that too, as he said it was a clean break and could be mended. And our mother's shoes went the same way; and our best sheet; and I might as well have used it to bury my poor mother, as would have been right.

He would go out of the house as jaunty as a rooster, pretending to look for work, but I knew where he was off to, I could tell by the smell of him when he came back. I would watch him swaggering down the lane and tucking his handkerchief back into his pocket; and soon enough Mrs. Burt gave up on her plan of consolation, and there were no more tea parties in the parlour; and she stopped the supply of milk and bread to us, and asked for her tumblers back, and for the rent to be paid, or she would have us all turned out, bag and baggage.

This was when our father began to tell me that I was almost a grown woman now and I was eating him out of house and home, it was time I went out into the world to earn my own bread, as my sister had done before me, although she had never sent enough of her wages back, the ungrateful slut. And when I asked who would look after the little ones, he said my next sister Katey would do it. She was nine years old, although halfway to ten. And I saw there was no help for it.

I did not have any notion about how to get a position, but I asked Mrs. Burt, she being the only person in the town that I knew. She now wanted to be rid of us, and who was to blame her; but she saw in me a hope of being repaid. She had a friend who knew the house-keeper at Mrs. Alderman Parkinson's, and she'd heard that they were short a pair of hands; so she told me to tidy myself up, and lent me a clean cap of her own, and took me there herself, and presented me to the housekeeper. She said I was a very willing and hard worker of good character, and she would vouch for it herself. Then she told about my mother having died on board ship and being buried at sea, and the housekeeper agreed that it was a shame, and looked at me more closely. I have noticed there is nothing like a death to get your foot in the door.

The housekeeper was called Mrs. Honey, although she was sweet only in name, being a dried-up woman with a pointed nose like a candle snuffer. She looked as if she lived on stale crusts and cheese parings, which she most likely had done in her life, being an English gentlewoman in distress who was only a housekeeper through the death of her husband, and being stranded in this country, and having no money of her own. Mrs. Burt told her I was thirteen, and I did not contradict her – she'd warned me beforehand that it would be best that way, as I would stand a better chance of being hired; and it was not entirely a lie, as I would be thirteen indeed in under a month's time.

Mrs. Honey looked at me with a pinched mouth, and said I was very scrawny, and she hoped I was not ill with anything, and what had my mother died of; but Mrs. Burt said nothing catching, and I was just a trifle small for my age and hadn't yet got my full growth, but I was very wiry, and she'd seen me carrying stacks of wood around just like a man.

Mrs. Honey took this for what it was worth, and sniffed, and asked if I was bad-tempered, as redheaded people frequently were; and Mrs. Burt said I had the sweetest temper in the world and had borne all my troubles with Christian resignation like a saint. This reminded Mrs. Honey to ask if I was a Catholic, as those from Ireland generally were; and if so she would have nothing to do with me, as the Catholics were superstitious and rebellious Papists who were ruining the country; but she was relieved to hear that I was not. And Mrs. Honey asked if I could sew, and Mrs. Burt said I could sew like the wind, and Mrs. Honey asked me directly if this was true; and I spoke up for myself, although nervous, and said I'd helped my mother make shirts from an early age, and could do the best button-holes, and mend stockings, and I remembered to say Ma'am.

Then Mrs. Honey hesitated, as if adding up sums in her head; and then she asked to look at my hands. Perhaps she wished to see if they were the hands of a person who had been working hard; but she needn't have bothered her head, as they were as red and rough as could be desired, and she appeared satisfied. You would have thought she was trading a horse; I was surprised she did not ask to look at my teeth, but I suppose if you pay out wages you want to get a good return on them.

The upshot was that Mrs. Honey consulted with Mrs. Alderman Parkinson, and sent word the next day that I was to come. My wages were to be board and a dollar a month, which was the lowest she could in conscience pay; but Mrs. Burt said I could command more once I had some training and had grown older. And a dollar bought more at that time than it does now. As for me, I was delighted to be earning money of my own, and thought it a fortune.

My father had the idea that I would go back and forth between the two houses, and sleep at home, which was what he called our two rickety rooms, and continue to get up first thing every morning and light the brute of a stove, and boil the kettle, and then tidy up at the end of the day and wash the laundry into the bargain, what laundry we were able to do, there not being any sort of copper and it was useless asking my father to spend money on even the worst kind of soap. But at Mrs. Alderman Parkinson's they wanted me to live in; and I was to come at the beginning of the week.

And although I was sorry to part with my brothers and sisters, I was thankful that I had to go away, because if not, it would soon have come to bones broken between myself and my father. The older I became, the less I was able to please him, and I myself had lost all of a child's natural faith in a parent, as he was drinking up the bread out of his own children's mouths, and soon he would force us to begging or thieving, or worse. Also his rages had returned, stronger than before my mother died. Already my arms were black and blue, and then one night he threw me against the wall, as he'd sometimes done with my mother, shouting that I was a slut and a whore, and I fainted; and after that I feared that he might someday break my spine, and make a cripple out of me. But after these rages he would wake up in the morning and say he couldn't remember a thing about it, and he hadn't been himself, and he didn't know what had got into him.

Although I was dog tired at the end of each day, I would lie awake at night brooding over it. It was the never knowing when he would go off his head like that and start rampaging about, and threaten to kill this or that person, including his own children, for no reason that anybody could see at all, apart from the drink.

I had begun to have thoughts about the iron cooking pot, and how heavy it was; and if it should happen to drop on him while he was asleep, it could smash his skull open, and kill him dead, and I would say it was an accident; and I did not want to be led into a grave sin of that kind, though I was afraid that the fiery red anger that was in my heart against him would drive me to it.

So as I made ready to go to Mrs. Alderman Parkinson's, I thanked God for taking me out of the path of temptation, and prayed that he would keep me out of it in the times ahead.

Mrs. Burt kissed me goodbye, and wished me well, and despite her fat mottled face and her smell of smoked fish I was glad of it, because in this world you have to take your bits and ends of kindness where you can find them, as they do not grow on trees. The little ones cried as I went away, carrying my small bundle including my mother's shawl, and I said I would come back and visit them; and at the time I meant it.

My father was not at home when I left. It was just as well, as I am sorry to say it would most likely have been curses both ways, although silent on my part. It is always a mistake to curse back openly at those who are stronger than you unless there is a fence between.

1 6 .

From Dr. Simon Jordan, care of Major C. D. Humphrey, Lower Union Street, Kingston, Canada West; to Dr. Edward Murchie, Dorchester, Massachusetts, The United States of America.

May 15th, 1859.

My dear Edward:

I am writing this by the light of the midnight oil, which we have so often burned together, in this damnably chilly house, which is fully equal to our London lodgings in that respect. But soon it will grow too hot, and the dank miasmas and summer diseases will be upon us, and I will complain about those in their turn.

I thank you for your letter, and for the welcome news it contains. So you have proposed yourself to the lovely Cornelia, and have been accepted! You will forgive an old friend for not expressing any great surprise, as the matter was writ large enough between the lines of your letters, and could easily be divined, without any great perspicacity on the reader's part. Please accept my earnest congratulations. From what I know of Miss Rutherford, you are a lucky dog. At moments like this I envy those who have found a safe haven, in which to bestow their hearts; or perhaps I envy them for having a heart to bestow. I often feel that I myself am without one, and possess in its stead merely a heart-shaped stone; and am therefore doomed to "wander lonely as a cloud," as Wordsworth has put it.

The news of your engagement will no doubt invigorate my dear mother, and spur her on to even greater matrimonial efforts on my behalf; and I have no doubt but that you will be used against me, as a prime example of rectitude, and as a stick to beat me with, at every opportunity. Well, no doubt she is in the right. Sooner or later I must set aside my scruples and obey the Biblical command to "be fruitful and multiply." I must give my stony heart into the keeping of some kindly damsel who will not mind too much that it is not a real heart of flesh, and who will also have the material means necessary to care for it; for hearts of stone are notoriously more demanding of their comforts than the other kind.

Despite this deficiency of mine, my dear mother continues her matrimonial scheming. She is currently singing the praises of Miss Faith Cartwright, whom you will remember encountering several years ago during one of your visits to us. She is supposed to have been much improved by a sojourn in Boston, which to my certain knowledge – and to yours too, my dear Edward, for you were with me as an undergraduate at Harvard – has never improved anyone else; but from the way my mother hymns the young lady's *moral* virtues, I fear that the rectification of the deficiencies in her other charms has not been among the improvements. Alas, it is a type of maiden other than the worthy and spotless Faith, who would have the power to transform your cynical old friend into the semblance of a lover.

But enough of my grumblings and repinings. I am heartily glad for you, my dear fellow, and will dance at your wedding with the greatest goodwill in the world, provided that I am in your vicinity when the nuptials take place.

You have been kind enough – in the midst of your raptures – to enquire as to my progress with Grace Marks. I have as yet little to report, but as the methods I am employing are gradual and cumulative in their effects, I did not expect rapid results. My object is to wake the part of her mind that lies dormant – to probe down below the threshold of her consciousness, and to discover the memories that must perforce lie buried there. I approach her mind as if it is a locked box, to which I must find the right key; but so far, I must admit, I have not got very far with it.

It would be helpful to me, if she were indeed mad, or at least a little madder than she appears to be; but thus far she has manifested a composure that a duchess might envy. I have never known any woman to be so thoroughly self-contained. Apart from the incident at the time of my arrival – which I was unfortunately too late to witness – there have been no outbursts. Her voice is low and melodious, and more culti-vated than is usual in a servant – a trick she has learned no doubt through her long service in the house of her social superiors; and she retains barely a trace of the Northern Irish accent with which she must have arrived, although that is not so remarkable, as she was only a child at the time and has now spent more than half her life on this continent.

She "sits on a cushion and sews a fine seam," cool as a cucumber and with her mouth primmed up like a governess's, and I lean my elbows on the table across from her, cudgelling my brains, and trying in vain to open her up like an oyster. Although she converses in what seems a frank-enough manner, she manages to tell me as little as possible, or as little as possible of what I want to learn; although I have managed to ascertain a good deal about her family situation as a child, and about her crossing of the Atlantic, as an emigrant; but none of it is very far out of the ordinary – only the usual poverty and hardships, etc. Those who believe in the hereditary nature of insanity might take some comfort in the fact that her father was an inebriate, and possibly an arsonist as well; but despite several theories to the contrary, I am far from being convinced that such tendencies are necessarily inherited.

As for myself, if it were not for the fascination her case affords, I might run mad myself, out of sheer boredom; there is little-enough society here, and none who share my sentiments and interests, with the possible exception of one Dr. DuPont, who is a visitor here like myself; but he is a devotee of the Scottish crackpot Braid, and a queer duck himself. As for amusements and recreations, there are few to be had; and I have decided to ask my landlady if I may dig in her back garden – which has been let go sadly to waste – and plant a few cabbages and so forth, just for the distraction and the exercise. You see what I am driven to, who have scarcely lifted a spade before in my life!

But it is now past midnight, and I must close this letter to you, and go to my cold and lonely bed. I send you my best

thoughts and wishes, and trust that you are living more prof-
itably, and are less perplexed, than is,

Your old friend,

Simon.

VI.

SECRET DRAWER

Hysterics – These fits take place, for the most part, in young, nervous, unmarried women. . . . Young women, who are subject to these fits, are apt to think that they are suffering from "all the ills that flesh is heir to;" and the false symptoms of disease which they show are so like the true ones, that it is often exceedingly difficult to detect the difference. The fits themselves are mostly preceded by great depression of spirits, shedding of tears, sickness, palpitation of the heart, &c. . . . The patient now generally becomes insensible, and faints; the body is thrown about in all directions, froth issues from the mouth, incoherent expressions are uttered, and fits of laughter, crying, or screaming, take place. When the fit is going off, the patient mostly cries bitterly, sometimes knowing all, and at other times nothing, of what has taken place. . . .

– Isabella Beeton,
Beeton's Book of Household Management, 1859-61.

My heart would hear her and beat,
　　Were it earth in an earthy bed;
My dust would hear her and beat,
　　Had I lain for a century dead;
Would start and tremble under her feet,
　　And blossom in purple and red.

– Alfred, Lord Tennyson,
Maud, 1855.

1 7 .

Simon is dreaming of a corridor. It's the attic passageway of his house, his old house, the house of his childhood; the big house they had before his father's failure and death. The maids slept up here. It was a secret world, one as a boy he wasn't supposed to explore, but did, creeping silent as a spy in his stocking feet. Listening at half-open doors. What did they talk about when they thought no one could hear?

When he was feeling very brave he would venture into their rooms, knowing they were downstairs. With a shiver of excitement he'd examine their things, their forbidden things; he'd slide open the drawers, touch the wooden comb with two broken teeth, the carefully rolled ribbon; he'd rummage in the corners, behind the door: the crumpled petticoat, the cotton stocking, only one. He'd touched it; it felt warm.

In his dream the passageway is the same, only bigger. The walls are taller, and yellower: glowing, as if the sun itself is shining through them. But the doors are closed, and also locked. He tries door after door, lifting the latch, pushing gently, but nothing yields.

There are people in there though, he can sense them. Women, the maids. Sitting on the edges of their narrow beds, in their white cotton shifts, their hair unbound and rippling down over their shoulders, their lips parted, their eyes gleaming. Waiting for him.

The door at the end opens. Inside it is the sea. Before he can stop himself, down he goes, the water closing over his head, a stream of silvery bubbles rising from him. In his ears he hears a ringing, a faint and shivery laughter; then many hands caress him. It's the maids; only they can swim. But now they are swimming away from him, abandoning him. He calls out to them, *Help me*, but they are gone.

He's clinging onto something: a broken chair. The waves are rising and falling. Despite this turbulence there is no wind, and the air is piercingly clear. Past him, just out of reach, various objects are floating: a silver tray; a pair of candlesticks; a mirror; an engraved snuffbox; a gold watch, which is making a chirping noise, like a cricket. Things that were his father's once, but sold after his death. They're rising up from the depths like bubbles, more and more of them; as they reach the surface they roll slowly over, like bloating fish. They aren't hard, like metal, but soft; they have a scaly skin on them, like an eel's. He watches in horror, because now they're gathering, twining together, re-forming. Tentacles are growing. A dead hand. His father, in the sinuous process of coming back to life. He has an overwhelming sense of having transgressed.

He wakes, his heart is pounding; the sheets and comforter are tangled around him, the pillows are on the floor. He's soaked with sweat. After he's lain quietly for a time, reflecting, he thinks he understands the train of association that must have led to such a dream. It was Grace's story, with its Atlantic crossing, its burial at sea, its catalogue of household objects; and the overbearing father, of course. One father leads to another.

He checks the time by his pocket-watch, which is on the small bedside table: for once, he's slept in. Luckily his breakfast is late; but the surly Dora should be arriving at any moment, and he doesn't want to be surprised by her in his nightshirt, caught out in sloth. He throws on his dressing-gown and seats himself quickly at his writing table, turning his back to the door.

He will record the dream he's just had in the journal he keeps for such purposes. One school of French *aliénistes* recommend the recording of dreams as a diagnostic tool; their own dreams, as well as those of their patients, for the sake of comparison. They hold dreams, like somnambulism, to be a manifestation of the animal life that continues below consciousness, out of sight, beyond reach of the will. Perhaps the hooks – the hinges, as it were – in the chain of memory, are located there?

He must reread Thomas Brown's work on association and suggestion, and Herbart's theory of the threshold of consciousness – the line that divides those ideas that are apprehended in full daylight from those others that lurk forgotten in the shadows below. Moreau de Tours considers the dream to be the key to the knowledge of mental illness, and Maine de Biran held that conscious life was only a sort of island, floating upon a much vaster subconscious, and drawing thoughts up from it like fish. What is perceived as being known is only a small part of what may be stored in this dark repository. Lost memories lie down there like sunken treasure, to be retrieved piecemeal, if at all; and amnesia itself may be in effect a sort of dreaming in reverse; a drowning of recollection, a plunging under. . . .

Behind his back the door opens: his breakfast is making its entrance. Assiduously he dips his pen. He waits for the thump of the tray, the clatter of earthenware on wood, but he does not hear it.

"Just set it on the table, will you?" he says, without turning.

There is a sound like air going out of a small bellows, followed by a shattering crash. Simon's first thought is that Dora has hurled the tray at him – she has always suggested, to his mind, a barely repressed and potentially criminal violence. He shouts involuntarily, leaps up, and whirls around. Lying full-length upon the floor is his landlady, Mrs. Humphrey, in a shambles of broken crockery and ruined food.

He hurries over to her, kneels, and takes her pulse. At least she is still alive. He rolls open an eyelid, sees the opaque white. Swiftly he undoes the none-too-clean bibbed apron which she is wearing, and which he recognizes as the one habitually worn by slovenly Dora; then he unbuttons the front of her dress, noticing as he does so that there is a button missing, with the threads still hanging in place. He rummages around inside the layers of cloth, and at last succeeds in cutting her stay-laces with his pocket-knife, releasing an odour of violet-water, autumn leaves, and humid flesh. There is more to her than he would have supposed, although she is far from plump.

He carries her into his bedroom – the settee in his sitting room is too small for the purpose – and extends her upon the bed, placing a pillow beneath her feet to cause the blood to run back into her head. He considers removing her boots – which haven't been cleaned yet today – but decides that this would be an unwarranted familiarity.

Mrs. Humphrey has neat ankles, from which he averts his eyes; her hair is dishevelled from the fall. Seen this way she is younger than he's thought; and, with her habitual expression of strained anxiety wiped away by unconsciousness, much more attractive. He sets his ear against her breast, listening: the heartbeat is regular. A simple case of fainting, then. He moistens a towel with water from the jug and applies it to her face and neck. Her eyelids twitch.

Simon pours half a glass of water from the bottle on his night-stand, adds twenty drops of sal volatile – a medication he always carries with him on his afternoon visits, in case of any similar flimsiness on the part of Grace Marks, who is said to be prone to fainting – and, supporting Mrs. Humphrey with one arm, holds the glass to her lips.

"Swallow this."

She gulps awkwardly, then lifts a hand to her head. There is a red mark, he notices now, on the side of her face. Perhaps her scoundrel of a husband is a brute as well as a sot. Though this looks more like a hard slap, and surely such a man as the Major would employ a closed fist. Simon feels a wave of protective pity for her that he cannot really afford. The woman is only his landlady; apart from that she's a complete stranger to him. He has no wish to alter this situation, despite an image that leaps into his mind, unbidden – aroused no doubt by the sight of a helpless woman extended upon his tumbled bed – of Mrs. Humphrey, semi-conscious and with her hands fluttering helplessly in the air, minus her stays and with her chemise half torn off, her feet – curiously, still in their boots – kicking spasmodically, making faint mewing noises while being savaged by a hulking figure that bears no resemblance at all to himself; although – from above, and from the back, which is his point of view during this sordid scene – the quilted dressing-gown looks identical.

He has always been curious about these manifestations of the imagination as he has been able to observe them in himself. Where do they come from? If they occur in him, they must occur as well in the majority of men. He is both sane and normal, and he has developed the rational faculties of his mind to a high degree; and yet he cannot always control such pictures. The difference between a civilized man and a barbarous fiend – a madman, say – lies, perhaps, merely in a thin veneer of willed self-restraint.

"You are quite safe," he says to her kindly. "You have had a fall. You must rest quietly until you feel better."

"But – I am on a bed." She gazes around her.

"It is my bed, Mrs. Humphrey. I was forced to carry you to it in the absence of any other suitable place."

The skin of her face is now flushed. She has noticed his dressing-gown. "I must leave at once."

"I beg you to remember that I am a doctor, and, for the time being, you are my patient. If you were to attempt to get up now, there might be a recurrence."

"Recurrence?"

"You collapsed, while carrying in" – it seems indelicate to mention it – "my breakfast tray. May I ask you – what has become of Dora?"

To his consternation, but not to his surprise, she begins to cry. "I could not pay her. I owed her three months' back wages; I had succeeded in selling some – some items of a personal nature, but my husband took the money from me, two days ago. He has not been back since. I do not know where he has gone." She makes a visible effort to control her tears.

"And this morning?"

"We had – words. She insisted on payment. I told her I could not, that it was not possible. She said in that case she would pay herself. She began to go through my bureau drawers, in search of jewellery, I suppose. Not finding any, she said she would have my wedding ring. It was gold, but very plain. I attempted to defend it from her. She said I was not honest. She . . . struck me. Then she took it, and said she would not be an unpaid slave to me any longer, and then she left the house. After that I prepared your breakfast myself, and carried it up. What else was I to do?"

So it was not the husband then, thinks Simon. It was that sow of a Dora. Mrs. Humphrey begins to cry again, gently, effortlessly, as if the sobs are a kind of birdsong.

"You must have some good woman friend you can go to. Or who can come to you." Simon is anxious to transfer Mrs. Humphrey from his own shoulders to those of someone else. Women help each other; caring for the afflicted is their sphere. They make beef tea and jellies. They knit comforting shawls. They pat and soothe.

"I have no friends in this place. We have only recently come to this city, having suffered – having undergone some financial difficulties in our previous abode. My husband discouraged visits. He did not want me going out."

A useful thought comes to Simon. "You must eat something. You will feel stronger."

At this she smiles wanly at him. "There is nothing in the house to eat, Dr. Jordan. Your breakfast was the last of it. I have not eaten for two days, ever since my husband left. What little there was, Dora ate up herself. I have had nothing but water."

And so Simon finds himself at the market, purchasing stores for the physical maintenance of his landlady, with his own money. He'd helped Mrs. Humphrey down the stairs to her own part of the house; she'd insisted on it, saying she could not afford to be found in the bedroom of her lodger in the event of her husband's return. He wasn't surprised to find that the rooms were essentially bare of furniture: a table and two chairs were all that remained in the parlour. But there was still a bed in the back bedroom, and onto it he had placed Mrs. Humphrey, in a state of nervous exhaustion. And starvation, too: no wonder she was so bony. He turned his mind away from the bed, and from the scenes of conjugal misery that must have been enacted upon it.

Then he went back upstairs to his own rooms, with a slop pail he'd located; the kitchen had been a shambles. He cleaned up the spilled breakfast and the broken dishes from his floor, noting that for once the now-ruined egg had been perfectly cooked.

He supposes he will have to give notice to Mrs. Humphrey, and change his lodgings, which will be an inconvenience; although preferable to the disruption of his life and work that would surely be the consequence if he were to stay. Disorder, chaos, the Bailiff's men coming for the furniture in his own chambers, no doubt. But if he leaves, what will become of the wretched woman? He does not want her on his conscience, which is where she will be if she starves to death on a street corner.

He buys some eggs, and some bacon and cheese, and some dirty-looking butter from an old farm woman at one of the stalls; and, at a shop, some tea twisted up in a paper. He would like bread, but there is none to be seen. He doesn't really know how to go about this. He's visited the market before, but only fleetingly, to obtain the vegetables with which he has been hoping to prod Grace's memory. Now he's on a different footing entirely. Where can he purchase milk? Why are there no apples? This is a universe he has never explored, having had no curiosity about where his food came from, as long as it did come. The other shoppers at the market are servants, their mistresses' shopping baskets over their arms; or else women of the poorer classes, in limp bonnets and bedraggled shawls. He feels they are laughing at him behind his back.

When he returns, Mrs. Humphrey is up. She's wrapped herself in a quilt and tidied her hair, and is sitting beside the stove, which is luckily alight – he himself would not know how to manage it – rubbing her hands together and shivering. He succeeds in making her some tea, and in frying some eggs and bacon, and in toasting a stale bun which he eventually found at the market. They eat these together, at the one remaining table. He wishes there were some marmalade.

"This is so good of you, Dr. Jordan."

"Think nothing of it. I could not let you starve." His voice is heartier than he intends, the voice of a jolly and insincere uncle who can scarcely wait to bestow the expected quarter-dollar on the grovelling poor-relation niece, pinch her cheek, and then make his getaway to the opera. Simon wonders what the bad Major Humphrey is doing right now, and curses him silently, and envies him. Whatever it may be, it is more enjoyable than this.

Mrs. Humphrey sighs. "I am afraid it will come to that. I am at the end of my resources." She is now quite calm, and is looking at her situation objectively. "The rent of the house must be paid, and there is no money. Soon they will come like vultures to pick over the bones, and I will be turned out. Perhaps I will even be arrested for debt. I would rather die."

"Surely there must be something you can do," says Simon. "To earn a living." She is clutching for her self-respect, and he admires her for it.

She gazes at him. Her eyes, in this light, are an odd shade of sea-green. "What do you suggest, Dr. Jordan? Fancy needlework? Women like me have few skills they can sell." There's a hint of malicious irony in her voice. Does she know what he was thinking as she lay unconscious on his unmade bed?

"I will advance you another two months' rent," he finds himself saying. He's a fool, a soft-hearted idiot; if he had any sense he would be out of here as if the Devil himself were in pursuit. "That should be sufficient to hold the wolves at bay, at least until you've had time to consider your prospects."

Her eyes fill with tears. Without a word, she lifts his hand from the table and presses it gently to her lips. The effect is only slightly dampened by the trace of butter that remains upon her mouth.

1 8 .

Today Dr. Jordan looks more disarranged than usual, and as if he has something on his mind; he does not seem to know quite how to begin. So I continue with my sewing until he's had time to gather himself together; and then he says, Is that a new quilt you are working on, Grace?

And I say, Yes it is, Sir, it is a Pandora's Box for Miss Lydia.

This puts him in an instructive mood, and I can see he is going to teach me something, which gentlemen are fond of doing. Mr. Kinnear was like that as well. And he says, And do you know who Pandora was, Grace?

And I say, Yes, she was a Greek person from days of old, who looked into a box she had been told not to, and a lot of diseases came out, and wars, and other human ills; for I had learnt it a long time ago, at Mrs. Alderman Parkinson's. Mary Whitney had a low opinion of the story, and said why did they leave such a box lying around, if they didn't want it opened.

He is surprised to find I know that, and says, But do you know what was at the bottom of the box?

Yes Sir, I say, it was hope. And you could make a joke of it, and say that hope was what you got when you scraped the bottom of the barrel, as some do who have to marry at last out of desperation. Or you could say it was a hope chest. But in any case it is all just a fable; although a pretty quilt pattern.

Well, I suppose we all need a little hope now and then, he says.

I am on the point of saying that I have been getting along without it for some time, but I refrain; and then I say, You do not look yourself today, Sir, I trust you are not ill.

And he smiles his one-sided smile, and says he isn't ill, only pre-occupied; but that if I would continue with my story, it would be a help to him, as it would distract him from his worries; but he does not say what these worries might be.

And so I go on.

Now, Sir, I say, I will come to a happier part of my story; and in this part I will tell you about Mary Whitney; and then you will under-stand why it was her name I borrowed, when I was in need of it; for she was never one to refuse a friend in need, and I hope I stood by her as well, when the time came for it.

The house of my new employment was very grand, and was known as one of the finest houses in Toronto. It was situated on Front Street, overlooking the Lake, where there were many other big houses; and it had a curved portico with white pillars at the front. The dining room was oval in shape, as was the drawing room, and a marvel to behold, although drafty. And there was a library as big as a ballroom, with shelves up to the ceiling all stuffed full of books in leather covers, with more words in them than you would ever want to read in your life. And the bedchambers had high tester bedsteads with hangings, and also netting to keep out the flies in summer, and dressing tables with looking glasses, and mahogany commodes, and chests of drawers all complete. They were Church of England, as all the best people were in those days, and also those who wanted to be the best, as it was Established.

The family consisted, first, of Mr. Alderman Parkinson, who was seldom visible, as he was much engaged in business and politics; he was the shape of an apple with two sticks stuck into it for legs. He had so many gold watch-chains and gold pins and gold snuffboxes and other trinkets, you could have got five necklaces out of him if he was melted down, with the earrings to match. Then there was Mrs. Alderman Parkinson, and Mary Whitney said she ought to have been the Alderman herself, as she was the better man. She was an imposing figure of a woman, and a very different shape out of her corsets than in them; but when she was firmly laced in, her bosom jutted out like a shelf, and she could have carried a whole tea service around on it and never spilt a drop. She came from the United States of America, and had been a well-to-do widow before being, as she said, swept off her feet by Mr. Alderman Parkinson; which must have been a sight to behold; and Mary Whitney said it was a wonder Mr. Alderman Parkinson had escaped with his life.

She had two grown sons who were away at college in the States; and also a spaniel dog named Bevelina, which I include as family because it was treated as such. I am fond of animals as a rule but this one took an effort.

Then there were the servants, which were many in number; and some left and others came while I was there, so I will not mention them all. There was Mrs. Alderman Parkinson's lady's maid, who claimed to be French although we had our doubts, and kept to herself; and Mrs. Honey the housekeeper, who had quite a large room at the back of the main floor, and so did the butler; and the cook and laundress lived next the kitchen. The gardener and stable-men lived in the outbuildings, as did the two kitchen maids, near the stable with the horses and three cows, where I went sometimes to help with the milking.

I was put in the attic, at the very top of the back stairs, and shared a bed with Mary Whitney, who helped in the laundry. Our room was not large, and hot in summer and cold in winter, as it was next the roof and without a fireplace or stove; and in it was the bedstead, which had a pallet mattress filled with straw, and a small chest, and a plain washstand with a chipped basin, and a chamber pot; and also a straight-backed chair, painted a light green, where we folded our clothes at night.

Down the passageway from us were Agnes and Effie, who were the chambermaids. Agnes was of a religious temperament, although kind-hearted and helpful. In her youth she had tried a preparation for taking the yellow off the teeth, but it took the white off as well, which may have been why she smiled so seldom, and took care to do it with her lips closed. Mary Whitney said she prayed so much because she was praying to God to get her white teeth back again, but so far no results. Effie had become very melancholic when her young man was transported to Australia for being in the Rebellion three years before; and when she got a letter saying he had died there, she attempted to hang herself by her apron strings; but they broke, and she was found on the floor half-choked and out of her mind, and had to be put away.

I knew nothing about the Rebellion, not having been in the country at the time, so Mary Whitney told me. It was against the gentry, who ran everything, and kept all the money and land for themselves; and it was led by Mr. William Lyon Mackenzie, who was a Radical, and after the Rebellion failed he escaped through ice and snow in women's clothing, and over the Lake to the States, and he could have been betrayed many times over but was not, because he was a fine man who always stood up for the ordinary farmers; but many of the Radicals had been caught and transported or hanged, and had lost their property; or else had gone south; and most of those left here were Tories, or said they were; so it was best not to mention politics, except among friends.

I said I understood nothing about politics, so would not think of mentioning it in any case; and I asked Mary if she was a Radical. And she said I was not to tell the Parkinsons, who had heard a different story, but her own father had lost his farm that way, which he had cleared himself with much labour; and they had burnt the log house he'd built with his own two hands, while fighting off the bears and other wild animals; and then he'd lost his life too, through illness caused by hiding in the winter woods; and her mother had died of grief. But their time would come, they would be revenged; and she looked very fierce as she said this.

I was pleased to be with Mary Whitney, as I liked her at once. Next to me she was the youngest one there, being sixteen; and she was a pretty and cheerful girl, with a tidy figure and dark hair and sparkling black eyes, and rosy cheeks with dimples; and she smelled like nutmegs or carnations. She asked all about me, and I told her about the journey in the ship, and about my mother dying, and sinking down into the sea among the icebergs. And Mary said that was very sad. And then I told her about my father, although keeping back the worst parts, because it is not right to speak ill of a parent; and how I feared he would want all of my wages; and she said I should not give him my money as he had not worked for it, and it would not benefit my sisters and brothers, as he would spend all on himself and most likely on the drink. I said I was afraid of him, and she said he could not get at me here, and if he tried, she would speak to Jim in the stables, who was a large man with friends. And I began to feel easier.

Mary said I might be very young, and as ignorant as an egg, but I was bright as a new penny, and the difference between stupid and ignorant was that ignorant could learn. And she said I looked like a good worker who would pull my weight, and we would get along fine together; and she'd had two other situations, and if you had to hire yourself out as a servant, it was as well at Parkinsons' as any-where, as they did not stint on the meals. And this was true, as I soon began to fill out and grow taller. Food was certainly easier to come by in the Canadas than on the other side of the ocean, and there was a greater variety of it; and even the servants ate meat every day, if only salt pork or bacon; and there was good bread, of wheat and also of Indian corn; and the house had its own three cows, and kitchen garden, and fruit trees, and strawberries, cur-rants, and grapes; and flower beds as well.

Mary Whitney was a fun-loving girl, and very mischievous and bold in her speech when we were alone. But towards her elders and betters her manner was respectful and demure; and because of that, and the brisk way she did her work, she was a general favourite. But behind their backs she made jokes about them, and imitated their faces and walks and ways. I was often astonished at the words that came out of her mouth, as many of them were quite coarse; it wasn't that I'd never heard such language before, as there was a suf-ficient store of it at home when my father was drunk, and on the ship coming over, and down by the harbour near the taverns and inns; but I was surprised to hear it from a girl, and one so young and pretty, and so neatly and cleanly dressed. But I soon got used to it, and put it down to her being a native-born Canadian, as she did not have much respect for degree. And sometimes when I would be shocked at her, she would say that I would soon be singing mournful hymns like Agnes, and going around with a mouth pulled down all glum and saggy like an old maid's backside; and I would protest, and we would end by laughing.

But it angered her that some people had so much and others so little, as she could not see any divine plan in it. She claimed that her grandmother had been a Red Indian, which was why her hair was so black; and that if she had half a chance she would run away to the woods, and go about with a bow and arrow, and not have to pin up her hair or wear stays; and I could come with her. And then we would fall to planning about how we would hide in the forest, and leap out upon travellers, and scalp them, which she had read about in books; and she said she would like to scalp Mrs. Alderman Parkinson, except it would not be worth the trouble as her hair was not her own, there were hanks and swatches of it kept in her dressing room; and she'd once seen the French maid brushing a heap of it, and thought it was the spaniel. But it was just our way of talking, and no harm was meant.

Mary took me under her wing from the very first. She soon guessed that I wasn't as old as I said I was, and she swore not to tell; and then she looked over my clothes, and said most of them were too small for me, and fit only for the scrap bag, and that I would never make it through the winter with only my mother's shawl, as the wind would go right through it like a sieve; and she would help me get the clothes I needed, as Mrs. Honey had told her I looked like a ragamuffin and I was to be made presentable, since Mrs. Alderman Parkinson had her name to keep up in the neighbourhood. But first I must be scrubbed like a potato, I was that filthy.

She said she would get the loan of Mrs. Honey's hip bath; and I was alarmed, as I had never been in a bath of any sort, and also I was afraid of Mrs. Honey; but Mary said her bark was worse than her bite, and in any case you could always hear her coming, as she clanked like a wagonful of old kettles because of all her keys; and if there was any argument she would threaten to bathe me outside, stark naked, under the pump in the back courtyard. I was shocked by this, and said I would not allow it; and she said of course she would never do such a thing, but the mere mention of it would obtain Mrs. Honey's consent.

Back she came quite soon, and said we could have the hip bath as long as we scoured it well out afterwards; and we took it to the laundry room, and pumped the water, and took the chill off it on the stove, and poured it in. I made Mary stand at the door to prevent anyone from coming in, and with her back turned, as I had never taken off all my clothes at once before, though I kept my shift on out of modesty. The water was not very warm, and by the time I'd finished I was shivering, and it was a good thing it was summertime or I would have caught my death of cold. Mary said I had to wash my hair as well; and though it was true that washing it too much would take all the strength out of your body, and she had known a girl who had faded away and died from too much hair washing, still it needed to be done every three or four months; and she looked at my head, and said at least I did not have any lice, but if any appeared I would need sulphur and turpentine put on, and she had this done once and smelled like rotten eggs for days afterwards.

Mary lent me a nightdress until mine should be dry, because she'd washed all my clothes; and she wrapped me up in a sheet so I could go out of the laundry and climb up the back stairs; and she said I looked very comical, just like a madwoman.

Mary asked Mrs. Honey to give me an advance on my wages, for a decent dress; and we got leave to go into the town the very next day. Mrs. Honey preached us a sermon before we set off, and said we were to behave modestly, and go and come back straight away, and not speak to any strangers, especially men; and we promised to do as she said.

I am afraid however that we went the long way round, and looked at the flowers in the fenced gardens of the houses, and at the shops, which were not nearly so many or so grand as in Belfast, from what I had briefly seen there. Then Mary said would I like to see the street where the whores lived; and I was frightened, but she said there was no danger. I was indeed curious to see the women who made a living by selling their bodies, because I thought if worst came to worst and if starving, I would still have something to sell; and I wanted to see what they looked like. So we went to Lombard Street, but as it was the morning there was not much to be seen. Mary said that there were several bawdy-houses there, although you couldn't tell them from the outside; but inside they were said to be very fancy, with Turkey carpets and crystal chandeliers and velvet curtains, and the whores lived in them with their own bedchambers, and with maids to bring them their breakfasts and clean their floors and make their beds and take out their slops, and all they had to do was put on their clothes and take them off again, and lie around on their backs, and it was easier work than a coal mine or a mill.

The ones in these houses were the better class of whore, and the more expensive, and the men were gentlemen, or at least good-paying customers. But the cheaper sort had to walk about outside, and make use of rooms rented by the hour; and many of them got diseases, and were old by the time they were twenty, and had to cover their faces with paint, so as to deceive the poor drunken sailors. And although they might look very elegant from a distance, with feathers and satins, up close you could see that their dresses were soiled and ill-fitting, as every stitch on their backs was rented by the day, and they scarcely had enough left over for their bread; and it was a dismal sort of life, and she wondered they did not throw themselves into the lake; which some did, and were often found floating about in the harbour.

I wondered how Mary knew so much about it; but she laughed, and said that I would hear a lot if I would keep my ears open, especially in the kitchen; but also a girl she'd known from the country had gone to the bad, and she used to meet her on the street; but what had become of her since she didn't know, and feared it was nothing good.

After that we went to King Street, to a dry-goods shop where ends of bales were sold cheaply; and there were silks and cottons and broadcloths and flannels, and satins and tartans, and everything you could desire; but we had to consider the price, and the use it was to be put to. In the end we bought a serviceable blue and white gingham, and Mary said she would help me make it up; though she was surprised, when the time came, to find I could sew so well and with such tiny stitches, and said I was wasted as a servant, and ought to set up as a dressmaker.

We bought the thread for the dress, and also the buttons, from a peddler who came round the next day, and was well known to all there. He was a great favourite with Cook, who made him a cup of tea and cut him a slice of cake while he opened up his pack and spread out his wares. His name was Jeremiah, and when he came up the drive to the back door he was followed by a band of five or six raggedy urchins, like a parade, and one was banging on a pot with a spoon; and all were singing,

Jeremiah, blow the fire,
Puff, puff puff;
First you blow it gently,
Then you blow it rough!

The racket brought us all to the window; and when they'd reached the back door, he gave them a penny to spend, and they ran off; and when Cook asked him what all that was about, he said he would rather have them following under his command, than pelting him with clots of mud and horse dung, which was their habit with peddlers, who could not chase them away without abandoning their packs; which if they did, would swiftly be pillaged by the little ruffians; so he'd chosen the wiser course, and employed them, and taught them the song himself.

This Jeremiah was a deft and nimble man, with a long nose and legs and a skin all browned by the sun, and a curling black beard, and Mary said that although he looked like a Jew or a gypsy, as many peddlers were, he was a Yankee with an Italian father who'd come over to work in the mills, in Massachusetts; and his last name was Pontelli, but he was well liked. He spoke good English, yet with something foreign in his voice; and he had piercing black eyes and a wide and handsome smile, and flattered the women shamelessly.

He had a great many things I wanted to buy, but could not afford to, even though he said he would take half the money now and leave the rest until the next time he came; but I do not like being in debt. He had ribbons and laces, as well as the thread and buttons, which were metal or mother-of-pearl or wood or bone, and I chose the bone; and white cotton stockings, and collars and cuffs, and cravats and handkerchiefs; and several petticoats, and two pairs of stays, used, but well washed and almost as good as new; and summer gloves in pale shades, most beautifully made. And earrings, silver and gold in colour, although Mary said they would rub off; and a real silver snuffbox; and bottles of scent that smelled like roses, very strong. Cook bought some, and Jeremiah said she scarcely needed it, as she smelled like a princess already; and she blushed and giggled even though she was nearing fifty and not of a graceful figure, and she said Onions, more like; and he said she smelled good enough to eat, and the way to a man's heart was through his stomach, and then he smiled with his large white teeth, which looked all the larger and whiter due to his dark beard, and gave Cook a hungry stare, and licked his lips, as if she herself was a delicious cake he longed to devour; at which she blushed even more.

Then he asked us if we had anything to sell, for as we knew, he gave good prices; and Agnes sold her coral earrings that she had from an aunt, as being vanity, but we knew she needed the money for her sister, who was in difficulties; and Jim from the stables came in, and said he would trade a shirt he had, and also a large coloured handkerchief, for another and finer shirt he liked better; and with a wooden-handled pocket-knife thrown into the bargain, it was done.

While Jeremiah was in the kitchen it was like a party, and Mrs. Honey came to find out what was making all the commotion. And she said, Well Jeremiah, I see you are up to your old pranks, taking advantage of the women again. But she smiled while saying it, which was a rare sight. And he said yes, that was what he was doing, there were so many pretty ones he could not resist, but none so pretty as her; and she bought two lawn handkerchiefs from him, although she did say he had to be brisk about it, and not take all day, as the girls had their work to do. And then she clanked away out of the kitchen.

Some wanted him to tell their fortunes by looking into their hands; but Agnes said it was meddling with the Devil, and that Mrs. Alderman Parkinson would not want word to get round of such gypsy doings in her kitchen. So he did not. But after much pleading, he did an imitation of a gentleman, with the voice and manners and all, at which we clapped our hands with joy, it was so lifelike; and he made a silver coin appear out of Cook's ear, and showed us how he could swallow a fork, or appear to. He said these were conjuring tricks he had learnt in the days of his wicked youth, when he was a wild lad and worked at fairs, before he'd become an honest trades-man and had his pocket picked and his heart broken fifty times over by cruel and pretty girls such as we were; and all present laughed.

But when he'd stowed everything away in his pack again, and had drunk his cup of tea and eaten his slice of cake, and said nobody made such good cakes as Cook did, and was going away, he motioned me over to him, and gave me an extra bone button, to go with the four I'd bought. He put it into my hand and folded my fingers over it, and his own fingers were hard and dry, like sand; but he peered into my hand swiftly first; and then he said, Five for luck; for people of that kind consider four an unlucky number, and odd numbers luckier than even ones. And he gave me a quick and intelligent look with his shining black eyes, and he said, quite low so that the others did not hear it, There are sharp rocks ahead. Which I suppose there always are, Sir, and there had certainly been enough of them behind, and I had survived them; so I was not too daunted by that.

But then he said the strangest thing of all to me. He said, You are one of us.

And then he shouldered his pack and took up his staff, and walked away; and I was left wondering what he'd meant. But after I had mulled it over, I decided he meant that I too was homeless, and a wanderer, like the peddlers and those who worked at fairs; for I couldn't imagine what else he might have had in mind.

We all felt a little stale and flat after he had gone; for it wasn't often that those of us in the back rooms and offices were allowed a treat like that, and a good look at such pretty things, and a chance to laugh and fun in the middle of the day.

But the dress came out very well, and because there were five buttons and not four, we used three at the neck and one on each of the sleeve cuffs; and even Mrs. Honey said what a difference it made in my appearance, and how trim and respectable I looked, now that I was decently dressed.

1 9 .

My father came round at the end of the first month, and wanted all my wages; but I could only give him a quarter, having spent the rest. And then he began to curse and swear, and seized me by the arm; but Mary set the stablehands onto him. And he came back at the end of the second month, and I gave him a quarter again, and Mary told him he wasn't to come any more. And he called her hard names, and she called him worse, and whistled for the men; and so he was chased off. I was of two minds about this, as I felt sorry for the little ones; and I tried to send them some money afterwards, through Mrs. Burt; but I do not think they received it.

I was set to work at first as a scullery maid, scouring out the pots and pans, but it was soon observed that the iron cauldrons were too heavy for me; and then our laundress left for a new position, and another one came who was not so brisk, and Mrs. Honey said I was to assist Mary with the rinsing and the wringing out, and the hanging up and the folding and the mangling and mending, and we were both very pleased. Mary said she would teach me what I needed to know, and as I was bright enough I would learn it quickly.

When I would make a mistake and become anxious about it, Mary would comfort me and say I should not take things so seriously, and if you never made a mistake you would never learn; and when Mrs. Honey spoke sharply to me and I was on the verge of tears, Mary would say I should not mind her, as that was her way, it was because she had swallowed a bottle of vinegar and it came out on her tongue. And also I should remember that we were not slaves, and being a servant was not a thing we were born to, nor would we be forced to continue at it forever; it was just a job of work. She said it was the custom for young girls in this country to hire themselves out, in order to earn the money for their dowries; and then they would marry, and if their husbands prospered they would soon be hiring their own servants in their turn, at the very least a maid-of-all-work; and that one day I would be the mistress of a tidy farmhouse, and independent, and I would look back on my trials and tribulations at the hands of Mrs. Honey as a fine joke. And one person was as good as the next, and on this side of the ocean folks rose in the world by hard work, not by who their grandfather was, and that was the way it should be.

She said that being a servant was like anything else, there was a knack to it which many never learnt, and it was all in the way of looking at it. For instance, we'd been told always to use the back stairs, in order to keep out of the way of the family, but in truth it was the other way around: the front stairs were there so that the family would keep out of our way. They could go traipsing up and down the front stairs in their fancy clothes and trinkets, while the real work of the place went on behind their backs, without them getting all snarled up in it, and interfering, and making a nuisance of themselves. They were feeble and ignorant creatures, although rich, and most of them could not light a fire if their toes were freezing off, because they didn't know how, and it was a wonder they could blow their own noses or wipe their own backsides, they were by their nature as useless as a prick on a priest – if you'll excuse me, Sir, but that was how she put it – and if they were to lose all their money tomorrow and be thrown out on the streets, they would not even be able to make a living by honest whoring, as they would not know which part was to go in where, and they would end up getting – I won't say the word – in the ear; and most of them did not know their own arse from a hole in the ground. And she said something else about the women, which was so coarse I will not repeat it, Sir, but it made us laugh very much.

She said that the trick to it was to have the work done without it ever being seen to be done; and if any of them was to surprise you at a task, you should simply remove yourself at once. In the end, she said, we had the better of them, because we washed their dirty linen and therefore we knew a good deal about them; but they did not wash ours, and knew nothing about us at all. There were few secrets they could keep from the servants; and if I was ever to be a chambermaid, I would have to learn to carry a bucket full of filth as if it was a bowl of roses, for the thing these people hated the most was to be reminded that they too had bodies, and their shit stank as much as anyone's, if not worse. And then she would say a poem: *When Adam delved and Eve span, Who was then the gentleman?*

As I've said, Sir, Mary was an outspoken young woman, and did not mince words; and she had very democratic ideas, which it took me some getting used to.

At the very top of the house was a large attic, divided up; and if you climbed the stairs, and then went along past the room where we slept, and down some other stairs, you were in the drying room. It was strung with lines, and had several small windows that opened out under the eaves. And the chimney from the kitchen ran up through this room. It was used to dry the clothes in winter, and when it was raining outside.

As a rule we did not do a wash if the weather threatened; but especially in the summer, the day could start fair and then cloud over all of a sudden, and thunder and rain; and the thunderstorms were very violent, with loud cracks of thunder and fiery flashes of lightning, so much that you would think the end of the world was come. I was terrified the first time it happened, and got under a table and began to cry, and Mary said it was nothing, only a thunderstorm; but then she told me several stories of men who had been out in their fields or even in their barns, and were struck dead by lightning, and also a cow standing under a tree.

When we had a wash hanging out and the first drops began to fall, we would rush out with the baskets and gather all in as quickly as we could, and then haul it up the stairs and hang it out anew in the drying room, as it could not be allowed to sit in the baskets for long because of mildew. I did love the smell of a laundry dried outside, it was a good fresh smell; and the shirts and the nightgowns flapping in the breeze on a sunny day were like large white birds, or angels rejoicing, although without any heads.

But when we hung the same things up inside, in the grey twilight of the drying room, they looked different, like pale ghosts of themselves hovering and shimmering there in the gloom; and the look of them, so silent and bodiless, made me afraid. And Mary, who was very quick in such matters, soon found this out, and would hide behind the sheets, and press up against them so there was the outline of her face, and give out a moaning sound; or she would get behind the nightshirts and make their arms move. Her object was to frighten me, and she would succeed, and I would shriek; and then we would chase up and down between the rows of washing, laughing and screaming, but trying not to laugh and scream too loud, and if I would catch her I would dart in and tickle her, for she was very ticklish; and sometimes we would try on Mrs. Alderman Parkinson's corsets, over top of our clothes, and walk around with our chests sticking out and looking down our noses; and we would be so overcome that we would fall backwards into the baskets of linens, and lie there gasping like fish until we had recovered our straight faces again.

These were just the high spirits of youth, which do not always take a very dignified form, as I am sure you have had cause to observe, Sir.

Mrs. Alderman Parkinson had more pieced quilts than I'd ever seen before in my life, as it was not so much the fashion on the other side of the ocean, and printed cottons were not so cheap and plentiful. Mary said that a girl did not consider herself ready for marriage here until she had three such quilts, made by her own hands; and the fanciest ones were the marriage quilts, such as the Tree of Paradise and the Flower Basket. Others, such as the Wild Goose Chase and the Pandora's Box, had a good many pieces, and took skill; and those such as the Log Cabin and the Nine Patch were for everyday, and were much faster to make. Mary had not begun on her own marriage quilt yet, as she did not have the time, being a servant; but she'd already finished a Nine Patch.

On a fine day in mid-September, Mrs. Honey said that it was time to take out the winter quilts and blankets, and to air them, in preparation for the cold weather; and to mend the rents and tears; and she gave this task to Mary and myself. The quilts were stored in the attic, away from the drying room, to avoid the damp, in a cedar chest, with a sheet of muslin in between each one and enough camphor to kill a cat, and the smell of it made me quite light-headed. We were to carry them downstairs and hang them out on the lines, and brush them down and see if the moths had been at them; for sometimes, despite cedar chests and camphor, the moths will get in, and the winter quilts had wool batts inside them instead of the cotton ones in the summer quilts.

The winter quilts were of deeper colours than the summer ones, with reds and oranges and blues and purples; and some of them had silks and velvets and brocade pieces in them. Over the years in prison, when I have been by myself, as I am a good deal of the time, I have closed my eyes and turned my head towards the sun, and I have seen a red and an orange that were like the brightness of those quilts; and when we'd hung a half-dozen of them up on the line, all in a row, I thought that they looked like flags, hung out by an army as it goes to war.

And since that time I have thought, why is it that women have chosen to sew such flags, and then to lay them on the tops of beds? For they make the bed the most noticeable thing in a room. And then I have thought, it's for a warning. Because you may think a bed is a peaceful thing, Sir, and to you it may mean rest and comfort and a good night's sleep. But it isn't so for everyone; and there are many dangerous things that may take place in a bed. It is where we are born, and that is our first peril in life; and it is where the women give birth, which is often their last. And it is where the act takes place between men and women that I will not mention to you, Sir, but I suppose you know what it is; and some call it love, and others despair, or else merely an indignity which they must suffer through. And finally beds are what we sleep in, and where we dream, and often where we die.

But I did not have these fancies about the quilts until after I was already in prison. It is a place where you have a lot of time to think, and no one to tell your thoughts to; and so you tell them to yourself.

Here Dr. Jordan asks me to pause a little so he can catch up with his writing; for he says he is much interested in what I have just related. I am glad of this, as I have enjoyed telling about those days, and if I had my own wish I would stay in them as long as I could. So I wait, and watch his hand moving over the paper, and think it must be pleasant to have the knack of writing so quickly, which can only be done by practice, like playing the piano. And I wonder if he has a good singing voice, and sings duets with young ladies in the evenings, when I am shut up alone in my cell. Most likely he does, as he is a handsome enough and friendly, and unmarried.

And so, Grace, he says, looking up, you consider a bed to be a dangerous place?

There is a different note in his voice; perhaps he is laughing at me up his sleeve. I should not speak to him so freely, and decide I will not, if that is the tone he is going to take.

Well of course not every time you get into it, Sir, I say, only on those occasions which I have mentioned. Then I keep silent, and continue to sew.

Have I offended you somehow, Grace? he says. I did not intend to.

I sew in silence for a few moments more. Then I say, I will believe you, Sir, and take you at your word; and hope such will be returned in future.

Of course, of course, he says warmly. Please do go on with your story. I should not have interrupted.

Surely you do not want to hear about such ordinary things, and daily life, I say.

I want to hear anything you may tell me, Grace, he says. The small details of life often hide a great significance.

I am not certain what he means by that, but I continue.

At last we had all of the quilts carried down and hung out in the sun, and brushed; and we took two of them inside again, to mend them. We stayed in the laundry, where there was no washing going forward, so it was cooler than the attic; and there was a large table where we could spread the quilts out.

One of them was quite strange-looking; it had four grey urns with four green willow trees growing out of them, and a white dove in each corner, or I believe they were intended for doves, although they looked more like chickens; and in the middle was a woman's name embroidered in black: Flora. And Mary said it was a Memorial Quilt, done by Mrs. Alderman Parkinson in the memory of a dear departed friend, as was then becoming the fashion.

And the other quilt was called Attic Windows; it had a great many pieces, and if you looked at it one way it was closed boxes, and when you looked at it another way the boxes were open, and I suppose the closed boxes were the attics and the open ones were the windows; and that is the same with all quilts, you can see them two different ways, by looking at the dark pieces, or else the light. But when Mary said the name I did not hear it right, and I thought she said Attic Widows, and I said, Attic Widows, that is a very odd name for a bed quilt. And then Mary told me what the right name was, and we had a fit of laughing, because we pictured an attic all full of widows, in their black dresses with their widow's caps and the weepers hanging down, pulling mournful faces and wringing their hands, and writing letters on their black-bordered writing paper, and dabbing at their eyes with their black-bordered handkerchiefs. And Mary said, And the boxes and chests in the attic would be stuffed to the brim with their dear deceased husbands' cut-off hair; and I said, And perhaps the dear deceased husbands are in the chests too.

And that set us off again. We could not stop laughing, even when we heard Mrs. Honey and her keys clanking along the hall. We buried our faces against the quilts, and by the time she'd opened the door Mary was composed again, but I was face down with my shoulders heaving, and Mrs. Honey said, What is the matter, girls, and Mary stood up and said, Please Mrs. Honey, it's just that Grace is crying about her dead mother, and Mrs. Honey said Very well then, you may take her down to the kitchen for a cup of tea, but don't be too long about it, and she said that young girls were often weepy but Mary must not indulge me and let it get out of control. And when she'd gone out we held on to each other, and laughed so much I thought we should die.

Now you may think it very thoughtless in us, Sir, to have made light of widows; and with the deaths in my own family, I should have known it was not a thing to joke over. And if there had been any widows nearby we would never have done it, as it is wrong to make fun of another's suffering. But there were no widows to hear us, and all I can say, Sir, is that we were young girls, and young girls are often silly in that way; and it is better to laugh than to burst.

Then I thought about widows – about widow's humps, and widow's walks, and the widow's mite in the Bible, which we servants were always being urged to give to the poor out of our wages; and also I thought about how the men would wink and nod when a young and rich widow was mentioned, and how a widow was a respectable thing to be if old and poor, but not otherwise; which is quite strange when you come to consider it.

In September the weather was beautiful, with days just like summer, and then in October many of the trees turned red and yellow and orange, as if they were on fire, and I could never stop looking at them. And one afternoon towards evening I was outside with Mary gathering in the sheets from the lines, and we heard a sound like many hoarse voices calling together, and Mary said, Look up, it's the wild geese flying south for the winter. The sky above was dark with them, and Mary said, The hunters will be out tomorrow morning. And it was sad to think that these wild creatures were about to be shot.

One night in late October a frightening thing happened to me. I would not tell you about this, Sir, except that you are a doctor and doctors know about it already, so you will not be shocked. I had been using the chamber pot, as I was already in my nightdress and ready to go to bed, so did not want to go outside to the privy in the dark;

and when I happened to look down, there was blood, and some on my nightdress also. I was bleeding from between the legs, and I thought I was dying, and burst into tears.

Mary coming into the room found me in this state, and said What has happened? and I said that I had a dreadful illness, and would surely die; and I had a pain in my stomach as well, which I'd ignored, thinking it was only from eating too much new bread, as it was a baking day. But now I remembered my mother, and how her death had begun with a stomach pain, and I cried harder.

Mary looked, and to do her credit she did not laugh at me; but explained all. You will wonder that I did not know this, considering how many children my mother had given birth to; but the fact is that I knew about babies and how they got out, and even how they got in, having seen dogs in the street; but not this other thing. I'd had no friends my own age, or I suppose I would have learnt it.

And Mary said, You are a woman now, which made me cry again. But she put her arms around me, and comforted me, better than my own mother could have done, for she was always too busy or tired or ill. Then she lent me her red flannel petticoat until I should get one of my own, and showed me how to fold and pin the cloths, and said that some called it Eve's curse but she thought that was stupid, and the real curse of Eve was having to put up with the nonsense of Adam, who as soon as there was any trouble, blamed it all on her. She also said that if the pain got too bad she would get me some willow bark to chew, and that would help; and she would heat a brick for me on the kitchen stove, and wrap it in a towel, for the ache. And I was very grateful to her, for she was indeed a good and kind friend.

And then she sat me down and combed out my hair, which was gentle and soothing, and she said, Grace, you will be a beauty, soon you will turn the men's heads. The worst ones are the gentlemen, who think they are entitled to anything they want; and when you go out to the privy at night, they're drunk then, they lie in wait for you and then it is snatch and grab, there's no reasoning with them, and if you must, you should give them a kick between the legs where they'll feel it; and it is always better to lock your door, and to use the chamber pot. But any kind of man will try the same; and they'll start promising things, they'll say they will do whatever you want; but you must be very careful what you ask, and you must never do anything for them until they have performed what they promised; and if there's a ring, there must be a parson to go with it.

I asked her innocently, Why was that, and she said it was because men were liars by nature, and would say anything to get what they wanted of you, and then they would think better of it and be off on the next boat. And now I saw that we were in the same story as the one Aunt Pauline used to tell about my mother, and I nodded wisely and said that she was right, although still not altogether certain what she meant. And she gave me a hug, and said I was a good girl.

On the night of October the 31st, which as you know, Sir, is All Hallows Eve, when they say the spirits of the dead come back from the grave, although it is only a superstition – on that night, Mary came to our room with something hidden in her apron, and she said, Look, I have got us four apples, I begged them from Cook. Apples were plentiful at that time of year and there were barrels of them already stored in the cellar. Oh, I said, are they for us to eat, and she said We will eat them after, but this is the night when you can find out who you will marry. She said she had got four, so that we would each have two chances at it.

She showed me a little knife she'd got from Cook also, or so she said. The truth is that she sometimes took things without asking, which made me nervous; though she said it was not stealing as long as you put the things back after. But sometimes she didn't do that either. She'd taken a copy of *The Lady of the Lake* by Sir Walter Scott out of the library where they had five of them, and she was reading it out loud to me; and she had a store of candle-ends which she'd taken one by one from the dining room, and she kept them hidden under a loose floorboard; and if she'd had them by permission, she wouldn't have done so. We were allowed our own candle, to undress by at night, but Mrs. Honey said we weren't to burn it up in a profligate way, each candle was to last us a week, and that was less light than Mary wanted to have. She had some Lucifer matches which she also kept hidden, so that when our official candle was blown out to save it, she could light another whenever she wanted; and she lit two of her candle-ends now.

Here is the knife and the apple, she said, and you must take the peel off in one long piece; and then without looking behind you, you must throw it over your left shoulder. And it will spell out the initial of the man you will marry, and tonight you will dream about him.

I was too young to be thinking of husbands, but Mary talked about them a great deal. When she'd saved up enough of her wages, she was going to marry a nice young farmer whose land was already cleared and a good house built; and if she could not get one of those, she would settle for one with a log house, and they would build a better house later. She even knew what kind of hens and cow they would have – she wanted white and red Leghorns, and a Jersey cow for the cream and cheese, which she said there was nothing better.

So I took the apple and pared it, and I got the peel off in one piece. Then I threw it behind me, and we looked at how it had fallen. There was no telling which way was up, but at last we decided that it was a J. And Mary began to tease, and to tell over the names of the men she knew whose names began with a J; and she said I would marry Jim from the stables, who had a squint, and stank horribly; or else Jeremiah the peddler, who was much handsomer, though I would have to tramp the country, and would have no house but the pack I carried on my back, like a snail. And she said I would cross water three times before it happened, and I said she was inventing it; and she smiled, because I'd guessed she was tricking me.

Then it was her turn, and she began to peel. But the peel on her first apple broke, and also on the second; and I gave her my extra one, but she was so nervous that she cut it in two almost as soon as she'd begun. And then she laughed, and said it was only a foolish old wives' tale, and she ate the third apple, and set the other two on the window ledge to keep until the morning, and I ate my own apple; and we turned to making fun of Mrs. Alderman Parkinson's corsets; but underneath all the funning she was upset.

And when we went to bed, I could tell that she hadn't gone to sleep, but was lying on her back beside me, staring up at the ceiling; and when I did go to sleep myself, I did not dream of husbands at all. Instead I dreamt of my mother in her winding sheet, drifting down through the cold water, which was blue-green in colour; and the sheet began to come undone at the top, and it waved as if in the wind, and her hair floated out, rippling like seaweed; but the hair was over her face so I could not see it, and it was darker than my mother's hair had been; and then I knew that this was not my mother at all, but some other woman, and she was not dead inside the sheet at all, but still alive.

And I was afraid; and I woke up with my heart beating very fast, and the cold sweat on me. But Mary was asleep now, breathing deeply, and the grey and pink light of the dawn was beginning; and outside the cocks had begun to crow, and all was as usual. And so I felt better.

20.

And so things went on through November, when the leaves fell from the trees and it became dark early, and the weather was grim and grey, with a hard driving rain; and then December came, and the ground froze up solid as rock, and there were flurries of snow. Our attic room was now very cold, especially in the mornings, when we had to get up in the dark and put our bare feet on the icy floor-boards; and Mary said that when she had a house of her own, she would have a braided rag rug beside every bed, and she herself would have a pair of warm felt slippers. We took our clothes into the bed with us, to warm them up before putting them on, and dressed underneath the bedclothes; and at night we would heat bricks on the stove and wrap them in flannel and put them in the bed, to keep our toes from turning to icicles. And the water in our basin was so cold that it would send the pain shooting up my arms when washing my hands; and I was glad we were two in a bed.

But Mary said this was nothing, as the real winter was not here and it would get much colder yet; and the only good of it was that they would have to build up the fires in the house, and burn them longer. And it was better to be a servant, in the daytime at least, because we could always warm ourselves in the kitchen, whereas the drawing room was as drafty as a barn and you could get no heat from the fireplace unless you stood right next to it, and Mrs. Alderman Parkinson lifted her skirts in front of it when alone in the room, to warm her backside; and last winter she'd set her petticoats alight, and Agnes the chambermaid heard the shouting, and rushed in and was frightened into hysterics, and Mrs. Alderman Parkinson had a blanket thrown over her, and was rolled on the floor like a barrel, by Jim from the stables. Luckily she was not burnt, but merely singed a little.

In the middle of December, my father sent my poor sister Katey to beg more of my wages; he would not come himself. I felt sorry for Katey, as the burden that had once been on me was now on her; and I brought her into the kitchen and warmed her by the stove, and asked a piece of bread from Cook, who said it was not her job to feed all of the starving orphans in the town, but gave it nevertheless; and Katey cried, and said she wished I was at home again. And I gave her a quarter of a dollar, and said she was to tell our father it was all I had, which I am sorry to say was a lie; but I had come to feel that the truth was not a thing I owed him. And I gave her ten cents for herself, and said she was to keep it safe in case of need, though she was in need enough already. Also I gave her a petticoat of mine, that was grown too small.

She said that our father had found no steady work, only odd jobs, but had the prospect of going north that winter, to cut trees; and had news of some free land farther west, and would go there once the spring had come. Which he did, and suddenly too, for Mrs. Burt came around and said my father had gone off without paying any-where near all he owed. At first she wanted me to make it good, but

Mary told her she could not force a girl of thirteen to pay a debt incurred by a grown man; and Mrs. Burt was not a bad woman at heart, and at the end she said it was not my fault.

I do not know what became of my father and the children. I never had a letter, and also heard nothing from them at the time of the trial.

As Christmastime came around, spirits rose; and the fires were built up larger, and hampers were delivered from the grocer, and great wedges of beef, and the carcass of a pig from the butcher, which was to be roasted whole; and bustling preparations were made in the kitchen; and Mary and I were called away from the laundry, to give a hand, and we stirred and mixed for Cook, and peeled and sliced the apples, and picked through the raisins and currants, and grated the nutmegs, and beat up the eggs as required; and we liked this very much, as there was a chance for a taste here and a nibble there, and whenever we could we scraped off a little sugar for ourselves; and Cook did not notice or say anything, as she had a great deal on her mind.

It was Mary and me who made the bottom crusts for all of the mince pies, although Cook did the top ones, as she said there was an art to it which we were too young to know; and she cut out stars for them, and other fancy designs. And she let us unwrap the Christmas cakes from the layers of muslin round them, and pour on the brandy and whisky, and wrap them up again; and the smell of it was one of the best things I can remember.

There were many pies and cakes needed, as it was the season of visiting, and of dinners and parties and balls. The two sons of the household came home from school, at Harvard in Boston; their names were Mr. George and Mr. Richard, and both seemed pleasant enough and fairly tall. I did not pay much attention to them, as to my mind they only made for more washing, and a great many more shirts to be starched and ironed; but Mary was always peeping out the upstairs window into the yard, to see if she could catch a glimpse of them as they rode away on their horses, or else listening in the passageway, while they sang duets with the ladies invited; and what she liked especially was *The Rose of Tralee*, because her name was in it – where it says, *Oh no, 'twas the truth in her eye ever dawning, That made me love Mary, the Rose of Tralee.* She had a good singing voice herself, too, and knew many of the songs off by heart; which the two of them would sometimes come into the kitchen and tease her to sing. And she called them young scamps, although both of them were some years older than she was.

On Christmas Day itself, Mary gave me a pair of warm mittens which she'd knitted. I'd seen her doing it, but she had been very sly, and had told me they were for a young friend of hers; and I never thought that the young friend she meant was myself. They were a beautiful dark blue, with red flowers embroidered on them. And I gave her a needle-case I'd made from five squares of red flannel, sewn together along the top; and it tied shut with two bits of ribbon. And Mary thanked me, and gave me a hug and a kiss, and said it was the best needle-case in the world, you could never buy such a thing in a store, and she'd never seen one like it, and she would treasure it always.

The snow had fallen heavily that day, and the people were out in their sleighs, with bells on the horses, and it sounded very pretty. And after the family had eaten their Christmas dinner the servants ate theirs, and had their own turkey and mince pies, and we sang some carols together, and were glad.

This was the happiest Christmas that I ever spent, either before or after.

Mr. Richard went back to school after the holidays, but Mr. George stayed at home. He'd caught a chill which had gone to his lungs, and was coughing a great deal; and Mr. and Mrs. Alderman Parkinson went about with long faces, and the doctor came, which alarmed me. But it was said he did not have consumption, only a feverish cold, and the lumbago, and must be kept quiet, and given hot drinks; and these he had in plentiful supply, as he was a great favourite with the servants. And Mary heated an iron button on the stove, which she said was the best thing for the lumbago, if you put it on the spot; and she took it up to him.

By the time he was better it was the middle of February, and he'd missed so much of the college term he said he would stay away until the next one; and Mrs. Alderman Parkinson agreed, and said he needed to build up his strength. And so there he was, being fussed over by all, and with time on his hands and not much he needed to do, which is a bad situation for a young man full of spirits. And there was no shortage of parties to go to, and girls to dance with, and their mothers to plan his wedding for him without his knowledge. I am afraid he was very much indulged, not least by himself. For if the world treats you well, Sir, you come to believe you are deserving of it.

Mary had told the truth about the winter. The snow at Christmastime had been heavy, but it was like a blanket of feathers, and the air appeared warmer after it had fallen; and the stablehands joked, and threw snowballs; but as they were soft, they broke when they hit.

But soon the real winter set in, and the snow began to come down in earnest. This time it was not soft but hard, like tiny stinging pellets of ice; and it was driven along by a keen and bitter wind, and piled up in thick drifts; and I feared we would all be buried alive. Icicles grew on the roof, and you had to be careful when passing underneath, as they could fall off, and were sharp and pointed; and Mary had heard of a woman who'd been killed by one, that went right through her body like a skewer. One day there was sleet, which covered all the tree branches with a coating of ice, and the next day they sparkled in the sun like a thousand diamonds; but the trees were weighted down by it, and many branches broke. And the entire world was hard and white, and when the sun shone it was so blinding that you had to shield your eyes, and not look at it too long.

We kept indoors as much as possible, as there was a danger of frostbite, especially in the fingers and toes; and the men went about with scarves tied over their ears and noses, and their breath came out in clouds. The family had their fur rugs in the sleigh, and their wraps and cloaks, and went visiting; but we did not have such warm garments. At night Mary and I put our shawls on top of the bedcovers, and wore our stockings and an extra petticoat to bed; though even so we were not warm. By morning the fires had died down, and our hot bricks had cooled, and we were shivering like rabbits.

On the last day of February the weather improved somewhat; and we ventured out on errands, having wrapped our feet up well in flannel cloths, inside the boots which we begged from the stable-hands; and we wound ourselves in as many shawls as we could find or borrow, and walked down as far as the harbour. It was frozen solid, with great blocks and slices of ice piled against the shore; and there was a place cleared of snow, where the ladies and gentlemen were skating. It was a graceful motion, as if the ladies were running on wheels underneath their dresses, and I said to Mary that it must be delightful. Mr. George was there, gliding over the ice hand in hand with a young lady in a fur scarf, and he saw us, and gave us a cheerful wave. I asked Mary if she had ever skated, and she said no.

About this time I began to notice a change in Mary. She was often late coming to bed; and when she did come, she no longer wanted to talk. She did not hear what I said to her, but appeared to be listening to something else; and she was constantly looking out through doorways, or windows, or over my shoulder. One night when she thought I was asleep, I saw her hiding something away in a handker-chief, under the floorboard where she kept her candle-ends and matches; and when I looked the next day, she being out of the room, I found that it was a gold ring. My first thought was that she had stolen it, which would be more than she'd ever stolen before, and very bad for her if she was caught; though there was no talk in the house of a missing ring.

But she did not laugh and fun as before, nor did she attend to her work in her usual brisk manner; and I became worried. But when I questioned her, and asked if there was some trouble, she would laugh, and say she did not know where I was getting such ideas. But her smell had changed, from nutmegs to salt fish.

The snow and ice began to melt, and a few birds returned, and they began to sing and call; so I knew it would soon be spring. And one day in late March, as we were carrying the clean wash up the back stairs in baskets, to hang it in the drying room, Mary said she was ill; and she ran downstairs and out into the back yard, behind the outbuildings. I set down my basket and followed her, just as I was, without my shawl; and I found her on her knees in the wet snow near the privy, which she had not had time to reach, as she had been overcome by a violent sickness.

I helped her up, and her forehead was damp and clammy, and I said she should be put to bed; but at that she became angry, and said it was something she'd eaten, it must have been yesterday's mutton stew, and now she was rid of it. But I'd eaten the very same thing myself, and felt perfectly well. She made me promise not to speak of it, and I said I would not. But when the same thing happened a few days later, and then again the next morning, I was truly alarmed; for I had seen my own mother in that condition very often, and I knew the milky smell of it; and I was well aware of what was wrong with Mary.

I thought it over, and turned it this way and that in my mind; and towards the end of April I taxed her with it, and swore very solemnly that if she would confide in me, I would not tell; for I believed she was in great need of confiding in someone, as she was restless at night, and had dark circles beneath her eyes, and was oppressed by the burden of her secret. Then she broke down and cried, and said my suspicions were all too true; and the man had promised to marry her, and had given her a ring, and for once in a way she'd believed him, as she'd thought he was not like other men; but he'd gone back on his promise, and now would not speak with her; and she was in despair and did not know what to do.

I asked her who the man was, but she would not tell me; and she said that as soon as it was known what sort of trouble she was in, she would be turned away, as Mrs. Alderman Parkinson held very strict views; and then what would happen to her? Some girls in her place would have gone back to their families, but she had none; and now no decent man would marry her, and she would have to go on the streets, and become a sailors' drab, as she would have no other way of feeding herself and the baby. And such a life would soon be the end of her.

I was very distressed on her behalf, and also on mine, for she was the truest and indeed the only friend I had in the world. I comforted her the best way I could, but I did not know what to say.

Throughout the month of May, Mary and I frequently talked about what she should do. I said there must be a workhouse or something of the sort that would take her in, and she said she knew of none, but even so, if young girls went to any such place they always died, as they got fever as soon as they were delivered; and she believed the babies in such places were secretly smothered, so as not to be a charge on the public purse; and she would sooner take her chances of dying elsewhere. We talked about some way of delivering the baby ourselves, and keeping it quiet, and giving it away as an orphan; but she said her condition would soon begin to show; and Mrs. Honey had very sharp eyes, and had already remarked that Mary was putting on flesh, and she could not hope to go long undetected.

I said she should try one last time to speak with the man in question, and appeal to his better nature. And she did so; but when she returned from the interview – which must have taken place nearby, as she was not gone long – she was angrier than she had ever been. She said he'd given her five dollars; and she'd said was that all his child was worth to him? And he said she would not catch him that way, and he doubted that it was even his own child, since she'd been so obliging with him, that he suspected she had been so for others; and if she threatened him with a scandal, or went to his family, he would deny it, and ruin whatever reputation she had left; and if she wanted a quick end to her troubles she could always drown herself.

She said she had once truly loved him, but did so no longer; and she threw the five dollars on the floor, and cried passionately for an hour; but I noticed her putting the money carefully away, under the loose board, afterwards.

The next Sunday she said she would not go to church, but for a walk by herself; and when she came back, she said she'd gone down to the harbour with the idea of throwing herself into the lake, and putting an end to her life. And I begged her with tears not to do such a wicked thing.

Two days later she said she'd been over to Lombard Street, and had heard there of a doctor who could help her; he was the doctor that the whores went to, when they needed it. I asked her in what way he might help, and she said I shouldn't ask; and I did not know what she meant, having never heard of such doctors. And she asked if I would lend her my savings, which amounted at that time to three dollars, which I'd been intending for a new summer dress. And I said I would lend it to her with all my heart.

She then brought out a piece of writing paper, which she'd obtained from the library downstairs, and a pen and ink, and she wrote: *If I die, my things are to go to Grace Marks.* And she signed it with her name. And then she said, Soon I may be dead. But you will still be alive. And she gave me a cold and resentful look, such as I'd seen her give to others behind their backs, but never to me.

I was much alarmed at this, and clutched her hand, and begged her not to go to this doctor, whoever he might be; but she said she must, and I was not to carry on, but I must put the pen and ink back secretly on the writing desk in the library, and go about my duties; and tomorrow she would steal away after the midday meal, and I was to say if asked that she'd just gone out to the privy, or that she was up in the drying room, or any excuse that came into my head; and then I was to slip away and join her, as she might be in difficulties coming home.

Neither one of us slept well that night; and the next day she did as she said she would, and managed to leave the house without detection, with the money knotted up in her handkerchief; and I followed soon after, and joined her. The doctor lived in a large-enough house, in a good neighbourhood. We went in by the servants' entrance; and the doctor himself met us. The first thing he did was to count the money. He was a big man in a black coat, and looked at us very severely; and he told me to wait in the scullery, and then said that if I told anything about it, he would deny ever having seen me. Then he took off his frock coat and hung it on a hook, and began rolling up his shirtsleeves, as if for a fight.

He looked very similar, Sir, to the head-measuring doctor that frightened me into a fit, just before you came here.

Mary went with him out of the room, her face as white as a sheet; and then I heard screams, and crying, and after a time the doctor pushed her in through the scullery door. Her dress was all damp, and clinging to her like a wet bandage, and she could scarcely walk; and I put my arms around her, and assisted her away from that place as best I could.

When we reached the house she was bent nearly double and holding her hands to her stomach; and said would I help her upstairs. Which I did, and she seemed very weak. I put her into her night-dress and into the bed, and she kept her petticoat on, crumpled up between her legs. And I asked her what had happened, and she said the doctor took a knife to her, and cut something inside; and he said there would be pain and bleeding, and it would last some hours, but that after this she would be all right again. And she'd given a false name.

It began to dawn on me that what the doctor had cut out of her was the baby, which I thought a most wicked thing; but I also thought it was either one corpse that way or two the other, because if not, she would certainly have drowned herself; so I could not find it within my heart to reproach her.

She was in great pain, and in the evening I warmed a brick and carried it upstairs; but she would not let me fetch anyone. And I said I would sleep on the floor, as she would be more comfortable that way; and she said I was the best friend she ever had, and that what-ever happened she would never forget me. I rolled myself up in my shawl, with my apron for a pillow, and lay down on the floor, which was very hard; and what with that, and with Mary's groans of agony, I could not sleep at first. But after a time it grew quieter, and I fell asleep, and did not wake up until daybreak. And when I did, there was Mary, dead in the bed, with her eyes wide open and staring.

I touched her, but she was cold. I stood stock-still with fear; but then I roused myself, and went along the hall, and woke Agnes the chambermaid, and fell into her arms weeping; and she said,

Whatever is the matter? I could not speak, but took her by the hand, and led her into our room, to where Mary was. Agnes laid hold of her, and shook her by the shoulder; and then she said, Good heavens, she is dead.

And I said, Oh Agnes, what shall I do? I did not know she was going to die, and now they will blame me, for not telling sooner that she was taken ill; but she made me promise not to. And I was sobbing, and wringing my hands.

Agnes lifted the bedcovers and looked beneath. The nightdress and petticoat were soaked through with blood, and the sheet was all red with it, and brown where it had dried. She said, This is a bad business, and she told me to stay there, and she went at once to fetch Mrs. Honey. I heard her footsteps going away, and it seemed to me she was gone a long time.

I sat on the chair in our room and looked at Mary's face; her eyes were open, and I could feel her looking back at me out of the corners of her eyes. I thought I saw her move, and I said, Mary, are you pretending? For she sometimes pretended she was dead, behind the sheets in the drying room, to frighten me. But she was not pretending.

Then I heard two sets of footsteps hurrying along the passage, and I was filled with dread. But I stood up. And Mrs. Honey came into the room; she did not look sad, she looked angry, and also disgusted, as if she could smell a bad smell. And there was indeed a smell in the room; it was the smell of wet straw, from the mattress, and also the salty smell of blood; you can smell something very similar in a butcher's shop.

And Mrs. Honey said, This is an outrage and a disgrace, I must go and tell Mrs. Parkinson. And we waited, and Mrs. Alderman Parkinson came, and said, Under my own roof, what a deceitful girl. And she looked straight at me, although she was talking about Mary.

Then she said, Why did you not inform me of this, Grace? And I said, Please Ma'am, Mary told me not to. She said she would be better in the morning. And I started to cry, and I said, I did not know she was going to die!

Agnes, who was very pious as I have told you, said The wages of sin is death.

Mrs. Alderman Parkinson said, That was wicked of you, Grace, and Agnes said, She is only a child, she is very obedient, she was just doing as she was told.

I thought Mrs. Alderman Parkinson would scold her for interfering, but she did not. She took hold of my arm gently, and looked into my eyes, and said, Who was the man? The scoundrel should be exposed, and made to pay for his crime. I suppose it was some sailor, down at the harbour, they have no more conscience than a flea. Do you know, Grace?

I said, Mary did not know any sailors. She was seeing a gentleman, and they were engaged. Only he broke his promise, and would not marry her.

And Mrs. Alderman Parkinson said sharply, What gentleman?

I said, Please Ma'am, I don't know. Only she said you would not like it at all, if you found out who it was.

Mary had not said this, but I had my own suspicions.

At that Mrs. Alderman Parkinson looked thoughtful, and paced to and fro the length of the room; and then she said, Agnes and Grace, we will not discuss this further, as it will only lead to unhappiness and added misery, and there is no sense in crying over spilt milk; and out of respect to the dead we will not say what Mary died of. We will say it was a low fever. That will be best for all.

And she looked at both of us very hard, and we curtsied. And all the time Mary was there on the bed, listening to us, and hearing about our plans to tell these lies about her; and I thought, She will not be easy in her mind about it.

I didn't say anything about the doctor, and they did not ask. Perhaps they didn't even consider such a thing. They must have thought it was only a lost baby, as women frequently have; and that Mary had died of it, as women frequently did. And you are the first person I have told about the doctor, Sir; but it is my true belief that it was the doctor that killed her with his knife; him and the gentleman between them. For it is not always the one that strikes the blow, that is the actual murderer; and Mary was done to death by that unknown gentleman, as surely as if he'd taken the knife and plunged it into her body himself.

Mrs. Alderman Parkinson left the room, and after a while Mrs. Honey came, and said we were to take the sheet from the bed, and her nightdress and petticoat, and wash the blood out of them; and wash the body, and take the mattress to be burnt, and see to it ourselves; and there was another mattress cover beside where the quilts were stored, and we could stuff that with straw; and we were to fetch a clean sheet. She asked if there was another nightdress for Mary to be dressed in, and I said there was, because Mary had two; but the other one was in the wash. Then I said I would give her one of mine. She said we were not to tell anyone of Mary's death until we'd got her looking presentable, with the quilt pulled up over her and her eyes closed, and her hair combed down and tidy. Then she went out of the room, and Agnes and myself did as she said; and Mary was light to lift, but heavy to arrange.

Then Agnes said, There is more to this than meets the eye, and I wonder who the man was. And she looked at me. And I said, Whoever he is, he is still alive and well, and most likely enjoying his breakfast at this very moment, and not having any thoughts in his head about poor Mary, no more than if she was a carcass hung up at the butcher's.

Agnes said, It is the curse of Eve which we must all bear, and I knew Mary would have laughed at that. And then I heard her voice, as clear as anything, right in my ear, saying *Let me in*. I was quite startled, and looked hard at Mary, who by that time was lying on the floor, as we were making up the bed. But she gave no sign of having said anything; and her eyes were still open, and staring up at the ceiling.

Then I thought with a rush of fear, But I did not open the window. And I ran across the room and opened it, because I must have heard wrong and she was saying *Let me out*. Agnes said, What are you doing, it's cold as an icicle out there, and I said The smell is making me sick. And she agreed that the room should be aired. I was hoping Mary's soul would fly out the window now, and not stay inside, whispering things into my ear. But I wondered whether I was too late.

Finally we had all done, and I bundled the sheet and the nightdress together and took them down to the laundry, and pumped a tub full of cold water, because it's the cold water you need to get out the blood, as the hot will set it. By good fortune the laundress was not in the laundry but in the main kitchen, heating the irons for the ironing, and gossiping with Cook. And I scrubbed, and much of the blood came out, making the water all red; and I ran that down the drain and pumped another tubful, and left the things to soak, with some vinegar poured in to help with the smell. Whether from the cold or the shock, my teeth by now were chattering; and as I ran back up the stairs I felt quite dizzy.

Agnes had been waiting in the room with Mary, all nicely laid out now with her eyes closed as if sleeping, and her hands crossed on her breast. I told Agnes what I'd done, and she sent me to tell Mrs. Alderman Parkinson that all was ready. And I did, and went back upstairs, and pretty soon here came the servants to see, crying some of them, and sad-faced, as was fitting; but still there is always a strange excitement around a death, and I could see that the blood was flowing more strongly through their veins than on ordinary days.

Agnes did the talking, and said it was a sudden fever, and for a woman as pious as she was, she lied very well; and I stood by Mary's feet, keeping silent. And one said, Poor Grace, to wake up in the morning and find her cold and stark in the bed beside you, with no warning at all. And another said, It makes your flesh creep to think of it, my own nerves would never stand it.

Then it was as if that had really happened; I could picture it, the waking up with Mary in the bed right beside me, and touching her, and finding she would not speak to me, and the horror and distress I would feel; and at that moment I fell to the floor in a dead faint.

They said I lay like that for ten hours, and no one could wake me, although they tried pinching and slapping, and cold water, and burning feathers under my nose; and that when I did wake up I did not seem to know where I was, or what had happened; and I kept asking where Grace had gone. And when they told me that I myself was Grace, I would not believe them, but cried, and tried to run out of the house, because I said that Grace was lost, and had gone into the lake, and I needed to search for her. They told me later they'd feared for my reason, which must have been unsettled by the shock of it all; and it was no wonder, considering.

Then I fell again into a deep sleep. When I woke, it was a day later, and I knew again that I was Grace, and that Mary was dead. And I remembered the night we'd thrown the apple peelings over our shoulders, and Mary's had broken three times; and it had all come true, as she had not married anyone at all, and now never would.

But I had no memory of anything I said or did during the time I was awake, between the two long sleeps; and this worried me.

And so the happiest time of my life was over and gone.

VII.

SNAKE FENCE

McDermot . . . was morose and churlish. There was very little to admire in his character. . . . [He] was a smart young fellow, so lithe that he would run along the top of a zigzag fence like a squirrel, or leap over a five-barred gate, rather than open or climb it. . . .

Grace was of a lively disposition and pleasant manners and may have been an object of jealousy to Nancy. . . . There is plenty of room for the supposition that instead of her being the instigator and promoter of the terrible deeds committed, she was but the unfortunate dupe in the whole dreadful business. There certainly did not appear to be anything in the girl's personality that would be likely to develop into an embodiment of concentrated iniquity that McDermot tried to make her out to have been, if he ever uttered one half of the statements attributed to him in his confession. His disregard for truth was well-known. . . .

– William Harrison,
"Recollections of the Kinnear Tragedy,"
written for the *Newmarket Era*, 1908.

Yet if you should forget me for a while
And afterwards remember, do not grieve;
For if the darkness and corruption leave

A vestige of the thoughts that once I had,
Better by far you should forget and smile
Than that you should remember and be sad.

– Christina Rossetti,
"Remember," 1849.

2 1 .

Simon takes his hat and stick from the Governor's wife's maid, and staggers out into the sunlight. It's too bright for him, too harsh, as if he's been closed up in a dark room for a long time, although the sewing room is far from dark. It's Grace's story that is dark; he feels as if he's just come from an abattoir. Why has this account of a death affected him so strongly? Of course he's known that such things happen; such doctors do exist, and it isn't as if he's never seen a dead woman. He's seen a great many of them; but they have been so thoroughly dead. They have been specimens. He has never caught them, as it were, in the act. This Mary Whitney, not yet – what? Seventeen? A young girl. Deplorable! He would like to wash his hands.

No doubt about it, the turn of events has caught him off guard. He'd been following her story with, he has to admit, a certain personal pleasure – he has his own happier days and the memories of them, and they too contain pictures of clean sheets and joyful holidays, and cheerful young maidservants – and then, at the centre of it, this dire surprise. She'd lost her memory, too; though only for some hours, and during a normal-enough fit of hysterics – but still, it may prove significant. It is the only memory she seems to have forgotten, so far; otherwise, every button and candle-end seems accounted for. But on second thought, he has no way of knowing that; and he has an uneasy sense that the very plenitude of her recollections may be a sort of distraction, a way of drawing the mind away from some hidden but essential fact, like the dainty flowers planted over a grave. Also, he reminds himself, the only witness who could corroborate her testimony – if this were a court of law – would be Mary Whitney herself, and she is not available.

Down the driveway to the left comes Grace herself, walking with her head lowered, flanked by two unsavoury-looking men he supposes to be prison guards. They're leaning very close to her, as if she's no murderess, but a precious treasure to be kept safe. He doesn't like the way they press up against her; but of course their lives would be very difficult if she were to escape. Although he's always known that she's taken back every evening and locked into a narrow cell, today it strikes him as incongruous. They've been talking together all afternoon as if in a parlour; and now he is free as air and may do whatever he likes, while she must be bolted and barred. Caged in a dreary prison. Deliberately dreary, for if a prison were not dreary, where would be the punishment?

Even the word *punishment* grates on him today. He can't get Mary Whitney out of his mind. Lying in her winding sheet of blood.

He has stayed longer than usual this afternoon. In half an hour he is due at the Reverend Verringer's, for an early supper. He does not feel hungry in the least. He decides to walk along by the lakeshore; the breeze there will do him good, and possibly restore his appetite.

It's just as well, he reflects, that he didn't continue as a surgeon. The most fearsome of his instructors at Guy's Hospital in London, the celebrated Dr. Bransby Cooper, used to say that for a good surgeon, as for a good sculptor, the ability to detach oneself from the business at hand was a prerequisite. A sculptor should not allow himself to be distracted by the transient charms of his model, but should regard her objectively, as merely the base material or clay from which his work of art was to be formed. Similarly, a surgeon was a sculptor of flesh; he should be able to slice into a human body as deliberately and delicately as if carving a cameo. A cold hand and a steady eye were what was required. Those who felt too deeply for the patient's suffering were the ones in whose fingers the knife slipped. The afflicted did not need your compassion, but your skill.

All very well, thinks Simon; but men and women are not statues, not lifeless like marble, although they often become so in the hospital surgery, after a harrowing period of noisy and leaky distress. He'd quickly discovered at Guy's that he was not fond of blood.

But he'd learned some worthwhile lessons nonetheless. How easily people die, for one; how frequently, for another. And how cunningly spirit and body are knit together. A slip of the knife and you create an idiot. If this is so, why not the reverse? Could you sew and snip, and patch together a genius? What mysteries remain to be revealed in the nervous system, that web of structures both material and ethereal, that network of threads that runs throughout the body, composed of a thousand Ariadne's clues, all leading to the brain, that shadowy central den where the human bones lie scattered and the monsters lurk. . . .

The angels also, he reminds himself. Also the angels.

In the distance he sees a woman walking. She's dressed in black; her skirt is a soft rippling bell, her veil blows out behind her like dark smoke. She turns, looks back briefly: it's Mrs. Humphrey, his sombre landlady. Fortunately she's walking away from him; or she may be deliberately avoiding him. Just as well, as he is not in the mood for conversation, and especially not for gratitude. He wonders why she insists on dressing quite so much like a widow. Wishful thinking, perhaps. So far there's been no news of the Major. Simon paces along the shore, picturing to himself what the Major must be doing – a racecourse, a bawdy-house, a tavern; one of the three.

Then he thinks, inconsequentially, about taking off his shoes and wading into the lake. He has a sudden memory of dabbling in the creek at the back of the property, as a young boy, in the company of his nursemaid – one of the young millhands turned servant, as were most of their maids then – and getting himself dirty, and being scolded by his mother, and the nursemaid too, for allowing it.

What was her name? Alice? Or was that later, when he was already at school, and in long trousers, and had gone up to the attic on one of his furtive escapades, and had been caught by the girl in her room? White-handed, as it were – he'd been fondling one of her shifts. She'd been angry with him, but couldn't express her anger, of course, as she'd wanted to keep her position; so she'd done the womanly thing, and burst into tears. He'd put his arms around her to console her, and they'd ended by kissing. Her cap had fallen off, and her hair came tumbling down; long dark-blonde hair, voluptuous, none too clean, smelling of curdled milk. Her hands were red, as she'd been hulling strawberries; and her mouth tasted of them.

There were red smears afterwards, on his shirt, from where she'd started to undo his buttons; but it was the first time he'd ever kissed a woman, and he'd been embarrassed, and then alarmed, and hadn't known what to do next. Probably she'd laughed at him.

What a raw boy he'd been then; what a simpleton. He smiles at the memory. It's a picture of more innocent days, and by the time the half-hour is up he feels much better.

Reverend Verringer's housekeeper greets him with a disapproving nod. If she were to smile, her face would crack like an eggshell.

There must be a school for ugliness, thinks Simon, where such women are sent to be trained. She shows him into the library, where a fire has been lit and two glasses of some unknown cordial set ready. What he would really like is a good stiff whisky, but there's no hope of that among the teetotalling Methodists.

Reverend Verringer has been standing among his leather bindings, but moves forward to welcome Simon. They sit and sip; the brew in the glass tastes like waterweed, with an undertone of raspberry beetles. "It is purifying to the blood. My housekeeper makes it herself, from an old recipe," says Reverend Verringer. Very old, thinks Simon; witches come to mind.

"Has there been any progress with – our mutual project?" asks Verringer.

Simon has known this question would be asked; nevertheless, he stumbles a little over the answer. "I have been proceeding with the utmost caution," he says. "Certainly there are several threads that are worth pursuing. I first needed to establish the grounds for trust, which I believe I have done. After that, I have sought to elicit a family history. Our subject appears to remember her life before arriving at Mr. Kinnear's, with a vividness, and a mass of circumstantial detail, that indicates the problem is not with her memory in general. I have learned about her journey to this country, and also the first year of her domestic service, which was not marked by any untoward episodes, with one exception."

"Which was?" asks Reverend Verringer, lifting his sparse eyebrows.

"Are you acquainted with a family called Parkinson, in Toronto?"

"I seem to remember them," says Verringer, "from my youth. He was an Alderman, as I recall. But he died some years ago; and the widow, I believe, returned to her native land. She was an American, like yourself. She found the winters too cold."

"That is unfortunate," says Simon. "I had hoped to speak with them, in order to corroborate certain supposed facts. Grace's first situation was with this family. She had a friend – a fellow-servant there – called Mary Whitney; which was, you may recall, the false name she herself gave, when escaping to the United States, with her – with James McDermott; if indeed it was an escape, and not a forced emigration of sorts. In any case this young woman died, under what I must term abrupt circumstances; and while sitting in the room with the body, our subject thought she heard her dead friend speak to her. An auditory hallucination, of course."

"It is not at all uncommon," says Verringer. "I myself have attended a great many deathbeds, and especially among the sentimental and the superstitious, it is counted a mark of dishonour *not* to have heard the deceased speak. If an angel choir is also audible, so much the better." His tone is dry, and possibly even ironic.

Simon is a little surprised: surely it is the duty of the clergy to encourage pious eyewash. "This was followed," he continues, "by an episode of fainting, and then by hysterics, mixed with what would appear to have been somnambulism; after which there was a deep and prolonged sleep, and subsequent amnesia."

"Ah," says Verringer, leaning forward. "So she has a history of such lapses!"

"We must not leap to conclusions," Simon says judiciously. "She herself is at present my only informant." He pauses; he does not wish to appear lacking in tact. "It would be exceedingly useful to me, in the formation of my professional opinion, if I were able to speak with those who knew Grace at the time of the – of the events in question, and who afterwards witnessed her comportment and behaviour in the Penitentiary, during the first years of her incarceration, and also in the Asylum."

"I myself was not present upon those occasions," says Reverend Verringer.

"I have read Mrs. Moodie's account," says Simon. "She has a great deal to say that interests me. According to her, Kenneth MacKenzie, the lawyer, visited Grace in the Penitentiary some six or seven years after she was imprisoned, and was told by Grace that Nancy Montgomery was haunting her – that her two bloodshot and blazing eyes were following her around, and appearing in such locations as her lap and her soup plate. Mrs. Moodie herself saw Grace in the Asylum – the violent ward, I believe – and portrays a gibbering mad-woman, shrieking like a phantom and running about like a singed monkey. Of course, her account was written before she could know that in less than a year Grace would be discharged from the Asylum as, if not perfectly sane, then sane enough to be returned to the Penitentiary."

"One does not have to be entirely sane for that," says Verringer, with a short laugh like a hinge creaking.

"I have thought of paying a visit to Mrs. Moodie," says Simon. "But I seek your advice. I am not sure how to question her, without casting aspersions on the veracity of what she has set down."

"Veracity?" says Verringer blandly. He doesn't sound surprised.

"There are discrepancies that are beyond dispute," says Simon. "For instance, Mrs. Moodie is unclear about the location of Richmond Hill, she is inaccurate on the subject of names and dates, she calls several of the actors in this tragedy by names that are not their own, and she has conferred a military rank on Mr. Kinnear that he appears not to have merited."

"A post-mortem medal, perhaps," Verringer murmurs.

Simon smiles. "Also, she has the culprits cutting Nancy Montgomery's body up into quarters before hiding it under the washtub, which surely was not done. The newspapers would hardly have failed to mention a detail so sensational. I am afraid the good woman did not realize how difficult it is to cut up a body, never having done so herself. It makes one wonder, in short, about other things. The motive for the murders, for example – she puts it down to wild jealousy on the part of Grace, who envied Nancy her possession of Mr. Kinnear, and lechery on the part of McDermott, who was promised a quid pro quo for his services as butcher, in the form of Grace's favours."

"That was the popular view at the time."

"No doubt," says Simon. "The public will always prefer a salacious melodrama to a bald tale of mere thievery. But you can see that one might have one's reservations also about the bloodshot eyes."

"Mrs. Moodie," says Reverend Verringer, "has stated publicly that she is very fond of Charles Dickens, and in especial of *Oliver Twist*. I seem to recall a similar pair of eyes in that work, also belonging to a dead female called Nancy. How shall I put it? Mrs. Moodie is subject to influences. You might like to read Mrs. Moodie's poem 'The Maniac,' if you are an aficionado of Sir Walter Scott. Her poem contains all the requirements – a cliff, a moon, a raging sea, a betrayed maiden chanting a wild melody and clad in unhealthily damp garments, with – as I recall – her streaming hair festooned with botanical specimens. I believe she ends by leaping off the picturesque cliff so thoughtfully provided for her. Let me see – " And closing his eyes, and beating time with his right hand, he recites:

> " 'The wind wav'd her garments, and April's rash showers
> Hung like gems in her dark locks, enwreath'd with wild flowers;
> Her bosom was bared to the cold midnight storm,
> That unsparingly beat on her thin fragile form;
> Her black eyes flash'd sternly whence reason had fled,
> And she glanc'd on my sight like some ghost of the dead,
> As she sang a loud strain to the hoarse dashing surge,
> That rang on my ears like the plaint of a dirge.
>
> "And he who had left her to madness and shame,
> Who had robb'd her of honour, and blasted her fame –
> Did he think in that hour of the heart he had riven,

The vows he had broken, the anguish he'd given?
And where was the infant whose birth gave the blow
To the peace of his mother, and madden'd her woe? . . .'"

He opens his eyes again. "Where indeed?" he says.

"You astonish me," says Simon. "You must have an extraordinary memory."

"For verse of a certain type, unfortunately yes; it comes from too much hymn-singing," says Reverend Verringer. "Though God himself chose to write a good deal of the Bible in poetry, which demonstrates his approval of the form as such, however indifferently it may be practised. Nevertheless, one cannot quibble with Mrs. Moodie's morals. But I am sure you take my meaning. Mrs. Moodie is a literary lady, and like all such, and indeed like the sex in general, she is inclined to – "

"Embroider," says Simon.

"Precisely," says Reverend Verringer. "Everything I say here is strictly confidential, of course. Although Tories at the time of the Rebellion, the Moodies have since seen the error of their ways, and are now staunchly Reform; for which they have been made to suffer, by certain malicious persons who are in a position to torment them with lawsuits and the like. I would not say a word against the lady. But I would also not advise a visit. I understand, by the by, that the Spiritualists have got hold of her."

"Indeed?" says Simon.

"So I hear. She was for a long time a sceptic, and her husband was the first convert of the two. No doubt she became tired of spending the evenings alone, while he was off listening to phantom trumpets, and conversing with the spirits of Goethe and Shakespeare."

"I take it you do not approve."

"Ministers of my denomination have been expelled from the Church for dabbling in these, to my mind, unholy proceedings," says Reverend Verringer. "It is true that some members of our Committee have partaken; are devotees, in fact; but I must bear with them, until this madness has run its course and they have come to their senses. As Mr. Nathaniel Hawthorne has said, the thing is a humbug, and if it is not, so much the worse for us; for the spirits who present themselves at table-turnings and the like, must be those who have failed to get into the eternal world, and are still cluttering up ours, like a kind of spiritual dust. It is unlikely that they wish us well, and the less we have to say to them the better."

"Hawthorne?" says Simon. He is surprised to find a clergyman reading Hawthorne: the man has been accused of sensualism, and – especially after *The Scarlet Letter* – of a laxity in morals.

"One must keep up with one's flock. But as to Grace Marks and her earlier behaviour, you would be better to consult Mr. Kenneth MacKenzie, who acted for her at the trial, and who, I understand, has a sound head on his shoulders. He is currently a partner in a Toronto law firm, having made a rapid professional rise. I shall address a letter of introduction to him; I am sure he will accommodate you."

"Thank you," says Simon.

"I am pleased to have had this chance to talk with you in private, before the advent of the ladies. But I hear them arriving now."

"The ladies?" says Simon.

"The Governor's wife and her daughters are favouring us with their company this evening," says Verringer. "The Governor himself is unfortunately away on business. Did I not inform you?" Two spots of colour appear, one on each of his pale cheeks. "Let us go to welcome them, shall we?"

Only one daughter is present. Marianne, says her mother, has been kept to her bed with a cold. Simon is alerted: he is familiar with such ruses, he knows the cabals of mothers. The Governor's wife has decided to give Lydia an unimpeded shot at him, without any distraction from Marianne. Perhaps he should reveal the smallness of his income immediately, so as to forestall her. But Lydia is a confection, and he doesn't wish to deprive himself of such an aesthetic pleasure too soon. As long as no declarations are made, no harm will be done; and he enjoys being gazed at by eyes as luminous as hers.

The season has now officially changed: Lydia has burst into spring bloom. Layers of pale floral ruffling have sprouted all over her, and wave from her shoulders like diaphanous wings. Simon eats his fish – overdone, but no one on this continent can poach a fish properly – and admires the smooth white contours of her throat, and what can be seen of her bosom. It's as if she is sculpted of whipped cream. She should be on the platter, instead of the fish. He's heard stories of a famous Parisian courtesan who had herself presented at a banquet in this way; naked, of course. He occupies himself with undressing and then garnishing Lydia: she should be garlanded with flowers – ivory-coloured, shell pink – and with perhaps a border of hothouse grapes and peaches.

Her pop-eyed mother is as finely strung as ever; she fingers the jet beads at her throat, and digs almost at once into the serious business of the evening. The Tuesday circle fervently longs to have Dr. Jordan address it. Nothing too formal – an earnest discussion among friends – friends of his too, she hopes she may assume – who are interested in the same important causes. Perhaps he could say a few words on the Abolition question? It is of such concern to them all.

Simon says he's not an expert on it – indeed, he isn't well informed at all, having been in Europe for the past few years. In that case, suggests Reverend Verringer, perhaps Dr. Jordan would be so kind as to share with them the latest theories concerning nervous illnesses and insanity? That too would be most welcome, as one of their long-standing projects, as a group, is the reform of public asylums.

"Dr. DuPont says he would be especially interested," says the Governor's wife. "Dr. Jerome DuPont, whose acquaintance you have already made. He has such breadth of, he has such a wide range of . . . of things that interest him."

"Oh, I would find that fascinating," says Lydia, looking at Simon from under her long dark lashes. "I hope you will!" She hasn't said much this evening; but then, she hasn't had much chance, except to refuse the offers of more fish that have been pressed upon her by Reverend Verringer. "I have always wondered what it would be like, to go mad. Grace won't tell me."

Simon has a picture of himself in a shadowy corner with Lydia. Behind a drapery; a heavy mauve brocade. If he were to encircle her waist with his arm – gently, so as not to alarm her – would she sigh? Would she yield, or push him away? Or both.

Back in his lodgings, he pours himself a large glass of sherry, from the bottle he keeps in the armoire. He hasn't had a drink all evening – the beverage at Verringer's supper party was water – but somehow he's as fuzzy-headed as if he had. Why did he agree to address the devilish Tuesday circle? What are they to him, or he to them? What can he say to them that would make any sense to them at all, considering their lack of expertise? It was Lydia, her admiration, her appeal. He feels as if he's been ambushed by a flowering shrub.

He's too exhausted to stay up late, and read and work as usual. He goes to bed, and sleeps at once. Then he's dreaming; an uneasy dream. He's in a fenced yard where laundry flaps on a line. No one else is there, which gives him a sensation of clandestine pleasure. The sheets and linens move in the wind, as if worn by invisible swelling hips; as if alive. As he watches – he must be a boy, he's short enough to be looking upwards – a scarf or veil of white muslin is blown from the line and undulates gracefully through the air like a long bandage unrolling, or like paint in water. He runs to catch it, out of the yard, down the road – he's in the country, then – and into a field. An orchard. The cloth has tangled in the branches of a small tree covered with green apples. He tugs it down and it falls across his face; and then he understands that it isn't cloth at all but hair, the long fragrant hair of an unseen woman, which is twining around his neck. He struggles; he is being closely embraced; he can scarcely breathe. The sensation is painful and almost unbearably erotic, and he wakes with a jolt.

2 2 .

Today I am in the sewing room before Dr. Jordan. There's no sense in wondering what has delayed him, as gentlemen keep their own hours; so I continue to sew, while singing a little to myself.

> Rock of ages, cleft for me,
> Let me hide myself in thee;
> Let the water and the blood,
> From thy riven side which flowed,
> Be of sin the double cure,
> Cleanse me from its guilt and power.

I like this song, as it makes me think of rocks, and water, and the seashore, which are outside; and thinking of a thing is next best to being there.

I did not know you could sing so well, Grace, says Dr. Jordan, coming into the room. You have a beautiful voice. He has dark circles under his eyes, and looks as if he hasn't slept a wink.

Thank you, Sir, I say. I used to have more occasion for it than I do now.

He sits down, and takes out his notebook and pencil, and also a parsnip, which he places on the table. It is not one I would have selected, having an orange tint, which means they are old.

Oh, a parsnip, I say.

Does it bring anything to mind? he asks.

Well, there is Fine words butter no parsnips, I say. Also they are very hard to peel.

They are kept in cellars, I believe, he says.

Oh no, Sir, I reply. Outside, in a hole in the ground with straw, as they are much improved by being frozen.

He looks at me in a tired fashion, and I wonder what has been causing his loss of sleep. Perhaps it is some young lady which is on his mind, and not returning his affection; or else he has not been eating regular meals.

Shall we continue with your story where we left off? he says.

I've forgotten just where that was, I say. This is not quite true, but I wish to see if he has really been listening to me, or just pretending to.

With Mary's death, he says. Your poor friend Mary Whitney.

Ah yes, I say. With Mary.

Well, Sir, the way in which Mary died was hushed up as much as possible. That she had died of a fever may or may not have been believed, but nobody said no to it out loud. Nor did anyone deny that she'd left her things to me, in view of what she had written down; though there were some raised eyebrows at her writing it, as if she'd known ahead of time that she was going to die. But I said rich people made their wills beforehand, so why not Mary; and then they said no more. Nor was anything said about the writing paper, and how she had got hold of it.

I sold her box, which was good quality, and also her best dress, to Jeremiah the peddler, who came around again just after her death; and I also sold him the gold ring which she kept hidden under the floor. I told him it was to pay for a decent burial, and he gave me a fair price and more. He said he'd seen death in Mary's face, but then, hindsight is always accurate. He also said he was sorry for her death, and would say a prayer for her, although what sort of a prayer I could not imagine, as he was a heathenish sort of man, with all his tricks and fortune-telling. But surely the form of a prayer does not matter, and the only distinction God makes is between good will and ill; or so I have come to believe.

It was Agnes who helped me with the burial. We put flowers from Mrs. Alderman Parkinson's garden into the coffin, having asked permission; and it being June, there were long-stemmed roses and peonies; and we chose only the white ones. I scattered the petals of them over her as well, and I slipped in the needle-case I'd made for her, but out of sight, as it might look wrong otherwise, being red; and I cut a piece off the back of her hair to remember her by, and tied it together with a thread.

She was buried in her best nightdress, and she didn't look dead in the least, but only asleep and very pale; and laid out all in white like that, she was just like a bride.

The coffin was pine boards and very plain, as I wanted a stone grave marker too for the money; but I had only enough for her name. I would have liked a poem, such as *From Earth's dark shadows though you flee, When in Heaven, remember me*, but it was greatly beyond my means. She was put with the Methodists on Adelaide Street, off in a corner right next to the paupers, but still within the churchyard, so I felt I had done all for her that I could. Agnes and two of the other servants were the only ones present, as a suspicion must have gone around that Mary had died under a shadow; and when they shovelled the dirt in on top of the coffin and the young minister said Dust to dust, I cried as if my heart would break. I was thinking of my poor mother as well, who'd had no proper burial with dirt on top the way it should be, but was just tossed into the sea.

It was very hard for me to believe that Mary was truly dead. I kept expecting her to come into the room, and when I lay in bed at night I sometimes thought I could hear her breathing; or she would be laughing just outside the door. Every Sunday I would lay flowers on her grave, not from Mrs. Alderman Parkinson's garden, as that was just the one special occasion, but wildflowers that I would pick in waste lots or beside the lakeshore or wherever I could find them growing.

Soon after Mary's death I left Mrs. Alderman Parkinson's. I didn't like to stay, as ever since Mary had died, Mrs. Alderman Parkinson and Mrs. Honey were not friendly towards me. They must have thought I'd helped Mary in her relations with the gentleman, whose name they believed I knew; and although I had not, it is hard to put an end to suspicion once it has begun. When I said I wished to leave my situation, Mrs. Alderman Parkinson did not protest, but instead had me into the library and asked very earnestly once more if I knew the man; and when I said I did not, she asked me to swear on the Bible that even if I did, I would never divulge it, and she would write me a good reference. I did not like being mistrusted in this manner, but I did as required, and Mrs. Alderman Parkinson wrote the reference, and said kindly that she never had any fault to find with my work, and gave me a present of two dollars upon leaving, which was generous, and found me another situation, with Mr. Dixon, who was also an Alderman.

At Dixon's I was paid more, as I was now trained and with a reference. Dependable servants were scarce, as many had left for the States after the Rebellion, and although there were new immigrants arriving all the time, the deficiency was not yet made up, and help was much in demand; and because of this, I knew that I did not have to stay in any place if I did not like it.

I found I did not like it at Mr. Dixon's, as I felt they knew too much of the story, and treated me strangely; so after half a year I gave notice, and went to Mr. McManus's; but I was not well suited there, as I was only one of two servants, the other being a hired man who talked a great deal about the end of the world, and the tribulation and the gnashing of teeth, and was not much company at meals. I stayed only three months, and was hired away by Mr. Coates, and stayed until some months after my fifteenth birthday; but there was another servant who was jealous of me, as I was more careful in my work than she was; so when I heard of the opportunity I went to Mr. Haraghy, at the same wages as at Coates's.

That went on well enough for a time, but I began to be uneasy, as Mr. Haraghy attempted liberties in the back passage while I was carrying out the dishes from the dining room; and although I remembered Mary's advice about kicking between the legs, I thought it would not be right to kick my employer, and might also lead to dismissal without a reference. But then one night I heard him outside the door of my attic chamber; I recognized his wheezy cough. He was fumbling with the latch of the door. I always locked myself in at night, but I knew that lock or no lock, sooner or later he would find a way of getting in, with a ladder if nothing else, and I couldn't sleep easy for thinking of it; and I needed my sleep, as I was very tired from the day's work; and once you are found with a man in your room you are the guilty one, no matter how they get in. As Mary used to say, there are some of the masters who think you owe them service twenty-four hours a day, and should do the main work flat on your back.

I believe Mrs. Haraghy suspected something of the sort. She was from a good family fallen upon hard times, and she'd had to take pot luck in the way of a husband; and Mr. Haraghy had made his fortune in hog butchering. I doubt it was the first time Mr. Haraghy had behaved in this way, because when I gave notice, Mrs. Haraghy did not even ask me why, but sighed, and said I was a good girl, and wrote me a reference right away on her best writing paper.

I went to Mr. Watson's. I could have done better if I'd had the time to look about me, but I'd felt speed was necessary, as Mr. Haraghy had come wheezing and panting into the scullery while I was scouring the pots, with my hands all covered with grease and smuts, and had attempted to seize hold of me despite it, and that was the sign of a desperate man. Mr. Watson was a shoemaker and in great need of help, with a wife and three children and a fourth on the way, and he had only one servant who was not up to all the washing, although a good plain cook; and so he was willing to pay me two dollars and fifty cents a month and a pair of shoes into the bargain. I needed shoes, as the ones I had from Mary's things did not fit properly and my own were almost worn through, and new shoes were very expensive.

I was there only a short time before I made the acquaintance of Nancy Montgomery, who came to visit, having grown up in the country with Mrs. Watson's cook Sally. Nancy was in Toronto to make some purchases at a dry-goods auction down at Clarkson's stores; she showed us some very pretty crimson silk which she'd bought for a winter dress, and I wondered what a housekeeper would be wanting with a dress like that; and some fine gloves, and an Irish linen tablecloth on behalf of her employer. She said it was better to buy at auction than from a store, as the prices were cheaper, and her master liked to stretch a penny. She had not taken the coach into town, but had been driven in by her master, which she said was much more comfortable, as you did not have to be jostled by strangers.

Nancy Montgomery was very handsome, dark-haired, and of about twenty-four years of age; she had beautiful brown eyes, and she laughed and joked much as Mary Whitney had done, and seemed very good-natured. She sat in the kitchen and took a cup of tea, and she and Sally talked over old times. They'd gone to school together north of the city, it being the first school in the district and conducted by the local minister on Saturday mornings, when the children could be spared from their work. It was held in a log house, more like a stable, said Nancy; and they had to walk to it through the forest, and were always afraid of bears, which were more numerous then; and one day they did see a bear, and Nancy ran away screaming, and climbed a tree. Sally said the bear was more frightened than Nancy was, and Nancy said it was probably a gentleman bear and it was running away from something dangerous that it had never seen before, but might have caught a glimpse of as she climbed the tree; and they laughed very much. They told about how the boys pushed over the privy at the back of the school while one of the girls was in it, and they hadn't warned the girl, but watched along with all of the others, and then they felt wrong about it afterwards. Sally said it was always the shy ones like that who got picked on, and Nancy said yes but you had to learn to stand up for yourself in this life; and I thought that was true.

While gathering her shawl and things together – she had a lovely parasol, pink in colour, although in need of cleaning – Nancy told me she was housekeeper to Mr. Thomas Kinnear, Esq., who lived in Richmond Hill, up Yonge Street past Gallow's Hill and Hogg's Hollow. She said she was in want of another servant to help her with the work, the house being large and the girl who was there before having left to get married. Mr. Kinnear was a gentleman of a fine Scottish family, and easygoing in his habits, and was not married; so there was less work, and no mistress of the household to carp and criticize, and would I be interested in the position?

She claimed to be lonely for some female company, as Mr. Kinnear's farm was a distance from the town; also she didn't like being there all by herself, a single woman alone with a gentlemen, as people would talk; and I thought this showed a right feeling. She said that Mr. Kinnear was a liberal master, and showed it when he was pleased; and that if I accepted, I'd be making a good bargain and taking a step up in the world. Then she asked what my wages were at present, and said she would pay three dollars a month; and I found this more than fair.

Nancy said she had business in the city in a week's time, and could wait until then to hear my decision; and I spent the week turning the matter over in my mind. I did worry about being out in the country, rather than in town, as I was now used to Toronto life – there was so much to see while walking out on errands, and sometimes there were shows and fairs, although you had to watch for thieves there; and outdoor preachers, and always a boy or a woman singing on the street for pennies. I'd seen a man eat fire, and another that could throw his voice, and a pig that could count, and a dancing bear with a muzzle on, only it was more like lurching, and the ragamuffins poked it with sticks. Also it would be muddier in the country, without the fine raised sidewalks; and no gas lighting at night, nor grand shops, and so many church spires, and smart carriages, and new brick banks, with pillars. But I reflected that if I did not like it in the country I could always come back.

When I asked Sally's opinion, she said she didn't know if it was a suitable position for a young girl like me; and when I asked her why not, she said Nancy had always been kind to her, and she didn't like to talk, and a person had to take her own chances, and least said soonest mended, and as she did not know anything for certain it would not be right for her to say any more; but she felt she'd done her duty by me in saying as much as she had, because I had no mother to advise me. And I didn't have the least idea of what she was talking about.

I asked her if she'd heard any harm spoken of Mr. Kinnear, and she said, Nothing that the world at large would call harm.

It was like a puzzle I could not guess; and it would have been better for all if she had spoken out more plainly. But the pay was higher than what I ever had before, which weighed heavily with me; and what weighed even more heavily was Nancy Montgomery herself. She resembled Mary Whitney, or so I then thought; and I'd been depressed in spirits ever since Mary's death. And so I decided to go.

23.

Nancy had given me the fare, and so on the day agreed I took the early coach. It was a long journey, as Richmond Hill was sixteen miles up Yonge Street. Directly north of the city the road was not too bad, although there was more than one steep hill where we had to get out and walk, otherwise the horses could not pull us up. Beside the ditches there were many flowers growing, daisies and such, with butterflies flying about, and these parts of the road were very pretty. I thought of picking a bouquet, but then, it would be sure to wilt along the way.

After a time the road was worse, with deep ruts and stones, and jolting and bumping enough to unhinge your bones, and dust fit to choke you on the tops of the hills, and mud in the low places, and logs laid crossways over the bogs. They said that when it rained the road was no better than a swamp, and in March, during the spring runoff, you could barely travel at all. The best time was the winter, when all was frozen hard and a sleigh could make good headway; but then there was the risk of blizzards, and of freezing to death if the sleigh overturned, and sometimes there were snowdrifts as high as a house, and your only chance was a little prayer and a great deal of whisky. All of this and more was told me by the man who sat squeezed beside me, who said he was a dealer in farm implements and seed grains, and claimed to know the road well.

Some of the houses we passed along the way were large and fine, but others were just log houses, low and poor-looking. The fences around the fields were of different kinds, snake fences of split rails, and others made of the tree roots pulled out of the ground, which looked like giant hanks of wooden hair. Every now and then there was a crossroads with a few houses close together and an inn, where the horses could be rested or changed and a glass of whisky taken. Some of the men hanging about had taken a good many more than one glass, and were shabbily dressed and impertinent, and came up to the coach where I sat, and tried to look under the rim of my bonnet. When we stopped at midday, the dealer in farm implements said would I care to go inside and take a glass with him and some refreshments, but I said no, as a respectable woman should not go into such places with a stranger. I had bread and cheese with me and could get a drink of water from the well in the courtyard, and that was enough for me.

For the journey I had put on my good summer things. I had a straw bonnet, trimmed with a blue ribbon bow from Mary's box, and my cap under it; and a cotton print dress with the drop-shouldered sleeves which were going out of style then, but I'd had no time to make it over; it was once red dots, but had washed to pink, and I had it as part wages from Coates's. Two petticoats, one torn but neatly mended, the other now too short, but who was there to see it? A cotton chemise and a pair of stays, used, from Jeremiah the peddler, and white cotton stockings, mended but still with good wear in them. The pair of shoes from Mr. Watson the shoemaker, which were not the best quality and did not fit, as the best shoes came from England. A summer shawl of green muslin, and a kerchief left to me by Mary, which had been her mother's – a white ground printed with small blue flowers, love-in-a-mist, folded into a triangle and worn around the neck to keep the sun off and prevent freckles. It was comforting to have such a remembrance of her. But I had no gloves. No one had ever given me any, and they were too dear for me to buy.

My winter things, my red flannel petticoat and my heavy dress, my wool stockings and my flannel nightdress, as well as two cotton for summer, and my summer working dress and clogs and two caps and an apron, and my other shift, were tied in a bundle with my mother's shawl and carried on top of the coach. It was well strapped down but I was anxious about it the entire journey, as I was worried that it would fall off and be lost in the road, and I kept looking behind.

Never look behind you, said the dealer in farm implements. Why not, said I. I knew you were not supposed to talk with strange men, but it was hard to avoid as we were crammed in so close together. Because the past is the past, he said, and regret is vain, let bygones be bygones. You know what became of Lot's wife, he went on. Turned to a pillar of salt she was, a waste of a good woman, not that they aren't all the better for a touch of salt, and he laughed. I was not sure what he meant but suspected it was nothing good, and thought I would not talk with him any further.

The mosquitoes were very bad, especially in the marshy places and at the edges of the forests, because although some of the land next the road had been cleared, there were still big stands of trees, and very tall and dark. The air in the forest had a different smell to it; it was cool and damp, and smelled of moss and of earth and old leaves. I did not trust the forest, as it was full of wild animals such as bears and wolves; and I remembered Nancy's story about the bear.

The dealer in farm implements said, Would you be afraid to go into the forest, Miss, and I said No I would not be afraid, but I would not go in there unless I had to. And he said Just as well, young women should not go into the forest by themselves, you never know what may happen to them; there was one found recently with her clothes torn off and her head at some distance from her body, and I said, Oh, was it the bears, and he said, The bears or the Red Indians, you know these woods are full of them, they could swoop out at any minute and have your bonnet off you in a trice and then your scalp, you know they like to cut off ladies' hair, they can sell it for a good price in the States. And then he said, I expect you have a good head of hair on you, underneath your cap; and all this time he was pressing up against me in a way I was finding offensive.

I knew he was lying, if not about the bears, then surely about the Indians, and he was only trying to horrify me. So I said, quite pert, I'd trust my head to the Red Indians sooner than I'd trust it to you, and he laughed; but I was in earnest. I'd seen Red Indians in Toronto, as they would sometimes go there to collect their treaty money; and others would come to the back door at Mrs. Alderman Parkinson's with baskets to sell, and fish. They kept their faces still and you could not tell what they were thinking, but they went away when told to. Still I was glad when we would come out of the forest again, and see the fences and houses and the washing hanging out, and smell the smoke from the cooking fires, and the trees being burnt for their ashes.

After a time we passed the remains of a building, just the foundations all blackened, and the dealer pointed it out, and told me it was the celebrated Montgomery's Tavern, which was where Mackenzie and his band of ragtags held their seditious meetings, and set out to march down Yonge Street, during the Rebellion. A man was shot in front of it, going to warn the Government troops, and it was burnt down afterwards. They hanged some of those traitors but not enough, said the dealer, and that cowardly rascal Mackenzie should be dragged back from the States, which was where he ran off to, leaving his friends to swing at the rope's end for him. The dealer had a flask in his pocket and by this time a strong dose of bottle courage, as I could tell by the smell of his breath, and when they are in that state it is just as well not to provoke them; and so I said nothing.

We reached Richmond Hill in the late afternoon. It did not look like much of a town; it was more like a village, with the houses strung out in a line along Yonge Street. I descended at the coaching inn there, which was the place agreed on with Nancy, and the coachman lifted my bundle down for me. The dealer in farm implements got down too, and asked where I was staying, and I said what he didn't know wouldn't hurt him. At that he took hold of my arm, and said I must come into the inn with him, and have a drink or two of whisky for old times' sake, as we had become so well acquainted in the coach; and I tried to pull my arm away, but he would not let go, and was becoming familiar, and was trying to encircle my waist; and several idle men were cheering him on. I looked around for Nancy, but she was nowhere to be seen. What a bad impression it would make, I thought, to be found struggling with a drunken man at an inn.

The door to the inn was standing open, and out of it at that moment came Jeremiah the peddler, with his pack on his back and his long walking-stick in his hand. I was very glad to see him, and called out his name; and he looked over in a puzzled way, and then hurried over.

Why, it is Grace Marks, he said. I did not expect to see you here.

Nor I you, I said, and I smiled; but was somewhat flustered because of the dealer in farm implements, who was still hanging on to my arm.

Is this man a friend of yours? said Jeremiah.

No he is not, I said.

The lady does not desire your company, said Jeremiah, in his pretend voice of an elegant gentleman; and the dealer in farm implements said I was no lady, and added some things which were not compliments, and also some hard words about Jeremiah's mother.

Jeremiah took his stick, and brought it down on the man's arm, and he let go of me; and then Jeremiah pushed him, and he staggered backwards against the wall of the inn, and sat down in a pat of horse dung; at which the others now jeered at him, as that sort will always jeer at those who are getting the worst of it.

Do you have a situation in the neighbourhood? asked Jeremiah, when I'd thanked him. I said I did, and he said he would come round and see what he could sell me; and just then a third man came up. Would your name be Grace Marks? he said, or something of the sort; I cannot remember his exact words. I said it was, and he said he was Mr. Thomas Kinnear, my new employer, and he'd come to fetch me. He had a light wagon with one horse – I found out later that his name was Charley, for Charley Horse; he was a bay gelding and very handsome, with such a beautiful mane and tail and large brown eyes, and I loved him dearly at first sight.

Mr. Kinnear had the ostler put my bundle in the back of the wagon – there were some packages in it already – and he said, Well you have not been in town five minutes and you have managed to attract two gentleman admirers; and I said they were not, and he said, Not gentlemen, or not admirers? And I was confused, and did not know what he wanted me to say.

Then he said, Up you go, Grace, and I said, Oh do you mean me to sit at the front, and he said, Well we can hardly have you in the back like a piece of luggage, and he handed me up to sit beside him. I was quite embarrassed, as I was not used to sitting beside a gentleman like him, and especially one who was my employer, but he didn't seem to give it a second thought, and got up on the other side and clicked to the horse, and there we were, driving up Yonge Street just as if I was a fine lady, and I thought that any of those looking out of their windows at us would have had something to gossip about. But as I later found, Mr. Kinnear was never a man to pay any attention to gossip, as he didn't care a pin what other people said about him. He had his own money and was not running for political office, and could afford to ignore such things.

What did Mr. Kinnear look like? asks Dr. Jordan.

He had a gentlemanly bearing, Sir, I say, and a moustache.

Is that all? says Dr. Jordan. You did not observe him very particularly!

I did not wish to gape at him, I say, and once in the wagon of course I did not look at him. I would have needed to turn my whole head, because of my bonnet. I suppose you have never worn a bonnet, have you Sir?

No I have not, says Dr. Jordan. He is smiling with his lopsided smile. I expect it is confining, he says.

It is that, Sir, I say. I did see his gloves though, on his hands holding the reins, pale-yellow gloves they were, soft leather and so well made they fit with scarcely a wrinkle, you'd think they were his own skin. I was all the more sorry that I did not have any gloves myself, and kept my hands tucked well in under the folds of my shawl.

I suppose you are very tired, Grace, he said, and I said Yes Sir, and he said, The weather is very warm, and I said Yes Sir, and so we went along, and to tell you the truth it was harder than riding in the bumping coach beside the farm implements dealer; I can't say why, as Mr. Kinnear was much more kind. But Richmond Hill was not a very big place and we were soon through it. He lived past the edge of the village, more than a mile to the north of it.

At last we were going past his orchard and up his driveway, which was curved and about a hundred yards long, and ran between two lines of maple trees of medium size. There was the house at the end of the drive, with a verandah along the front of it and white pillars, a big house but not as big as Mrs. Alderman Parkinson's.

From the back of the house came the sound of chopping. There was a boy sitting on the fence – he was perhaps fourteen years old –

and when we drove up he jumped down and came to hold the horse; he had red hair, raggedly cut, and the freckles to go with it. Mr. Kinnear said to him, Hello Jamie here is Grace Marks come all the way from Toronto, I found her at the inn, and the boy looked up at me and grinned, as if he thought there was something funny about me; but he was only shy and awkward.

There were flowers planted in front of the verandah, white peonies and pink roses, and a gracefully dressed lady with a triple flounce was cutting them; she had a flat basket over her arm to put them in. When she heard our wheels and the horse's hooves on the gravel, she straightened up and shaded her eyes with her hand, and I saw she was wearing gloves; and then I recognized that this woman was Nancy Montgomery. She was wearing a bonnet the same pale colour as her dress, it was as if she'd put on her best clothes to go out front and cut the flowers. She waved a hand daintily in my direction, but she made no move to come over to me; and something squeezed tight about my heart.

Getting up into the wagon was one thing but getting down was another, because Mr. Kinnear did not help me down, he swung out by himself and hurried up the walk towards the front of the house and bent his head down towards Nancy's bonnet, leaving me to sit in the wagon like a sack of potatoes, or else scramble down unaided, which is what I did. A man had come out from the back; he was holding an axe, so it must have been him doing the chopping. He had a thick-woven jacket over one shoulder and his shirt had the sleeves rolled up and was open at the neck with a red bandanna tied around, and he had loose trousers tucked into his boot-tops. He was dark-haired and slender and not very tall, and did not appear to be more than one-and-twenty. He said nothing, but stared at me, suspicious and frowning a little, almost as if I was an enemy of his; yet he did not seem to be looking at me at all, but at someone else right behind me.

The boy Jamie said to him, This is Grace Marks, but he still didn't say anything; and then Nancy called, McDermott, take the horse in, won't you, and Grace's things, take them to her room and you can show her where it is. At that he flushed up as if in anger, and jerked his head curtly for me to come with him.

I stood there for an instant with the late sunlight in my eyes, looking at Nancy and Mr. Kinnear beside the peonies; they were surrounded by a golden haze, as if gold dust had fallen down out of the sky all over them, and I heard her laughing. I was hot and tired and hungry, and covered with dust from the road, and she had not given me one word of greeting.

Then I followed the horse and wagon towards the back of the house. The boy Jamie walked along beside me, and he said shyly, Is it big, Toronto, is it very grand, I have never been there, but I only said Grand enough. I could not find it in me to answer him about Toronto, because right then I was bitterly sorry I had ever left it.

When I close my eyes I can remember every detail of that house as clear as a picture – the verandah with the flowers, the windows and the white pillars, in the bright sunlight – and I could walk every room of it blindfolded, though at that moment I had no particular feeling about it and only wanted a drink of water. It is strange to reflect that of all the people in that house, I was the only one of them left alive in six months' time.

Except for Jamie Walsh, of course; but he was not living there.

24.

McDermott showed me to the room that was to be mine, which was off the winter kitchen. He was not very civil about it, all he said was You're to sleep in here. While I was untying my bundle Nancy came in, and now she was all smiles. She said I am very glad to see you Grace, I am glad you have come. She sat me down at the table in the winter kitchen, which was cooler than the summer kitchen as the stove was not lit, and she showed me where I could wash my face and hands at the sink, and then she gave me a glass of small beer and some cold beef from the larder, and said You must be tired after your journey, it is very fatiguing, and sat with me while I ate, as gracious as could be.

She had on a very handsome pair of earrings, which I could tell were real gold, and I wondered how she could afford them, on the salary of a housekeeper.

After I'd finished refreshing myself she showed me over the house and outbuildings. The summer kitchen was entirely separate from the main house, so as not to heat it up, a sensible arrangement which ought to be adopted by all. Each of the kitchens had a flagged floor and a good-sized iron stove with a flat apron in the front for keeping things warm, which was the latest model then; and each kitchen had its own sink with a pipe running out to the cesspool, and its own scullery and larder. The pump for the water was in the courtyard between the two kitchens; I was pleased it was not an open well, as such wells are more dangerous, things can fall down into them and they often harbour rats.

Behind the summer kitchen was the stable, adjoining the carriage house, where the wagon was kept. There was enough room in the carriage house for two carriages but Mr. Kinnear had only the one light wagon, I suppose a real carriage would have been useless on those roads. In the stable there were four stalls, but Mr. Kinnear kept only one cow and two horses, Charley Horse and a colt who was to be a riding horse when grown. The harness room was off the winter kitchen, which was unusual, and also inconvenient.

There was a loft room over the stable, and that was where McDermott slept. Nancy told me he'd been there only a week or so, and although he was prompt enough when Mr. Kinnear was giving the orders he appeared to have a grudge against her, and was impertinent; and I said that possibly his grudge was against the world, because he had been short with me as well. Nancy said as far as she was concerned he could mend his ways or be off out of it, because there was lots more where he came from, as out-of-work soldiers were to be had for the asking.

I have always liked the smell of a stable. I patted the colt's nose and said Good day to Charley, and I greeted the cow as well because it would be my job to milk her and I hoped we would start off on good terms. McDermott was setting out straw for the animals; he did not speak to us much more than a grunt, and he gave Nancy a scowling look and I could see there was no love lost, and when we were going out of the stable Nancy said, He is more surly than ever, well he can suit himself and welcome, it's a smile or the open road for him, or more likely the bottom of a ditch, and then she laughed; and I hoped he had not overheard it.

After that we saw the henhouse and the henyard, which had a woven willow fence around it to keep the chickens in, although it was not much good at keeping the foxes and the weasels out, and the raccoons too, which were known to be great stealers of eggs; and the kitchen garden, which was well planted but needed hoeing; and quite far back along a path was the privy.

Mr. Kinnear had a good deal of land, a pasture field which was kept for the cow and horses, and a little orchard down by Yonge Street, and several other fields which were worked or in the midst of being cleared of trees. It was Jamie Walsh's father who looked after that, said Nancy; they had a cottage on the grounds about a quarter of a mile away. From where we were standing we could just see the rooftop and chimney sticking up above the trees. Jamie himself was a bright and promising boy, who ran errands for Mr. Kinnear; and he could play the flute; or he called it a flute, but it was more like a fife. Nancy said he would come over some evening and play for us, as he liked to do it, and she did enjoy a little music herself, and was learning to play the piano. That surprised me, as it was not the usual thing for a housekeeper. But I said nothing.

In the courtyard between the two kitchens there were three lines strung up for the washing. There was no separate laundry room, but the things for the washing, the coppers and the washtub and scrubbing board, were at present in the summer kitchen beside the stove, all good quality; and I was pleased to see they did not make their own soap but used bought soap, which is far easier on the hands.

They did not keep a pig and I was just as glad, for pigs are too clever for their own good, and fond of escaping from their pens, as well as having a smell that is not at all agreeable. There were two cats which lived in the stable, to keep down the mice and rats, but no dog, Mr. Kinnear's old dog Fancy having died. Nancy said she would feel easier with a dog about the place to bark at strangers, and Mr. Kinnear was looking for a good dog to go hunting with him; he was not a great sportsman in that way but liked to shoot a duck or two in the autumn, or else a wild goose, which were very numerous although too stringy for her taste.

We went back into the winter kitchen, and along the passageway that led from it to the entrance hall, which was large, with a fireplace and stag's horns over it, and a good green wallpaper, and a fine Turkey carpet. The trapdoor to the cellar was in this hall, and you had to lift up a corner of the carpet to get to it, which I thought was an odd place as the kitchen would have been more convenient; but the kitchen did not have a cellar under it. The cellar stairs were too steep for comfort, and the cellar below was divided into two parts by a half-wall, the dairy on one side, which was where they kept the butter and the cheeses, and on the other side the place where they stored the wine and beer in barrels, and the apples, and the carrots and cabbages and beets and potatoes in boxes of sand in the winter, and the empty wine barrels as well. There was a window, but Nancy said I should always take a candle or a lantern as it was quite dark below and you could trip and fall down the stairs and break your neck.

We did not go down into the cellar at that time.

Off the hall was the front parlour, with its own stove and two pictures, one a family group, I suppose they were ancestors as their faces were stiff and their dress was old-fashioned, the other a large fat bull with short legs; also the piano, which was not a pianoforte but only a straight-backed parlour piano, and the globe lamp which took the best whale oil, brought up from the States; they did not have kerosene for lamps then. Behind that was the dining room, also with a fireplace, with silver candlesticks and the good china and plate in a locked cabinet, and a picture of dead pheasants over the mantelpiece, which I did not think would be agreeable while eating. This room connected with the parlour through a set of double doors and was also reached by a single door from the passageway, for carrying in the food from the kitchen. On the other side of the passageway was Mr. Kinnear's library, but we did not go into it at that time as he was reading in it, and behind that was a small study or office with a desk, which was where he wrote his letters and transacted any business he might have.

There was a fine staircase from the front hall, with a polished bannister; we went up it, and on the second floor there was Mr. Kinnear's bedchamber with a large bedstead, and his dressing room adjoining, and dressing table with an oval mirror, and a carved wardrobe, and in the bedchamber, a picture of a woman without any clothes on, on a sofa, seen from the back and looking over her shoulder, with a sort of turban on her head and holding a peacock-feather fan. Peacock feathers inside the house are bad luck, as everyone knows. These were only in a picture, but I would never have allowed them in any house of mine. There was another picture, also of a naked woman taking a bath, but I did not have the chance to examine it. I was a little taken aback at Mr. Kinnear having two naked women in his bedchamber, as at Mrs. Alderman Parkinson's it was mostly landscapes or flowers.

Down the hall towards the back there was Nancy's own bedchamber, which was not as large; and each room had a carpet. By rights these carpets should have been beaten and cleaned and stored for the summer, but Nancy had not got around to it, being short of help. I did wonder at her chamber being on the same floor as Mr. Kinnear's, but there was no third floor to the house, nor attic, not like Mrs. Alderman Parkinson's house, which was much grander. There was also a chamber for guests if any. At the end of the passageway was a closet, for such things as winter clothing, and a well-stocked linen cupboard with a good many shelves; and beside

Nancy's bedchamber was a tiny room which she called her sewing room, and it had in it a table and a chair.

After we had seen the upstairs of the house, we went back downstairs and discussed my duties; and I thought to myself it was a mercy it was the summer, as otherwise I would have all those fires to lay and light, as well as the grates and stoves to clean and polish; and Nancy said of course I would not begin that very day, but the next one, and I would no doubt wish to retire early, as I must be wearied out. As this was indeed the case, and as the sun was setting, I did so.

And then everything went on very quietly for a fortnight, says Dr. Jordan. He is reading aloud from my Confession.

Yes Sir, it did, I say. More or less quietly.

What is *everything*? How did it go on?

I beg your pardon, Sir?

What did you do every day?

Oh, the usual, Sir, I say. I performed my duties.

You will forgive me, says Dr. Jordan. Of what did those duties consist?

I look at him. He is wearing a yellow cravat with small white squares. He is not making a joke. He really does not know. Men such as him do not have to clean up the messes they make, but we have to clean up our own messes, and theirs into the bargain. In that way they are like children, they do not have to think ahead, or worry about the consequences of what they do. But it is not their fault, it is only how they are brought up.

25.

The next morning I woke at dawn. My little bedchamber was close and hot, as the summer weather had begun; and it was dim also, as the shutters were kept closed at night in case of intruders. The windows were closed too, because of the mosquitoes and flies; and I thought that I must get a piece of muslin to put over the window, or else over my bed, and would speak to Nancy about it. I slept only in my shift, because of the heat.

I got out of bed and opened the window and the shutters to get some light, and turned back the bedclothes to air them, and then I put on my work dress and apron, and pinned up my hair, and set my cap in place. I intended to do a better job with my hair later, when I could use the mirror over the kitchen sink, there being no mirror in my room. I turned up my sleeves, slipped on my clogs, and unlatched the bedroom door. I always kept it locked, for if anyone was to break into the house, my bedchamber would be the first they would arrive at.

I liked being early to rise; that way I could pretend for a little while that the house was my own. The first thing I did was, I emptied my chamber pot into the slop pail; and then with the pail I went out by the door of the winter kitchen, noting in my mind that the floor was in need of a good scrubbing, as Nancy had let things get behind and there was considerable mud that had been tracked in and not dealt with. The air outside in the courtyard was fresh; there was a pink glow in the east, and a pearly grey mist rising from the fields. Somewhere nearby a bird was singing – I thought it was a wren – and farther off there were crows calling. In the early dawn, it is as if everything is beginning anew.

The horses must have heard the kitchen door open, because they whinnied; but it was not my duty to feed them or let them out to pasture, although I would have been glad to do it. The cow mooed as well, as her udder was no doubt full, but she would have to wait because I could not do everything at once.

I went along the path, past the henyard and the kitchen garden and back through the dew-sprinkled weeds, pushing aside the gauzy spiderwebs that were woven in the night. I would never kill a spider. Mary Whitney said it would bring bad luck, and she was not the only one to say so. When I found one inside the house I would pick it up on the end of the broom and shake it off outside, but I must have killed some of them by accident, because I got the bad luck anyway.

I reached the privy and emptied the slop pail, and so forth.

And so forth, Grace? asks Dr. Jordan.

I look at him. Really if he does not know what you do in a privy there is no hope for him.

What I did was, I hoisted my skirts and sat down above the buzzing flies, on the same seat everyone in the house sat on, lady or lady's maid, they both piss and it smells the same, and not like lilacs neither, as Mary Whitney used to say. What was in there for wiping was an old copy of the Godey's Ladies' Book; I always looked at the pictures before using them. Most were of the latest fashions, but some were of duchesses from England and high-society ladies in New York and the like. You should never let your picture be in a magazine or newspaper if you can help it, as you never know what ends your face may be made to serve, by others, once it has got out of your control.

But I do not say any of this to Dr. Jordan. And so forth, I say firmly, because And so forth is all he is entitled to. Just because he pesters me to know everything is no reason for me to tell him.

Then I carried the slop bucket to the pump in the courtyard, I say, and I primed the pump with water from the bucket that was kept there for the purpose, as with a pump you have to pour some in before you can get any out, and Mary Whitney used to say that was exactly how men viewed the flattering of a woman, when they had low ends in view. Once I had the pump going I rinsed out the slop pail, and washed my face, then cupped my hands to drink. The water from Mr. Kinnear's well was good, with no taste of iron or sulphur. By this time the sun was coming up, and burning off the mist, and I could tell it was going to be a fair morning.

Next I went into the summer kitchen and started the fire in the stove. I cleaned out the ashes from the day before and saved them for sprinkling into the privy, or else for the kitchen garden, where they help to keep off the snails and slugs. The stove was a new one but it had its own opinions, and when first lit, it threw black smoke out at me like a witch on fire. I had to coax it, I fed it bits of old newspapers – Mr. Kinnear liked his papers, and took several – and also slivers of kindling; and it coughed, and I blew in through the grate, and finally the fire caught and began blazing away. The firewood was split in pieces too big for the stove and I had to cram them in with the poker. I would have to speak to Nancy about it later, and she would speak to McDermott, who was the one responsible.

Then I went out into the yard and pumped a bucketful of water and lugged it back to the kitchen and filled the kettle from it with the dipper, and set it on the stove to boil.

Then I got two carrots from the bin in the harness room off the winter kitchen, old carrots they were, and put them in my pocket and headed out to the barn with the milking pail. The carrots were for the horses, and I gave them furtively; they were only horse carrots but I hadn't asked permission about them. I kept an ear out for sounds of McDermott stirring his bones up above in the loft, but there wasn't a rustle out of him, he was dead to the world or acting it.

Then I milked the cow. She was a good cow, and took to me right away. There are some cows very bad-tempered that will hook you with a horn or give you a good kick, but this was not one of them, and once I had my forehead into her flank she settled right down to the business. The barn cats came mewing around for milk, and I gave them some. Then I said goodbye to the horses, and Charley put his head down towards my apron pocket. He knew where the carrots were kept, all right.

On the way out I heard a strange noise coming from up above. It was as if someone was hammering furiously with two hammers, or beating on a wooden drum. At first I could not make it out at all; but as I listened, I realized it must be McDermott, step-dancing on the bare boards of the loft. He sounded skilful enough; but why was he dancing all by himself up there, and so early in the morning? Perhaps it was from sheer joy, and the overflow of animal spirits; but somehow I did not think so.

I carried the milk back to the summer kitchen and took off some fresh milk for the tea; then I covered the milk pail with a cloth because of the flies, and let it stand so the cream would rise. I wished to make butter from it later in the day if there were no thunderstorms about, as butter will not come when there's thunder. Then I took a moment to tidy my own room.

It was not much of a room to speak of, not papered and no pictures in it nor even any curtains. I gave it a quick sweep with the broom, and rinsed out the chamber pot and slid it under the bed. There were rolls of slut's wool under there, enough for a whole sheep, and you could see it hadn't been swept out for a long time. I shook up the mattress and straightened the sheets and plumped the pillow, and pulled the quilt up over. It was an old threadbare quilt, though a fine one when first made, a Wild Goose Chase it was; and I thought of the quilts I would make for myself, after I'd saved up enough wages and was married, and with a house of my own.

It gave me satisfaction to have a tidied room. When I came into it later, at the end of the day, it would be neat and trim, just as if a servant had made it up for me.

Then I took the egg basket and half a pail of water and went out to the henhouse. James McDermott was in the yard, sousing his dark head under the pump, but he must have heard me behind him; and as his face came up out of the water, for a moment he had a lost look to him, wild and frantic, like a half-drowned child, and I wondered who he thought was in pursuit of him. But then he saw who it was, and gave a jaunty wave, which was at least a friendly sign and the first one he'd given me. I had both hands full, so merely nodded.

I poured out the water for the hens, into their trough, and let them out of the henhouse, and while they were drinking and fighting over who was to go first, I went in and gathered their eggs – big eggs they were, it being the time of year for it. Then I scattered grain for them and the kitchen waste from the day before. I was not that fond of hens, as I have always preferred an animal with fur to a gaggle of frowsy, cackling birds scratching in the dirt; but if you want their eggs you have to put up with their unruly ways.

The rooster hacked at my ankles with his spurs, to chase me away from his wives, but I gave him a kick and almost lost the clog off my foot while doing it. One rooster a flock keeps the hens happy, they say, but one was too many as far as I was concerned. Mind your manners or I'll wring your neck, I told him; although in fact I could never bear to do anything of the sort.

By this time McDermott was watching over the fence, with a big grin on his face. He was better looking when smiling, I had to give him that, although he was so dark and had a rogue's twist to the mouth. But perhaps, Sir, I am imagining that in view of what came later.

Would that be me you're addressing? said McDermott. No it would not, I said with a cool manner as I walked by him. I thought I could tell what he had in mind, and it was not original. I did not want any of that kind of trouble, and to keep a cordial distance would be best.

The kettle was boiling at last. I set the porridge pot on the stove, with the porridge in it that was already soaking; then I made the tea and left it to steep while I went out into the yard and pumped another pail of water and carried it back in, and lifted the big copper pot onto the back of the stove and filled it up, as I needed a good supply of it heated, for the dirty dishes and such.

At this time Nancy came in, wearing a cotton gingham dress and an apron, not a fancy dress as she'd worn the afternoon before. She said Good morning and I gave it in return. Is the tea made, she said, and I said it was. Oh I feel I am scarcely alive in the morning until I've had my cup of tea, she said, and so I poured it out for her.

Mr. Kinnear will take his tea upstairs, she said, but I already knew this as she'd laid out the tea tray the night before with a small teapot and the cup and saucer; not the silver tray with the family crest, but one of painted wood. And, she added, he will want a second cup when he comes down, before his breakfast, as that is his custom.

I put on the fresh milk in a little jug, and the sugar, and picked up the tray. I will take it up, said Nancy. I was surprised, and said that at Mrs. Alderman Parkinson's, the housekeeper would never have thought of carrying a tea tray up the stairs, as it was beneath her position and a job for the maids. Nancy stared at me for a moment and was not pleased; but then she said that of course she only took the tray up when short of help and there was no one else to do it, and she'd got into the habit of it lately. So I proceeded.

The door to Mr. Kinnear's bedchamber was at the top of the stairs. There was nowhere near it where I could set down the tray, so I balanced it with one arm while knocking. Your tea, Sir, I said. There was a mumbling from inside and I went in. It was dark in the room, so I set the tray down on the round low table beside the bed and went over to the window and opened the curtains just a little. Those curtains were dark-brown brocade with a satiny feel to them and a fringe, and they were soft to the touch; but in my opinion it is better to have a white curtain, a cotton or a muslin, in summer, as white does not absorb the heat and bring it into the house as much, and also looks a good deal cooler.

I could not see Mr. Kinnear, as he was in the darkest corner of the room with his face in shadow. His bed did not have a patchwork quilt but a dark bedspread that matched the curtains; it was thrown back, and he had only the sheet over him. His voice came to me as you might say from underneath it. Thank you, Grace, he said. He was always one to say please and thank you. I must say he knew how to speak.

You're welcome, Sir, I said, and he was indeed welcome from my heart. I never begrudged doing things for him, and even though he paid me for doing them, it was as if I did them freely. There's beautiful eggs this morning, Sir, I said. Would you want one of them for your breakfast?

Yes, he says, in a hesitating way. Thank you, Grace. I'm sure it will do me good.

I did not like the way he said this, as he was talking as if he was ill. But Nancy hadn't mentioned anything about it.

When I went back downstairs I said to Nancy, Mr. Kinnear wants an egg for his breakfast. And she said, I will take one also. He will have his fried, with bacon, but I cannot eat a fried egg, mine should be boiled. We will have breakfast together, in the dining room, as he requires me to keep him company, he does not like to eat alone.

I found this a little curious, although not unheard of. Then I said, Is Mr. Kinnear ill at all?

Nancy laughed a little, and said, Sometimes he fancies he is. But it's all just in his head. He wants to be fussed over.

I wonder why he never married, I said, a fine man like him. I was getting out the frying pan, for the eggs, and it was just an idle question, I did not mean anything by it; but she replied in an angry tone, or it sounded angry to me. Some gentlemen do not have an inclination for the married state, she said. They are very pleased with themselves the way they are, and think they can get along well enough without it.

I suppose they can at that, I said.

Certainly they can, if rich enough, she said. If they want a thing, all they have to do is pay for it. It's all one to them.

Now here is the first falling-out that I had with Nancy. It was when I was doing up Mr. Kinnear's room, on the first day, and I had my bed apron on, to keep the dirt and smuts from the stove away from the white sheets. Nancy was hovering about, and telling me where the things were to be put, and how to tuck in the corners of the sheets, and how to air out Mr. Kinnear's nightshirt, and how his brushes and dressing things were to be laid out on the dressing table, and how often the silver backs of them should be polished, and which of the shelves he liked to have his folded shirts and his linens put on, ready for wearing; and she was acting as if I had never done any of these things before.

And I reflected then, as I have done since, that it is harder to work for a woman who has once been a servant herself, than one who has not; because those who have been servants will have their own ways of doing things, and they will also know the shortcuts, such as the dropping of a few dead flies down behind the bedstead, or the sweeping of a little sand or dust under the carpet, which would never be noticed unless those places were closely inspected; and they will have sharper eyes, and will be more likely to find you out in such matters. Not that I was such a slattern as a rule, but we all have days when we are in a hurry.

And when I would say about a thing, that this was not the way it was done at Mrs. Alderman Parkinson's, Nancy replied sharply that she did not care, as I was not at Mrs. Alderman Parkinson's now. She didn't like to be reminded that I'd once worked in such a grand house, and mixed with better than her. But I have thought since that the reason for all her fussing was that she did not wish to leave me by myself in Mr. Kinnear's room alone, in case he should come into it.

To take her mind off her fidgeting, I asked her about the picture on the wall; not the one with the peacock-feather fan, but the other one, of a young lady taking a bath, in a garden, which was an odd place for it, with her hair tied up, and a maid holding a large towel ready for her, and several old men with beards peering at her from behind the bushes. I could tell by the clothing that it was in ancient times. Nancy said it was an engraving, and that the colouring was done by hand, and it was a copy of a famous painting about Susannah and the Elders, which was a Bible subject. And she was very proud of knowing so much.

But I was annoyed with her because of all the picking and carping she had been doing, and I said that I knew my Bible backwards and forwards – which was not far from the truth – and that this was not one of the stories in it. So it could not be a Bible subject.

And she said it was; and I said it wasn't, and I was willing to have it put to the test; and she said I was not there to argue about pictures, but to make the bed. And at that moment Mr. Kinnear came into the room. He must have been listening in the passageway, as he seemed amused. What, he said, are you discussing theology, and so early in the morning too? And he wanted to be told all about it.

Nancy said it was nothing for him to be bothered about, but he still desired to know, and said, Well, Grace, I see Nancy wishes to keep it a secret from me, but you must tell me; and I was shy, but at length I asked him whether the picture was of a Biblical subject, as Nancy had said. And he laughed, and said that strictly speaking it was not, as the story was in the Apocrypha. And I was surprised, and asked what that might be; and I could tell that Nancy had never heard the word before either. But she was put out because she'd been wrong, and was frowning in a sulky manner.

Mr. Kinnear said I was very inquisitive for such a young person, and soon he would have the most learned maidservant in Richmond Hill, and he would have to put me on display, and charge money for me, like the mathematical pig in Toronto. Then he said the Apocrypha was a book where they'd put all the stories from Biblical times that they'd decided should not go into the Bible. I was most astonished to hear this, and I said, Who decided? Because I'd always thought that the Bible was written by God, as it was called the Word of God, and everyone termed it so.

And he smiled, and said that though perhaps God wrote it, it was men who wrote it down; which was a little different. But those men were said to have been inspired; which meant that God had spoken to them, and told them what to do.

So I asked did they hear voices, and he said yes. And I was glad that someone else had done so, although I said nothing about it, and in any case the voice I had heard, that one time, had not been God's but Mary Whitney's.

He asked if I knew the story of Susannah, and I said no; and he said she was a young lady who had been falsely accused of sinning with a young man, by some old men, because she refused to commit the very same sin with them; and she would have been executed by being stoned to death; but luckily she had a clever lawyer, who was able to prove that the old men had been lying, by inducing them to give contradictory evidence. Then he said what did I think the moral of it was? And I said the moral was, that you should not take baths outside in the garden; and he laughed, and said he thought the moral was that you needed a clever lawyer. And he said to Nancy, This girl is no simpleton after all; by which I guessed she had been telling him that I was one. And Nancy looked daggers at me.

Then he said that he'd found a shirt ironed and put away with a button missing; and that it was very aggravating to put on a clean shirt, only to find you couldn't do it up properly because of a lack of buttons; and would we please mind that it did not happen again. And he took up his gold snuffbox, which was what he'd come for, and went out of the room.

But now Nancy had been in the wrong twice, for that shirt must have been washed and ironed by her, before I was ever anywhere near; and so she gave me a list of chores as long as your arm, and went flouncing out of the room and down the stairs, and out into the yard, and began scolding McDermott for not cleaning her shoes properly that morning.

I said to myself that there was trouble ahead, and I would have to guard my tongue; because Nancy did not like being crossed, and most of all she did not like being put in the wrong by Mr. Kinnear.

When she hired me away from Watson's, I thought we would be like sisters or at least good friends, the two of us working together side by side, as I had done with Mary Whitney. Now I knew that this was not the way things were going to be.

2 6 .

I had now been a servant for three years, and could act the part well
enough by that time. But Nancy was very changeable, two-faced you
might call her, and it wasn't easy to tell what she wanted from one
hour to the next. One minute she would be up on her high horse and
ordering me about and finding fault, and the next minute she would
be my best friend, or pretend to be, and would put her arm through
mine, and say I looked tired, and should sit down with her, and have
a cup of tea. It is much harder to work for such a person, as just
when you are curtsying and Ma'am-ing them, they turn around and
upbraid you for being so stiff and formal, and want to confide in
you, and expect the same in return. You cannot ever do the correct
thing with them.

The next day was a fine fair day with a breeze, and so I did the
wash, and high time too as clean things were running short. It was
hot work, as I had to keep the fire in the summer kitchen stove
going at a brisk rate; and I'd had no chance to sort and soak the
things the night before; but I could not risk waiting, as at that time
of year there could be a quick change in the weather. So I scrubbed

and rubbed, and got it all hung up nicely at last, with the napkins and the white pocket-handkerchiefs neatly spread out on the grass to bleach. There were snuff stains, and ink stains, and grass stains on a petticoat of Nancy's – I wondered how she had got them, but she had most likely slipped and fallen down – and several spots of mildew, on things that had been in the dampness at the bottom of the pile; and wine stains on the tablecloth, from a supper party, which had not been covered with salt at the time, as they should have been; but by dint of a good bleaching fluid made from lye and chloride of lime, which I'd learnt from the laundress at Mrs. Alderman Parkinson's, I got them out mostly, and trusted to the sunlight to do the rest.

I stood for a moment admiring my handiwork; for there is a great deal of pleasure to be had in a wash all clean, and blowing in the wind, like pennants at a race, or the sails of a ship; and the sound of it is like the hands of the Heavenly Hosts applauding, though heard from far away. And they do say that cleanliness is next to Godliness; and sometimes, when I have seen the pure white clouds billowing in the sky after a rain, I used to think that it was as if the angels themselves were hanging out their washing; for I reasoned that someone must do it, as everything in Heaven must be very clean and fresh. But these were childish fancies, as children like to tell themselves stories about things that are not visible; and I was scarcely more than a child at the time, although I thought myself a grown woman, having my own money that I earned myself.

While I was standing there, Jamie Walsh came around the corner of the house, and asked if there were any errands to be run; and he said to me, quite shyly, that if he was sent into the village by Nancy or Mr. Kinnear, and if there was any little thing I should want, he would be glad to buy the same for me, and fetch it back, if I would give him the money. Although awkward, he was as polite as he knew how to be, and even removed his hat, which was an old straw one and had been his father's most likely, as it was too big for him. I said it was thoughtful of him, but that I did not need anything at the moment. But then I remembered that there was no ox gall in the house, for setting the dyes in the wash, and I would need some to do the dark colours; for the things I had done that morning had all been white. I went with him to Nancy, and she had several other items for him to buy, and Mr. Kinnear had a message to be delivered nearby to one of his gentleman friends, and so off he went.

Nancy told him to come back in the afternoon, and bring his flute with him; and when he was gone, she said that he played so beautiful it was a pleasure to hear it. She was in a good temper again by this time, and helped me get the dinner, which was a cold one, with ham and pickles, and a salad from the kitchen garden; for there were lettuces and chives to be had. But she ate in the dining room with Mr. Kinnear, as before, and I had to make do with McDermott for my own company.

It is uncomfortable watching another person eat, and listening to them as well, especially if they have a tendency to guzzle; but McDermott did not seem inclined to conversation, having reverted to a sullen mood; so I asked him whether he enjoyed dancing.

What makes you ask that, he said suspiciously; and not wanting to let on that I'd been overhearing him at his practice, I said it was known of him that he was a good dancer.

He said maybe he was and maybe he wasn't, but he seemed pleased; and so then I set to work to draw him out, and asked him about his own life, before he came to work at Mr. Kinnear's. He said, Who would care to hear about that? I said that I would, as all such stories were of interest to me; and he soon began to tell.

He said his family was respectable enough, being from Waterford in the south of Ireland, and his father had been a steward; but he himself had been a scapegrace, and never one to lick the boots of the rich, and was always getting into mischief, which he appeared rather proud of than otherwise. I asked if he had a mother living, and he said whether he did or didn't it was all the same to him, as she'd had a bad opinion of him, and told him he was going straight to the Devil; and she could be dead for all he knew or cared about it. But his voice was not so sturdy as his words.

He'd run away from home at a young age, and joined the army in England, claiming he was several years older than he was; but it being too hard a life to his mind, and too much discipline and hard treatment, he'd deserted, and stowed away on a ship bound for America; and when discovered, he'd worked out the rest of his passage; but had landed in Canada East rather than the United States. And then he'd got a job on the boats that plied up and down the St. Lawrence River, and then on the Lake boats, which were glad to have him, as he was very strong, with a grand lot of endurance, and could work without stopping, just like a steam engine; and that was well enough for a time. But it became too monotonous; and as he had a love of variety, he'd enlisted again for a soldier, with the Glengarry Light Infantry, which had got such a bad reputation among the farmers, as I knew from Mary Whitney, having burnt a good many farmhouses during the Rebellion, and turned women and children out into the snow, and done worse to them besides, that was never printed in the papers. So they were an unruly bunch of men, and given to dissipation, and to gaming and drink and the like; which he accounted manly virtues.

But the Rebellion was over by then, and there was not much to be done; and McDermott was not a regular soldier, but acted as personal servant to Captain Alexander Macdonald. It was a soft life with decent pay, and he was sorry when that regiment was disbanded, and he was thrown on his own resources. He went to Toronto and lived idly on the money he had saved; but then his funds dwindled, and he knew he would have to look about him; and it was in search of a position that he'd gone north up Yonge Street, and had come as far as Richmond Hill. He heard in one of the taverns that Mr. Kinnear was in need of a man, and had presented himself, and it was Nancy that hired him; but he thought he would be working for the gentleman himself, and doing for him in person as he had for Captain Macdonald; but was annoyed to find that a woman was set over him instead, and one who never gave him a moment's rest from her tongue, and found fault constantly.

I believed all he said; but afterwards, when I had added up the times in my head, I felt he must be several years older than the twenty-one he gave himself; either that, or he'd been lying. And when I heard later from others in the neighbourhood, including Jamie Walsh, that McDermott had a strong reputation as a liar and braggart, I was not at all surprised.

Then I began to think I'd been wrong to show such an interest in his story; as he had mistaken this for an interest in his person. Having had several glasses of beer, he now began to make sheep's eyes at me, and asked if I had a sweetheart, as a pretty girl like me might be expected to have one. I should have replied that my sweetheart was six feet tall and an expert at boxing; but I was too young to know any better, so instead I told the truth. I said I did not have a sweetheart, and furthermore I had no inclinations that way.

He said that was a pity, but there was a first time for everything, and I only needed breaking in, like a colt, and then I would go as good as the rest of them, and he was the man for the job. I was very annoyed by this, and got up at once and began to clear the dishes with a great clattering, and said I would thank him to keep such offensive remarks to himself, as I was not a mare. Then he said he didn't mean it, and it was all in fun, and he'd just wanted to see what sort of a girl I might be. I said that what sort of a girl I might be was not any business of his, at which he became quite sulky, as if I was the one who had insulted him, and went out into the courtyard, and began to chop the firewood.

After I'd washed up the dishes, which had to be done carefully because of all the flies about, which would walk on the clean dishes if not covered up by a cloth, and leave their dirty flyspecks; and after I'd been outside to see how my laundry was drying, and had sprinkled the pocket-handkerchiefs and table napkins with water, to make them bleach out better; then it was time to skim the cream off the milk, and to make the butter.

I did this outside, in the shade cast by the house, to get some air; and as the churn was the kind that was worked by a foot pedal, I was able to sit in a chair while doing it, and attend to some of the mending at the same time. Some people have churns that are worked by a dog, which is penned up in a cage and made to run on a treadmill with a hot coal under its tail; but I consider this to be cruel. While I was sitting there waiting for the butter to come, and sewing a button onto one of Mr. Kinnear's shirts, Mr. Kinnear himself came past me on his way to the stable. I made to get up, but he told me to remain where I was, as he would rather have good butter than a curtsy.

Always busy I see, Grace, he said. Yes Sir, I said, the Devil finds work for idle hands to do. He laughed, and said, I trust you do not mean me, as my hands are idle enough, but not nearly devilish enough for my liking; and I was confused, and said Oh no Sir, I did not mean you. And he smiled, and said it was becoming for a young woman to blush.

There was no reply to that, so I said nothing; and he went on past; and shortly he came by on Charley, and rode down the drive. Nancy had come out to see how I was getting on with the butter, and I asked where Mr. Kinnear was going. To Toronto, she said; he goes there every Thursday, and stays overnight, to do some business at the bank and also some errands; but first he will go to Colonel Bridgeford's, whose wife is away from home, and the two daughters as well, so he can visit safely, but when she is there he is not received.

I was surprised at this, and asked why; and Nancy said that Mr. Kinnear was considered a bad influence by Mrs. Bridgeford, who thought she was the Queen of France, and that nobody else was fit to lick her shoes; and she laughed. But she did not sound very amused.

Why, what has he done? I asked. But just then I could feel the butter coming – there is a thick feel to it – so I did not pursue it.

Nancy helped me with the butter, and we salted the most of it, covered it in cold water to store, and pressed some fresh into the moulds; two had a thistle design, and the third had the Kinnear crest, with the motto *I Live In Hope*. Nancy said that if Mr. Kinnear's elder brother in Scotland was to die, who was really only a half-brother, then Mr. Kinnear would come into a big house and lands there; but she said he was not expecting it, and claimed to be happy enough as he was, or that is what he said when feeling in good health. But there was no love lost between him and the half-brother, which is usual in such cases; and I guessed that Mr. Kinnear had been packed off to the Colonies, to get him out of the way.

When we had the butter done, we carried it down the cellar stairs into the dairy; but we left some of the buttermilk above, to make into biscuits later. Nancy said she didn't much like the cellar, as it always smelled of earth, and of mice and old vegetables; and I said that perhaps it could be given a good airing-out someday, if we could get the window open. And we went back upstairs, and after I'd gathered in my washing we sat outside on the verandah, mending away together like the best friends in the world. Later I came to notice that she was always affability itself when Mr. Kinnear was not present, but jumpy as a cat when he was, and when I was in the same room with him; but I was not aware of it then.

As we sat there, along came McDermott, running along the top of the snake fence, agile as a squirrel, and zigging and zagging. I was amazed, and said, What on earth is he doing, and Nancy said, Oh, he does that sometimes, he says it is for the exercise but really he just wants to be admired, you should not pay any attention. And so I pretended not to; but secretly I watched, as he was in reality very nimble; and after he had run back and forth, he jumped down, and then leapt entirely over the fence, using only one hand on it to steady himself.

So there I was, pretending not to watch, and there he was, pretending not to be watched; and you may see the very same thing, Sir, at any polite gathering of society ladies and gentlemen. There is a good deal that can be seen slantwise, especially by the ladies, who do not wish to be caught staring. They can also see through veils, and window curtains, and over the tops of fans; and it is a good thing they can see in this way, or they would never see much of anything. But those of us who do not have to be bothered with all the veils and fans manage to see a good deal more.

In a little time Jamie Walsh appeared; he'd come through the fields, and had brought his flute with him as requested. Nancy greeted him warmly, and thanked him for coming. She sent me to fetch Jamie a mug of beer; and while I was drawing it, McDermott came in, and said he would have one too. Then I could not resist, and said, I did not know you had monkey blood in you, you was leaping about like one. And he did not know whether to be pleased that I had seen him, or angry at being called a monkey.

He said that when the cat was away the mice would play, and when Kinnear was in town, then Nancy always liked her little parties, and he supposed the Walsh boy would now be screeching on his tin whistle; and I said that was quite right, and I would give myself the pleasure of hearing it; and he said that to his mind it was no pleasure; and I said he could suit himself. At that he caught hold of my arm, and looked at me very earnestly, and said he hadn't meant to offend me, before; but having been so long among rough men, whose manners were not of the best, he was inclined to forget himself, and did not know how to speak; and he hoped I would forgive him, and that we could be friends. I said I was always ready to be friends, with any who were sincere; and as for forgiveness, was it not ordained in the Bible? And I certainly hoped that I could forgive, as I myself hoped to be forgiven in future. Which I said very calm.

After that I took the beer to the front verandah, and some bread and cheese for our supper to have with it, and I sat out there with Nancy and Jamie Walsh while the sun declined, and it became too dark to sew. It was a lovely and windless evening, and the birds were twittering, and the trees in the orchard near the road were golden in the late sunlight, and the purple milkweed flowers that grew beside the drive smelled very sweetly; and also the last few peonies beside the verandah, and the climbing roses; and the coolness came down out of the air, while Jamie sat and played on his flute, so plaintively it did your heart good. After a while McDermott came skulking around the side of the house like a tamed wolf, and leant against the side of the house, and listened also. And there we were, in a kind of harmony; and the evening was so beautiful, that it made a pain in my heart, as when you cannot tell whether you are happy or sad; and I thought that if I could have a wish, it would be that nothing would ever change, and we could stay that way forever.

But the sun cannot be stopped in its path, except by God, and he has done that only once, and will not do it again until the end of the world; and on this night it went down as usual, leaving behind it a deep-red sunset; and for a few moments the front of the house was all pink with it. Then in the dusk the fireflies came out, for it was their time of year; and they shone in the low bushes and grasses, on and then off, like stars glimpsed through cloud. Jamie Walsh caught one in a glass tumbler, and held his hand over the top, so I could see it up close; it flashed slowly, with a cool greenish fire; and I thought, if I could have two fireflies on my ears, for earrings, I would not care at all about Nancy's gold ones.

Then the darkness deepened, and came out from behind the trees and bushes, and up through the fields, and the shadows lengthened and joined together; and I thought it looked like water, coming up through the ground, and rising slowly up like the sea; and I fell into a reverie, and was remembering back to the time I crossed the great ocean, and how at that time of day the sea and the sky were the same indigo, so you could not tell where the one left off and the other one began. And into my memory there floated an iceberg, as white as white could be; and despite the warmth of the evening I felt a chill.

But then Jamie Walsh said he must be getting home, as his father would be looking for him; and I remembered I had not milked the cow or shut up the hens for the night, and hurried to do both by last light. When I came back into the kitchen, Nancy was still there, and had lighted a candle. I asked why she hadn't gone to bed, and she said she was afraid to sleep alone when Mr. Kinnear was not at home, and would I sleep upstairs with her.

I said I would, but asked what she was afraid of. Was it robbers? Or perhaps, I said, she was afraid of James McDermott? But I meant it as a joke.

She said archly that from what she could make out from the look in his eyes, I had more cause to be afraid of him than she did, unless I was in need of a new beau. And I said I was more afraid of the old rooster in the henyard, than I was of him; and as for beaus, I had no more use for them than the man in the moon.

And so she laughed, and the two of us went up to bed in a very companionable fashion; but I made sure that all was locked up first.

VIII.

FOX AND GEESE

Everything went on very quietly for a fortnight, except the housekeeper several times scolding McDermott for not doing his work properly, and she gave him a fortnight's warning. . . . He often after this told me he was glad he was going, as he did not wish any longer to live with a parcel of w___s, but would have satisfaction before he went, and he told me he was positive that Kinnear and the housekeeper, Nancy, slept together; I was determined to find it out, and I was afterwards convinced that they did so, for her bed was never slept in except when Mr. Kinnear was absent, and then I slept with her.

– Confession of Grace Marks,
Star and Transcript, Toronto, November 1843.

"Grace Marks was . . . a pretty girl, and very smart about her work, but of a silent, sullen temper. It was very difficult to know when she was pleased. . . . After the work of the day was over, she and I generally were left to ourselves in the kitchen, [the housekeeper] being entirely taken up with her master. Grace was very jealous of the difference made between her and the housekeeper, whom she hated, and to whom she was often very insolent and saucy. . . . 'What is she better than us?' she would say, 'that she is to be treated like a lady, and eat and drink of the best? She is not better born than we are, or better educated. . . .'

"The good looks of Grace had interested me in her cause; and though there was something about the girl that I could not exactly like, I had been a very lawless, dissipated fellow, and if a woman was young and pretty, I cared very little about her character. Grace was sullen and proud, and not very easily won over to my purpose; but in order to win her liking, if possible, I gave a ready ear to all her discontented repinings."

– James McDermott,
to Kenneth MacKenzie, as retold by
Susanna Moodie, *Life in the Clearings*, 1853.

Yet half I seemed to recognize some trick
   Of mischief happened to me, God knows when –
   In a bad dream perhaps. Here ended, then,
Progress this way. When, in the very nick
Of giving up, one time more, came a click
   As when a trap shuts – you're inside the den!

– Robert Browning,
"'Childe Roland to the
Dark Tower Came,'" 1855.

2 7 .

Today when I woke up there was a beautiful pink sunrise, with the mist lying over the fields like a white soft cloud of muslin, and the sun shining through the layers of it all blurred and rosy like a peach gently on fire.

In fact I have no idea of what kind of a sunrise there was. In prison they make the windows high up, so you cannot climb out of them I suppose, but also so you cannot see out of them either, or at least not onto the outside world. They do not want you looking out, they do not want you thinking the word *out*, they do not want you looking at the horizon and thinking you might someday drop below it yourself, like the sail of a ship departing or a horse and rider vanishing down a far hillside. And so this morning I saw only the usual form of light, a light without shape, coming in through the high-up and dirty grey windows, as if cast by no sun and no moon and no lamp or candle. Just a swathe of daylight the same all the way through, like lard.

I took off my prison nightdress, which was coarse-woven and of a yellowed colour; I should not say it was mine, because we own nothing here and share all in common, like the early Christians, and the nightdress you wear one week, next to your skin while you sleep, may two weeks previous have been lying close to the heart of your worst enemy, and washed and mended by others who do not wish you well.

As I dressed myself and tidied back my hair there was a tune going through my head, a little song that Jamie Walsh used to play sometimes upon his flute:

Tom, Tom, the piper's son,
Stole a pig and away he run,
And all the tune that he could play
Was over the hills and far away.

I knew I'd remembered it wrong, and the real song said the pig was eat and Tom was beat, and then went howling down the street; but I didn't see why I shouldn't make it come out in a better way; and as long as I told no one of what was in my mind, there was no one to hold me to account, or correct me, just as there was no one to say that the real sunrise was nothing like the one I'd invented for myself, but was instead only a soiled yellowish white, like a dead fish floating in the harbour.

At least in the Lunatic Asylum you could see out better. When you were not muffled up in a darkened room.

Before breakfast there was a whipping, out in the courtyard; they do it before breakfast, as if those being whipped have eaten first, they are likely to spew up their food, and that makes a mess, as well as being a waste of good nourishment; and the keepers and guards say they like the exercise at that time of day, as it gives them an appetite. It was only a routine whipping, and nothing unusual, so we were not summoned to watch it; two or three only, and all of them men; the women do not get whipped so frequently. The first was young, by the tenor of his screaming; I can tell these things, having had a good deal of practice. I tried not to listen, and thought instead about the pig that was stolen by Tom the thief, and how it got eaten; but the song did not say who ate it, whether it was Tom himself or those who caught him. Set a thief to catch a thief, as Mary Whitney used to say. I wondered, was it a dead pig to begin with? Most likely not; most likely it had a rope around its neck or a ring through its nose, and was forced to run away with Tom. That would make the most sense, as it would save the carrying of it. In the whole song, the poor pig was the only one who did no wrong, but it was also the only one who died. Many songs, I have noticed, are unfair in this way.

At breakfast, all was silent except for the munching of bread and the slurping of tea, and the shuffling of feet and the snuffling of noses, and the drone of the Bible being read out, which today was Jacob and Esau and the mess of pottage, and the lies that were told and the blessing and birthright that was sold, and the deceptions and disguises that were practised, which God did not mind at all but the contrary. Just as old Isaac was feeling his hairy son, which was not his son at all but a skinned goat, Annie Little gave me a hard pinch on the thigh, under the table where it could not be seen. I knew what she was about, she wanted to make me scream so I would be punished or else thought to be having another attack of insanity, but I was ready for her, as I was expecting something of the sort.

In the washhouse yesterday, as we stood at the sink, she leant over and whispered to me, Doctor's pet, spoiled whore; because the word has gone round, and all know about the visits of Dr. Jordan, and some think I am having too much attention paid to me, and have grown proud with it. If they think that here, they will take you down a peg or two; and it would not be the first time, as they resent my service in the Governor's house as well; but they're afraid to act too openly, thinking I might have the ear of some in power. There is no place like a prison for small jealousies, and I've seen some come to blows, and even close to murder, over nothing more than a piece of cheese.

But I knew better than to complain of her to the matrons. Not only do they view such tale-tellers with disgust, preferring a quiet life for themselves; but also they might not believe me, or might say they did not, as the Warden says a convict's word is not sufficient evidence; and then too, Annie Little would be sure to be revenged on me in some other way. One ought to bear all patiently, as part of the correction we are subject to; unless a way can be found, of tripping up your enemy without detection. Hair pulling is not advisable, as the racket brings the keepers, and then both sides are punished for creating a disturbance. Dirt slipped into the food by means of the sleeve, as with magicians, may be accomplished without much fuss, and may bring some satisfaction. But Annie Little was in the Asylum with me, her crime being manslaughter, having struck and killed a stableboy with a log of wood; and she was said to suffer from nervous excitement, and was sent back here at the same time as me; but should not have been, as I do not think she is right in the head; so I resolved to forgive her this time, unless she did worse. And the pinch appeared to have relieved her feelings.

Then it was time for the keepers, and our walk out through the gate, Ah Grace, out for your promenade with your two beaus, ain't you the lucky one. Oh no, we're the lucky ones, we're the lucky boys ourselves, with such a morsel on our arms, says the one. What do you say Grace, says the other, let's just nip up a side alley, into a back stable, down on the hay, it won't take long if you lie still, and quicker yet if you wriggle about. Or why lie down at all, says the one, back her up against the wall and heave-ho and hoist the petticoats, it's a quick jump standing up, as long as your knees don't give out on you; come Grace, just give us the word and we're your lads, one as good as the other and why settle for one when there's two standing ready? Standing ready all the time, here, give us a hand and you can test the truth of it. Nor we won't charge you a penny neither, says the other, what's a good time between old friends?

You're no friends of mine, I say, with your filthy talk, you were born in the gutter and you'll die in it too. Oh ho, says the one, that's what I like, a little high spirits in a woman, a little fire, they say it comes with the redness of the hair. But is it red where it most counts, says the other, a fire in a treetop is no use at all, it must be in a fireplace to cast enough heat, in a little cookstove, you know why God made women with skirts, it's so they can be pulled up over their heads and tied at the top, that way you don't get so much noise out of them, I hate a screeching slut, women should be born without mouths on them, the only thing of use in them is below the waist.

Shame on you, says I, as we walk around a puddle and across the street, to talk that way, your own mother was a woman or at least I suppose she was. And bad cess to her, says the one, the whoring old witch, the only part of me she ever liked to see was my bare bum covered with stripes, she's burning in Hell this moment and I'm only sorry it wasn't me put her there, but a drunken sailor whose pocket she tried to pick, and who knocked her on the head with a bottle. Well, says the other, my own mother was an angel to be sure, a saint on earth according to her own reckoning, and would never let me forget it; and I don't know which is the worse.

I'm a philosopher, says the one, it's moderation for me, not too thin and not too fat, and best not to waste God's gifts to us, speaking of which Grace, you're ripe enough to be picked, why stay on the tree untasted, you'll just fall off and rot at the foot of it in any case. True enough, says the other, why let the milk go sour in the bowl, a sweet nut should be cracked while there's still some goodness in it, as there's nothing worse than a fusty old nut. Come, you're making my mouth water for you already, you're enough to turn an honest man into a cannibal, I'd like to get a strong grip on you with my teeth, just what you might call a nibble, a small bite out of the ham end, you'd not miss it, you've enough on you and to spare. Right you are, says the one, look, she's got a waist like a willow but she's taking on fat below, it's all the fine cooking they do at the prison, cream-fed she is, would you just take a feel of it, that's a haunch fit for the Pope's own table. And he took to kneading and prodding, with the one hand that was hidden by the folds of my gown.

I'll thank you not to take liberties, I say, pulling away. I'm all for liberties myself, says the one, being a republican at heart, having no use for the Queen of England except what Nature intended, and though she's got a fine pair of bosoms on her and I'd pay her the compliment of giving them a squeeze at any time she might request it, she's got no chin to her at all, no more than a duck; and what I say is, no man is better than the next, and it's share and share alike and none preferred; and once you've given it out to one of us, why then, the others must all take their turns like true democrats, and why should that little runt McDermott be allowed to enjoy what is denied to his betters?

Yes, said the other, you gave him liberties enough, a fine time you had of it I've no doubt, with him sweating away at it all night in the tavern in Lewiston with barely a pause to refresh himself, for they say he was a prime athlete, and a dab hand with the axe as well, and could climb up a rope like a monkey. Right you are, said the other, and at last the cunning fellow tried to climb into Heaven, and ended by making such a high leap into the air that he stayed up there for two hours, and could not be made to come down of his own accord, no matter how they called, but had to be fetched. And he danced while he was up there, a spry jig with the ropemaker's daughter, as lively as a rooster with its neck fresh wrung, so it did your heart good to see it.

And stiff as a board he was afterwards too, I'm told, said the one; but that's just what the ladies like. And here they laughed very much, and thought they'd made the finest joke in the world; but it was cruel in them, to laugh at a man simply for being dead; and bad luck also, for the dead don't like being laughed at; and I assured myself that they had their own ways of protecting against injury, and would deal with the keepers in good time, either above the ground or beneath it.

I spent the morning mending some blonde lace of Miss Lydia's, that she'd torn at a party; she does tend to be careless about her clothes, and ought to be told that such fine clothes as hers are do not grow on trees. It was delicate work and a strain on the eyes, but I got it done at last.

Dr. Jordan came as usual in the afternoon, and seemed fatigued, and also troubled in mind. He hadn't brought any vegetable with him, to ask me what I might think of it; and I was a little taken aback, as I had become used to this part of the afternoon, and had enjoyed wondering what he would bring next, and what it was he wanted me to say about it.

So I said, Sir, you are without any item today.

And he said, Item, Grace?

Any potato or carrot, I said. Or onion. Or beet, I added.

And he said, Yes, Grace, I have determined upon a different plan.

What is that, Sir? I said.

I have decided to ask you, what it is that you yourself would like me to bring.

Well Sir, I said. That is indeed a different plan. I would have to consider it.

So he said I was welcome to do that; and meanwhile, had I had any dreams? As he was looking forlorn, and as it were at a loss, and as I suspected that not all was going well with him, I did not say that

I could not remember. Instead I said that I had indeed had a dream. And what was it about, said he, brightening up considerably, and fiddling with his pencil. I told him I'd dreamt about flowers; and he wrote that down busily, and asked what sort of flowers. I said that they were red flowers, and quite large, with glossy leaves like a peony. But I did not say that they were made of cloth, nor did I say when I had seen them last; nor did I say that they were not a dream.

And where were they growing, said he.

Here, I said.

Here, in this room? said he, looking very alert.

No, I said, outside in the yard, where we take our walks for exercise. And he wrote that down as well.

Or I suppose he wrote it down. I cannot be certain, because I never see what he writes down; and sometimes I imagine that whatever he is writing down, it cannot possibly be anything that has come out of my mouth, as he does not understand much of what I say, although I try to put things as clearly as I can. It's as if he is deaf, and has not yet learnt to read lips. But at other times he appears to understand quite well, although like most gentlemen he often wants a thing to mean more than it does.

When he'd finished writing I said, I have thought of what I would like you to bring next time, Sir.

And what is that, Grace, said he.

A radish, I said.

A radish, he replied. A red radish? And why have you chosen a radish? And he frowned, as if it was a matter for weighty thought.

Well Sir, said I, the other things you have brought have not been for eating, or so it seemed; because most of them would need to be cooked first; and you took them away again with you, except for the apple you brought the first day, and very nice it was too. But I thought that if you brought a radish, it could be eaten with no preparation; and they are now in season; and it is very seldom we get anything fresh in the Penitentiary, and even when I eat in the kitchen of this house, I do not get such garden stuff, as it is reserved for the family. So it would be a rare treat; and I would take it very kindly in you, if you would bring a little salt as well.

He gave a sort of sigh, and then he said, Did they have radishes at Mr. Kinnear's?

Oh yes, Sir, I said, they did; but by the time I reached that place they were past their prime; as a radish is best early in the season, for when the hot weather comes they will go soft and maggoty, and go to seed.

He did not write this down.

As he was preparing to leave, he said, Thank you for telling me your dream, Grace. Perhaps you will tell me another one soon. And I said, Perhaps I will, Sir. And then I said, I will try hard to remember them, if it will help you, Sir, with the trouble you are in; for I was feeling pity towards him, he looked so out of sorts. And he said, What makes you think I am in trouble, Grace? And I said, Those who have been in trouble themselves are alert to it in others, Sir.

He said it was a kind thought in me; then he hesitated a moment, as if to tell me more; but he thought better of it, and nodded goodbye. He always gives the same small nod when he goes out.

I had not finished my quilting block for the day, as he had not been in the room with me as long as usual; and so I remained seated, and continued to sew. After a short while Miss Lydia came in.

Dr. Jordan has left? she said. I said that he had. She was wearing a new dress which I helped sew, of a violet ground, with a white design of small birds and flowers, very becoming to her, and a skirt on it like a half a pumpkin; and I thought she had most likely meant to have more of an audience for it than just myself.

She sat down in the chair opposite me, where Dr. Jordan had been sitting, and began to sort through the sewing basket. I cannot find my thimble, I believe I put it in here, she said. Then, Oh, he has forgotten about the scissors; I thought he was not supposed to leave them within your reach.

We do not bother much about that, I said. He knows I would not hurt him.

She sat for a little with the sewing basket in her lap. Did you know you have an admirer, Grace? she said.

Oh, who is that, I said, thinking it would be a stableboy or some such young lad, who might have heard my story and found it romantic.

Dr. Jerome DuPont, she said. He is staying at present with Mrs. Quennell. He says you have lived a remarkable life, and he finds you of considerable interest.

I do not know any such gentleman. I expect he reads the newspapers, and is on a tour, and views me as a sight that must be seen, I said a little sharply, for I suspected her of making fun of me. She is of a fun-loving nature, and sometimes goes too far with it.

He is a man of serious pursuits, said she. He is studying Neuro-hypnotism.

What is that? I said.

Oh, it is like Mesmerism, but much more scientific, said she, it is all to do with the nerves. But he must know you, or at least he has seen you, as he says you are still quite handsome. Perhaps he passed you in the street, as you are on your way here in the mornings.

Perhaps, I said; thinking what a spectacle I made, with a smirking ruffian to either side.

He has such dark eyes, she said, they burn right into you, as if he could see inside. But I'm not sure I like him. Of course he's old. He's like Mama and the rest of them, I suppose he goes to their table-rappings and séances. I don't believe in it, and neither does Dr. Jordan.

Did he say so? I said. He is a man of sense then. It's not a thing that should be meddled with.

A man of sense, that is so cold, she said; and sighed. A man of sense makes him sound like a banker. Then she said, Grace, he talks with you more than any of us put together. What sort of man is he really?

A gentleman, I said.

Well, I knew that much, she said shortly. But what is he like?

An American, I said, which was another thing she knew. Then I relented, and said, He seems like a proper-enough young man.

Oh I would not want him to be too proper, she said. Reverend Verringer is too proper.

Privately I agreed that this was so, but as Reverend Verringer is trying to get a pardon for me, I said, Reverend Verringer is a man of religion, and it is required of them to be proper.

I think Dr. Jordan is very sarcastic, said Miss Lydia. Is he very sarcastic with you as well, Grace?

I don't suppose I would know it if he was, Miss, I said.

She sighed again, and said, He is going to address one of Mama's Tuesdays. I do not usually attend them as it is so tedious, although Mama says I should take more interest in serious matters concerning the welfare of society, and Reverend Verringer says the same; but this time I will go, as I'm sure it will be thrilling to hear Dr. Jordan talk about asylums. Though I would prefer him to invite me to tea in his chambers. With Mama, and Marianne, of course, as I must have a chaperone.

It is always advisable, I said, for a young girl.

Grace, sometimes you are an old stick, she said. And I am no longer a young girl really, I am nineteen. I suppose it's nothing to you, you've done all sorts of things, but I have never been to tea in a man's chambers before.

Just because you've never done a thing before, Miss, I said, is no good reason to do it. But if your mother would be going, I am sure it would be respectable enough.

She stood up, and trailed her hand along the top of the sewing table. Yes, she said. It would be respectable enough. She appeared discouraged by this thought. Then she said, Will you help me with my new dress? For the Tuesday circle; as I would like to make an impression with it.

I said I would help her gladly; and she said I was a treasure, and she hoped they would never let me out of prison, as she would like me always to be there, to help her with her dresses. Which I suppose was a compliment of a sort.

But I did not like the drifting look in her eyes, or the falling note in her voice; and I thought, there will be trouble ahead; as is always the case, when one loves, and the other does not.

2 8 .

On the next day, Dr. Jordan brings me the promised radish. It is washed, with the leaves cut off, and quite fresh and crisp, not rubbery the way they go when left to sit about. He's forgotten the salt, but I do not mention this, as it is not right to look a gift horse in the mouth. I eat the radish quickly – I've learnt the habit of bolting my food in prison, as it must be eaten before it is snatched away – and I relish the sharpness of it, which is like the peppery smell of a nasturtium. I ask him how he came by it; and he says it is from the market; although he has it in mind to make a small kitchen garden himself at the house where he lodges, as there is the place for it, and he has already begun the digging. Now that is a thing I envy.

Then I say, I thank you from the bottom of my heart, Sir, this radish was like the nectar of the Gods. He looks surprised to hear me use such an expression; but that's only because he doesn't remember that I have read the poetry of Sir Walter Scott.

Because he was so thoughtful as to bring me this radish, I set to work willingly to tell my story, and to make it as interesting as I can, and rich in incident, as a sort of return gift to him; for I have always believed that one good turn deserves another.

When I left off last time, Sir, I believe Mr. Kinnear had rode away to Toronto, and then Jamie Walsh came over and played his flute, and there was a lovely sunset, and then I went off to sleep with Nancy, as she was afraid of robbers with no man in the house. She did not count McDermott, as he did not sleep in the house itself; or perhaps she did not account him a man; or perhaps she thought he was more likely to side with the robbers, and not against them. She did not say.

So there we were, going up the staircase with our candles. Nancy's bedchamber, as I have said, was at the back of the house, and was much larger and finer than mine, although she had no separate dressing room like Mr. Kinnear's. But she had a commodious bedstead, with a fine quilt on it, a summer one in light pinks and blues on a white ground; it was a Broken Staircase. She had a wardrobe, with her dresses in it, and I wondered how she could have saved up enough money to buy so many; but she said Mr. Kinnear was a generous master when the mood took him. Also she had a dressing table with an embroidered runner on it, roses and lilies with the buds of each, and a sandalwood box with her earrings and a brooch, and also her pots of creams and potions were kept there; for before going to bed she greased the skin of her face like a boot. She had a bottle of rose-water too, and let me try some, which smelled most delicious; for on this evening she was all sociability; and a saucerful of hair pomade, of which she rubbed in a little, and said it gave the hair a shine; and she asked me to brush out her hair for her, just like a lady's maid, which I did with pleasure. She had lovely long hair, a dark brown, and wavy. Oh Grace, she said, that feels most luxurious, you have a good touch; and I was flattered. But I remembered Mary Whitney, and how she used to brush out my own hair; for indeed I had never forgotten her for long.

There we are, snug as two peas in a pod, she said, very friendly, when we were once in bed. But as she blew out the candle she sighed, and it was not the sigh of a happy woman, but of one who is trying to make the best of things.

Mr. Kinnear came back on the morning of the Saturday. He'd meant to return on the Friday, but had been delayed by business in Toronto, or so he said; and had stopped part of the way back, at an inn which was not far north of the first toll gate; and Nancy was none too pleased to hear that, as the place had a bad reputation and was said to countenance loose women, or so she told me in the kitchen.

I replied that a gentleman can stay at such places without any risk to his reputation, as I was trying to calm her. She was very agitated, because Mr. Kinnear had met with two of his acquaintances on the way home, Colonel Bridgeford and Captain Boyd, and had invited them to dine; and it was Jefferson the butcher's day to come, but he had not yet done so, and there was no fresh meat in the house.

Oh Grace, said Nancy, we will have to kill a chicken, just step out and request McDermott to do it. I said that surely we would need two chickens, as there would be six to dine, with the ladies; but she was annoyed, and said there would be no ladies, as the wives of these gentlemen never condescended to darken the door of the house, and she herself would not be taking dinner with them in the dining room, as all they would do was drink and smoke and tell stories about what fine deeds they'd done in the Rebellion, and they would stay too long and play cards after, and it was bad for Mr. Kinnear's health, and he would catch a cough, as was always the case when these men came to visit. She allowed him a poor constitution when it suited her.

When I went out to look for James McDermott, he was nowhere to be found. I called, and I even went so far as to go up the ladder into the loft over the stables where he slept. He was not there; but he had not run off, as his things were still in the loft, such as he had; and I didn't think he would go away without the pay that was owed him. As I came down the steps there was Jamie Walsh, and he looked at me curiously, thinking I suppose that I'd been visiting McDermott; but when I asked where McDermott could have gone, as he was needed, Jamie Walsh smiled at me again, and was friendly, and said he did not know, but that he might have gone across the road to Harvey's, who was a coarse fellow who lived in a log house, more like a shack, with a woman not his wife – I knew her by sight, her name was Hannah Upton, and she had a rough look to her and was generally avoided. But Harvey was an acquaintance of McDermott's – I won't say friend – and the two of them were in the habit of drinking together; and Jamie then said was there any errands to be run.

I went back into the kitchen and said McDermott could not be found, and Nancy said she'd had enough of his lazy ways, he was always going off when required and leaving her in the lurch, and I would have to kill the chicken myself. I said, Oh no, I could not do that, I've never done it before and don't know how; as I had an aversion to shedding the blood of any living thing, although I could pluck a bird well enough once killed; and she said not to be a silly goose, it was easy enough, just take the axe and knock it on the head, and then give it a strong whack right through the neck.

But I could not bear the thought of it, and began to cry; and I am sorry to say – for it is wrong to speak ill of the dead – that she gave me a shake and a slap, and pushed me out the kitchen door into the courtyard, and told me not to come back without a dead bird, and in a hurry too, as we did not have much time to prepare, and Mr. Kinnear liked his meals on time.

I went into the henyard and caught a plump young fowl, a white one, crying all the time, and tucked it securely under my arm, and went towards the woodpile and the chopping block, wiping my tears with my apron; for I did not see how I could bring myself to do such a thing. But Jamie Walsh followed me, and asked kindly what was the matter; and I said could he please just kill the chicken for me; and he said there was nothing easier, and he would be glad to do so as I was so squeamish and tender-hearted. So he took the bird from me and neatly chopped off its head, and it ran about with only a neck for a moment, and then lay kicking in the dirt; and I thought it was very pathetic. And then we plucked it together, sitting side by side on a rail of the fence, and making the feathers fly; and then I thanked him sincerely for his help, and said I did not have anything to give him for it, but would remember it for the future. And he grinned awkwardly and said he would help me willingly at any other time I might need it.

Nancy had come out at the last part of this, and was standing at the kitchen door with her hand up to shade her eyes, waiting impatiently for the bird to be readied for cooking; so I cleaned it as fast as I could, holding my breath against the smell and keeping the giblets in case wanted for gravy, and rinsed it under the pump, and brought it in. And she said in the kitchen, as we were stuffing it, Well I see you have made a conquest, and I said what did she mean, and she said, Jamie Walsh, he has a bad case of puppy love, it is written all over his face, he used to be my admirer but now I see he is yours. And I saw she was trying to be friends with me again, after having lost her temper; so I laughed, and said he was not much of a catch for me, as he was only a boy, and with red hair like a carrot and freckled as an egg too, although tall for his age. And she said, Well, a worm will always turn; which I thought mysterious; but did not ask her what she meant, in case she should think me ignorant.

We had to get the stove good and hot in the summer kitchen, to roast the chicken; so we did the rest of the work in the winter one. To be served with the chicken we prepared a dish of creamed onions and carrots; and for the dessert there were strawberries, with our own cream, and our own cheese after. Mr. Kinnear kept the wine in the cellar, some in a barrel and some in bottles; and Nancy sent me down to bring up five bottles of it. She never did like going down there; she said there were too many spiders.

In the midst of all our bustling, James McDermott sauntered in, as cool as you please; and when Nancy asked him where he'd got himself off to, using a warm tone of voice, he said that since he'd finished the morning's chores before he left, it was none of her damned business; and if she must know, he'd been on a special errand of Mr. Kinnear's, entrusted to him before Mr. Kinnear left for Toronto; and Nancy said she would see about that, and he had no right to come and go, and to vanish off the face of the earth, just when he might be wanted most; and he said how was he to know, he could not read the future; and she said that if he could, he would see that he would not spend much more of it in this house. But as she was occupied at the moment, she would speak to him later, and just now he might look after Mr. Kinnear's horse, which was in need of grooming after the long ride, if he didn't consider such a thing too far beneath His Royal Highness. And he went off to the stables with a scowling face.

Colonel Bridgeford and Captain Boyd arrived as promised, and behaved as Nancy said they would; and there were loud voices from the dining room, and much laughter; and Nancy had me wait on table. She did not wish to do it herself, but sat in the kitchen, and had a glass of wine, and poured one for me as well; and I thought she was resentful of these gentlemen. She said she did not think Captain Boyd was a real Captain, as some of them had taken up such titles just for having got their two legs around a horse on the day of the Rebellion; and I asked, what about Mr. Kinnear, as some in the neighbourhood called him Captain as well; and she said she did not know about it, as he never styled himself in that manner, and his visiting card said plain Mr.; however, if he had been a Captain, it would certainly have been on the Government side. And this was another thing she appeared to resent.

She poured herself a second glass of wine, and said that Mr. Kinnear sometimes teased her about her name, and called her a fiery little Rebel, because her last name was Montgomery, which was the same as John Montgomery who'd owned the tavern where the rebels met together, and which was now a ruin; and he'd boasted that when his enemies were burning in Hell, he would be keeping a tavern again on Yonge Street; which afterwards turned out to be true, Sir, at least as to the tavern; but at that time he was still in the United States, having escaped in a daring manner from the Kingston Penitentiary. So it is a possible thing to be done.

Nancy poured herself a third glass of wine, and said that she was getting too fat, and whatever would she do, and put her head down on her arms; but it was time for me to carry in the coffee, so I could not ask her why she had become so melancholy all of a sudden. In the dining room they were very merry, having consumed all five bottles and called for more; and Captain Boyd said where had Mr. Kinnear found me, and were there any more growing on the tree that I came from, and if so were they ripe yet; and Colonel Bridgeford said what had Tom Kinnear done with Nancy, was she locked up in a cupboard somewhere with the rest of his Turkish harem; and Captain Boyd said I should look to my fine blue eyes, or Nancy might scratch them out, if old Tom so much as winked at me sideways. It was all in fun, but still I hoped that Nancy had not heard.

On the Sunday morning, Nancy said I should go to church with her. I said that I didn't have a good-enough dress, though this was an excuse – I did not much want to go, among strangers, where I would be sure to be stared at. But she said she would lend me a dress of hers, which she did, though she took care that it was one of her second best, and not so fine as what she herself put on. And she lent me a bonnet as well, and said I looked very proper; and also she let me wear a pair of her gloves, which did not however fit as they should, as Nancy had large hands. Also we each wore a light shawl of patterned silk.

Mr. Kinnear was nursing a headache, and said he would not go – he was never much of a church man in any case – but said McDermott could drive us in the wagon, and fetch us again later, it being understood that he would not attend the service, as he was a Catholic and the church was Presbyterian. It was the only church built there so far, and many who were not by rights members of that church attended it, as being better than nothing; and it had the only graveyard in town as well, so held a monopoly of the dead as well as of the living.

We sat up in the wagon as fine as anything, and the day was bright and fair, with the birds singing, and I felt at peace with the world, as much as I ever did, which was fitting for the day. As we walked into the church Nancy put her arm through mine, out of friendship I believed. Some heads were turned, but I thought it was because I was new to them. There were all different sorts of people there, the poorer farmers and their wives, and servants, and the tradesmen of the town, as well as those who from their dress and from their positions in the front pews thought themselves gentry, or next door to it. We sat on the benches at the back, which was the proper thing.

The minister looked like a heron, with a pointed beak of a nose and a long skinny neck, and a tuft of hair sticking up from the top of his head. The sermon was on the subject of Divine Grace, and how we could be saved by it alone, and not through any efforts on our own part, or any good works we might do. But this did not mean we should stop making efforts, or doing good works; but we could not count on them, or be certain that we had been saved, just because we were respected for our efforts and good works; because Divine Grace was a mystery, and the recipients of it were known to God alone; and although Scripture said that by their fruits you would know them, the fruits meant were spiritual fruits, and not visible to any but God alone; and although we must and should pray for Divine Grace, we should not be so puffed up with vanity as to believe that our prayers might have any effect, because man proposes but God disposes, and it was not up to our puny sinful and mortal souls to determine the course of events. The first would be last and the last would be first, and some that had been warming themselves by worldly fires for many years would soon find themselves roasting in something a good deal hotter, much to their indignation and surprise; and there were many whited sepulchres walking around in our midst, fair on the outside but filled with rot and corruption within; and we should beware of the woman sitting at the door of her house, which Proverbs 9 warns of, or of any such who might tempt us by saying that stolen waters are sweet, and bread eaten in secret is pleasant; because as Scripture tells, the dead are there, and her guests are in the depths of Hell; and above all we should guard against complacency, like the Foolish Virgins, and should not let our lamps go out; because no man knew the day and the hour thereof; and we must await in fear and trembling.

He went on in this way for some time, and I found myself examining the bonnets of the ladies present, as much as I could see of them from the back; and the flowers on their shawls; and I said to myself that if you could not get Divine Grace by praying for it, or any other way, or ever know if you had it or not, then you might as well forget about the whole matter, and go about your own business, because whether you would be damned or saved was no concern of yours. There is no use crying over spilt milk if you don't know whether the milk is spilt or not, and if God alone knew, then God alone could tidy it up if necessary. But thinking about such matters makes me drowsy, and the minister had a droning voice; and I was on the verge of nodding off, when we were all on our feet singing *Abide With Me*, or so I recall; which was not very well sung by the congregation, but at least it was music, which is always a consolation.

Nancy and I were not greeted warmly by any as we went out, but rather avoided; although some of the poorer sort nodded; and there were whisperings as we went past; which I found odd, as although I was an unknown, Nancy herself must have been familiar to them; and though the gentry or those who fancied themselves such need not notice her, she did not deserve such treatment from the farmers and their wives, and from the others there who hired out as servants. Nancy held her head up high, and did not look to left or right; and I thought, These are cold and proud people, and not good neighbours. They are hypocrites, they think the church is a cage to keep God in, so he will stay locked up there and not go wandering about the earth during the week, poking his nose into their business, and looking into the depths and darkness and doubleness of their hearts, and their lack of true charity; and they believe they need only be bothered about him on Sundays when they have their best clothes on and their faces straight, and their hands washed and their gloves on, and their stories all prepared. But God is everywhere, and cannot be caged in, as men can.

Nancy thanked me for going to church with her, and said she'd been glad of the company. But she wanted me to give the dress and bonnet back that very day, as she was concerned that they might get soiled.

Later that week, McDermott came into the kitchen for the midday dinner with a long and sullen face. Nancy had given him his notice, and he was to leave at the end of the month. He said he was just as glad, as he did not like being ordered about by a woman, and had never been thus while in the army or on the boats; but when he'd complained about it, Mr. Kinnear only said that Nancy was the mistress of the house, and was paid to arrange things, and McDermott should take his orders from her, as Mr. Kinnear could not bother himself about trifling details. So that was bad; but it was much worse, considering what type of a woman she was. And he did not care to stay any longer with such a parcel of whores.

I was shocked by this, and thought it was just McDermott's fashion, and the way he talked, and exaggerated, and lied; and I asked him indignantly what he meant by that. And he said did I not know that Nancy and Mr. Kinnear slept together, as bold as brass, and lived in secret as man and wife, though they were no more married than he was; although it was no secret, as all the neighbourhood knew of it. I was much surprised, and said so; and McDermott said I was an idiot, and despite my Mrs. Alderman Parkinson this and Mrs. Alderman Parkinson that, and my city notions, I was not so knowing as I thought myself, and could scarcely see the nose before my own face; and as for the whorishness of Nancy, anyone but a simpleton such as me would have found it out at once, as it was only the common knowledge that Nancy had a baby when she was working over at Wrights', by a young layabout who ran off and left her, only the baby died. But Mr. Kinnear hired her and took her in anyway, which no respectable man would have done; and it was clear from the first what he'd had in mind, because once the horse was out of the stable it was no good shutting the barn door, and a woman once on her back was like a turtle in the same plight, she could scarcely turn herself right side up again, and was fair game for all.

Although I still protested, it came to me that for once he was telling the truth; and I saw in a flash the meaning of the averted heads at church, and the whisperings, and also many other small things I had not taken much notice of; as well as the fine dresses and the gold earrings, which were the wages of sin, you might say; and even the warning of Mrs. Watson's cook Sally, which was given to me before

I had ever consented to be hired. After that I kept my eyes and ears open, and went about the house like a spy, and made sure that Nancy's bed was never slept in, when Mr. Kinnear was at home. And I was ashamed of myself for letting myself be tricked and imposed on in this fashion, and for being so blind and foolish.

2 9 .

I am sorry to say that after this I lost much of the respect I'd once felt for Nancy, as being older, and the mistress of the house; and I let my scorn show, and answered her back more than was wise, and there were arguments between us which came to raised voices, and on her side to a slap or two; for she had a quick temper and a flat hand. But I so far remembered my place as not to strike her back; and if I'd held my tongue, my ears would have rung less often. So I take some of the blame upon myself.

Mr. Kinnear did not seem to notice the discord. If anything he became kinder to me than before, and would stop beside me when I was at my various chores, and ask me how I was getting on, and I would always tell him, Very well Sir, because there is nothing such a gentleman would wish to get rid of sooner than a discontented servant – you are paid to smile, and it does well to remember it. And he would tell me I was a good girl and a brisk worker. And once when I was lugging a bucket of water up the stairs, for Mr. Kinnear's bath which he'd asked to be filled in his dressing room, he said why was McDermott not doing that, as it was too heavy for me. I said it was my task to do; and he wanted to take the bucket from me, and carry it up himself, and put his hand over mine on the handle. Oh no Sir, said I, I cannot allow it; and he laughed, and said it was up to him what would be allowed or not, for he was master of the house, was he not? Which I had to say yes. And as we were standing thus, close together on the stairs with his hand on mine, Nancy came into the downstairs hall, and saw us; which did nothing to improve her disposition towards me.

I have often thought that all would have gone better if there had been a separate staircase for the servants at the back of the house, as was usual; but there was none. And that meant we were all obliged to live too close together, and in one another's pockets, which was not a desirable thing; as you could scarcely cough or laugh in that house without it being heard, especially from the downstairs hall.

As for McDermott, he became more brooding and vengeful by the day; and he said that Nancy planned to turn him off before the month was up, and to withhold his wages, but that he would not stand for it; and if she treated him so, she would soon treat me the same way, and that we should join together and demand our rights. And when Mr. Kinnear was away, and Nancy was visiting with her friends the Wrights – for they were among the neighbours who were still friendly towards her – he dipped more frequently into Mr. Kinnear's whisky, which was bought by the keg and thus in plentiful supply, and none to take account if some went missing. At these times he would say that he hated all Englishmen, and though Kinnear was a lowland Scot it was the same thing, they were all thieves and whores, and stealers of land, and ground down the poor wherever they went; and both Mr. Kinnear and Nancy deserved to be knocked on the head and thrown down into the cellar, and he was the man for the deed.

But I thought this was just a way of talking, as he was always a boaster, and saying what great things he would do; and my own father when drunk had often threatened to serve my mother in this way, but had never in fact done so. The best thing at such times was just to nod and agree with him, and to take no further notice.

Dr. Jordan looks up from the notes he is making. So you did not believe him, at first? he says.

Not at all, Sir, I say. Nor would you, if you yourself had been listening. I took it all for idle threats.

Before he was hanged, McDermott said that you were the one who put him up to it, says Dr. Jordan. He claimed you intended to murder Nancy and Mr. Kinnear by putting poison into their porridge, and that you repeatedly urged him to help you; which he very piously refused to do.

Who told you such a lie? I say.

It is written in McDermott's Confession, says Dr. Jordan; which I knew very well, having read the selfsame thing myself, in the Governor's wife's scrapbook.

Just because a thing has been written down, Sir, does not mean it is God's truth, I say.

He laughs his bark of a laugh, Hah, and tells me I am quite right about that. All the same, Grace, he says, what do you say to it?

Well Sir, I say, I think it is one of the silliest things I have ever heard.

Why is that, Grace? says he.

I allow myself to smile. If I wanted to put poison into a bowl of porridge, Sir, why would I have needed any help from such as him? I could have done it all by myself, and put some in his own porridge too, into the bargain. It would not take any more strength than the adding of a spoonful of sugar.

You are very cool about it, Grace, says Dr. Jordan. Why do you think he said that about you, if it was false?

I suppose he wanted to shift the blame, I say slowly. He never did like being put in the wrong. And perhaps he wanted me to keep him company on the journey. The road to death is a lonely highway, and longer than it appears, even when it leads straight down from the scaffold, by way of a rope; and it's a dark road, with never any moon shining on it, to light your way.

You seem to know a good deal about it, Grace, for one who has never been there, says he, with his uneven smile.

I have not been there, I say, except in dreams; but I have looked along it many a night. I too was condemned to be hanged, and thought I would be; and it was only by luck, and the skill of Mr. MacKenzie, who pleaded my extreme youth, that I was got off. When you believe that you yourself are soon to go the same road, you must take your bearings of it.

True enough, says he in a thoughtful voice.

Nor do I blame poor James McDermott, I say. Not for such a wish. I would never blame a human creature for feeling lonely.

The next Wednesday was my birthday. As things had cooled between Nancy and myself, I did not expect her to acknowledge it, although she knew the date well enough, as I'd told her my age when hired, and when I would turn sixteen; but to my surprise, when she came into the kitchen in the morning she was very friendly, and wished me a happy birthday, and went around to the front of the house herself and picked a little bouquet of roses, from the trellises there, and put them into a glass for me to have in my room. And I was so grateful for the kindness from her, which was rare enough by that time, what with our quarrelling, that I almost cried.

Then she said I could have the afternoon free, as it was my birthday. And I thanked her very much. But I said I wouldn't know what to do with myself, as I had no friends in the neighbourhood to visit, and there were no real shops, and nothing to see; and perhaps I should just stay at home, and sew, or clean the silver, as I'd been planning to do. And she said I could stroll into the village if I liked, or go for a pleasant walk in the countryside around; and I could borrow her straw hat.

But later I learnt that Mr. Kinnear intended to be at home all that afternoon; and I suspected that Nancy wanted me out of the way so she could spend time with him alone, without worrying about whether I would come suddenly into the room or up the stairs, or whether Mr. Kinnear would wander back into the kitchen where I was, and hang about there, asking this and that, as he had been tending to do of late.

However, after I'd taken in the dinner for Mr. Kinnear and Nancy, which was cold roast beef and a salad, as the weather was hot, and had eaten my own dinner with McDermott in the winter kitchen, and had cleaned up the dishes, and washed my hands and face, I took off my apron and hung it up, and put on Nancy's straw hat and my white and blue kerchief for keeping the sun off the neck; and McDermott, who was still sitting at the table, asked where I was going. And I said it was my birthday, and therefore Nancy had given me leave to go out for a walk. He said he would come with me, as there were many rough men and vagabonds on the roads that I needed protection from. It was on the tip of my tongue to say that the only one such I knew of was sitting right there in the kitchen with me; but as McDermott had made an effort to be civil, I bit my tongue and thanked him for his kind thoughts, but said it was not required.

He said he would come in any case, as I was young and flighty and did not know what was good for me; and I said it was not his birthday, and he had the chores to do; and he said birthday be damned, he did not give a pin for birthdays, and he saw it as no cause for celebration, as he was not overly thankful to his mother for having given birth to him; and even if it was his birthday, Nancy would never give him any time off for it. And I said he should not begrudge it to me, as I had not asked for it and wanted no special favours. And I left the kitchen as soon as I could.

I had no idea in my mind of where I should go. I did not want to walk into the main part of the village, where there was no one I knew; and it struck me at once how very solitary I was, as I had no friends here except Nancy, if she could be called a friend, being such a weathervane, a friend one day and the next quite turned against me; and perhaps Jamie Walsh, but he was a mere boy. There was Charley, but he was a horse, and although a good listener and a comfort, of not much avail when I needed advice.

I did not know where my family was, which was the same as having none; not that I ever wished to see my father again, but I would have been glad of some news of the children. There was Aunt Pauline, and I could have written her a letter, if I'd been able to afford the postage; for this was before the reforms, and to send a letter far across the sea was very expensive. If you looked at things in the cold light of day, I was indeed alone in the world, with no prospects before me except the drudgery I'd been doing; and although I could always find a different situation, still it would be the same sort of work, from dawn to dusk, with always a mistress to be ordering me about.

So thinking, I walked down the driveway, keeping up a brisk-enough pace while McDermott might be watching; and indeed when I turned once, there he was, leaning in the kitchen doorway. For if I loitered, he might take it as an invitation to join me. But when I reached the orchard, I thought myself out of sight, and slowed down. I usually kept a firm-enough grip on my feelings, yet there is something depressing to the spirits about a birthday, espe-cially when alone; and I turned into the orchard, and sat down with my back against one of the big old stumps that were left over from the forest when it was cleared. The birds were singing around me, but I reflected that the very birds were strangers to me, for I did not even know their names; and that seemed to me the saddest of all, and the tears began to roll down my cheeks; and I did not dry them, but indulged myself in weeping for several minutes.

But then I said to myself, What can't be cured must be endured; and I looked around at the white daisies and the Queen Anne's lace, and at the purple globes of the milkweed flowers, which smelled so sweetly and were covered with orange butterflies; and then I looked up at the branches of the apple tree above me, where the small green apples were already forming, and at the patches of blue sky visible beyond, and attempted to cheer myself up, by reflecting that only a benevolent God, who had our good at heart, would have created so much beauty, and that whatever burdens were laid upon me were surely trials, to test my strength and faith, as with the early Christians, and Job, and the martyrs. But as I have said, thoughts about God often make me drowsy; and I fell asleep.

It is a strange thing, but however deeply asleep I may be, I can always sense when there is a person come close, or watching me. It's as if there is a part of me that never sleeps at all, but keeps one eye a little open; and when I was younger I used to think this was my guardian angel. But perhaps it comes from my early days, when to sleep past my time for getting up, and starting the work of the house, would be the occasion for shouts on the part of my father, and harsh words, and I would find myself hauled up out of sleep by one arm, or else by the hair. In any case, I was dreaming that a bear had come out of the forest, and was looking at me. Then I woke with a start, just as if a hand had been laid on me; and there was a man standing quite near, against the sun so I couldn't see his face. I gave a little shriek, and began to scramble up. But then I saw it was not a man, but only Jamie Walsh; and I remained where I was.

Oh Jamie, I said, you startled me.

I didn't mean to, he said. And he sat down beside me under the tree. Then he said, What are you doing here in the middle of the day? Won't Nancy be after you? For he was a very inquisitive boy, and always asking questions.

I explained about my birthday, and said it was kind of Nancy to give me the entire afternoon to myself. And he wished me a happy birthday. Then he said, I saw you crying.

And I said, Where were you, to be spying on me like that?

He said he often came to the orchard, when Mr. Kinnear wasn't looking; and later in the season, Mr. Kinnear sometimes stood on the verandah and used his telescope, to make sure the boys around were not robbing his orchard; but the apples and pears were still too green for that. Then he said, Why are you sad, Grace?

I felt I would cry again, and said simply, I have no friends here.

Jamie said, I am your friend. Then he paused, and said, Do you have a sweetheart, Grace? And I said I did not. And he said, I would like to be your sweetheart. And in a few years, when I'm older and have saved the money for it, we will be married.

I could not keep myself from smiling at that. I said, making a joke of it, But are you not in love with Nancy. And he said, No, though I like her well enough. Then he said, So what do you say to it?

But Jamie, I said, I am a great deal older than you; and I spoke as if teasing. For I could not believe he was in earnest.

A year and a bit, he said. A year is nothing.

Still, you are only a boy, I said.

I am taller than you, he said. Which was true. But I don't know why it is, a girl of fifteen or sixteen is accounted a woman, but a boy of fifteen or sixteen is still a boy. I did not say this however, seeing it was a sore point with him; so I thanked him gravely for his offer, and told him I would consider it, as I did not wish to hurt his feelings.

Come, he said, as it is your birthday, I will play you a tune. And he took out his fife, and played *The Soldier Boy to the Wars Has Gone*, very nicely and with feeling, although a trifle shrill on the top notes. And then he played *Believe Me If All These Endearing Young Charms*. And I could tell that these must have been some new pieces that he was practising, and he was proud of them; so I told him how lovely it was.

After that he said he would make me a daisy crown, in honour of the day; and the two of us set to making daisy chains, and were very busy and industrious over them, just like small children; and I don't think I'd enjoyed myself more since the times with Mary Whitney. When we were finished, he very solemnly put one chain around my hat, and another around my neck, for a necklace, and said I was the May Queen; and I said I would have to be the July Queen, as it was July, and we laughed. And he asked if he could give me a kiss on the cheek; which I said yes, but only one; and he did it. And I told him that he had made my birthday a fine occasion after all, because he'd taken my mind off all of my worries; and he smiled at that.

But the time had gone flying by, and the afternoon was now over. As I came back up the drive I saw Mr. Kinnear standing on the verandah, and looking at me with his telescope; and as I approached the back door, he walked around the side of the house, and said, Good afternoon, Grace.

I returned it, and he said, Who was that man with you in the orchard? And what were you doing with him?

I could hear in his voice what sort of suspicions he was entertaining; and I said it was only young Jamie Walsh, and we were making daisy chains because it was my birthday. And he accepted that, but was none too pleased all the same. And when I went into the kitchen to begin the preparations for supper, Nancy said, What is that wilted flower doing in your hair? It looks very silly.

There was one, which had got caught when I was taking off the daisy necklace.

But these two things together took some of the innocence out of the day.

So I set about cooking the supper; and when McDermott came in later with an armful of wood for the stove, he said in a sneering manner, So, you were rolling about in the grass, and kissing the errand boy, he should have his brains knocked out for that, and I'd do it for him myself if he wasn't such a baby. It's clear you prefer the boys to the men, such a fine cradle-robber you are. And I said, I was doing no such thing. But he did not believe me.

I felt as though my afternoon had not been mine at all, and not a kind and private thing, but had been spied upon by every one of them – with Mr. Kinnear included, which I did not think he would have stooped so low – exactly as if they'd all been lined up in a row at the door of my chamber, and taking turns at looking through the keyhole; which made me very sad, and also angry.

3 0 .

Several days now passed without event. I had been at Mr. Kinnear's almost two weeks, but it seemed a good deal longer, for time was hanging heavy on my hands, as it does tend to do, Sir, when a person is not happy. Mr. Kinnear was away on horseback, I believe he had gone over to Thornhill, and Nancy had gone visiting to her friend Mrs. Wright's. Jamie Walsh had not been over to the house of late, and I wondered if McDermott had threatened him, and told him to keep away.

I do not know where McDermott was; I expect he was asleep in the barn. I was not on good terms with him, as he'd started in that morning on what fine eyes I had, all the better to make eyes at young lads who still had their milk teeth, and I'd told him to keep his conversation to himself as he was the only one in the room who enjoyed it, and he'd said I had a tongue in my head like a viper, and I said that if he wanted someone who wouldn't answer back, why didn't he go out to the barn and make love to the cow, which is the kind of thing Mary Whitney would have said, or so I told myself.

I was in the kitchen garden, picking the new peas and turning the anger over in my mind – for I was still angry over the suspicions and prying I had been subject to, as well as McDermott's bitter teasing – when I heard a tuneful whistling, and I saw a man coming up the drive with a pack on his back and a weather-beaten hat on his head, and a long walking-stick in his hand.

It was Jeremiah the peddler. I was so glad to see a face from better times that I dropped the peas out of my apron in a heap on the ground, and waved, and ran down the drive to meet him. For he was an old friend, or so I thought of him by then. In a new country, friends become old friends very quickly.

Well, Grace, he said, I told you I would come.

And I am very glad to see you, Jeremiah, I said.

I walked with him to the back door of the house, and I said, What do you have with you today? For I always loved to see the contents of a peddler's pack, even if most of the things were beyond my means.

He said, Aren't you going to invite me into the kitchen, Grace, out of the sun where it is cool? And I remembered that this was the way it was done at Mrs. Alderman Parkinson's, and I did so; and once he was inside I sat him down at the kitchen table, and got him some small beer from the pantry, and a cup of cold water; and I cut him a slice of bread and cheese. I was quite the busybody, as I felt that he was a guest of a kind, and I was by way of being the hostess, and so should do the hospitable thing. And I had a glass of beer too, to keep him company.

Here's to your good health, Grace, he said. I thanked him and returned it. And are you happy here? he said.

The house is a very beautiful one, I said, with pictures and a piano. For I did not like to speak ill of anyone, and especially not my master and mistress.

But in a quiet and removed situation, he said, regarding me with his bright and shining eyes. He had eyes like blackberries, and the air of being able to see more than most could; and I could tell he was trying to look into my mind; but in a kindly way. For I believe he always had a regard for me.

It is quiet, I said. But Mr. Kinnear is a liberal gentleman.

And with a gentleman's tastes, he said, giving me a shrewd look. They say in the neighbourhood that he has a hankering after the servant-girls, especially those close to home. I hope you will not end up like Mary Whitney.

I was startled at that, for I thought I was the only one to know the truth about that affair, and which gentleman it was, and how close to home, and I'd never told a living soul. How did you guess it? I said.

He put his finger alongside his nose, to signify silence and wisdom; and said, The future lies hid in the present, for those that can read it. And since he already knew so much, I unburdened myself to him, and told him everything I have told you, Sir, even the part where I heard Mary's voice, and fainted, and ran about the house with no recollection of it; except about the doctor, as I felt Mary would not want it known. But I believe Jeremiah guessed about it, for he was a great man for divining what was meant, even when not spoken out loud.

That is a sad story, said Jeremiah, when I had done. As for you, Grace, a stitch in time saves nine. You know that Nancy was the servant of the house, not so long ago, and did all the rough and dirty work that you do now.

This was very direct, and I looked down. I did not know that, I said.

Once a man gets a habit it is hard to break, he said. It's like a dog gone to the bad – once a sheep is killed, the dog will get a taste for it, and must kill another.

Have you been travelling very much, I said; as I did not like this talk of killing.

Yes, he said, I am always on the move. I was lately down in the States, where I can buy notions cheap, and sell them up here for more; for that is how we peddlers earn our bread. We must be paid for our shoe leather.

And what is it like there? I said. Some say it is better.

In many ways it is the same as here, he said. There are rogues and scoundrels everywhere, but they use a different sort of language to excuse themselves; and there they pay a great lip service to democracy, just as here they rant on about the right order of society, and loyalty to the Queen; though the poor man is poor on every shore. But when you cross over the border, it is like passing through air, you wouldn't know you'd done it; as the trees on both sides of it are the same. And it's generally through the trees I go, and by night; as paying the Customs duties on my goods would be an inconvenience to me; and also the price to such good customers as you would have to go up, he said with a smile.

But are you not breaking the law? said I. And what would become of you if caught?

Laws are made to be broken, he said, and these laws were not made by me or mine, but by the powers that be, and for their own profit. But I am harming no one. A man with any spirit in him likes a challenge, and to outwit others; and as to being caught, I'm an old fox, and have been at it a few too many years for that. Also I am a lucky man, as can be read inside my hand. And he showed me a cross on the palm of his right hand, and one on the left as well, both of them in the shape of an X; and he said he was protected both asleep and awake, as the left hand was the hand of dreams. And I looked into my own hands, but could not see any such crosses.

Luck can run out, I said. I hope you will be careful.

Why Grace, do you have a tender concern for my safety? said he with a smile; and I looked down at the table. Indeed, he said more seriously, I have thought about giving up this line of work, as there is now more competition than formerly, and with the improvement of the roads, many go into the towns to make their purchases, instead of staying at home and buying from me.

I was disappointed to hear he might stop the peddling, as it meant he would not be coming any more with his pack. But what would you do then? I said.

I could go about the fairs, he said, and be a fire-eater, or else a medical clairvoyant, and trade in Mesmerism and Magnetism, which is always a draw. As a younger man I was in partnership with a woman who knew the business, as the thing is generally worked in couples; I was the one who made the passes and also took in the money, and she was the one to have a muslin veil put over her, and go into a trance, and speak in a hollow voice, and tell the people what was wrong with them, for a fee of course. It is wellnigh fool-proof, for as they can't see inside their own bodies, who's to say whether you are right or not? But the woman got tired of it, or else of me; and went off down the Mississippi on one of the boats. Or I could become a preacher, he continued. Below the border there's a great demand for it, more so than here, in particular during the summers, when the preaching is done outdoors, or in tents; and the people there love to fall down in fits, and talk in tongues, and be saved once a summer, or more if available; for which they are willing to show their gratitude by a liberal scattering of coinage. That's a promising line of work, and rightly carried on, it pays a good deal more than this.

I did not know you were religious, I said.

Nor am I, said he; but so far as I can tell it is not required. Many of the preachers there have no more faith in God than a stone.

I said it was wicked of him to say so, but he only laughed. So long as the people get what they come for, what does it matter? he said. I would give full measure. A faithless preacher with a good manner and voice will always convert more than a limp-handed long-faced fool, no matter how Godly. Then he struck a solemn pose, and intoned, Those strong in the faith know, that in the Lord's hands even the infirm vessel is put to right use.

I see you have made a study of it already, I said, for he did sound exactly like a preacher; and he laughed again. But then he looked more earnest, and leant across the table. I think you should come away with me, Grace, he said. I don't like the feel of things.

Come away? I said. What do you mean?

You would be safer with me than you are here, he said.

At that I gave a shiver, for it was close to what I myself had been feeling, although I did not know it until then. But what would I do? I said.

You could travel with me, he said. You could be a medical clairvoyant; I would teach you how, and instruct you in what to say, and put you into the trances. I know by your hand that you have a talent for it; and with your hair down you would have the right look. I promise you'd earn more that way in two days than you do scrubbing the floors here in two months. You would need a different name, of course; a French one or something foreign, because the people on this side of the ocean would find it hard to believe that a woman with the plain name of Grace had mysterious powers. The unknown is always more wonderful to them than the known, and more convincing.

I said, wouldn't that be a deception and a cheat? And Jeremiah said, no more than at the theatre. For if people wish to believe a thing, and long for it and depend on it to be true, and feel the better for it, is it cheating to help them to their own belief, by such an insubstantial thing as a name? Is it not rather a charity, and a human kindness? And when he put the thing that way, it had a better light on it.

I said that a new name would pose no problem for me, as I had no great attachment to my own, it having been my father's. And he smiled, and said, Let us shake hands on it then.

I won't conceal from you, Sir, that the idea was greatly tempting; for Jeremiah was a handsome man, with his white teeth and dark eyes, and I recalled that I was supposed to marry a man with a J to his name; and I thought also of the money I might have, and the clothes I could buy with it, and perhaps some gold earrings as well; and I would also see many other places and towns, and not always be doing the same hard and dirty chores. But then I remembered what had happened to Mary Whitney; and although Jeremiah seemed kindly, appearances can be deceptive, as she found to her cost. What if things went wrong, and I was left in the lurch by myself in a strange place?

Would we be married, then? I said.

What would be the need of that? he said. Marriage never did any good, as far as I can see; for if the two are of a mind to keep together, they will; and if not, then one of them will run off, and that's the long and short of it.

This alarmed me. I think I had better stay here, I said. In any case I am too young to be married.

Consider it, Grace, he said. For I wish you well, and am willing to help you, and care for you. And I tell you truly that you are surrounded by dangers here.

At this moment McDermott entered the room, and I wondered if he had been listening outside the door, and for how long; for he seemed very angry. He asked Jeremiah who the Devil he might be, and what the Devil he was doing in the kitchen.

I said that Jeremiah was a peddler, and well known to me from former days; and McDermott looked at the pack – which was opened by this time, for Jeremiah had opened it up as we were talking, although he had not spread out all of the things – and said that was all very well, but Mr. Kinnear would be annoyed to find out that I had been wasting good beer and cheese on a common rogue of a peddler. He said this not because he cared two straws about what Mr. Kinnear might think, but only to insult Jeremiah.

And I replied that Mr. Kinnear was generous-minded, and would not refuse an honest man a cold drink on a hot day. And at that McDermott scowled even more, for he did not like it if I praised Mr. Kinnear.

Then Jeremiah, to get between and make the peace, said that he had some shirts, which although used were good ones, and a bargain; and they were just the size to fit McDermott; and although McDermott grumbled, Jeremiah brought them out, and displayed their qualities; and I knew McDermott was in need of some new shirts, having torn one of his past mending, and ruined another by letting it lie muddied and damp, so that the mildew got into it. And I saw that his attention was caught, and silently brought a mug of beer for him.

The shirts were marked H. C., and Jeremiah said they'd belonged to a soldier, a gallant fighter too; but not a dead one, for it was bad luck to wear the clothes of the dead; and he named a price, for all four. McDermott said he could only manage three at that price, and named a lower, and so they went on until Jeremiah said well, he would do it, he would give the four for the price of three, but not a penny less, although it was highway robbery and he would be bankrupt in no time if things went on this way; and McDermott was very pleased with himself to think he'd made such a tight bargain. But I could see by the twinkle in Jeremiah's eye that he was only pretending to let McDermott get the better of him, and in fact had come out of it very well.

Now, Sir, these were the very same shirts that figured so largely at the trial; and there was much confusion over them, firstly because McDermott said he'd got them from a peddler, and then changed his tune and said, From a soldier. But in a sense both were true; and I believe he turned the story that way because he did not want Jeremiah standing in court against him, knowing he was a friend of mine, and would help me, and would testify against McDermott's character; or so he must have thought. And secondly, because the newspapers could not get the number of shirts right. But there were four of them, not three, as they said; for two were in McDermott's carpetbag, and one was found covered with blood behind the kitchen door; which was the one McDermott had on when he was disposing of Mr. Kinnear's body. And the fourth was on Mr. Kinnear himself, because James McDermott put it there. So that makes four, not three.

I walked with Jeremiah partway down the drive, with McDermott looking on with a baleful scowl from the kitchen doorway; but I didn't care what he thought, as he was not my owner. When the time came to part, Jeremiah looked very earnestly at me, and said he would come back soon for my answer, and he hoped for my sake as well as his own that it would be yes. And I thanked him for his good wishes. Just knowing I could go away if I wanted to made me feel safer, and happier as well.

When I went back into the house, McDermott said it was a good riddance, and he didn't like the man, as he had a low foreign look about him; and he supposed he'd come sniffing around after me like a dog after a bitch in heat. I did not reply to this remark, as I found it very coarse, and was surprised by the violence of his expression; and I asked him to kindly remove himself from the kitchen, as it was now time for me to busy myself with the supper.

It was only then I remembered the peas that I'd dropped in the garden, and went outside to pick them up.

31.

Several days later, the doctor paid us a visit. Dr. Reid was his name, an elderly gentleman, or so he appeared; but with doctors it is hard to tell, as they put on grave faces and carry many sorts of illnesses about with them, in their leather satchels where they keep the knives, and this makes them old before their time; and as with crows, when you see two or three of them gathered together you know there is a death in the offing, and they are discussing it. With the crows they are deciding which parts they will tear open and make off with, and so it is with the doctors.

I do not mean you, Sir, as you have no leather bag or knives.

When I saw the doctor coming up the drive in his one-horse gig, I felt my heart beat painfully, and I thought I was about to faint; but I did not do so, as I was downstairs by myself and would have to answer for anything that might be needed. Nancy would be no help; she was upstairs lying down.

On the day before, I'd assisted her in fitting the new dress she was making, and so I'd spent an hour kneeling on the floor with my mouth full of pins while she turned around and viewed herself in front of the mirror. She remarked that she was getting too plump, and I said it was a good thing to have a bit of flesh, as it did not do to be all skin and bones, and that the young ladies nowadays were starving themselves because of the fashion, which was to be pale and sickly, and they laced their stays in so tight they fainted as soon as looked at. Mary Whitney used to say that no man wanted a skeleton, they liked something to take a hold of, some at the front and some at the back and the more arse the better; but I did not repeat this to Nancy. The dress she was making was a light cream-coloured American print with sprigs and buds, and a tucked bodice coming to a point below the waist, and three layers of flounced ruffles to the skirt; and I told her it was very becoming.

Nancy frowned at herself in the mirror, and said all the same her waist was getting too big, and if it kept on she would need a new pair of stays, and soon she would be a great fat fishwife.

I bit my tongue, and did not say that if she would keep her thumbs out of the butter she'd stand less chance of it. Half a loaf of bread she'd gobbled before breakfast, and spread with butter thick as tar, and plum jam on top of it. And the day before I'd seen her eating a slice of pure fat trimmed off the ham in the pantry.

She'd asked me to lace her stays just a little tighter, and then fit the waist again; but as I was doing so she said she felt unwell. It was no wonder, considering what she'd been eating, though I'd set it down as well to the tightness of the lacing. But this morning she'd also had a spell of dizziness, or so she said; and this after hardly any breakfast, and no tight lacing at all. So I was beginning to wonder what was the matter, and thought that perhaps the doctor had been summoned for Nancy.

When I saw the doctor coming, I was outside in the yard, pumping another pail of water for the wash; for it was a fine morning, with the air hard and clear, and bright hot sunlight, and a good drying day.

Mr. Kinnear went out to greet the doctor, who tied up his horse to the fence, and then they both went into the house by the front door. I went on with what I was doing and soon had the wash hanging up on the line, which was a white wash, consisting of shirts and nightdresses and petticoats and the like, but no bedsheets; and all the while I was wondering what business the doctor had with Mr. Kinnear.

The two of them had gone into Mr. Kinnear's little office, and shut the door; and after a moment's consideration I went quietly into the adjoining library to dust the books; but I was unable to hear anything from inside the office except a murmuring of voices.

I was imagining all sorts of things, such as Mr. Kinnear coughing up blood and gasping his last, and I was working myself up into a state over him; so when I heard the office door handle turning I went quickly along through the dining room into the front parlour with my duster and cloth, as it is always best to know the worst. Mr. Kinnear showed Dr. Reid to the front entrance, and the doctor said that he was sure they would have the pleasure of Mr. Kinnear's company for many years to come, and that Mr. Kinnear had been reading too many medical journals, which gave him ideas, and caused him to imagine things; and that there was nothing wrong with him that a healthy diet and regular hours would not cure; but for the sake of his liver he should limit his drink. This speech relieved me; yet I reflected that it was a thing a doctor may say to a man who is dying, to spare him the worry.

I looked cautiously out of the parlour, through the side window. Dr. Reid went over to his horse and gig, and the next thing I knew there was Nancy, with her shawl clutched around her and her hair half down, in conversation with him. She must have crept down the stairs without my hearing her, which meant she didn't wish Mr. Kinnear to hear her either. I thought she might be trying to find out what was wrong with Mr. Kinnear, if anything; but then it came to me that she could also be consulting him about her own sudden illness.

Dr. Reid drove off, and Nancy turned towards the back of the house. I heard Mr. Kinnear calling for her from the library; but as she was still outside, and might not want it known what she'd been doing, I went in to him myself. Mr. Kinnear did not look any the worse than usual, and was reading a copy of *The Lancet*, from the large pile of them he kept on a shelf. I'd sometimes peered into them myself while cleaning the room, but could not make head nor tail of a great deal that was in there, except that some of it was about bodily functions that ought not to be set down in print, even with all of the fancy names.

Well, Grace, said Mr. Kinnear. And where is your mistress?

I said she was not at all well, and was lying down upstairs, but if there was anything to be brought to him, I could do it myself. He said he wanted some coffee, if it was not too much trouble. I said it was not, although it might take a time, for I would have to build the fire up again; and he said when it was ready I should bring it in to him; and he thanked me, as always.

I went across the courtyard to the summer kitchen. Nancy was there, seated at the table and looking tired and sad, and quite pale. I said I hoped she was feeling better, and she said she was, and then asked me what I was doing, as I was stirring up the fire, which was nearly out. I said that Mr. Kinnear wanted me to make him some coffee, and to take it in to him.

But I always take in his coffee, said Nancy. Why did he ask you?

I said I was sure it was because she herself was not there. I was only trying to spare her the work, I said, as I knew she was ill.

I will take it in, she said. And Grace, this afternoon I would like you to scrub this floor. It is very dirty and I am tired of living in a pigpen.

I did not think the dirtiness of the floor had anything to do with it, but that I was being punished by her, for having gone into Mr. Kinnear's office by myself; which was most unjust, as I had only been attempting to help her.

Although the day had begun so fine and clear, by noon it had become very oppressive and glowering. There was no breeze moving anywhere, and the air was damp, and the sky had covered over with clouds of a sullen yellowish grey, but bright behind them, like heated metal; and it had a blank and foreboding look to it. In such weather it is often hard to breathe. But nonetheless, in the middle of the afternoon, when if things had been as usual I would have been sitting down, outside perhaps to catch a breath of air, with some mending, to give my feet a rest as I was on the two of them the most part of every day, I was down on my knees instead, scrubbing the stone floor of the summer kitchen. It did need a cleaning but I would just as soon have done it in cooler weather, as it was hot enough to fry an egg; and the sweat was pouring off me like water off a duck, if you'll excuse me for putting it that way, Sir. I was worried about the meat in the meat safe in the pantry, as there were more flies than was usual buzzing around it. If I was Nancy, I would never have ordered such a big slab of meat in such hot weather, as I was sure it would go off, which would be a waste and a shame; and it ought to have been put down in the cellar, for the coolness. But I knew it was no use my making any suggestions to her, as I would only get my head bitten off.

The floor was dirty as a stable, and I wondered when it had last been given a good cleaning. I'd swept it first, of course, and now I was washing it in the proper way, kneeling down with each knee on an old clout because of the hardness of the stone, and with my shoes and stockings off, because to do a good job you have to get right down to it, and my sleeves rolled up past the elbows and my skirt and petticoats pulled back between my legs and tucked behind into the sash of my apron, which is what you do, Sir, to save your stockings and clothes, as anyone knows who has ever scrubbed a floor. I had a good bristle brush for the scrubbing and an old cloth to wipe up, and I was working from the far corner, moving backwards towards the door; for you don't want to scrub yourself into a corner, Sir, when doing a task like this.

I heard someone come into the kitchen behind me. I'd left the door open to get what air there was, and so the floor would dry faster. I thought it must be McDermott.

Don't walk on my clean floor, you with your mucky boots, I said to him; and I kept on scrubbing.

He didn't answer, but neither did he go away. He stayed standing in the doorway, and it came to me that he was watching my bare ankles and legs, dirty as they were, and – if you'll excuse me, Sir – my backside moving back and forth with the scrubbing, like a dog waggling its rump.

Don't you have anything better to do? I said to him. You're not paid to stand there and gawp. I turned my head to look at him over my shoulder, and it wasn't McDermott at all, but Mr. Kinnear himself, with a smirk on him as if he thought it a good joke. I scrambled to my feet, tugging my skirt down with one hand, with the brush in the other, and the dirty water dripping onto my dress.

Oh I am sorry, Sir, I said. But I thought, why couldn't he have the decency to say who he was?

No harm done, he said, a cat may look at a queen; and at that minute Nancy came in through the doorway, with her face as white as chalk and green around the gills, but her eyes as sharp as needles.

What is it? What are you doing here? She said it to me, but she meant it for him.

Scrubbing the floor, I said. Ma'am. As you ordered me to. What does it look like to her, I thought. Dancing?

You're talking back, said Nancy, I am sick of your insolence. But I was not, I was only answering her own question.

Mr. Kinnear said, as if he was apologizing – but what had he done? – he said, All I wanted was a second cup of coffee.

I will make it, said Nancy. Grace, you may go.

Where am I to go, Ma'am? I said. With the floor only half done.

Anywhere out of here, said Nancy. She was very angry with me. And for God's sake pin up your hair, she added. You look like a common slut.

Mr. Kinnear said, I will be in the library, and he went away.

Nancy poked at the fire in the stove as if stabbing it. Close your mouth, she said to me, you'll catch flies. And you'll keep it closed in future if you know what's good for you.

I thought about throwing the scrubbing brush at her, and the bucket too for good measure, the dirty water and all. I pictured her standing there, with the hair streaming down over her face, like someone drowned.

But then all at once it came over me what was the matter with her. I'd seen it often enough before. The eating of strange foods at odd times, the sickness and the green tinge around the mouth, the way she was plumping out, like a raisin in hot water, and her quirkiness and irritation. She was in a delicate condition. She was in the family way. She was in trouble.

I stood there gaping at her, as if I'd been kicked in the stomach. Oh no, oh no, I thought. I felt my heart going hard like a hammer. It cannot be.

That evening Mr. Kinnear was at home, and he and Nancy took their supper in the dining room, and I carried it in. I scanned his face, looking for a consciousness there, of Nancy's condition: but he did not know. What would he do when he found out, I wondered. Boot her into the ditch. Marry her. I had no idea, and could not rest easy with either of these futures. I wished Nancy no harm, and did not want her cast out, a waif on the common highway and a prey to wandering scoundrels; but all the same it would not be fair and just that she should end up a respectable married lady with a ring on her finger, and rich into the bargain. It would not be right at all. Mary Whitney had done the same as her, and had gone to her death. Why should the one be rewarded and the other punished, for the same sin?

I cleared the things off the table as usual after they had gone into the parlour. By this time it was hot as an oven, with grey clouds blotting out the light, although it was not yet sunset; and still as the grave, with no wind, but heat lightning flickering on the horizon, and a faint growling of thunder. When the weather is like that you can hear your own heart beat; it is like hiding, and waiting for someone to come and find you, and you don't know who that person will be. I lit a candle so I could see to eat my own supper, which I took with McDermott, cold roast beef it was, as I couldn't bear to cook anything hot for us. We ate it in the winter kitchen, and with it we had beer, and some of the bread which was still fresh enough and very nice, with a slice or two of cheese. Then I washed up the supper things and dried them, and put them away.

McDermott was cleaning the shoes; he'd been sullen during our supper, and said why couldn't we have proper cooked food, like the steaks with new peas the others had eaten, and I said new peas did not grow on trees, and he ought to know who would have the first choice of them, as there had only been enough for two; and in any case I was Mr. Kinnear's servant, not his; and he said that if I was his I would not last long, as I was such a foul-tempered witch, and the only cure for me was the end of a belt; and I said ill words butter no parsnips.

I could hear the sound of Nancy's voice from the parlour, and I knew she must be reading out loud. She liked to do it, as she thought it was genteel; but she always pretended that Mr. Kinnear required it of her. They had the parlour window open, even though the moths would get in that way, and that is why I could hear her.

I lit another candle and told McDermott I was going to bed, to which he said nothing but only gave a grunt; and he took up his own candle and went out. When he was gone I opened the door to the passageway and looked along it. The light from the globe lamp was falling through the half-open parlour door, making a light patch on the passage floor, and Nancy's voice was coming out into the hall as well.

I went quietly along the passageway, leaving my candle on the kitchen table, and stood leaning against the wall. I wanted to hear the story she was reading. It was *The Lady of the Lake*, which Mary Whitney and I had once read together, and it made me sad to recall it. Nancy read it well enough, though slowly, and sometimes stumbling over a word.

The poor madwoman had just been shot by mistake, and was expiring, while speaking several lines of verse; and I thought it a very melancholy part; but Mr. Kinnear did not agree, for he said it was a wonder anyone could move an inch in romantic landscapes such as those of Scotland, without being accosted by madwomen, who were always jumping in front of arrows and bullets not intended for them, which had the virtue at least of putting an end to their caterwauling and misery; or else they were constantly throwing themselves into the ocean, at such a rate that the sea soon would be so clogged with their drowned bodies, as to constitute a serious hazard to shipping. Then Nancy said he lacked a proper feeling; and Mr. Kinnear said no, he did not, but it was well known that Sir Walter Scott had put so many corpses into his books for the sake of the ladies, because the ladies must have blood, there is nothing delights them so much as a weltering corpse.

Nancy told him gaily to be quiet and behave himself, or she would have to punish him and stop reading, she would play the piano instead; and Mr. Kinnear laughed and said he could endure any form of torture but that. There was the sound of a little slap, and a rustling of cloth, and I decided she must be sitting on his knee. For a time there was quiet, until Mr. Kinnear asked Nancy if the cat had got her tongue, and why was she so pensive.

I leant forward, as I thought she must be about to inform him of her condition, and then I would know which way things were going to fall; but she did not. Instead she told him that she was worried about the servants.

Which of the servants, Mr. Kinnear wanted to know; and Nancy said both of them, and Mr. Kinnear laughed and said of course there were three servants in the house, not two, as she was a servant herself; and Nancy said it was kind of him to remind her of that; and she must now leave him, as she had her duties in the kitchen to attend to, and there was another sound of rustling, and of struggling too, as if she was trying to get up. Mr. Kinnear laughed some more and said she should stay where she was, it was her master's command, and Nancy said bitterly that she supposed that was what she was paid for; and then he soothed her, and asked her what was worrying her about the servants. Was the work getting done, was the main thing, he said, and he did not much care who cleaned his boots as long as they were clean, as he paid good wages and expected to get value for his money.

Yes, Nancy said, the work was getting done, but in the case of McDermott, only because she stood over him with a whip; and when she scolded him for being lazy, he was insolent with her, and she had given him his notice. Mr. Kinnear said he was a surly black-browed rascal, and he'd never liked him. And then he said, What about Grace. And I strained my ears, the better to hear what Nancy said.

She said that I was tidy and quick about my work, but that I had lately become very quarrelsome, and she was thinking of giving me my notice; and when I heard that, my face went hot all over. Then she said there was something about me that made her quite uneasy, and she wondered whether I was quite right, as she'd several times heard me talking out loud to myself.

Mr. Kinnear laughed, and said that was nothing – he often talked to himself, as he was the best conversationalist he knew; and I was certainly a handsome girl, as I had a naturally refined air and a very pure Grecian profile, and that if he put me in the right clothes and told me to hold my head high and keep my mouth shut, he could pass me off for a lady any day.

Nancy said she certainly hoped he would never say such flattering things to me, as it would turn my head, and give me ideas above my station, which would be no favour to me. Then she said he never had such agreeable opinions of her; and he said something I couldn't hear, and there was more silence and rustling. And then Mr. Kinnear said that it was time for bed. So I made my way quickly back to the kitchen, and sat down at the table; for it would not have done for Nancy to catch me listening.

But I did listen afterwards, once they'd gone up; and I heard Mr. Kinnear saying, I know you're hiding, come out right now, you dirty girl, do as I say, or I will have to catch you, and when I do . . .

And then a laugh from Nancy, and then a little scream.

The thunder was coming closer. I've never liked a thunderstorm, and did not then. When I went to bed, I secured my shutters so none of the thunder could get in, and pulled the covers up over my head, although it was so hot; and I thought I would never get to sleep. But I did; and was awakened in the pitch darkness by a tremendous crashing, as if the end of the world had come. A violent storm was raging, with a sound of drums and roaring, and I was beside myself with terror, and cowered in my bed praying for it to be over, shutting my eyes against the flashes of light that came in through the cracks in the shutters. The rain was pouring down like ten thousand,

and the house working in the wind like grinding teeth; and I was sure that every next minute we would split in two like a ship at sea, and sink down into the earth. And then, right next to my ear, I heard a voice whispering: *It cannot be.* I must have been frightened into a fit, because after that I lost consciousness altogether.

Then I had a very strange dream. I dreamt that all was quiet again, and that I got out of bed in my nightdress, and unlatched my chamber door, and walked across the floor of the winter kitchen in my bare feet, and out into the courtyard. The clouds had been swept away, and the moon was shining brightly, and the leaves of the trees looked like feathers of silver; and the air was cooler, with a touch to it like velvet; and there were crickets chirping. I could smell the wet garden smell, and the sharp tang of the henhouse; and also I could hear Charley whinnying softly from the stable, which meant he knew there was someone close by. I stood there in the yard beside the pump, with the moonlight falling over me like water; and it was as if I could not move.

Then two arms stole around me from the back, and began caressing me. They were a man's arms; and I could feel the mouth of this same man on my neck and cheek, kissing me ardently, and his body pressed up against my back; but it was like the game of blind man's buff, that children play, as I could not tell who it was, nor could I turn and look. I caught a scent of road dust and leather, and thought it might be Jeremiah the peddler; then it changed to a smell of horse dung, so I thought it was McDermott. But I could not rouse myself to push him away. Then it changed again, and was the odour of tobacco, and of Mr. Kinnear's fine shaving soap, and I was not surprised, as I had been half expecting something of the sort from him; and all the while the mouth of the unknown man was on my neck, and I could feel his breath stirring my hair. And then I felt it was not any of these three, but another man, someone I knew well and had long been familiar with, even as long ago as my childhood, but had since forgotten; nor was this the first time I'd found myself in this situation with him. I felt a warmth and a drowsy languor stealing over me, and urging me to yield, and surrender myself; as to do so would be far easier than to resist.

But then I heard the neighing of a horse; and it came to me that this was not Charley, nor the colt in the barn, but a different horse altogether. A great fear came over me, and my body went entirely cold, and I stood as if paralyzed with fear; for I knew that the horse was no earthly horse, but the pale horse that will be sent at the Day of Reckoning, and the rider of it is Death; and it was Death himself who stood behind me, with his arms wrapped around me as tight as iron bands, and his lipless mouth kissing my neck as if in love. But as well as the horror, I also felt a strange longing.

At this the sun came up, not little by little as it does when we are awake, Sir, but all at once, with a great blare of light. If it had been a sound, it would have been the blowing of many trumpets; and the arms that were holding me melted away. I was dazzled by the brightness; but as I looked up, I saw that in the trees by the house, and also in the trees of the orchard, there were a number of birds perching, enormous birds as white as ice. This was an ominous and baleful sight, as they appeared crouched as if ready to spring and destroy; and in that way they were like a gathering of crows, only white. But as my sight cleared, I saw that they were not birds at all. They had a human form, and they were the angels whose white robes were washed in blood, as it says at the end of the Bible; and they were sitting in silent judgment upon Mr. Kinnear's house, and on all within it. And then I saw that they had no heads.

In the dream, I then lost consciousness, from sheer terror; and when I came to myself, I was in my own bed, in my small chamber, with the quilt drawn up to my ears. But after I rose – for it was already dawn – I found that the hem of my nightdress was wet, and my feet had the marks of earth and grass on them; and I thought I must have been walking around outside without knowing I was doing so, as had happened to me once before, on the day that Mary Whitney died; and my heart sank within me.

I proceeded to dress as usual, vowing to keep my dream to myself, because who was there I could trust with it, in that house? If I told it as a warning, I would only be laughed at. But when I went outside to pump the first pail of water, there was all the laundry I had done the day before, blown into the trees by the tempest during the night. I'd forgotten to bring it in; it was very unlike me to forget a thing like that, especially a white laundry, which I'd worked so hard at, getting out the spots; and this was another cause of foreboding to me. And the nightdresses and shirts which were stuck in the trees did indeed look like angels without heads; and it was as if our own clothing was sitting in judgment upon us.

I could not shake the feeling that there was a doom on the house, and that some within were fated to die. If I'd been given the chance right then, I would have taken the risk, and gone off with Jeremiah the peddler; and indeed I wanted to run after him, and better for me if I had; but I didn't know where he had gone.

Dr. Jordan is writing eagerly, as if his hand can scarcely keep up, and I have never seen him so animated before. It does my heart good to feel I can bring a little pleasure into a fellow-being's life; and I think to myself, I wonder what he will make of all that.

IX.

HEARTS AND GIZZARDS

During the evening James Walsh came in, and brought his flute with him, Nancy said, we might as well have some fun, as Mr. Kinnear was away. Nancy said to McDermott, you have often bragged about your dancing, come let us have a dance, he was very sulky all the evening, and said he would not dance. About ten o'clock we went to bed. I slept with Nancy that night; before we went to bed McDermott said to me that he was determined to kill her that night, with the axe, when in bed. I entreated him not to do so that night, as he might hit me instead of her. He said, damn her; I'll kill her then, first thing in the morning. I got up early on the Saturday morning, and when I went into the kitchen McDermott was cleaning the shoes, the fire was lighted, he asked me where was Nancy, I said she was dressing, and I said, are you going to kill her this morning. He said he would. I said, McDermott, for God's sake don't kill her in the room, you'll make the floor all bloody. Well, says he, I'll not do it there, but I'll knock her down with the axe the moment she comes out.

– Confession of Grace Marks,
Star and Transcript, Toronto, November 1843.

"That cellar presented a dreadful spectacle. . . . [Nancy] Mont-gomery was not dead, as I had thought; the blow had only stunned her. She had partially recovered her senses, and was kneeling on one knee as we descended the ladder with the light.

I don't know if she saw us, for she must have been blinded with the blood that was flowing down her face; but she certainly heard us, and raised her clasped hands, as if to implore mercy.

"I turned to Grace. The expression of her livid face was even more dreadful than that of the unfortunate woman. She uttered no cry, but she put her hand to her head, and said –

"'God has damned me for this.'

"'Then you have nothing more to fear,' says I. 'Give me that handkerchief off your neck.' She gave it without a word. I threw myself upon the body of the housekeeper, and planting my knee on her breast, I tied the handkerchief round her throat in a single tie, giving Grace one end to hold, while I drew the other tight enough to finish my terrible work. Her eyes literally started from her head, she gave one groan, and all was over. I then cut the body in four pieces, and turned a large washtub over them."

– James McDermott,
to Kenneth MacKenzie, as retold by
Susanna Moodie, *Life in the Clearings*, 1853.

. . . the death, then, of a beautiful woman is, unquestionably, the most poetical topic in the world. . . .

– Edgar Allan Poe,
"The Philosophy of Composition," 1846.

3 2 .

The heat of summer has come without warning. One day it was still cold spring, with gusting showers and chilly white clouds remote above the glacial blue of the lake; then suddenly the daffodils withered, the tulips burst open and turned inside out as if yawning, then dropped their petals. Cesspool vapours rise from back yards and gutters, and a mist of mosquitoes condenses around every pedestrian's head. At noon the air shimmers like the space above a heated griddle, and the lake glares, its margin stinking faintly of dead fish and frog spawn. At night Simon's lamp is besieged by moths, which flutter around him, the soft touch of their wings like the brushing of silken lips.

He is dazed by the change. Living through the more gradual seasons of Europe, he'd forgotten these brutal transitions. His clothing is heavy as fur, his skin seems always damp. He's under the impression that he smells like bacon fat and soured milk; or perhaps it's his bedchamber that smells this way. It hasn't been thoroughly cleaned for far too long, nor the sheets changed: no suitable maid-of-all-work has yet been located, though Mrs. Humphrey details her efforts along these lines to him every morning. According to her, the departed Dora has been spreading stories around the town – among all the potential servant-girls, at least – about how Mrs. Humphrey has not paid her, and is about to be turned out bag and baggage, on account of having no money; and also about how the Major has run off, which is even more disgraceful. So of course, she tells Simon, it stands to reason that no servants wish to take their chances in such a household. And she smiles a rueful smile.

She herself has been cooking the breakfasts, which they continue to share at her table – her suggestion, to which he's agreed, as it would be humiliating for her to have to carry a tray up. Today Simon listens to her with fretful inattention, toying with his humid toast, and with his egg that he now takes fried. At least with a fried egg there are no surprises.

Breakfast is all she can manage; she is subject to fits of nervous prostration and headache, brought on by the reaction to shock – or so he assumes, and has told her – and by afternoon is invariably stretched out on her bed, with a wet cloth pressed to her forehead, giving off a strong smell of camphor. He can't let her starve herself to death, so although for the most part he eats his meals at the wretched inn, from time to time he attempts to feed her.

Yesterday he bought a chicken from a rancorous crone in the market, but not until he got it home did he discover that although it had been plucked, it had not been cleaned. He could not face the task – he'd never cleaned a chicken before in his life – and thought of disposing of the avian corpse. A walk by the lakeshore, a swift fling of the arm . . . But then he recalled that it was only a dissection, after all, and he'd dissected worse than chickens; and once he had his scalpel in hand – he's kept the tools of his former trade with him, in their leather satchel – he was all right again, and managed a neat incision. After that, things got worse, but he'd come through it all right by holding his breath. He cooked the chicken by cutting it into pieces and frying it. Mrs. Humphrey came to the table, saying she felt a little better, and ate a good deal of it for one so fragile; but when the washing up had to be done she suffered a relapse, and Simon was left to do it himself.

The kitchen is even greasier than it was when he first entered it. Dust rolls have gathered under the stove, spiders in the corners, breadcrumbs beside the sink; a family of beetles has moved into the pantry. It is alarming how quickly one descends into squalor. Something must be done soon, some slave or lackey acquired. In addition to the dirt, there is the question of appearances. He cannot continue to live alone in this house with his landlady: especially not such a tremulous landlady, and one deserted by her husband. If it becomes generally known and people begin to talk – no matter how groundless such talk would be – then his reputation and professional standing may suffer. Reverend Verringer has made it plain that the enemies of the Reformers will use any means, however base, to discredit their opponents, and in case of a scandal he'd be given his discharge in short order.

He could at least do something about the state of the house, if he could summon the will for it. In a pinch he could sweep the floors and stairway, and dust the furniture in his own rooms; but there would still be no hiding the odour of muted disaster, of slow and dispirited decay, that breathes from the limp curtains and accumulates in the cushions and woodwork. The advent of the summer heat has made it worse. He remembers with nostalgia the clatter of Dora's dustpan; he has gained a new respect for the Doras of this world, but although he longs for such household problems to resolve themselves, he has no idea how this may be accomplished. Once or twice he's thought of asking Grace Marks for advice – how a maid should properly be hired, how a chicken should properly be cleaned – but he has thought better of it. He must retain his position of all-knowing authority in her eyes.

Mrs. Humphrey is talking again; the subject is her gratitude to him, as it often is while he is eating his toast. She waits until his mouth is full, then launches in. His gaze wanders over her – the pale oval of her face, her stringent and bloodless hair, her crackling black silk waist, her abrupt white edgings of lace. Underneath her stiff dress there must be breasts, not starched and corset-shaped, but made of soft flesh, with nipples; he finds himself idly guessing what colour these nipples would be, in sunlight or else in lamplight, and how large. Nipples pink and small like the snouts of animals, of rabbits or mice perhaps; or the almost-red of ripening currants; or the scaly brown of acorn caps. His imagination runs, he notes, to wildwood details, and to things hard or alert. In reality this woman does not attract him: such images arrive unsummoned. His eyes feel squeezed – not a headache yet, but a dull pressure. He wonders if he's running a low fever; this morning he examined his tongue in the mirror for telltale blanching and spots. A bad tongue looks like cooked veal: greyish white, with a scum on it.

The life he's leading is not healthy. His mother is right, he should marry. Marry or burn, as St. Paul says; or search out the usual remedies. There are houses of ill repute in Kingston, as everywhere, but he cannot avail himself of them as he might in London or Paris. The town is too small and he is too conspicuous, his position too precarious, the Governor's wife too pious, the enemies of Reform too ubiquitous. It's not worth the risk, and in any case the houses here are bound to be depressing. Sadly pretentious, with a provincial idea of the alluring in their wistfully upholstered furnishings. Too much brocade and fringe. But also briskly utilitarian – run on the North American mill-town factory principle of quick processing, and dedicated to the greatest happiness of the greatest number, no matter how grim and minimal the quality of that happiness may be. Soiled petticoats, whores' sunless flesh pallid as uncooked pastry and smudged by the thick tarry fingers of sailors; and by those, more manicured, of the occasional Government legislator, travelling through, sheepishly incognito.

It's just as well he must avoid these places. Such experiences drain the mental energies.

"Are you ill, Dr. Jordan?" asks Mrs. Humphrey, as she hands him a second cup of tea, which she has poured for him without being asked. Her eyes are motionless, green, marine, the pupils small and black. He wakes with a start. Has he been asleep?

"You were pressing your hand to your forehead," she says. "Do you have a pain there?"

She has a habit of materializing outside his door while he's trying to work, asking if there is anything he needs. She is solicitous of him, tender almost, yet there is something cringing about her, as if she's waiting for a slap, a kick, a flat-handed blow, which she knows with dreary fatalism will surely come sooner or later. But not from him, not from him, he protests silently. He is a mild-tempered man, he has never been given to outbursts, to rampages and violence. There is no news of the Major. He thinks of her naked feet, shell-thin, exposed and vulnerable, tied together with – where has this come from? – an ordinary piece of twine. Like a parcel. If his sub-threshold consciousness must indulge in such exotic poses, it ought to be able to supply at least a silver chain. . . .

He drinks the tea. It tastes of marshes, the roots of bulrushes. Tangled and obscure. He's had some intestinal problems lately, and has been dosing himself with laudanum; fortunately he has a good supply. He suspects the water in this house; perhaps his intermittent digging in the yard has disturbed the well. His plan of a kitchen garden has come to nothing, though he's turned over a satisfying amount of mud. After his days spent wrestling with shadows, he finds it a curious relief to get his hands into something real, such as earth. But it's getting too hot for that.

"I must go," he says, and stands up, pushing back his chair, wiping his mouth brusquely, making a show of bustle, although in fact he has no appointment until the afternoon. Useless to stay in his room, to try to work; at his desk he will only doze, but with his ears alert, like a drowsing cat's, attuned to the sound of footsteps on the stairs.

He goes out, wanders at random. His body feels insubstantial as a bladder, emptied of will. He is carried along beside the lakeshore; he squints into the immense morning light, passing here and there the solitary fishermen as they cast their lures into the tepid and indolent waves.

Once he's with Grace, things are a little better, as he can still delude himself by flourishing his own sense of purpose. Grace at least represents to him some goal or accomplishment. But today, listening to her low, candid voice – like the voice of a childhood nurse reciting a well-loved story – he almost goes to sleep; only the sound of his own pencil hitting the floor pulls him awake. For a moment he thinks he's gone deaf, or suffered a small stroke: he can see her lips moving, but he can't interpret any of the words. This however is only a trick of consciousness, for he can remember – once he sets his mind to it – everything she's been saying.

On the table between them lies a small and dispirited white turnip, which both of them have so far ignored.

He must concentrate his intellectual forces; he can't afford to flag now, give in to lethargy, lose hold of the thread he's been following over the course of these past weeks, for at last they are approaching together the centre of Grace's narrative. They are nearing the blank mystery, the area of erasure; they are entering the forest of amnesia, where things have lost their names. In other words, they are retracing (day by day, hour by hour) the events which immediately preceded the murders. Anything she says now may be a clue; any gesture; any twitch. She knows; she knows. She may not know that she knows, but buried deep within her, the knowledge is there.

The trouble is that the more she remembers, the more she relates, the more difficulty he himself is having. He can't seem to keep track of the pieces. It's as if she's drawing his energy out of him – using his own mental forces to materialize the figures in her story, as the mediums are said to do during their trances. This is nonsense, of course. He must refuse to indulge such brain-sick fancies. But still, there was something about a man, in the night: has he missed it? One of those men: McDermott, Kinnear. In his notebook he has pencilled the word *whisper*, and underlined it three times. Of what had he wished to remind himself?

My dearest Son. I am alarmed that I have not heard from you for so long. Are you perhaps unwell? Where there are mists and fogs, there are bound to be infections; and I understand that the situation of Kingston is quite low, with many nearby swamps. One cannot be too careful in a garrison town, as soldiers and sailors are promiscuous in their habits. I hope you will take the precaution of keeping indoors as much as possible during this intense heat, and not going out in the sun.

Mrs. Henry Cartwright has purchased one of the new domestic Sewing Machines, for the use of her servants; and Miss Faith Cartwright was so intrigued by it, that she has tried it herself, and was able to hem a petticoat with it, in very little time; which she most thoughtfully brought over yesterday, so that I might see the stitching, as she knows I am interested in the modern inventions. The Machine works tolerably well, though there is room for improvement – snarls of thread occur more often than is desirable, and must be cut or untangled – but such devices are never perfected at first; and Mrs. Cartwright says that her husband is of the opinion, that the shares in the company which manufactures these machines, would prove a most sound investment over time. He is a most affectionate and considerate Father, and has given much study to the future welfare of his daughter, who is his only surviving Child.

But I will not bore you with talk of money, as I know you find it tedious; although, dear Son, it does keep the larder supplied, and is the means for coming by those small comforts, which make the difference between a threadbare existence, and a life of modest ease; and as your dear Father used to say, it is a substance which does not grow on trees. . . .

Time is not running at its usual unvarying pace: it makes odd lurches. Now, too quickly, it's evening. Simon sits at his desk, the notebook open before him, and stares stupidly out through the darkening square of window. The hot sunset has faded, leaving a purple smear; the air outside vibrates with insect whines and amphibious peepings. His entire body feels swollen, like wood in rain. From the lawn comes a scent of withering lilacs – a singed smell, like sunburned skin. Tomorrow is Tuesday, the day when he must address the Governor's wife's little salon, as promised. What can he possibly say? He must jot down a few notes, organize some sort of coherent presentation. But it's no use; he can't accomplish anything of importance, not tonight. He can't think.

Moths beat against the lamp. He sets aside the question of the Tuesday meeting, and turns instead to his unfinished letter. *My dear Mother. My health continues excellent. Thank you for sending the embroidered watch-case made for you by Miss Cartwright; I am surprised you were willing to part with it, even though as you say it is too large for your own watch; and it is certainly exquisite. I expect to finish my work here quite soon. . . .*

Lies and evasions on his side, and on hers, plottings and enticements. What does he care about Miss Faith Cartwright and her endless and infernal needlework? Every letter his mother sends him contains news of yet more knitting, stitching, and tedious crocheting.

The Cartwright household must by this time be covered all over – every table, chair, lamp, and piano – with acres of tassel and fringe, a woolwork flower heavily abloom in every nook of it. Does his mother really believe that he can be charmed by such a vision of himself – married to Faith Cartwright and imprisoned in an armchair by the fire, frozen in a kind of paralyzed stupor, with his dear wife winding him up gradually in coloured silk threads like a cocoon, or like a fly snarled in the web of a spider?

He crumples the page, drops it onto the floor. He will write a different letter. *My dear Edward. I trust you are in good health; I myself am still in Kingston, where I continue to . . .* But continue to what? What exactly is he doing here? He can't sustain his usual jaunty tone. What can he write to Edward, what trophy or prize can he show? What clue, even? His hands are empty; he has discovered nothing. He has been travelling blindly, whether forward he cannot say, without learning anything except that he has not yet learned anything, unless he counts the extent of his own ignorance; like those who have searched fruitlessly for the source of the Nile. Like them, he must take into account the possibility of defeat. Hopeless dispatches, scrawled on pieces of bark, sent out in cleft sticks from the swallowing jungle. *Suffering from malaria. Bitten by snake. Send more medicine. The maps are wrong.* He has nothing positive to relate.

In the morning he will feel better. He will collect himself. When it is cooler. For the moment, he goes to bed. In his ears there's a simmering of insects. The damp heat settles down on his face like a hand, and his consciousness flares up for a moment – what is it he is on the verge of remembering? – then gutters out.

Suddenly he starts awake. There's light in the room, a candle, floating in the doorway. Behind it a glimmering figure: his landlady, in a white gown, a pale shawl wrapped around her. In the candlelight her long loose hair looks grey.

He pulls the sheet up over him; he is not wearing a nightshirt. "What is it?" he says. He must sound angry, but in fact he's frightened. Not of her, surely; but what the Devil is she doing in his bedroom? In future he must lock the door.

"Dr. Jordan, I am so sorry to disturb you," she says, "but I heard a noise. As if of someone attempting to break in through a window. I was alarmed."

There's no trembling in her voice, no quavering. The woman has a very cool nerve. He tells her he will come downstairs with her in a minute, and check the locks and shutters; he asks her to wait in the front room. He fumbles into his dressing-gown, which sticks immediately to his moist skin, and shuffles through the darkness towards the door.

This must stop, he tells himself. *This can't go on*. But nothing has been going on, and therefore nothing can stop.

33 .

It's the middle of the night, but time keeps going on, and it also goes round and around, like the sun and the moon on the tall clock in the parlour. Soon it will be daybreak. Soon the day will break. I can't stop it from breaking in the same way it always does, and then from lying there broken; always the same day, which comes around again like clockwork. It begins with the day before the day before, and then the day before, and then it's the day itself. A Saturday. The breaking day. The day the butcher comes.

What should I tell Dr. Jordan about this day? Because now we are almost there. I can remember what I said when arrested, and what Mr. MacKenzie the lawyer said I should say, and what I did not say even to him; and what I said at the trial, and what I said afterwards, which was different as well. And what McDermott said I said, and what the others said I must have said, for there are always those that will supply you with speeches of their own, and put them right into your mouth for you too; and that sort are like the magicians who can throw their voice, at fairs and shows, and you are just their wooden doll. And that's what it was like at the trial, I was there in the box of the dock but I might as well have been made of cloth, and stuffed, with a china head; and I was shut up inside that doll of myself, and my true voice could not get out.

I said that I remembered some of the things I did. But there are other things they said I did, which I said I could not remember at all.

Did he say, I saw you outside at night, in your nightgown, in the moonlight? Did he say, Who were you looking for? Was it a man? Did he say, I pay good wages but I want good service in return? Did he say, Do not worry, I will not tell your mistress, it will be our secret? Did he say, You are a good girl?

He might have said that. Or I might have been asleep.

Did she say, Don't think I don't know what you've been up to? Did she say, I will pay you your wages on Saturday and then you can be gone out of here, and that will be the end of it and good riddance?

Yes. She did say that.

Was I crouching behind the kitchen door after that, crying? Did he take me in his arms? Did I let him do it? Did he say Grace, why are you crying? Did I say I wished she was dead?

Oh no. Surely I did not say that. Or not out loud. And I did not really wish her dead. I only wished her elsewhere, which was the same thing she wished for me.

Did I push him away? Did he say I will soon make you think better of me? Did he say I will tell you a secret if you promise to keep it? And if you do not, your life will not be worth a straw.

It might have happened.

I'm trying to remember what Mr. Kinnear looked like, so I can tell Dr. Jordan about him. He was always kind to me, or so I will say. But I can't rightly remember. The truth is that despite everything I once thought about him, he has faded; he's been fading year by year, like a dress washed over and over, and now what is left of him? A faint pattern. A button or two. Sometimes a voice; but no eyes, no mouth.

What did he really look like, when he was in the flesh? Nobody wrote it down, not even in the newspapers; they told all about McDermott, and about me as well, and our looks and appearance, but not about Mr. Kinnear, because it is more important to be a murderess than the one murdered, you are more stared at then; and now he's gone. I think of him asleep and dreaming in his bed, in the morning when I bring in his tea, with his face hidden by the tumbled sheet. In the darkness here I can see other things, but I can't see him at all.

I tell over his pieces, counting. The gold snuffbox, the telescope, the pocket-compass, the pen-knife; the gold watch, the silver spoons that I polished, the candlesticks with the family crest. *I Live In Hope.* The tartan vest. I don't know where they have gone.

I'm lying on the hard and narrow bed, on the mattress made of coarse ticking, which is what they call the covering of a mattress, though why do they call it that as it is not a clock. The mattress is filled with dry straw that crackles like a fire when I turn over, and when I shift it whispers to me, *hush hush*. It's dark as a stone in this room, and hot as a roasting heart; if you stare into the darkness with your eyes open you are sure to see something after a time. I hope it will not be flowers. But this is the time they like to grow, the red flowers, the shining red peonies which are like satin, which are like splashes of paint. The soil for them is emptiness, it is empty space and silence. I whisper, *Talk to me*; because I would rather have talking than the slow gardening that takes place in silence, with the red satin petals dripping down the wall.

I think I sleep.

I'm in the back passage, feeling my way along the wall. I can scarcely see the wallpaper; it used to be green. Here are the stairs going up, here is the bannister. The bedroom door is half open, and I can listen. Bare feet on the red-flower carpet. I know you're hiding from me, come out at once or I'll have to find you and catch you, and when I've got hold of you, then who knows what I will do.

I'm keeping very still behind the door, I can hear my own heart. Oh no, oh no, oh no.

Here I come, I am coming now. You never obey me, you never do what I say, you dirty girl. Now you will have to be punished.

It is not my fault. What can I do now, where can I turn?

You must unlock the door, you must open the window, you must let me in.

Oh look, oh look at all the spilt petals, what have you done?

I think I sleep.

I'm outside, at night. There are the trees, there is the pathway, and the snake fence with half a moon shining, and my bare feet on the gravel. But when I come around to the front of the house, the sun is just going down; and the white pillars of the house are pink, and the white peonies are glowing red in the fading light. My hands are numb, I can't feel the ends of my fingers. There's the smell of fresh meat, coming up from the ground and all around, although I told the butcher we wanted none.

On the palm of my hand there's a disaster. I must have been born with it. I carry it with me wherever I go. When he touched me, the bad luck came off on him.

I think I sleep.

I wake up at cock crow and I know where I am. I'm in the parlour. I'm in the scullery. I'm in the cellar. I'm in my cell, under the coarse prison blanket, which I likely hemmed myself. We make everything we wear or use here, awake or asleep; so I have made this bed, and now I am lying in it.

It is morning, and time to get up; and today I must go on with the story. Or the story must go on with me, carrying me inside it, along the track it must travel, straight to the end, weeping like a train and deaf and single-eyed and locked tight shut; although I hurl myself against the walls of it and scream and cry, and beg to God himself to let me out.

When you are in the middle of a story it isn't a story at all, but only a confusion; a dark roaring, a blindness, a wreckage of shattered glass and splintered wood; like a house in a whirlwind, or else a boat crushed by the icebergs or swept over the rapids, and all aboard powerless to stop it. It's only afterwards that it becomes anything like a story at all. When you are telling it, to yourself or to someone else.

3 4 .

From the Governor's wife, Simon accepts a cup of tea. He doesn't much like tea, but considers it a social duty to drink it in this country; and to greet all jokes about the Boston Tea Party, of which there have been too many, with an aloof but indulgent smile.

His indisposition appears to have passed. Today he's feeling better, although in need of sleep. He's managed to get through his little talk to the Tuesday group, and feels he's acquitted himself well enough. He began with a plea for the reform of mental asylums, too many of which remain the dens of squalor and iniquity they'd been in the last century. This was well received. He then continued with some remarks about the intellectual turmoil in this field of study, and about the contending schools of thought amongst alienists.

First he dealt with the Material school. Such practitioners held that mental disturbances were organic in origin – due, for instance, to lesions of the nerves and brain, or hereditary conditions of a definable kind, such as epilepsy; or to catching diseases, including those that are sexually transmitted – he was elliptical here, consider-ing the presence of ladies, but everyone knew what he meant. Next he described the approach of the Mental school, which believed in causes that were much harder to isolate. How to measure the effects of shock, for example? How to diagnose amnesias with no discernible physical manifestation, or certain inexplicable and radical alterations of the personality? What, he asked them, was the role played by the Will, and what by the Soul? Here Mrs. Quennell leaned forward, only to lean back when he said he did not know.

Next he proceeded to the many new discoveries which were being made – Dr. Laycock's bromide therapy for epileptics, for example, which should put paid to a great many erroneous beliefs and superstitions; the investigation of the structure of the brain; the use of drugs in both the induction and the alleviation of hallucinations of various sorts. Pioneer work was constantly going forward; here he would like to mention the courageous Dr. Charcot of Paris, who had recently dedicated himself to the study of hysterics; and the investigation of dreams as a key to diagnosis, and their relation to amnesia, to which he himself hoped in time to make a modest contribution. All of these theories were in the early stages of their development, but much might soon be expected of them. As the eminent French philosopher and scientist Maine de Biran had said, there was an inner New World to be discovered, for which one must "plunge into the subterranean caverns of the soul."

The nineteenth century, he concluded, would be to the study of Mind what the eighteenth had been to the study of Matter – an Age of Enlightenment. He was proud to be part of such a major advance in knowledge, if only in a very small and humble way.

He wished it was not so damnably hot and humid. He was drenched by the time he concluded, and is still conscious of a marshy smell, which comes from his hands. It must be the digging; he'd done another spell of it this morning, before the heat of the day.

The Tuesday group applauded politely, and Reverend Verringer thanked him. Dr. Jordan, he said, was to be congratulated upon the edifying remarks with which he had honoured them today. He had given them all a great deal to think about. The Universe was indeed a mysterious place, but God had blessed man with a mind, the better to understand whatever mysteries were truly within his comprehension. He implied that there were others, which weren't. This seemed to please everyone.

Afterwards, Simon was thanked individually. Mrs. Quennell told him he'd spoken with heartfelt sensibility, which made him feel slightly guilty, as his chief goal had been to get the occasion over with as quickly as possible. Lydia, very fetching in a crisp and rustling summer ensemble, was breathless in her praise, and as admiring as any man might wish; but he could not shake the notion that she hadn't really understood a single word he'd said.

"Most intriguing," says Jerome DuPont now, at Simon's elbow. "I notice you said nothing about prostitution, which, along with drink, is surely one of the major social ills afflicting our age."

"I did not wish to bring it in," says Simon, "considering the company."

"Naturally enough. I would be interested in your opinion of the view held by some of our European colleagues, that the penchant for it is a form of insanity. They link it to hysteria and neurasthenia."

"I am aware of it," says Simon, smiling. In his student days, he used to argue that if a woman has no other course open to her but starvation, prostitution, or throwing herself from a bridge, then surely the prostitute, who has shown the most tenacious instinct for self-preservation, should be considered stronger and saner than her frailer and no longer living sisters. One couldn't have it both ways, he'd point out: if women are seduced and abandoned they're supposed to go mad, but if they survive, and seduce in their turn, then they were mad to begin with. He'd said that it seemed to him a dubious piece of reasoning; which got him the reputation either of a cynic or of a puritanical hypocrite, depending on his audience.

"I myself," says Dr. DuPont, "tend to place prostitution in the same class as the homicidal and religious manias; all may be considered, perhaps, as an impulse to play-act which has run out of control. Such things have been observed in the theatre, among actors who claim that they become the character they are acting. Female opera singers are especially prone to it. There's a Lucia on record who actually did kill her lover."

"It's an interesting possibility," says Simon.

"You do not commit yourself," says Dr. DuPont, gazing at Simon with his dark, lustrous eyes. "But you will go so far as to admit that women in general have a more fragile nervous organization, and consequently a greater suggestibility?"

"Perhaps," says Simon. "Certainly it is generally believed."

"It makes them, for instance, a good deal easier to hypnotize."

Ah, thinks Simon. Each to his own hobby-horse. Now he's getting to it.

"How is your fair patient, if I may call her that?" says Dr. DuPont. "Are you making progress?"

"Nothing definitive yet," says Simon. "There are several possible lines of enquiry which I hope to follow up."

"I would be honoured if you would permit me to try my own method. Just as a sort of experiment; a demonstration, if you like."

"I am at a crucial point," says Simon. He doesn't wish to appear rude, but he does not want this man interfering. Grace is his territory; he must repel poachers. "It might upset her, and undo weeks of careful preparation."

"At your convenience," says Dr. DuPont. "I expect to remain here for another month at least. I should be pleased to be of help."

"You are staying with Mrs. Quennell, I believe," says Simon.

"A most generous hostess. But infatuated with the Spiritualists, as are many these days. An entirely groundless system, I assure you. But then, the bereaved are so easily imposed upon."

Simon refrains from saying that he doesn't need any assurance. "You have attended some of her . . . her evenings – should I call them séances?"

"One or two. I am, after all, a guest; and the delusions involved are of considerable interest, to the clinical enquirer. But she is far from closing her mind to science, and is even prepared to fund legit-imate research."

"Ah," says Simon.

"She would like me to attempt a session of Neuro-hypnosis, with Miss Marks," says Dr. DuPont blandly. "On behalf of the Committee. You would have no objection?"

Curse them all, thinks Simon. They must be getting impatient with me; they think I am taking too long. But if they meddle too much, they will upset the apple cart, and ruin everything. Why can't they leave me to my own devices?

❧

Today is the Tuesday meeting, and as Dr. Jordan is speaking at it I did not see him in the afternoon, since he had to prepare. The Governor's wife asked if I could be spared for a little extra time, as they were short hands and she would like me to help with the refreshments, as I have often done. Of course it was a request in form only, as Matron had to say yes, and did so; and I was to take my supper in the kitchen after, just like a real servant, as the supper at the Penitentiary would be over by the time I got back. I was looking forward to it, as it would be like the old times, when I was free to come and go, and there was more variety in my days, and such treats to look forward to.

I knew however that I'd have to put up with some slights, and hard looks, and spiteful remarks as to my character. Not from Clarrie, who has always been a friend to me although a silent one, and not from Cook, who is used to me by now. But one of the upstairs maids resents me, as I have been in this house longer, and know its ways, and enjoy the confidence of Miss Lydia and Miss Marianne, which she does not; and she is bound to make some allusion to murders, or strangling, or some such distasteful thing. Also there is Dora, who has been coming in to help in the laundry, but not permanent and only paid by the hour. She is a large person with strong arms, and useful for the carrying of the heavy baskets of wet sheets; but untrustworthy, as she is always telling tales of her former mistress and master, who she says never paid what they owed her, and carried on in scandalous ways besides, with him so far gone with drink he was no better than an imbecile, and blacked his wife's eye for her more than once; and her taking sick at the drop of a hat, and Dora wouldn't be surprised to find there was drink at the bottom of her vapours and headaches, as well.

But although Dora says all these things, she has accepted to go back there, and to be the maid-of-all-work again, and indeed has already begun; and when Cook asked her why she would do it, considering they are such disreputable people, she gave a wink and said that money talks, and loudly too; and that the young doctor who boards there has paid out her back wages, and begged almost upon his bended knee to have her back, as no one else was to be found. And he is a man who likes his peace and quiet and for things to be clean and tidy, and is willing to pay for it, although the landlady cannot, her husband having run off on her, so that now she was no more than a grass widow, and a pauper at that. And Dora said she won't take orders from her any more, as she was always a carping and peevish mistress, but only from Dr. Jordan, as he who pays the piper calls the tune.

Not that he is up to any good either, she says, having the air of a poisoner about him, as so many doctors do have, with their bottles and potions and pills, and she thanks the good Lord every day that she isn't a rich old lady under his care, or she would not be long for this world; and he has a strange habit of digging in the garden, although it is now much too late to plant anything, but he goes at it like a sexton, and has turned over almost the whole of the yard, nonetheless; and then it's her who has to sweep up the mud he tracks in, and scrub the dirt out of his shirts in the wash, and heat up the water for his bath.

I was astonished to realize that this Dr. Jordan she was talking about was the same one as my Dr. Jordan; but I was curious as well, for I hadn't known all those things about his landlady, or indeed anything about her at all. So I asked Dora, what sort of a woman was she, and Dora said, Skinny as a rail and pale as a corpse, with long hair so yellow it was almost white, but despite that and her fine-lady ways, no better than she should be, although Dora did not yet have proof of it; but this Mrs. Humphrey had a wild rolling to the eye, and a twitchy manner, and those two things together always meant warm work behind closed doors; and that Dr. Jordan should watch himself, because if ever she saw a determination to get a man's trousers off him, it was there in the eyes of Mrs. Humphrey; and they took breakfast together every morning now, which to her mind was unnatural. Which I thought was coarse, at least the part about the trousers.

And I think to myself, if that is what she says about those she works for, behind their backs, then, Grace, what will she say of you? I catch her looking me over with her small pink eyes, and devising what sensational tales she will tell her friends if any, about taking her tea with a celebrated murderess, who ought by rights to have been strung up long since, and cut into slabs by the doctors, like butchers dressing a carcass, and what was left of me after they'd finished done up into a bundle, just like a suet pudding, and left to moulder in a dishonoured grave, with nothing growing on it but thistles and nettles.

But I am all for keeping the peace, and so I say nothing. For if I was to get into a fight with her, I know sure enough who would be blamed.

We had orders to keep our ears open for the end of the meeting, which would be signalled by applause, and a speech to thank Dr. Jordan for his edifying remarks, which is what they say to everyone who speaks on these occasions; and that would be our signal to bring up the refreshments; and so one of the maids was told to listen at the parlour door. Down she came after a while, and said the thanks were being given; and so we counted to twenty, and then sent up the first urn of tea, and the first trays of cakes. I was kept below, cutting up the pound cake, and arranging it on a round platter, for which the Governor's wife had given instructions that there was to be a rose or two in the centre; and very nice it looked. Then word came down that I was to bring in that particular plate myself, which I found odd; but I tidied my hair and carried the pound cake up the stairs, and in through the parlour door, expecting no harm.

There amongst the others was Mrs. Quennell with her hair like a powder puff, wearing pink muslin, which was far too young for her; and the Governor's wife in grey; and Reverend Verringer looking down his nose as usual; and Dr. Jordan, somewhat wan and limp, as if his talk had worn him out; and Miss Lydia, in the dress I'd helped her with, and pretty as a picture she was.

But who should I see, looking straight at me with a little smile, but Jeremiah the peddler! He was considerably trimmed as to hair and beard, and got up like a gentleman, in a beautifully cut sand-coloured suit, with a gold watch-chain across the vest; and holding a cup of tea in the best mincing gentleman's manner, just as he used to do when imitating the same, in the kitchen at Mrs. Alderman Parkinson's; but I'd have known him anywhere.

I was so taken aback that I gave a little shriek, and then stood stock-still, with my mouth open like a haddock, and almost dropped the plate; and indeed several pieces of the pound cake slid off it onto the floor, and the roses as well. But not before Jeremiah had set down his cup, and laid his forefinger alongside his nose, as if scratching it; which I don't believe anyone saw, as they were all looking at me; by which gesture of his I knew that I was to button my lip, and not say anything, or give him away.

So I did not, but excused myself for dropping the cake, and set the platter on the side table, and knelt down to retrieve the spilt cake into my apron. But the Governor's wife said, Never mind that at present, Grace, I wish to introduce you to someone. And she took me by the arm, and led me forward. This is Dr. Jerome DuPont, she said, he is a noted medical practitioner, and Jeremiah nodded to me, and said, How do you do, Miss Marks. I was still confused, but managed to keep my composure; the Governor's wife saying to him, She is often startled by strangers. And to me, Dr. DuPont is a friend, he will not hurt you.

At which I nearly laughed out loud, but instead said, Yes, Ma'am, and looked down at the floor. She must have feared a repetition of that other time, when the head-measuring doctor came here, and I screamed so much. But she need not have worried.

I must look into her eyes, said Jeremiah. It is often an indication as to whether or not the procedure will be efficacious. And he lifted my chin, and we gazed at each other. Very good, he said, all solemn and sedate, just as if he was what he pretended to be; and I had to admire him. Then he said, Grace, have you ever been hypnotized? And he kept hold of my chin for a moment, to steady me, and give me time to control myself.

I should certainly hope not, Sir, I said, with some indignation. I do not even know rightly what it is.

It is an entirely scientific procedure, he said. Would you be willing to try it? If it would help your friends, and the Committee. If it is decided by them that you should. And he gave my chin a little squeeze, and moved his eyes up and down very quickly, to signal to me that I should say yes.

I will do anything within my power, Sir, I said; if that is what is wanted.

Good, good, he said, just as pompous as a real doctor. But in order for it to be successful, you must repose your trust in me. Do you think you can do that, Grace?

Reverend Verringer and Miss Lydia, and Mrs. Quennell and the Governor's wife, were all beaming at me with encouragement. I will try, Sir, I said.

Then Dr. Jordan stepped up, and said he thought I'd had enough excitement for one day, and care must be taken of my nerves, as they were delicate and must not be damaged; and Jeremiah said, Of course, of course. But he looked well pleased with himself. And although I have an esteem for Dr. Jordan, and he has been kind to me, I thought he looked a poor fish beside Jeremiah, like a man at a fair who's had his pocket picked, but does not yet know it.

As for me, I could have laughed with glee; for Jeremiah had done a conjuring trick, as surely as if he'd pulled a coin from my ear, or made believe to swallow a fork; and just as he used to do such tricks in full view, with everyone looking on but unable to detect him, he had done the same here, and made a pact with me under their very eyes, and they were none the wiser.

But then I recalled that he'd once travelled about as a Mesmerist, and done medical clairvoyance at fairs, and really did know the arts of such things, and might put me into a trance. And that brought me up short, and gave me pause to consider.

3 5 .

"It is not the question of your guilt or innocence that concerns me," says Simon. "I am a doctor, not a judge. I simply wish to know what you yourself can actually remember."

They have come at last to the murders. He's reviewed all the documents at his disposal – the accounts of the trial, the opinions of the newspapers, the Confessions, even Mrs. Moodie's overblown rendition. He is fully prepared, and also tense: how he conducts himself today will determine whether Grace will at last crack open, revealing her hoarded treasures, or whether she will instead take fright and hide, and shut herself up like a clam.

What he's brought with him today is not a vegetable. Instead it's a silver candlestick, supplied by Reverend Verringer, and similar – he hopes – to the type used in the Kinnear household, and purloined by James McDermott. He hasn't yet produced it; it's in a wicker basket – a shopping basket, actually, borrowed from Dora – which he has placed unobtrusively by the side of his chair. He isn't entirely sure what he plans to do with it.

Grace continues her stitching. She does not look up. "Nobody has cared about that before, Sir," she says. "They told me I must be lying; they kept wanting to know more. Except for Mr. Kenneth MacKenzie the lawyer. But I am sure that even he did not believe me."

"I will believe you," says Simon. It is, he realizes, a fairly large undertaking.

Grace tightens her mouth a little, frowns, says nothing. He plunges in. "Mr. Kinnear left for the city on the Thursday, did he not?"

"Yes, Sir," says Grace.

"At three o'clock? On horseback?"

"That was the exact time, Sir. He was to be back on the Saturday. I was outside, sprinkling the linen handkerchiefs laid out in the sun to bleach. McDermott brought the horse round for him. Mr. Kinnear was riding Charley, as the wagon was down in the village getting a fresh coat of paint put on it."

"Did he say anything to you at that time?"

"He said, 'Here's your favourite beau, Grace, come and kiss him goodbye.'"

"Meaning James McDermott? But McDermott was not going anywhere," says Simon.

Grace looks up at him with a blank expression which verges on contempt. "He meant the horse, Sir. He knew I was very fond of Charley."

"And what did you do?"

"I went over and stroked Charley, Sir, on the nose. But Nancy was watching from the winter kitchen door, and she'd heard what he said, and did not like it. Nor did McDermott. But there was no harm in it. Mr. Kinnear only enjoyed a tease."

Simon takes a deep breath. "Had Mr. Kinnear ever made improper advances to you, Grace?"

She looks at him again; this time there's a faint smile. "I don't know what you mean by improper, Sir. He never used foul language to me."

"Did he ever touch you? Did he take liberties?"

"Only what was usual, Sir."

"Usual?" says Simon. He is baffled. He does not know how to say what he means, without being too explicit: Grace has a strong dash of prude in her.

"With a servant, Sir. He was a kind-enough master," says Grace primly. "And liberal when he wished to be."

Simon lets his impatience get the better of him. What does she mean? Is she saying she got paid for favours? "Did he put his hands inside your clothing?" he says. "Were you lying down?"

Grace stands up. "I have heard enough of that kind of talk," she says. "I do not have to stay here. You are just like them at the Asylum, and the prison chaplains, and Dr. Bannerling and his filthy ideas!"

Simon finds himself apologizing to her, and no wiser into the bargain. "Please sit down," he says, when she has been soothed. "Let us go back to the chain of events. Mr. Kinnear rode away at three o'clock on Thursday. Then what happened?"

"Nancy said we was both to leave after the next day, and she had the money to pay us. She said that Mr. Kinnear was in agreement with her."

"Did you believe that?"

"As regards McDermott, I did. But not as regards myself."

"Not yourself?" says Simon.

"She was afraid that Mr. Kinnear would come to like me better than her. As I've said, Sir, she was in the family way, and it often happens like that with a man; they'll change from a woman in that condition to one who is not, and it's the same with cows and horses; and if that happened, she'd be out on the road, her and her bastard. It was plain she wanted me out of the way, and gone before Mr. Kinnear came home. I don't believe he knew a thing about it."

"What did you do then, Grace?"

"I cried, Sir. In the kitchen. I did not want to leave, and I had no new situation to go to. It had been so sudden, I'd had no time to seek for one. And I was afraid she would not pay me after all, and send me off with no reference, and then what would I do? And McDermott feared the same."

"And then?" says Simon, when she does not continue.

"It was at this time, Sir, that McDermott said he had a secret, and I promised not to tell; and you know, Sir, that once having promised such a thing, I was bound by it. Then he said he was going to kill Nancy with the axe, and strangle her as well, and shoot Mr. Kinnear when he came back, and take the valuables; and I was to help him, and go with him, if I knew what was good for me, as otherwise I would be blamed for all. If I hadn't been so upset I would have laughed at him, but I did not; and to tell you the truth, we'd both had a glass or two of Mr. Kinnear's whisky, which we saw no reason not to help ourselves, seeing as we were to be turned away in any case. Nancy was over to the Wrights', and so we had a free hand."

"Did you believe McDermott would do as he said?"

"Not altogether, Sir. On the one hand, I thought he was just bragging, about what a fine man he was and what he could do, which was a thing he was prone to when drunk; and my father was the same way. But at the same time he seemed in earnest, and I was afraid of him; and I had a strong feeling as if it was fated, and it couldn't be avoided, no matter what I did."

"You did not warn anyone? Nancy herself, when she came back from her visit?"

"Why would she have believed me, Sir?" says Grace. "It would have sounded too stupid, if I said it out loud. She would think I was getting back at her, because she told me to leave; or that it was a servants' quarrel, and I was paying back McDermott. There was only my word for it, which he could easily deny, and say I was nothing but a silly hysterical girl. At the same time, if McDermott really meant it he might have killed the both of us right there and then; and I did not want to be killed. The best I could do was to try to delay him until Mr. Kinnear got back. At first he said he was going to do it that very night, and I persuaded him not to."

"How did you manage to do that?" says Simon.

"I said that if Nancy was killed on the Thursday, that would mean a whole day and a half of having to account for her where-abouts to anyone who might enquire. Whereas if he left it till later, there would be less suspicion aroused."

"I see," says Simon. "Very sensible."

"Please don't make fun of me, Sir," says Grace with dignity. "It is very distressing to me, and doubly so considering what I am being asked to remember."

Simon says he didn't mean it that way. He seems to be spending a lot of time apologizing to her. "And what happened then?" he asks, trying to sound kind, and not too eager.

"Then Nancy came back from her visit, and was quite cheerful. It was always her way, after she'd been in a temper, to pretend as if nothing had happened and we were all the best of friends; at least when Mr. Kinnear was not present. So she acted as if she hadn't told us to leave, or given us any hard words, and all went on as usual. We had supper together in the kitchen, cold ham, and potatoes made into a salad, with chives from the garden, the three of us; and she laughed and chattered. McDermott was sullen and silent, but that was no change; and then Nancy and I went to bed together, as was always the case when Mr. Kinnear was away, on account of her fear of burglars; and she suspected nothing. But I made very sure the bedchamber door was locked."

"Why was that?"

"As I've said, I always lock the door when I sleep. But also, McDermott had some foolish notion of creeping about the house at night with the axe. He wanted to kill Nancy while asleep. I said he should not do that, as he might hit me by mistake; but it was hard to convince him. He said he didn't want her looking at him when he did it."

"I can understand that," says Simon drily. "And then what happened?"

"Oh, the Friday began right as rain, to the outward eye, Sir. Nancy was very gay and light-hearted, and did not scold at all, or not as much as usual; and even McDermott was less sullen, in the morning, as I told him if he went around with such a hangdog face then Nancy was sure to suspect he was up to no good.

"In the middle of the afternoon young Jamie Walsh came over with his flute, as Nancy had asked him to. She said that as Mr. Kinnear was away we would all have a party, to celebrate. What was to be celebrated I am not sure; but in her good mood Nancy was very lively, and liked a song and dance. We had a fine supper, with cold roast chicken, and beer to wash it down; and then Nancy told Jamie to play for us, and he asked me if there was a tune I would especially wish to have, and was very attentive and kind to me, which McDermott did not like, and told him to stop making sheep's eyes at me, as it was enough to turn the stomach; and poor Jamie flushed bright red. Then Nancy told McDermott not to tease the boy, and couldn't he remember being young once himself; and she told Jamie he would grow up handsome, she could always tell a thing like that – much handsomer than McDermott with his scowling and pouting, and in any case handsome is as handsome does; and McDermott threw her a look of pure hate, which she affected not to see. Then she sent me down into the cellar to get more whisky, as by that time we had emptied the decanters upstairs.

"Then we laughed and sang; or Nancy laughed and sang, and I joined in. We sang *The Rose of Tralee*, and I remembered Mary Whitney, and wished very much that she was there, as she would know what to do, and would help me out of my difficulties. McDermott would not sing, as the dark mood was on him; nor would he dance when Nancy urged him, and said now was his chance to make good his boasts about what a nimble dancer he was. She wanted us all to part friends, but he was having none of that.

"After a time the life went out of the party. Jamie said he was tired of playing, and Nancy said it was time for bed; and McDermott said he would walk Jamie back to his own house, across the fields, I suppose to make sure he was well and truly gone. But by the time McDermott was come back, Nancy and I were upstairs already, in Mr. Kinnear's room, with the door locked."

"Mr. Kinnear's room?" says Simon.

"It was Nancy's idea," says Grace. "She said his bed was bigger, and cooler in the hot weather, and I had a habit of kicking in my sleep; and in any case Mr. Kinnear would not find it out, as it was us who made up the beds, not him; and even if he did discover it, he would not care, but would no doubt like the idea of two serving-maids in his bed at once. She had drunk several glasses of whisky, and was talking recklessly.

"And I did warn Nancy, after all, Sir. While she was brushing out her hair, I said, McDermott wants to kill you. She laughed, and said, I expect he does. I would not mind killing him, either. There is no love lost between us. He is in earnest, I said. He is never in earnest about anything, she said lightly. He is always bragging and boasting, and it is all just air.

"So then I knew there was nothing I could do, to save her.

"Once she was in the bed, she fell asleep at once. I sat brushing out my own hair, in the light of a single candle, with the naked woman in the picture looking out at me, the one who was taking a bath outdoors, and the other one with the peacock feathers; and they were both smiling at me, in a way I did not like."

"That night Mary Whitney appeared to me in a dream. It was not the first time; she'd come before, but never to say anything; she would be hanging up the wash and laughing, or paring an apple, or hiding behind a sheet on the line up in the attic, which were all things she used to do before her trouble came; and when I dreamt about her in that way I would wake up comforted, as if she was still alive and happy.

"But those were scenes of the past. This time she was in the room with me, the very room where I was, which was Mr. Kinnear's bedchamber. She was standing beside the bed in her nightdress, with her hair down, as when she was buried; and on the left side of her body I could see her heart, bright red through the white of her dress. But then I saw it was not a heart after all, but the red felt needle-case I made for her that Christmas, which I'd put in the coffin with her, under the flowers and the scattered petals; and I was glad to see she still had it with her, and hadn't forgotten me.

"She was holding a glass tumbler in her hand, and inside it was a firefly, trapped and glowing with a cold and greenish fire. Her face was very pale, but she looked at me and smiled; and then she took her hand from the top of the glass, and the firefly came out and darted about the room; and I knew that this was her soul, and it was trying to find its way out, but the window was shut; and then I could not see where it was gone. Then I woke up, with the tears of sadness running down my face, because Mary was lost to me once more."

"I lay there in the darkness, with the sound of Nancy's breathing; and in my ears I could hear my own heart, trudging and trudging, as if on a long and weary road that I was doomed to walk along whether I wanted to or not, and who could tell when I would get to the end of it. I was afraid to go to sleep again, for fear I might have another such dream; and my fears were not in vain, for that is indeed what happened.

"In this new dream, I dreamt I was walking in a place I had never been before, with high walls all around made of stone, grey and bleak as the stones of the village where I was born, back across on the other side of the ocean. On the ground there were loose grey pebbles, and out of the gravel there were peonies growing. They came up with just the buds on them, small and hard like unripe apples, and then they opened, and there were huge dark-red flowers with glossy petals, like satin; and then they burst in the wind and fell to the ground.

"Except for being red, they were like the peonies in the front garden on the first day I came to Mr. Kinnear's, when Nancy was cutting the last of them; and I saw her in the dream, just as she was then, in her pale dress with the pink rosebuds and the triple-flounced skirt, and her straw bonnet that hid her face. She was carrying a flat basket, to put the flowers in; and then she turned, and put her hand up to her throat as if startled.

"Then I was back in the stone yard, walking, with the toes of my shoes going in and out under the hem of my skirt, which was blue and white stripes. I knew I'd never had a skirt like that before, and at the sight of it I felt a great heaviness and desolation. But the peonies were still coming up from the stones; and I knew they shouldn't be there. I reached out my hand to touch one and it had a dry feel, and I knew it was made of cloth.

"Then up ahead I saw Nancy, on her knees, with her hair fallen over and the blood running down into her eyes. Around her neck was a white cotton kerchief printed with blue flowers, love-in-a-mist, and it was mine. She was holding out her hands to me for mercy; in her ears were the little gold earrings I used to envy. I wanted to run to her and help her, but I could not; and my feet kept walking at the same steady pace, as though they were not my own feet at all. When I was almost up to Nancy, to where she was kneeling, she smiled. Only the mouth, her eyes were hidden by the blood and hair, and then she came apart into patches of colour, she scattered, a drift of red and white cloth petals across the stones.

"Then it was dark suddenly, and a man was standing there with a candle, blocking the stairs that went up, and the cellar walls were all around me, and I knew I would never get out."

"You dreamt this before the event?" says Simon. He is writing feverishly.

"Yes Sir," says Grace. "And many times since." Her voice has dropped to a whisper. "That was why they put me away."

"Away?" Simon prompts.

"Into the Asylum, Sir. Because of the bad dreams." She has laid her sewing aside, and is looking down at her hands.

"Only the dreams?" Simon asks gently.

"They said they were not dreams at all, Sir. They said I was awake. But I do not wish to say any more about it."

36.

"On the Saturday morning I woke up at dawn. Outside in the henhouse the cock was crowing; he had a hoarse and rattling sort of crow, as if there was a hand tightening around his neck already, and I thought, You know you're for the stewpot soon. Soon you will be a carcass. And although I was thinking about the rooster, I will not deny that I was thinking about Nancy as well. It sounds cold and perhaps it was. I felt light-headed, and detached from myself, as if I was not really present, but only there in body.

"I know these are odd thoughts to confess to, Sir, but I will not lie and conceal them, as I could easily do, having never told this to anyone before. I wish to relate everything just as it happened to me, and those were the thoughts I had.

"Nancy was still asleep, and I took care not to disturb her. I felt she might as well have her sleep out, and the longer she stayed in bed the longer it would be before anything bad happened, either to her or to me. As I crept cautiously out of Mr. Kinnear's bed she groaned and rolled over, and I wondered whether she was having a bad dream.

"The night previous, I'd put my nightdress on in my own room off the winter kitchen before going upstairs with my candle, so I went in there and dressed as usual. Everything was the same but not the same, and when I went to wash my face and do my hair, my own face in the mirror over the kitchen sink was not like my face at all. It looked rounder and whiter, with two great startled staring eyes, and I didn't wish to look at it.

"I went into the kitchen and opened the window shutters. The glasses and plates from the night before were still on the table, and they looked very lonely and forlorn, as if some great and sudden disaster had overtaken all who had eaten and drunk from them, and here was I, coming upon them by accident, many years later; and I felt very sad. I gathered them up and carried them into the scullery.

"When I came back out there was a strange light in the kitchen, as if there was a film of silver over everything, like frost only smoother, like water running thinly down over flat stones; and then my eyes were opened and I knew it was because God had come into the house and this was the silver that covered Heaven. God had come in because God is everywhere, you can't keep him out, he is part of everything there is, so how could you ever build a wall or four walls or a door or a shut window, that he could not walk right through as if it was air.

"I said, What do you want here, but he did not answer, he just kept on being silver, so I went out to milk the cow; because the only thing to do about God is to go on with what you were doing anyway, since you can't ever stop him or get any reasons out of him. There is a Do this or a Do that with God, but not any Because.

"When I came back with the pails of milk I saw McDermott in the kitchen. He was cleaning the shoes. Where is Nancy, he said.

"She is dressing, I said. Are you going to kill her this morning?

"Yes, he said, damn her, I will take the axe now and go knock her on the head.

"I laid my hand on his arm, and looked up into his face. Surely you will not, surely you cannot bring yourself to do such a wicked thing, I said. But he didn't understand me, he thought I was taunting him. He thought I was calling him a coward.

"You will see in a minute what I can do, he said angrily.

"Oh, for God's sake don't kill her in the room, I said, you will make the floor all bloody. It was a foolish thing to say but that is what came into my mind, and as you know, Sir, it was my job to clean the floors in that house, and there was a carpet in Nancy's room. I'd never tried to get blood out of a carpet but I'd got it out of other things, and it is not a task to be sneezed at.

"McDermott gave me a scornful glance, as if I was a halfwit, and indeed I must have sounded like one. Then he went outside the house, and picked up the axe from beside the chopping block.

"I could not think what to do. I went into the garden, to gather some chives, as Nancy had ordered an omelette for breakfast. On the bolted lettuces the snails were making their lacework. I knelt down and watched them, with their eyes on little stems; and I reached out my hand for the chives, and it was as if my hand was not mine at all, but only a husk or skin, with inside it another hand growing.

"I tried to pray, but the words would not come, and I believe that is because I had ill-wished Nancy, I had indeed wished her dead; but I did not do so right then. But why did I need to pray, when God was right there, hovering above us like the Angel of Death over the Egyptians, I could feel his cold breath, I could hear the beating of his dark wings, inside my heart. God is everywhere, I thought, so God is in the kitchen, and God is in Nancy, and God is in McDermott, and in McDermott's hands, and God is in the axe too. Then I heard a dull sound from within, like a heavy door closing shut, and after that I can remember no more for a time."

"Nothing about the cellar?" says Simon. "Not about seeing

McDermott dragging Nancy by the hair, to the trapdoor, and throwing her down the stairs? It was in your Confession."

Grace clutches her two hands to the sides of her head. "That is what they wanted me to say. Mr. MacKenzie told me I had to say it, to save my own life." For once she is trembling. "He said it was not a lie, as that is what must have happened, whether I could remember it or not."

"Did you give James McDermott the kerchief from around your neck?" Simon sounds more like a courtroom lawyer than he wishes to, but he presses on.

"The one that was used to strangle poor Nancy? It was mine, I know that. But I have no recollection of giving it to him."

"Nor of being down in the cellar?" says Simon. "Nor of helping him to kill her? Nor of wanting to steal the gold earrings off the corpse, as he says you wished to do?"

Grace covers her eyes with a hand, briefly. "All that time is dark to me, Sir," she says. "And in any case, there were no gold earrings taken. I won't say I didn't think of it later, when we were packing up; but having a thought is not the same as doing it. If we were all on trial for our thoughts, we would all be hanged."

Simon has to admit the justice of this. He tries a different line. "Jefferson the butcher testified that he spoke with you that morning."

"I know he did, Sir. But I cannot remember it."

"He says he was surprised, as it was not you who ordinarily gave the orders, but Nancy; and he was further surprised when you said that no fresh meat was wanted for the week. He found it most peculiar."

"If it was me, Sir, and acting in my right mind, I'd of had my wits about me, and ordered the meat as usual. It would have been less suspicious."

Simon has to agree. "Well then," he says, "what is the next thing you remember?"

"I found myself standing at the front of the house, Sir, where the flowers were. I felt quite dizzy, and had a headache. I was thinking, I must open the window; but that was foolish, as I was already outside. It must have been about three o'clock. Mr. Kinnear was coming up the driveway, with his light wagon all new-painted, yellow and green. McDermott came out from the back, and we both helped with the packages, and McDermott gave me a threatening look; and then Mr. Kinnear went into the house, and I knew he was looking for Nancy. A thought came into my head – You won't find her there, you will have to look below, she is a carcass – and I became very frightened.

"Then McDermott said to me, I know you will tell, and if you do, your life is not worth a straw. I was confused by this. What have you done? I said. You know very well, he said with a laugh. I did not know; but now I suspected the worst. Then he made me promise I would help to kill Mr. Kinnear, which I did say I would; for if not, I could see by his eyes he would have killed me as well. Then he took the horse and wagon to the stable.

"I went into the kitchen, to go about my duties as if nothing was wrong. Mr. Kinnear came in, and asked, Where was Nancy? I said she had gone to town in the stagecoach. He said that was strange, as he'd passed it on the way and did not see her. I asked him if he would like something to eat, and he said yes, and asked, had Jefferson come with the fresh meat; and I said no. He said that was curious, and then said he would have some tea and toast and eggs.

"And so I made it. I brought it to him in the dining room, where he sat waiting, reading a book which he had brought with him from town. It was the newest Godey's Ladies' Book, which poor Nancy liked to have, for the fashions; and although Mr. Kinnear always pretended it was only ladies' fripperies, he himself often took a peek at it when Nancy was not nearby, as there were things in it other than dresses; and he liked to look at the new styles of undergarments, and to read the articles on how a lady should behave, which I would often catch him chuckling over on those occasions when I brought in his coffee.

"I went back into the kitchen, and McDermott was there. He said, I think I'll go and kill him now. But I said, Good gracious McDermott, it is too soon, wait till it is dark.

"Then Mr. Kinnear went upstairs and had a nap, with all his clothes on, and so McDermott had to wait, whether he wanted to or not. Even he was not up to the shooting of a sleeping man. McDermott stuck to me all afternoon, as close as glue, because he was certain that I would run away and tell. He had the gun with him, and kept fiddling with it. It was the old double-barrelled shotgun that Mr. Kinnear kept to shoot ducks with, but it was not loaded with duck-shot. He said he had two lead bullets in it – one he'd found, the other one he'd made from a piece of lead; and that he'd got the powder for it across the way at his friend John Harvey's, although Hannah Upton, the hard-faced bitch – she was the woman who lived with Harvey – had told him he couldn't have it. But he'd taken it anyway, and be damned to her. By this time he was very excited and nervous, and swaggering as well, and proud of his own daring. He was cursing a good deal, but I did not object to it, being afraid."

"About seven o'clock Mr. Kinnear came down, and had his tea, and was quite uneasy about Nancy. Now I will do it, said McDermott, you must go in there and ask him to come into the kitchen, so I can shoot him on the stone floor. But I said I would not.

"He said in that case he would do it himself. He'd get him to come, by telling him there was something wrong with his new saddle, it was all cut to ribbons.

"I wanted nothing to do with it. I took the tea tray across the courtyard to the back kitchen, which was the one with the stove lit, as I was going to do the washing up in there; and as I was setting down the tray I heard the report of a gun.

"I ran into the front kitchen and saw Mr. Kinnear lying dead on the floor, and McDermott standing over him. The gun was on the floor. I attempted to run out, and he yelled and swore, and said I must open the trapdoor in the hall. I said, I won't; he said, You shall. So I did, and McDermott threw the body down the stairs.

"I was so frightened that I ran out of the front door onto the lawn, and around past the pump to the back kitchen, and then McDermott came out of the front kitchen door with the gun, and fired at me, and I fell onto the ground in a dead faint. And that is all I can remember, Sir, until much later in the evening."

"Jamie Walsh testified that he came into the yard about eight o'clock, which must have been right after you fainted. He said McDermott still had the gun in his hand, and claimed to have been shooting birds."

"I know it, Sir."

"He said you were standing by the pump. He said you told him that Mr. Kinnear was not back yet, and that Nancy was gone over to the Wrights'."

"I cannot account for it, Sir."

"He said you were well, and in good spirits. He said you were better dressed than usual, and were wearing white stockings. He implied they were Nancy's."

"I was there in the courtroom, Sir. I heard him say it; although the stockings were my own. But by then he had forgot all of his former loving sentiments towards me, and only wished to damage me, and to hang me if possible. But there is nothing I can do about what other people say."

Her tone is so dejected that Simon feels a tender pity for her. He has an impulse to take her in his arms, to soothe her, to stroke her hair.

"Well, Grace," he says briskly, "I can see you are tired. We will continue with your story tomorrow."

"Yes, Sir. I hope I will have the strength."

"Sooner or later we will get to the bottom of it."

"I hope so, Sir," she says wanly. "It would be a great relief to me, to know the whole truth at last."

3 7 .

The leaves of the trees are already taking on an August look – lustreless, dusty, and limp – although it isn't yet August. Simon walks back slowly through the wilting afternoon heat. He carries with him the silver candlestick; he didn't think to use it. It's dragging on his arm; in fact, both of his arms hold a curious tension, as if he's been pulling hard on a heavy rope. What was he expecting? The missing memory, of course: those few crucial hours. Well, he hadn't got it.

He finds himself remembering an evening long ago, when he was still an undergraduate at Harvard. He'd gone to New York on an excursion with his father, who was still rich then and also still alive; they'd seen the opera. It was Bellini's *Sonnambula*: a simple and chaste village girl, Amina, is found asleep in the count's bedroom, having walked there unconsciously; her fiancé and the villagers denounce her as a whore, despite the Count's protests, which are based on his superior scientific knowledge; but when Amina is seen walking in her sleep across a perilous bridge, which collapses behind her into the rushing stream, her innocence is proven beyond a doubt and she awakes to restored happiness.

A parable of the soul, as his Latin teacher had pointed out so sententiously, *Amina* being a crude anagram for *anima*. But why, Simon has asked himself, was the soul depicted as unconscious? And, even more intriguingly: while Amina slept, who was doing the walking? It's a question which now holds implications for him which are far more pressing.

Was Grace unconscious at the time she claimed, or was she fully awake, as Jamie Walsh testified? How much of her story can he allow himself to believe? Does he need a grain of salt, or two, or three? Is it a real case of amnesia, of the somnambulistic type, or is he the victim of a cunning imposture? He cautions himself against absolutism: why should she be expected to produce nothing but the pure, entire, and unblemished truth? Anyone in her position would select and rearrange, to give a positive impression. In her favour, much of what she's told him accords with her printed Confession; but is that really in her favour? Possibly it accords too well. He wonders if she's been studying from the same text he himself has been using, the better to convince him.

The difficulty is that he wants to be convinced. He wants her to be Amina. He wants her to be vindicated.

He must be careful, he tells himself. He must draw back. Looked at objectively, what's been going on between them, despite her evident anxiety over the murders and her surface compliance, has been a contest of wills. She hasn't refused to talk – far from it. She's told him a great deal; but she's told him only what she's chosen to tell. What he wants is what she refuses to tell; what she chooses perhaps not even to know. Knowledge of guilt, or else of innocence: either could be concealed. But he'll pry it out of her yet. He's got the hook in her mouth, but can he pull her out? Up, out of the abyss, up to the light. Out of the deep blue sea.

He wonders why he's thinking in such drastic terms. He means her well, he tells himself. He thinks of it as a rescue, surely he does.

But does she? If she has anything to hide, she may want to stay in the water, in the dark, in her element. She may be afraid she won't be able to breathe, otherwise.

Simon tells himself to stop being so extreme and histrionic. It may well be that Grace is a true amnesiac. Or simply contrary. Or simply guilty.

She could of course be insane, with the astonishingly devious plausibility of the experienced maniac. Some of her memories, especially those of the day of the murders, would suggest a fanaticism of the religious variety. However, those same recollections could as easily be interpreted as the naive superstitions and fears of a simple soul. What he wants is certainty, one way or the other; and that is precisely what she's withholding from him.

Perhaps it's his methods that have been at fault. Certainly his technique of suggestion has not been productive: the vegetables have been a dismal failure. Perhaps he's been too tentative, too accommodating; perhaps something more drastic may be in order. Perhaps he should encourage Jerome DuPont in his neuro-hypnotic experiment, and arrange to witness it himself, and even choose the questions. He distrusts the method. Still, something new might emerge; something might be discovered which he's so far been unable to discover by himself. It would at least be worth trying.

He reaches the house, and fumbles in his pocket for the key, but Dora opens the door for him. He regards her with disgust: a woman so porcine, and, in this weather, so distinctly sweaty, should not be permitted out in public. She's a libel on the entire sex. He himself has been instrumental in bringing her back to work here – he's practically bribed her to do it – but this doesn't mean he likes her any better than he ever did. Nor she him, judging from the venomous look she gives him, out of her small red eyes.

"Herself wants to see you," she says, jerking her head towards the back of the house. Her manners are as democratic as ever.

Mrs. Humphrey was strongly opposed to Dora's return, and can hardly bear to be in the same room with her, which is not surprising. However, Simon had pointed out that he cannot be expected to function without tidiness and order, and someone must do the work of the house, and as no one else was to be had at the moment, Dora would have to do. As long as Dora was paid, he'd said, she would be tractable enough, although politeness would be too much to expect; all of which has proven to be the case.

"Where is she?" says Simon. He shouldn't have said *she*; it sounds too intimate. *Mrs. Humphrey* would have been better.

"Lying on the sofa, I guess," says Dora with contempt. "Same as always."

But when Simon enters the parlour – still eerily bare of furniture, although some of the original pieces have mysteriously reappeared – Mrs. Humphrey is standing by the fireplace, with one arm and hand draped gracefully over the white mantelpiece. The hand with the lace handkerchief. He smells violets.

"Dr. Jordan," she says, breaking her pose, "I thought you might care to dine with me tonight, as a poor recompense for all the efforts you have made on my behalf. I do not like to seem deficient in gratitude. Dora has prepared a little cold chicken." She enunciates each word carefully, as if it's a speech she has memorized.

Simon declines, with as much politeness as he can summon. He thanks her very much, but this evening he is engaged. This verges on the truth: he has half accepted an invitation of Miss Lydia's, to join a party of young people in a rowing excursion on the inner harbour.

Mrs. Humphrey accepts his refusal with a gracious smile, and says that they will do it another time. Something in the way she's holding her body – that, and the slow deliberation of her speech –

strikes him as odd. Has the woman been drinking? Her eyes have a fixed stare, and her hands are trembling slightly.

Once upstairs, he opens his leather satchel. Everything seems in order. His three bottles of laudanum are there: none is emptier than it should be. He uncorks them, tastes the contents: one is almost pure water. She's been raiding his supplies, God only knows for how long. The afternoon headaches take on a different significance. He should have known: with a husband like that she was bound to seek out a crutch of some kind. When in funds she no doubt buys it, he thinks; but cash has been scarce, and he has been careless. He ought to have locked his room, but now is too late to begin.

There is, of course, no way he can mention it to her. She is a fastidious woman. To accuse her of theft would be not only brutal, but vulgar. Still, he's been taken.

Simon goes on the rowing trip. The night is warm and calm, and there's moonlight. He drinks a little champagne – there only is a little – and sits in the same rowboat as Lydia, and flirts with her in a half-hearted way. She at least is normal and healthy, and pretty too. Possibly he should propose to her. He thinks she might accept. Cart her home to propitiate his mother, hand her over, let the two of them work on his well-being.

It would be one way of deciding his own fate, or settling his own hash; or getting himself out of harm's way. But he won't do it; he's not that lazy, or weary; not yet.

X.

LADY OF THE LAKE

We then commenced packing up all the valuable things we could find; we both went down into the cellar; Mr. Kinnear was lying on his back in the wine-cellar; I held the candle; McDermott took the keys and some money from his pockets; nothing was said about Nancy; I did not see her, but I knew she was in the cellar, and about 11 o'clock, McDermott harnessed the horse; we put the boxes in the wagon and started off for Toronto; he said he would go to the States and he would marry me. I consented to go; we arrived at Toronto, at the City Hotel, about 5 o'clock; awoke the people; had breakfast there; I unlocked Nancy's box and put some of her things on, and we left by the boat at 8 o'clock, and arrived at Lewiston, about 3 o'clock; went to the tavern; in the evening we had supper at the public table, and I went to bed in one room and McDermott in another; before I went to bed, I told McDermott I would stop at Lewiston, and I would not go any further; he said he would make me go with him, and about 5 o'clock in the morning, Mr. Kingsmill, the High Bailiff, came and arrested us, and brought us back to Toronto.

– Confession of Grace Marks,
Star and Transcript, Toronto, November 1843.

He meets, by heavenly chance express,
    The destined maid; some hidden hand
Unveils to him that loveliness
    Which others cannot understand.
His merits in her presence grow,
    To match the promise in her eyes,
And round her happy footsteps blow
    The authentic airs of paradise. . . .

– Coventry Patmore,
The Angel in the House, 1854.

3 8 .

What McDermott told me later was that after he'd fired the gun at me, and I'd fallen down in a dead faint, he pumped a bucket of cold water and threw it over me, and gave me some water with peppermint to drink, and I revived immediately, and was as good as new and quite cheerful, and stirred up the fire and cooked supper for him, which was ham and eggs, with tea after, and a shot of whisky to steady us; and we ate it together with a good will, and clinked our glasses, and drank to the success of our venture. But I can't remember any of that at all. I could not have acted so heartlessly, with Mr. Kinnear lying dead in the cellar, not to mention Nancy, who must have been dead too, though I didn't know for certain what had become of her. But McDermott was a great liar.

I must have lain unconscious for a long time, for when I woke up the light was already fading. I was lying on my back, on the bed in my own bedchamber; and my cap was off and my hair was all disarranged and down about my shoulders, and also it was damp, and the upper part of my dress as well, and that must have been from the water that James had thrown over me; so that part at least of what he said was true. I lay there on the bed, trying to remember what had happened, as I couldn't recollect how I'd got into the room. James must have carried me in, for the door was standing open, and if I'd walked in by myself I would have locked it.

I meant to get up and latch the door, but my head was aching and the room was very hot and airless; and I fell asleep again, and must have tossed restlessly, for when I woke the bedclothes were all rumpled and the coverlet had fallen off onto the floor. This time I woke suddenly and sat bolt upright, and despite the heat I was in a cold sweat. The reason for it was that there was a man standing in the room looking down at me. It was James McDermott, and I thought he had come in to strangle me in my sleep, having killed the others. My voice was all dried up in my throat with terror, and I couldn't speak a word.

But he said, quite kindly, did I feel better now after my rest; and I found my voice again and said I did. I knew it would be a mistake to show too much fear, and to lose control of myself; for then he'd think he couldn't trust me or depend on me to keep my nerve, and would be afraid I would break down and begin crying or screaming when there were others present, and tell everything; which was why he had shot at me; and if he thought that, he would do away with me as quick as winking, rather than have any witness.

Then he sat down on the side of the bed, and said now it was time for me to keep my promise; and I said what promise, and he said I knew very well, for I had promised him myself in exchange for the killing of Nancy.

I could not remember having said any such thing; but as I was now convinced he was a madman, I thought he had twisted around something I had indeed said, some thing that was innocent enough, or only what anyone would say; such as I wished she was dead, and that I would give anything for it. And Nancy had been very harsh with me, from time to time. But that is only what servants are always saying, out of their masters' hearing; for when you can't answer back to their faces, you must give vent to your feelings in some other way.

But McDermott had turned this around to mean what I never intended, and now he wished to hold me to a bargain I hadn't made. And he was in earnest, as he put a hand on my shoulder, and was pushing me backwards onto the bed. And with the other hand he was pulling up my skirt; and I could tell by the smell of him that he'd been into Mr. Kinnear's whisky, and heavily too.

I knew that the only way was to humour him. Oh no, I said, laughing, not in this bed, it is too narrow and not at all comfortable for two people. Let us go to some other bed.

To my surprise he thought that was a fine idea, and said it would give him great pleasure to sleep in Mr. Kinnear's bed, where Nancy had so often played the whore; and I reflected that once I'd given in to him, he would consider me a whore as well, and would hold my life very cheap indeed, and would most likely kill me with the axe and throw me into the cellar, as he had often said a whore was good for nothing but to wipe your dirty boots on, by giving them a good kicking all over their filthy bodies. So I planned to delay, and to put him off as long as I could.

He pulled me to my feet, and we lit the candle that was in the kitchen, and climbed the stairs; and then we went into Mr. Kinnear's room, that was all tidy and with the bed neatly made up, as I had done it myself that very morning; and he threw back the covers, and pulled me down beside him. And he said, No straw for the gentry, nothing but goose feathers for them, no wonder Nancy liked to spend so much time in this bed; and for a moment he seemed over-awed, not by what he'd done, but by the grandeur of the bed he was in. But then he fell to kissing me, and said, Now my girl, it's time, and began unbuttoning my dress; and I remembered that the wages of sin is death, and I felt faint. But I knew that if I fainted I was as good as dead, with him in the state he was in.

I burst into tears, and I said, No, I can't, not here, in a dead man's bed, it isn't right, with him in the cellar stark and stiff; and I began to sob and cry.

He was very annoyed, and said I must stop at once, or he would slap my face for me; but he did not. What I had said had cooled his ardour, as they say in books; or as Mary Whitney would say, he'd mislaid the poker. For at that moment Mr. Kinnear, dead as he was, was the stiffer man of the two of them.

He pulled me up off the bed, and yanked me down the hallway by one arm, and I was still wailing and howling for all I was worth. If you don't like that bed, said he, I shall do it in Nancy's, for you are as great a slut as she was. And I could see which way the wind was blowing, and I thought my last hour had come; and I expected at any moment to be thrown down, and dragged along by the hair.

He flung open the door, and hauled me into the room, which was in disarray, just as Nancy had left it, for I hadn't tidied the room, there being no need and indeed no time to do so. But when he pulled back the coverlet, the sheet was all spattered with dark blood, and there was a book lying there in the bed, covered with blood also. At which I let out a scream of terror; but McDermott stopped, and looked at it, and said, I'd forgot about that.

I asked him what in Heaven's name it was, and what it was doing there. He said it was the magazine that Mr. Kinnear had been reading, and he'd carried it with him out to the kitchen, where he was shot; and in falling he'd clapped his hands to his breast, still holding the book; and it therefore received the first spurts of blood. And McDermott had thrown it into Nancy's bed, to get it out of sight, and also because it belonged there, having been brought from town for her, and also because Kinnear's blood was on Nancy's head, for if she had not been such a bloody great whore and shrew, all would have been different, and Mr. Kinnear needn't have died. So it was a sign. And at that he crossed himself, which was the only time I ever saw him do anything so Papist.

Well, I thought him as mad as a moose in heat, as Mary Whitney used to say; but the sight of the book had sobered him up, and all notions of what he'd been about to do had gone right out of his head. And I held the candle down close, and turned the book over with my thumb and finger, and it was indeed the Godey's Ladies' Book which Mr. Kinnear had so enjoyed reading, earlier in the day. And at this memory I nearly burst into tears in earnest.

But there was no telling how long McDermott's present mood would hold. So I said, That will confuse them; when they find it, they will not be able to guess at all how it came here. And he said yes, it would give them something to puzzle their brains over; and he laughed in a hollow sort of way.

Then I said, We had better hurry, or someone may come while we are here; we must make haste, and pack up the things. For we will have to travel by night, or someone will see us on the road, with Mr. Kinnear's rig, and will know something is wrong. It will take us a long time to reach Toronto, I said, in the dark; and also Charley Horse will be tired, having made the trip once today already.

And McDermott agreed, as one half asleep; and we commenced searching through the house, and packing up the things. I did not want to take very much, only the lightest and most valuable items, such as Mr. Kinnear's gold snuffbox, and his telescope and pocket-compass, and his gold pen-knife, and any money we could find; but McDermott said, in for a penny, in for a pound, and he might as well be hanged for a goat as for a sheep; and in the end we ransacked the house, and took the silver plate and candlesticks, and the spoons and forks and all, even the ones with the family crest on; for McDermott said they could always be melted.

I looked into Nancy's box, and at her dresses; and I thought, There is no need for them to go to waste, poor Nancy has no further use for them. So I took the box and all in it, and her winter things too; but I left the dress that she'd been sewing, because it seemed too close to her altogether, as it was not finished; and I'd heard that the dead would come back to complete what they had left undone, and I didn't want her missing it, and following after me. For by this time I was almost certain she was dead.

Before leaving, I tidied up the house, and washed the dishes, the plates from supper and all; and I put Mr. Kinnear's bed in order, and pulled the coverlet up over Nancy's bed, although I left the book in it, not wanting to get Mr. Kinnear's blood on my hands; and I emptied her chamber pot, as I did not think it a nice thing to leave, as being somehow disrespectful. And meanwhile McDermott was harnessing Charley, and loading the boxes and the carpetbag into the wagon; though one time I found him sitting outside on the step, and staring vacantly in front of him. So I told him to pull himself together, and be a man. For the last thing I wanted was to be stuck there in that house with him, especially if he'd gone completely out of his mind. And when I told him to be a man, it had an effect, for he shook himself, and got up, and said I was right.

The last thing I did was to take off the clothes I'd been wearing that day; and I put on one of Nancy's dresses, the pale one with the white ground and the small floral print, which was the same one she had on the first day I came to Mr. Kinnear's. And I put on her petticoat with the lace edging, and my own spare clean petticoat, and Nancy's summer shoes of light-coloured leather, which I had so often admired, although they did not fit very well. And also her good straw bonnet; and I took her light cashmere shawl, although I did not think I would need to wear it, as the night was warm. And I put some rosewater behind my ears and on my wrists, from the bottle of it on her dresser; and the smell of it was a comfort of sorts.

Then I put on a clean apron, and stirred up the fire in the summer kitchen stove, which still had some embers left in it, and burnt my own clothes; I didn't like the thought of wearing them ever again, as they would remind me of things I wished to forget. It may have been my fancy, but a smell went up from them like scorching meat; and it was like my own dirtied and cast-off skin that I was burning.

While I was doing this, McDermott came in, and said he was ready, and why was I wasting time. I told him I could not find my large white kerchief, the one with the blue flowers on it, and that I needed it to keep the sun off my neck, while we would be crossing the Lake on the ferry the following day. At that he laughed in an astonished way, and said it was downstairs in the cellar, keeping the sun off Nancy's neck; as I ought to remember, seeing as how I myself had pulled it tight and tied the knot. At this I was very shocked; but did not wish to contradict him, as it is dangerous to contradict mad people. So I said I had forgot.

It was about eleven o'clock at night when we set out; a beautiful night, with enough of a breeze to be cooling, and not too many mosquitoes. There was half a moon, and I couldn't remember whether it was waxing or waning; and as we went down the driveway between the rows of maples and past the orchard, I looked behind me, and saw the house standing there all peaceful and lighted up by the moonlight, as if it was gently glowing. And I thought, who would guess from looking at it what lies within. And then I sighed, and readied myself for the long drive.

We went quite slowly, even though Charley knew the road; but he knew also that this was not his true driver, and that there was something amiss; for several times he stopped, and would not go forward until urged with the whip. But when we'd gone several miles along the road, and were past the places that he knew best, he settled into it; and along we went, past the fields all silent and silvery, and the snake fences like darker braid alongside, with the bats flickering overhead, and the dense patches where there was woodland; and once an owl crossed our path, as pale and soft as a moth.

At first I was afraid we would meet someone we knew, and they would ask where we were going on such a furtive errand; but there was not a living soul. And James became bolder and more cheerful, and started talking about what we would do when we reached the States, and how he would sell the things, and buy a small farm, and then we would be independent; and if we did not have enough money at first, we would hire ourselves out as servants, and save up our pay. And I said neither yes nor no, as I did not intend to stay with him any more than a minute, once we were safe across the Lake and among people.

But after a time he fell silent, and there was only the sound of Charley's hooves on the road, and the rustling of the slight wind. I thought I might jump down from the wagon, and run off into the woods; but knew I would not get far, and even if I did, I would then be eaten by the bears and wolves. And I thought, I am riding through the Valley of the Shadow of Death, as it says in the Psalm; and I attempted to fear no evil, but it was very hard, for there was evil in the wagon with me, like a sort of mist. So I tried to think about something else. And I looked up at the sky, which did not have a cloud in it, and was filled with stars; and it seemed so close I could touch it, and so delicate I could put my hand right through it, like a spiderweb spangled with dewdrops.

But then as I looked, a part of it began to wrinkle up, like the skin on scalding milk; but harder and more brittle, and pebbled, like a dark beach, or like black silk crêpe; and then the sky was only a thin surface, like paper, and it was being singed away. And behind it was a cold blackness; and it was not Heaven or even Hell that I was looking at, but only emptiness. This was more frightening than anything I could think of, and I prayed silently to God to forgive my sins; but what if there was no God to forgive me? And then I reflected that perhaps it was the outer darkness, with the wailing and the gnashing of teeth, where God was not. And as soon as I had this thought, the sky closed over again, like water after you have thrown a stone; and was again smooth and unbroken, and filled with stars.

But all the time the moon was descending, and the wagon was moving along. And gradually I became drowsy, and the night air was cool, so I drew the cashmere shawl around myself; and I must have nodded off asleep, and let my head fall against McDermott; for the last I remembered was the feel of him settling the shawl tenderly around my shoulders.

The next thing I knew I was flat on my back on the ground, in the weeds at the side of the road, with a heavy weight on top of me holding me down, and there was a hand feeling up under my petticoats; and I began to struggle, and to scream. Then a hand came over my mouth, and the voice of James said angrily, what did I mean, causing such an uproar, did I want us to be discovered? I became quiet, and he took away his hand, and I told him to get off, and to let me up at once.

Then he was very angry; for he claimed I had asked him to stop the wagon, so I could get down and relieve myself by the roadside; and having done so, that I had spread out my own shawl, not two minutes before, and had invited him to join me on it like the hot bitch I was, at the same time saying I would now fulfil my promise.

I knew I had done no such thing, having been sound asleep, and I said so. And he said he would not be made a fool of, and I was a damned slut and a demon, and Hell was too good for me, as I had led him on, and enticed him, and caused him to damn his own soul into the bargain; and I began to cry, not feeling I deserved such hard words. And he said crocodile tears would not avail this time, as he'd had a bellyful of them; and he proceeded to wrench at my skirts, holding my head down by the hair. So I bit him hard on the ear.

He roared out, and I thought he might kill me there and then. But instead he let go of me, and got up, and helped me up as well; and said I was a good girl after all, and he would wait until he had married me, as it was better that way, and more proper; and he had just been testing me. Then he said I certainly had good strong teeth, as I had drawn blood; which seemed to please him.

I was much surprised at this, but said nothing, as I was still all alone with him on an empty road, with many miles to go.

3 9 .

And so we went on through the night, and at last the sky grew lighter; and we reached Toronto a little after five in the morning. McDermott said we would go to the City Hotel, and rouse the people up, and make them cook breakfast for us, as he was almost starved with hunger. I said that was not a good plan, and we should wait until many people were about, as if we did as he said we would be very noticeable, and would be remembered. And he said why must I always be arguing with him, it was enough to drive a man into a frenzy, and he had money in his pocket which was as good as the next man's, and if he wanted a breakfast and could pay for it, then he would have it.

It is remarkable, I have since thought, how once a man has a few coins, no matter how he came by them, he thinks right away that he is entitled to them, and to whatever they can buy, and fancies himself cock of the walk.

We did as he said; not so much for the breakfast, I now believe, but because he wanted to show me who was master. What we had was bacon and eggs; and it was a wonder to see how he strutted, and swaggered, and ordered the servant about, and said his egg was not well-enough cooked. But I could scarcely eat two bites; I was shivering with apprehension, because of all the attention he was calling to himself.

Then we found that the next ferry did not leave for the States until eight o'clock, and we would have to wait in Toronto another two hours or so. I felt this was very dangerous, as Mr. Kinnear's horse and wagon were sure to be known by some in the town, as he had come there very often. So I made McDermott leave the wagon in the most out-of-sight place I could find, on a small side street, although he wanted to drive it about, and preen himself; but I found later that despite my precautions it had been noticed.

It wasn't until the sun had come up that I got a good look at McDermott in a bright light, and realized he had got Mr. Kinnear's boots on. And I asked, did he take them off the body, as it lay in the cellar; and he said yes, and the shirt too was Kinnear's, off the shelves in his dressing room, as it was a fine one, and better quality than any shirt he'd ever owned. He'd thought to take the one off the body as well, but it was covered in blood, and he'd thrown it behind the door. I was horrified, and asked how could he do such a thing; and he said what did I mean, as I was wearing Nancy's dress and bonnet myself. And I said it was not the same thing, and he said it was; and I said at least I had not taken the boots off a corpse. And he said it made no difference; and in any case, he hadn't wanted to leave the corpse naked, so he'd dressed it in his own shirt.

I asked which one had he put on Mr. Kinnear, and he said it was one of those he'd bought from the peddler. I was distressed, and said, Now Jeremiah will be blamed, as it will be traced; and I would be sorry for that, as he was a friend of mine.

McDermott said much too close a friend, in his opinion; and I said what did he mean by that? And he said that Jeremiah had looked at me in a way he didn't like, and that no wife of his would be allowed to hobnob with any Jew peddlers, and gossip with them at the back door, and flirt in that way; and if she did, he would black her eyes, and knock her head about her shoulders for her.

I was becoming angry; and I was on the point of saying that Jeremiah was not a Jew, but even if he was, I would marry a Jew peddler any day, rather than marry him; but I knew that if we had a quarrel it would not be to the good of either, especially if it came to slaps and screaming. So I held my tongue; for it was my plan to get safe across to the States without incident, and then give McDermott the slip, and be quit of him.

I told him to change his costume, and I would do the same; for if people came asking after us, it might throw them off. We did not think that would happen at least until Monday, for we did not know that Mr. Kinnear had invited some friends to Sunday dinner. And so I changed my dress, at the City Hotel, and James put on a light summer jacket of Mr. Kinnear's. And he told me with a bit of a sneer that I looked very elegant, and quite the lady, with my pink parasol and all.

Then he went to get himself shaved; and this was the moment I could have run for help. But he had several times told me that we must hang together or we would hang separately; and although I felt myself innocent, I knew that appearances were against me. And even if he was to be hanged and I not, and even though I desired no more of his company, and was afraid of him, still I did not wish to be the means of betraying him. There is something despicable about betrayal; and I'd felt his heart beating next to mine, and however undesired, still it was a human heart; and I did not wish to have any part in stilling it forever, unless I should be forced to it. And I reflected as well, that in the Bible it is written, *Vengeance is mine, saith the Lord*. I did not feel it was my place to take such a serious thing as vengeance into my own hands; and so I stayed where I was until he came back.

By eight o'clock we were on board the steamer *Transit*, with the wagon, and Charley Horse, and the boxes and all, and pulling out of the harbour; and I was much relieved. The day was fair, with a fine breeze, and the sun sparkling on the blue waves; and by this time James was in high spirits, and very proud of himself; and I was afraid that if he got out of my sight, he would go about boasting, and strutting in his new clothes, and showing off Mr. Kinnear's gold trinkets; but he was eager to keep me in view, in case I should tell someone what he had done, and he stuck by me like a leech.

We were on the lower deck, because of Charley, as I didn't wish to leave him alone; he was nervous, and I suspected he'd never been on a steamer before; and the noise of the engine, and the paddle-wheel going around, must have been frightening to him. So I stayed with him and fed him crackers, which he loved because of the salt. A young girl and a horse will always attract attention from admiring youths, who will pretend to be interested in the horse; and soon we did; and I found myself having to answer questions.

James had told me to say that we were brother and sister, and had left our unpleasant relations, with whom we had quarrelled; so I chose to be Mary Whitney, and said that he was David Whitney, and we were on our way to Rochester. The young fellows did not see any reason why they should not flirt with me, as James was only my brother, and so they did; and I thought it my part to return their sallies with good humour, though it told against me at the trial; and at the time I got some black looks from James. But I was only attempting to allay suspicion, both theirs and his; and underneath my show of happiness I was very downhearted.

We stopped at Niagara, but it was nowhere near the Falls, so I was unable to see them. James went ashore, and made me come with him, and he ate a beefsteak. I did not take any refreshment, as I was nervous the whole time we were there. But nothing happened, and we went on.

One young fellow pointed to another steamer in the distance, and said it was the *Lady of the Lake*, a United States vessel which until recently was thought to be the fastest boat on the Lake; but she had just lost a trial-of-speed race to the new Royal Mail Standard boat, the *Eclipse*, which outran her by four minutes and a half. And I said didn't that make him proud, and he said no, because he had a dollar bet on the *Lady*. And all present laughed.

Then something came clear to me which I used to wonder about. There is a quilt pattern called Lady of the Lake, which I thought was named for the poem; but I could never find any lady in the pattern, nor any lake. But now I saw that the boat was named for the poem, and the quilt was named for the boat; because it was a pinwheel design, which must have stood for the paddle going around. And I thought that things did make sense, and have a design to them, if you only pondered them long enough. And so perhaps it might be with recent events, which at the moment seemed to me entirely senseless; and finding out the reason for the quilt pattern was a lesson to me, to have faith.

Then I remembered Mary Whitney reading that poem with me, and how we would skip through the dull courtships, and move on to the exciting parts, and the fighting; but the place I recalled best was the poor woman who'd been stolen away from the church on her wedding day, kidnapped for a nobleman's pleasure, and had gone mad from it, and wandered about picking wildflowers, and singing to herself. And I considered that I too was being kidnapped after a fashion, though not on my wedding day; and I feared I might end up in the same plight.

Meanwhile we were coming into Lewiston. James had attempted to sell the horse and wagon to those on board, against my better judgment; but he asked far too low a price, which aroused suspicion. And because he'd offered them for sale, the Customs Officer in Lewiston put a duty on them, and detained them because we did not have the money to pay it. But although James was angry at first, he soon passed it off as being of little importance, and told me we would sell some of the other things, and come back the next day for the rig. But I was quite anxious about it, as it meant we would have to spend the night there; and although we were in the United States, and should think ourselves safe, as we were in a foreign country now; yet that never stopped the slavers up from the States from seizing runaway slaves they said were theirs; and altogether it was far too close for comfort.

I tried to make him promise not to sell Charley Horse, though he could do as he liked with the wagon. But he said, Horse be damned; and I believe he was jealous of the poor horse, because I was so fond of him.

The scenery in the United States was much the same as that of the countryside we had just come from, but it was indeed a different place, as the flags were different. I remembered what Jeremiah told me about borders, and how easy it was to cross them. The time when he had said that to me, in the kitchen at Mr. Kinnear's, seemed very long ago, and in a different lifetime; but in reality it was just over a week before.

We went to the nearest tavern, which was not a hotel at all, as was said in the broadsheet poem about me, but only a cheap inn by the wharf. There James soon swilled down a lot more beer and brandy than was good for him; and then we had supper, and he drank yet more. And when it was time to retire, he wanted us to pretend we were man and wife, and to take a room together; for, he said, it would be half the cost. But I saw what he was after, and said that as we had started on the boat as brother and sister, we could not change now, in case any remembered us from the boat. So he was given a room with another man in it, and I had one to myself.

But he tried to push his way into my room, saying we would be married soon enough anyway. And I said we would not, and I would sooner marry the Devil himself, than him; and he said he would have my promise off me anyway. Then I said I would scream, which would be a different thing in a houseful of people than in one with only two corpses. And he told me for God's sake to shut my mouth, and called me a slut and a whore; and I said he should think of some new words to use, because I was heartily tired of those. And he left in a foul temper.

I resolved to get up very early, and dress, and steal away. For if I was forced in some way to marry him, I would be dead and buried in one shake of a lamb's tail; as if he was suspicious of me at present, he would be more so later. And once he'd got me into a farmhouse, in a strange neighbourhood with no friends about, I would not give two pins for my own life, as it would be a knock on the head for me, and six feet deep in the kitchen garden, and I would be making the potatoes and carrots grow, a great deal sooner than I cared to think.

Happily there was a door that latched, and so I latched it; and then I took off my clothes, all except my shift, and folded them neatly across the back of the chair, as I used to do in the little room at Mrs. Alderman Parkinson's where I slept with Mary. Then I blew out the candle and slid myself in between the sheets, which were nearly clean for a wonder; and I closed my eyes.

On the insides of my eyelids I could see the water moving, the blue heaps of the waves as we came across the Lake, with the light sparkling on them; only they were much bigger waves, and darker, like rolling hills; and they were the waves of the ocean which I had voyaged across three years before, though it seemed like a century. And I wondered what would become of me, and comforted myself that in a hundred years I would be dead and at peace, and in my grave; and I thought it might be less trouble altogether, to be in it a good deal sooner than that.

But the waves kept moving, with the white wake of the ship traced in them for an instant, and then smoothed over by the water. And it was as if my own footsteps were being erased behind me, the footsteps I'd made as a child on the beaches and pathways of the land I'd left, and the footsteps I'd made on this side of the ocean, since coming here; all the traces of me, smoothed over and rubbed away as if they had never been, like polishing the black tarnish from the silver, or drawing your hand across dry sand.

On the edge of sleep I thought: It's as if I never existed, because no trace of me remains, I have left no marks. And that way I cannot be followed.

It is almost the same as being innocent.

And then I slept.

4 0 .

This is what I dreamt, as I lay asleep between the nearly clean sheets, in the tavern at Lewiston.

I was walking up the long curved drive to Mr. Kinnear's, between the rows of maple trees that were planted at either side. I was seeing it all for the first time, although I also knew I had been there before, as is the way in dreams. And I thought, I wonder who lives in that house?

Then I knew that I was not alone on the driveway. Mr. Kinnear was walking behind me, to the left; he was there to make sure no harm came to me. And then the lamp came on in the parlour window, and I knew that Nancy was inside, waiting to welcome me back from my journey; for I had been on a journey, I was sure of it, and had been absent a long time. Only it was not Nancy, but Mary Whitney who was waiting; and I felt so happy, to know I would see her again, restored to health and laughing, as she was before.

I saw how beautiful the house was, all white, with the pillars at the front, and the white peonies in flower by the verandah glimmering in the dusk, and the lamplight blooming in the window.

And I longed to be there, although in the dream I was there already; but I had a great yearning towards this house, for it was my real home. And as I felt that, the lamp was dimmed and the house went dark, and I saw that the fireflies were out and glowing, and there was the smell of milkweed blossoms from the fields all around, and the warm damp air of the summer evening against my cheek, so mild and soft. And a hand was slipped into mine.

And just then there was a knocking at the door.

XI.

FALLING TIMBERS

The girl, instead of exhibiting any traces of broken rest and a guilty conscience, appears quite calm, with her eye full and clear as though she slept sound and undisturbed – her only anxiety appears to get some of her clothes sent to her, and her box. Of the former she never had but few – she wears at the present time the murdered woman's frock, and the box that she asks for belonged to the same poor sufferer.

– *Chronicle and Gazette*,
Kingston, August 12th, 1843.

"But though I have repented of my wickedness with bitter tears, it has pleased God that I should never again know a moment's peace. Since I helped Macdermot to strangle [Nancy] Montgomery, her terrible face and those horrible bloodshot eyes have never left me for a moment. They glare upon me by night and day, and when I close my eyes in despair, I see them looking into my soul – it is impossible to shut them out. . . . at night – in the silence and loneliness of my cell, those blazing eyes make my prison as light as day. No, not as day – they have a terribly hot glare, that has not the appearance of anything in this world. . . ."

– Grace Marks,
to Kenneth MacKenzie, as retold by
Susanna Moodie, *Life in the Clearings*, 1853.

It was not love, although her rich beauty was a madness to him; nor horror, even while he fancied her spirit to be imbued with the same baneful essence that seemed to pervade her physical frame; but a wild offspring of both love and horror that had each parent in it, and burned like one and shivered like the other. . . . Blessed are all simple emotions, be they dark or bright! It is the lurid intermixture of the two that produces the illuminating blaze of the infernal regions.

– Nathaniel Hawthorne,
"Rappaccini's Daughter," 1844.

4 1 .

To Dr. Simon Jordan, care of Major C. D. Humphrey, Lower Union Street, Kingston, Canada West; from Mrs. William P. Jordan, Laburnum House, Loomisville, Massachusetts, The United States of America.

August 3rd, 1859.

My Dearest Son:

I am in the greatest state of apprehension, at not having had a letter from you, for so long. Do send me at least one word, to let me know that no disaster has befallen you. In these evil days, with a calamitous War looming ever nearer in the distance, a Mother's chief hope is that her dearest ones, of which I have only you remaining, should be safe and sound. Perhaps it would be best if you would remain in that country, to avoid the inevitable; but it is only a weak Mother's heart that urges it, as I cannot in all conscience advocate cowardice, when so many other Mothers will surely be prepared to face whatever Fate may have in store.

I do so long to see your welcome face once more, dear Son. The slight cough, which has troubled me ever since the time of your birth, has increased of late, and is in the evenings quite violent; and I am in an agony of nerves, every day that you are away from us, for fear that I should be taken away suddenly, in the middle of the night perhaps, without having the opportunity of bidding you a last fond farewell, and giving you a last Mother's Blessing. Should War be avoided, which we must all hope for, I do so pray that I may see you well settled, and in a home of your own, before that inevitable date. But do not let my doubtless idle fears and fancies take you away from your studies and researches, and your Lunatics, or whatever you are doing, which I am sure is very important.

I hope you are eating a nourishing diet, and keeping up your strength. There is no blessing like a solid constitution, and if one has not inherited it, then even more care must be taken. Mrs. Cartwright says she is so thankful that her daughter has never been sick a day in her life, and is as strong as a horse. The inheritance of a sound mind in a healthy body would be the best legacy of all, to leave to one's children; one which your own poor Mother was, alas, not able to provide, to her own dear Boy, though not for lack of wishing. But we must all content ourselves with the lot in life, in which Providence has seen fit to place us.

My faithful Maureen and Samantha send their respect and love to you, and beg to be remembered. Samantha says that her strawberry preserves, which you loved so much as a Boy, continue as good as ever, and you should hurry back for a taste of them, before she "crosses over the river," as she puts it; and my poor Maureen, who may soon be as crippled as your

Mother, says she cannot eat a spoonful, without thinking of you, and remembering happier times; and they are both most anxious for the renewed sight of your ever-welcome countenance; as is, to a thousandfold extent,

Your always loving and devoted,

Mother.

4 2 .

Simon is in the upstairs corridor again, in the attic, where the maids live. He senses them waiting behind their closed doors, listening, their eyes shining in the semi-darkness; but they don't make a sound. His footsteps in their thick schoolboy boots ring hollowly on the boards. Surely there ought to be some kind of carpet here, or matting; everyone in the house must be able to hear him.

He opens a door at random, hoping to find Alice, or was her name Effie? But he's back at Guy's Hospital. He can smell it, almost taste it – that dense, heavy smell of damp stone, damp wool, halitosis, and septic human flesh. It's the smell of trial and disapproval: he is going to be examined. Before him is a draped table: he must make a dissection, although he is only a student here, he hasn't been taught, he doesn't know how. The room is empty, but he knows he's being watched, by those who are there to judge him.

It's a woman, under the sheet; he can tell by the contours. He hopes she isn't too old, as that would be somehow worse. A poor woman, dead of some unknown disease. No one knows where they get the cadavers; or no one knows for certain. Dug up in the graveyard by moonlight, goes the student joke. No, not by moonlight, you fool: by the Resurrection Men.

Step by step he approaches the table. Does he have his instruments ready? Yes, here is the candlestick; but he has no shoes on, and his feet are wet. He must lift off the sheet, then lift off her skin, whoever she is, or was, layer by layer. Strip back her rubbery flesh, peel her open, gut her like a haddock. He's shaking with terror. She will be cold, inflexible. They keep them on ice.

But under the sheet there's another sheet, and under that another one. It looks like a white muslin curtain. Then there's a black veil, and then – can it be? – a petticoat. The woman must be down there somewhere; frantically he rummages. But no; the last sheet is a bed-sheet, and there's nothing under it but a bed. That, and the form of someone who's been lying here. It's still warm.

He is failing desperately, failing his examination, and so publicly too; but now he doesn't mind that. It's as if he's been reprieved. It will be all right now, he will be taken care of. Outside the door, which is the same one he came in by, there's a green lawn, with a stream flowing beyond it. The sound of the running water is very soothing. There's a quick indrawn breath, and the smell of strawberries, and a hand touches his shoulder.

He wakes, or dreams he wakes. He knows he must still be asleep, because Grace Marks is bending over him in the close darkness, her loosened hair brushing his face. He isn't surprised, nor does he ask how she has managed to come here from her prison cell. He pulls her down – she is wearing only a nightdress – and falls on top of her, and shoves himself into her with a groan of lust and no manners, for in dreams everything is permitted. His spine jerks him like a hooked fish, then releases him. He gasps for air.

Only then does he realize he's not dreaming; or not dreaming the woman. She's really here, in the flesh, lying motionless beside him in the suddenly too-quiet bed, arms at her sides like an effigy; but she is not Grace Marks. Impossible now to mistake her boniness, her bird's ribcage, her smell of singed linen and camphor and violets. The opium taste of her mouth. It's his thin landlady, whose first name he doesn't even know. When he entered her she made no sound, either of protest or delight. Is she even breathing?

Tentatively he kisses her again, then again: small kisses. It's the alternative to taking her pulse. He works his way around until he finds a vein, the one in her neck, throbbing. Her skin is warm, a little sticky, like syrup; the hairs behind her ear smell of beeswax.

Not dead then.

Oh no, he thinks. What next? What have I done?

4 3 .

Dr. Jordan has gone off to Toronto. I don't know how long he will be gone; I hope it's not very long, as I have become quite used to him somehow, and fear that when he goes away, as he is bound to do sooner or later, there will be a sad emptiness in my heart.

What should I tell him, when he comes back? He will want to know about the arrest, and the trial, and what was said. Some of it is all jumbled in my mind, but I could pick out this or that for him, some bits of whole cloth you might say, as when you go through the rag bag looking for something that will do, to supply a touch of colour.

I could say this:

Well, Sir, they arrested me first, and James next. He was still asleep in his bed, and the first thing he did when they woke him up was to try to blame it on Nancy. If you find Nancy you will know all about it, he said, it was her fault. I thought this was very stupid of him, as although she hadn't yet been discovered, they were bound to ferret her out sooner or later, if only by the smell; and indeed they did so, the very next day. James was trying to pretend he didn't know where she was, or even that she was dead; but he should have held his tongue about her.

It was still the early morning when they arrested us. They hustled us out of the Lewiston tavern at great speed. I believe they were afraid the men there might stop them, and attract a mob, and rescue us, as they might have done if McDermott had thought to shout out that he was a revolutionary, or a republican, or some such, and he had his rights, and down with the British; because there was still considerable high feelings then, on the side of Mr. William Lyon Mackenzie and the Rebellion, and there were those in the States that wanted to invade Canada. And the men that arrested us had no real authority. But McDermott was too cowed to protest, or else he lacked the presence of mind; and when they'd got us as far as the Customs, and said we were wanted on suspicion of murder, then our party was allowed to proceed, and to set sail without further ado.

I was very glum going back across the Lake, although the weather was fair and the waves not large; but I cheered myself up, by telling myself that Justice would not let me be hanged for something I hadn't done, and I would only have to tell the story as it happened, or as much of it as I could remember. As for McDermott's chances, I did not rate them very high; but he was still denying all, and saying we only had Mr. Kinnear's things with us because Nancy had refused to pay us what we were owed, and so we had paid ourselves. He said if anyone had killed Kinnear it was most likely a tramp; and there had been a suspicious-looking man hanging around, who'd said he was a peddler, and sold him some shirts; and they should be looking for that one, and not an honest man like himself, whose only crime was to wish to better his lot in life through hard work and immigration. He certainly could lie, but never very well; and he wasn't believed, and might just as well have kept his mouth shut; and I thought it wrong in him, Sir, that he was trying to put the murder off on my old friend Jeremiah, who'd never done any such thing in his life, that I knew of.

They put us into the jail in Toronto, locked up in cells, like animals in a cage, but not so close together that we could speak; and then they examined us separately. They asked me a good many questions; and I was quite frightened, and not at all sure what I should say. I had no lawyer at this time, as Mr. MacKenzie only came into it much later. I asked for my box, which they made such a fuss over in the newspapers, and sneered at me for referring to it as mine, and for having no clothes of my own to speak of; but although it was true this box and the clothes in it had once been Nancy's, they were hers no longer, as the dead have no use for such things.

They held it against me as well that I was at first calm and in good spirits, with full and clear eyes, which they took for callousness; but if I'd been weeping and crying, they would have said it showed my guilt; for they'd already decided I was guilty, and once people make their minds up that you have done a crime, then anything you do is taken as proof of it; and I don't think I could have scratched myself or wiped my nose without it being written up in the newspapers, and malicious comment made on it, in high-sounding phrases. And it was at this time that they called me McDermott's paramour, and also his accomplice; and they wrote also that I must have helped to strangle Nancy, as it would take two to do the job. The newspaper journalists like to believe the worst; they can sell more papers that way, as one of them told me himself; for even upstanding and respectable people dearly love to read ill of others.

The next thing, Sir, was the Inquest, which was held very soon after we were brought back. It was to determine how Nancy and Mr. Kinnear had died, whether by accident or murder; and for that I had to be examined in court. By now I was thoroughly terrified, as I could see that feeling was running very much against me; and the jailers in Toronto made cruel jokes when they brought in my food, and said they hoped when they hanged me that the scaffold would be high, as that way they would get a good look at my ankles. And one of them tried to take advantages, and said I might as well enjoy it while I had the chance, as where I was going I'd never have no fine brisk lover like himself between my knees; but I told him to keep his filthy self to himself; and it would have come to worse, except that his fellow-jailer came along and said that I hadn't been tried yet, much less condemned; and if the first one valued his position he should keep away from me. Which he did mostly.

I will tell Dr. Jordan about this, as he likes to hear about such things, and always writes them down.

Well, Sir, I will continue – the day of the Inquest came, and I took care to appear neat and tidy, for I knew how much appearances count, as when you are applying for a new position, and they always look at your wrists and cuffs, to see if you are of clean habits; and they did say in the newspapers that I was decently dressed.

The Inquest was held in the City Hall, with a number of Magistrates present, all staring and frowning; and an immense crowd of spectators, and Press men, pushing and shoving and jostling, so as to be in a better position to see and hear; and these had to be reprimanded several times, for disruption. I didn't see how they could get any more people into the room, which was stuffed to bursting, but more and more kept trying to thrust themselves forward.

I tried to control my trembling, and to face what was to come with as much courage as I could lay hold of, which by that time, to tell you the truth, Sir, was not very much. McDermott was there, looking as surly as ever, which was the first time I had seen him since we were arrested. The newspapers said he showed *sullen doggedness and reckless defiance*, which was their way of putting it, I suppose. But it was nothing different from the way he always looked at the breakfast table.

Then they started in to question me about the murders, and I was at a loss. For as you know, Sir, I could not rightly remember the events of that terrible day, and did not feel I had been present at them at all, and had lain unconscious for several parts of it; but I was well aware that if I said this I would be laughed to scorn, since Jefferson the butcher testified that he'd seen me and conversed with me, and said I'd told him we would not be needing any fresh meat; which they made a joke of later, because of the bodies in the cellar, in a broadsheet poem they were hawking about at the time of McDermott's hanging; and I thought it was very coarse and common, and disrespectful of a fellow-being's mortal struggle.

So I said that the last time I'd seen Nancy was around dinner-time, when I looked out of the kitchen door and saw her putting the young ducks in; and after that, McDermott said she'd gone into the house, and I said she was not there, and he told me to mind my own business. Then he said she'd gone over to Mrs. Wright's. I told them I was suspicious, and asked McDermott about her several times, when we were travelling to the States, at which he said she was all right; but I did not positively know of her death, until she was discovered on the Monday morning.

I then told how I heard a shot, and saw Mr. Kinnear's body lying on the floor; and how I screamed and rushed about, and how McDermott shot at me, and I fainted and fell down. I did remember that part of it. And indeed they found the ball from the gun, in the wood of the summer kitchen door frame, which showed I was not lying.

We were bound over for trial, which was not to take place until November; and so I was three weary months penned up in the Toronto jail, which was worse than being here in the Penitentiary, as I was all by myself in a cell, and people coming on the pretence of some errand or other, but really to gawk and gape. And I was in a very miserable state.

Outside, the seasons changed, but all I knew of it was the difference in the light that shone through the small barred window, which was too high on the wall for me to see out of it; and the air that would come in, bringing the scents and odours of all I was missing. In August there was the smell of fresh-mown hay, and then the smell of grapes and peaches ripening; and in September the apples, and in October the fallen leaves, and the first cold foretaste of snow. There was nothing for me to do, except sit in my cell, and worry about what was going to happen, and whether indeed I would be hanged, as the jailers told me every day, and I must say they enjoyed every word of death and disaster that came out of their mouths. I don't know whether you have noticed it, Sir, but there are some that take pleasure in the distress of a fellow-mortal, and most especially if they think that fellow-mortal has committed a sin, which adds an extra relish. But which among us has not sinned, as the Bible tells us? I would be ashamed myself, to take such delight in the sufferings of others.

In October they gave me a lawyer, which was Mr. MacKenzie. He was not very handsome, and had a nose like a bottle. I thought he was very young and untried, as this was his first case; and sometimes his manner was a little too familiar for my taste, as he appeared to wish to be shut up in the cell with me alone, and offered to comfort me, with frequent pattings of the hand; but I was glad to have anyone at all, to plead my case and to put things in as good a light as possible; so I said nothing about it, but did my best to smile and behave gratefully. He wanted me to tell my story in what he called a coherent way, but would often accuse me of wandering, and become annoyed with me; and at last he said that the right thing was, not to tell the story as I truly remembered it, which nobody could be expected to make any sense of; but to tell a story that would hang together, and that had some chance of being believed. I was to leave out the parts I could not remember, and especially to leave out the fact that I could not remember them. And I should say what must have happened, according to plausibility, rather than what I myself could actually recall. So that is what I attempted to do.

I was by myself a great deal, and spent many a long hour dwelling on my future ordeal; and if I came to be hanged, what it would be like; and how long and lonely the road of death might be, that I could well be forced to travel along; and what awaited me at the other end of it. I prayed to God, but got no answer; and I consoled myself by reflecting that this silence of his was just another of his mysterious ways. I tried to think over all of the things I'd done wrong, so I could repent of them; such as choosing the second-best sheet for my mother, and not staying awake when Mary Whitney was dying. And when I myself came to be buried, it might not be in a sheet at all, but cut up into pieces, and bits and fragments, as they say the doctors did to you if you were hanged. And that was my worst fear.

Then I attempted to cheer myself, by recalling earlier scenes. I remembered Mary Whitney, and how she'd had her marriage and her farmhouse planned out, with the curtains chosen and all, and how it came to nothing, and how she died in agony; and then the last day of October came around, and I remembered the night we'd peeled the apples, and how she'd said I would cross the water three times, and then get married to a man whose name began with a J. All of that seemed now like a childish game, and I no longer had any belief in it. Oh Mary, I would say, how I long to be back in our little cold bedroom at Mrs. Alderman Parkinson's, with the cracked washbasin and the one chair, instead of here in this dark cell, in danger of my life. And it did seem to me at times that a little comfort came back to me in return; and once I heard her laughing. But you often imagine things, when you are alone so much.

It was at this time that the red peonies first began growing.

The last time I saw Dr. Jordan, he asked if I recalled Mrs. Susanna Moodie, when she'd come to visit the Penitentiary. That would have been seven years ago, shortly before they put me into the Lunatic Asylum. I said that I did recall her. He asked me what I thought of her, and I said she looked like a beetle.

A beetle? said Dr. Jordan. I saw that I had astonished him.

Yes, a beetle, Sir, I said. Round and fat and dressed in black, and a quick and scuttling sort of walk; and black, shiny eyes too. I do not mean it as an insult, Sir, I added, for he'd given one of his short laughs. It was just the way she looked, in my opinion.

And do you remember the time she visited you, just a short time after that, in the Provincial Asylum?

Not well, Sir, I said. But we had many visitors there.

She describes you as shrieking and running about. You were confined on the violent ward.

That may be, Sir, I said. I do not recall behaving in a violent manner towards others, unless they did so first to me.

And singing, I believe, said he.

I enjoy singing, I said shortly; for I was not pleased by this line of questioning. A good hymn tune or ballad is uplifting to the spirits.

Did you tell Kenneth MacKenzie that you could see the eyes of Nancy Montgomery following you around? he said.

I have read what Mrs. Moodie wrote down about that, Sir, I said. I don't like to call anyone a liar. But Mr. MacKenzie put a misconstruction upon what I told him.

And what was that?

I said red spots, at first, Sir. And that was true. They looked like red spots.

And after?

And after, when he pressed me for an explanation, I told him what I thought they were. But I did not say eyes.

Yes? Go on! said Dr. Jordan, who was trying to appear calm; he was leaning forward, as if waiting for some great secret. But it was no great secret. I would have told him earlier, if he'd asked me.

I did not say eyes, Sir; I said peonies. But Mr. MacKenzie was always more fond of listening to his own voice than to someone else's. And I suppose it's more the usual thing, to have eyes following you around. It is more what is required, under the circumstances, if you follow me, Sir. And I guess that was why Mr. MacKenzie misheard it, and why Mrs. Moodie wrote it down. They wanted to have things done properly. But they were peonies, all the same. Red ones. There is no mistake possible.

I see, said Dr. Jordan. But he looked as puzzled as ever.

Next he will want to know about the trial. It began on the 3rd of November, and so many people crushed into the courthouse that the floor gave way. When I was put into the dock, at first I had to stand, but then they brought me a chair. The air was very close, and there was a constant buzzing of voices, like a swarm of bees. Different people got up, some in my favour, to say I'd never been in trouble before, and was a hard worker, and of good character; and others spoke against me; and there were more of these. I looked around for Jeremiah the peddler, but he was not there. He at least would have understood something of my plight, and would have tried to help me out of it, for he'd said there was a kinship between us. Or so I believed.

Then they brought in Jamie Walsh. I was hoping for some token of sympathy from him, but he gave me a stare filled with such reproach and sorrowful anger, that I saw how it was with him. He felt betrayed in love, because I'd gone off with McDermott; and from being an angel in his eyes, and fit to be idolized and worshipped, I was transformed to a demon, and he would do all in his power to destroy me. With that my heart sank within me, for of everyone I knew at Richmond Hill, I had been counting on him to say a good word for me; and he looked so young and fresh, and unspoiled and innocent, that a pang went through me, for I valued his good opinion of me, and it was a grief to lose it.

He got up to testify, and was sworn in; and the way he took the oath on the Bible, very solemn but with hard rage in his voice, did not bode me any good. He told about our party the night before, and playing the flute, and how McDermott had refused to dance, and walked him partway home; and how Nancy was alive when he'd left us, and on her way upstairs to bed. And then he told how he'd come over the next afternoon, and seen McDermott with a double-barrelled gun in his hand, which he claimed he'd been using to shoot birds. He said I was standing by the pump with my hands folded, wearing white cotton stockings; and when asked where Nancy was, I laughed in a teasing manner, and said he was always wanting to know things; but that Nancy had gone to Wrights', where there was someone ill, with a man who'd come to fetch her.

I remember none of this, Sir, but Jamie Walsh gave his testimony in a straightforward manner which it was difficult to doubt.

But then his emotions overcame him, and he pointed at me, and said, "She has got on Nancy's dress, the ribbons under her bonnet are also Nancy's, and the tippet she has on, and also the parasol in her hand."

At that there was a great outcry in the courtroom, like the uprush of voices at the Judgment Day; and I knew I was doomed.

When my turn came, I said what Mr. MacKenzie had told me to say, and my head was all in a turmoil, trying to remember the right answers; and I was pressed to explain why I hadn't warned Nancy and Mr. Kinnear, once I knew James McDermott's intentions. And Mr. MacKenzie said it was for fear of my life, and despite his nose he was very eloquent. He said that I was little more than a child, a poor motherless child and to all intents and purposes an orphan, cast out upon the world with nobody to teach me any better; and I'd had to work hard for my bread, from an early age, and was industry itself; and I was very ignorant and uneducated, and illiterate, and little better than a halfwit; and very soft and pliable, and easily imposed upon.

But despite everything he could do, Sir, it went against me. The jury found me guilty of murder, as an accessory both before and after the fact, and the judge pronounced sentence of death. I'd been made to stand up to hear the sentence; but when he said Death, I fainted, and fell on the railing made of pointed spikes that was all around the dock; and one of the spikes went into my breast, right next to my heart.

I could show him the scar.

4 4 .

Simon has taken the morning train for Toronto. He's travelling second class; he's been spending too much money of late, and feels the need to economize.

He's looking forward to his interview with Kenneth MacKenzie: through it, he may uncover some detail or other, something Grace has failed to mention, either because it might show her in a bad light or because she has genuinely forgotten it. The mind, he reflects, is like a house – thoughts which the owner no longer wishes to display, or those which arouse painful memories, are thrust out of sight, and consigned to attic or cellar; and in forgetting, as in the storage of broken furniture, there is surely an element of will at work.

Grace's will is of the negative female variety – she can deny and reject much more easily than she can affirm or accept. Somewhere within herself – he's seen it, if only for a moment, that conscious, even cunning look in the corner of her eye – she knows she's concealing something from him. As she stitches away at her sewing, outwardly calm as a marble Madonna, she is all the while exerting her passive stubborn strength against him. A prison does not only lock its inmates inside, it keeps all others out. Her strongest prison is of her own construction.

Some days he would like to slap her. The temptation is almost overwhelming. But then she would have trapped him; then she would have a reason for resisting him. She would turn on him that gaze of a wounded doe which all women keep in store for such occasions. She would cry.

Yet he doesn't feel she dislikes their conversations. On the contrary, she appears to welcome them, and even to enjoy them; much as one enjoys a game of any sort, when one is winning, he tells himself grimly. The emotion she expresses most openly towards him is a subdued gratitude.

He's coming to hate the gratitude of women. It is like being fawned on by rabbits, or like being covered with syrup: you can't get it off. It slows you down, and puts you at a disadvantage. Every time some woman is grateful to him, he feels like taking a cold bath. Their gratitude isn't real; what they really mean by it is that he should be grateful to them. Secretly they despise him. He recalls with embarrassment, and a kind of shrivelling self-loathing, the puppyish condescension he used to display when paying out his money to some pitiful shopworn streetgirl – the beseeching look in her eyes, and how large and rich and compassionate he felt himself to be, as if the favours about to be conferred were his, not hers. What contempt they all must have kept hidden, under their thanks and smiles!

The whistle shouts; grey smoke blows past the window. To the left, across flat fields, is the flat lake, dimpled like hammered pewter. Here and there is a log shanty, a line of washing flapping, a fat mother no doubt cursing the smoke, a clutch of staring children. Freshly cut trees, then old stumps; a smouldering bonfire. The occasional bigger house, red brick or white clapboard. The engine pounds like an iron heart, the train moves relentlessly westward.

Away from Kingston; away from Mrs. Humphrey. Rachel, as he has now been entreated to call her. The more miles he is able to put between himself and Rachel Humphrey, the lighter and less troubled in spirit he feels. He's gotten himself in too deep with her. He's floundering – images of quicksand come to mind – but he can't see how to extricate himself, not yet. Having a mistress – for that's what she's become, he supposes, and it hasn't taken long! – is worse than having a wife. The responsibilities involved are weightier, and more muddled.

The first time was an accident: he was ambushed in his sleep. Nature took advantage of him, creeping up on him as he lay entranced, without his daytime armour; his own dreams turned against him. This is the very thing Rachel claims of herself: she was sleepwalking, she says. She thought she was outdoors in the sunlight, gathering flowers, but somehow she found herself in his room, in the darkness, in his arms, and already then it was too late, she was lost. *Lost* is a word she uses a lot. She has always been of a sensitive nature, she's told him, and subject to somnambulism even as a child. They used to have to lock her into her room at night, to prevent her wandering around in the moonlight. He doesn't for an instant believe this story, but for a refined woman of her class he supposes it's a way of saving face. What was really in her mind at the time, and what she is thinking now, he scarcely dares to guess.

Almost every night since, she's come to his room in her nightdress, with a white ruffled peignoir thrown over it. The ribbons at the throat untied, the buttons open. She carries a single candle: she looks young in the dusk. Her green eyes gleam, her long fair hair is down around her shoulders like a shining veil.

Or if he stays out late, walking by the river in the cool of night as he's increasingly inclined to do, she'll be there waiting for him when he returns. His initial reaction is one of ennui: there is a ritual dance to be gone through, and it is one that bores him. The encounter begins with tears, quivering, and reluctance: she sobs, she reproaches herself, she pictures herself as ruined, wallowing in shame, a soul condemned. She's never been anybody's mistress before, she has never stooped so low, indulged in such abasement; if her husband discovers them, what will become of her? It is always the woman who's blamed.

Simon lets her go on in this vein for a time; then he comforts her, and assures her in the vaguest of terms that all will be well, and says he doesn't think any the less of her for what she has so inadvertently done. Then he adds that nobody need know, provided they are discreet. They must take great care never to betray themselves by word or glance, in front of others – especially Dora, because Rachel must know how servants gossip – a caution that isn't only for her protection, but for his. He can imagine what Reverend Verringer would have to say; among others.

She cries more at the thought of discovery; she writhes with humiliation. He doesn't think she's been taking the laudanum any more, or at least not so much; otherwise she wouldn't get so worked up. Her behaviour would not be so reprehensible if she were a widow, she goes on. If the Major were dead, she would not be betraying her marriage vows; but as it is. . . . He tells her the Major has treated her abominably, and is a cad, a scoundrel, a dog, and deserves even worse from her. He has kept a semblance of caution: he's made no offers of instant marriage, should the Major suddenly and accidentally topple off a cliff and break his neck. Inwardly he wishes him a long and healthy life.

He dries her eyes with her own handkerchief – always a clean one, freshly ironed, smelling of violets, tucked conveniently into her sleeve. She winds her arms around him, presses close, and he feels her breasts pushing against him, her hips, the full length of her body. She has an astonishingly tiny waist. Her mouth grazes his neck. Then she draws back, aghast at herself, with a gesture of nymph-like coyness, and bends away from him in an attitude of flight; but by this time he is no longer bored.

Rachel is unlike any woman he's ever had before. To begin with, she's a respectable woman, his first; and respectability in a woman, as he's now discovered, complicates things considerably. Respectable women are by nature sexually cold, without the perverse lusts and the neurasthenic longings that drive their degenerate sisters into prostitution; or so goes the scientific theory. His own explorations have suggested to him that prostitutes are motivated less by depravity than by poverty, but nevertheless they must appear as their clients wish to imagine them. A whore must feign desire and then pleasure, whether she feels them or not; such pretences are what she's paid for. A cheap whore is cheap not because she's ugly or old, but because she's a bad actress.

With Rachel however things are reversed. Her pretence is a pretence of aversion – it's her part to display resistance, his to overcome it. She wishes to be seduced, overwhelmed, taken against her will. At the moment of her climax – which she attempts to disguise as pain – she always says *no*.

In addition, she implies, by her shrinking and clinging, her abject imploring, that she's offering him her body as a kind of payment – something she owes him in return for the money he's spent on her behalf, as in some overdone melodrama featuring evil bankers and virtuous but penniless maidens. Her other game is that she is trapped, at the mercy of his will, as in the obscene novels obtainable at the seedier bookstalls of Paris, with their moustache-twirling Sultans and cowering slave-girls. Silvery draperies, chained ankles. Breasts like melons. Eyes of gazelles. That such configurations are banal does not rob them of their power.

What idiocies has he uttered, in the course of these nightly debauches? He can hardly remember. Words of passion and burning love, of how he cannot resist her, which – strange to say – he himself actually believes at the time. During the day, Rachel is a burden, an encumbrance, and he wishes to be rid of her; but at night she's an altogether different person, and so is he. He too says no when he means yes. He means more, he means further, he means deeper. He would like to make an incision in her – just a small one – so he can taste her blood, which in the shadowy darkness of the bedroom seems to him like a normal wish to have. He's driven by what feels like uncontrollable desire; but apart from that – apart from himself, at these times, as the sheets toss like waves and he tumbles and wallows and gasps – another part of himself stands with folded arms, fully clothed, merely curious, merely observing. How far, exactly, will he go? How far in.

The train pulls into the station at Toronto, and Simon attempts to put such thoughts behind him. At the station he hires a gig, and directs the driver to his chosen hotel; not the best one – he doesn't want to squander money unnecessarily – but not a hovel either, as he has no wish to be bitten by fleas and robbed. As they move through the streets – hot and dusty, crowded with vehicles of all descriptions, lumbering wagons, coaches, private carriages – he looks around him with interest. Everything is new and brisk, bustling and bright, vulgar and complacent, with a smell of fresh money and fresh paint about it. Fortunes have been made here in a very short time, with more in the making. There are the usual shops and commercial buildings, and a surprising number of banks. None of the eating establishments looks at all promising. The people on the sidewalks appear prosperous enough for the most part, without the hordes of destitute beggars, the swarms of rickety, dirty children, and the platoons of draggled or showy prostitutes that disfigure so many European cities; yet such is his perversity that he would rather be in London or Paris. There he would be anonymous, and would have no responsibilities. No ties, no connections. He would be able to lose himself completely.

XII.

SOLOMON'S TEMPLE

"I looked at her in astonishment. 'Good God!' thought I, 'can this be a woman? A pretty, soft-looking woman too – and a mere girl! What a heart she must have!' I felt equally tempted to tell her that she was a devil, and that I would have nothing more to do with such a horrible piece of business; but she looked so handsome, that somehow or another I yielded to the temptation. . . ."

– James McDermott,
to Kenneth MacKenzie, as retold by
Susanna Moodie, *Life in the Clearings*, 1853.

. . . for it is the fate of a woman
Long to be patient and silent, to wait like a ghost that is
speechless,
Till some questioning voice dissolves the spell of its silence.
Hence is the inner life of so many suffering women
Sunless and silent and deep, like subterranean rivers
Running through caverns of darkness. . . .

– Henry Wadsworth Longfellow,
"The Courtship of Miles Standish," 1858.

4 5 .

The law offices of Bradley, Porter, and MacKenzie are located in a new and somewhat pretentious red-brick building on King Street West. In the outer office a lank youth with colourless hair sits at a high desk, scrabbling with a steel-nibbed pen. When Simon enters he jumps up, scattering inkdrops like a dog shaking itself.

"Mr. MacKenzie is expecting you, Sir," he says. He places a reverent parenthesis around the word *MacKenzie*. How young he is, thinks Simon; this must be his first position. He ushers Simon along a carpeted passageway, and knocks at a thick oak door.

Kenneth MacKenzie is in his inner sanctuary. He's framed himself with polished bookshelves, expensively bound professional volumes, three paintings of racehorses. On his desk is an inkstand of Byzantine convolution and splendour. He himself isn't quite what Simon has been expecting: no heroic delivering Perseus, no Red Cross Knight. He's a short, pear-shaped man – narrow shoulders, a comfortable little belly swelling under his tartan vest – with a pocked and tuberous nose, and, behind his silver spectacles, two small but observant eyes. He rises from his chair, hand outstretched, smiling; he has two long front teeth like a beaver's. Simon tries to imagine what he must have looked like, sixteen years ago, when he was a young man – younger than Simon is now – but fails in the attempt. Kenneth MacKenzie must have looked middle-aged even as a five-year-old.

This is the man, then, who once saved the life of Grace Marks, against considerable odds – cold evidence, outraged public opinion, and her own confused and implausible testimony. Simon is curious to find out exactly how he managed it.

"Dr. Jordan. A pleasure."

"It is kind of you to spare me the time," says Simon.

"Not at all. I have Reverend Verringer's letter; he speaks very highly of you, and has told me something of your proceedings. I am glad to be of help in the interests of science; and as you have heard, I am sure, we lawyers always welcome a chance to show off. But before we get down to it – " A decanter is produced, cigars. The sherry is excellent: Mr. MacKenzie does himself well.

"You are no relation to the famous rebel?" Simon asks, by way of beginning.

"None at all, though I would almost rather claim kin than not; it isn't the disadvantage now that it once was, and the old boy has long since been pardoned, and is seen as the father of reforms. But feeling ran high against him in those days; that alone could have put a noose around Grace Marks' neck."

"How so?" says Simon.

"If you've read back over the newspapers, you'll have noticed that those which supported Mr. Mackenzie and his cause were the only ones to say a good word for Grace. The others were all for hanging her, and William Lyon Mackenzie as well, and anyone else thought to harbour republican sentiments."

"But surely there was no connection!"

"None whatsoever. There is never any need for a connection, in such matters. Mr. Kinnear was a Tory gentleman, and William Lyon

Mackenzie took the part of the poor Scots and Irish, and the emigrant settlers generally. Birds of a feather, was what they thought. I sweated blood at the trial, I can tell you. It was my first case, you know, my very first; I'd just been called to the bar. I knew it would be the making or the breaking of me, and, as things turned out, it did give me quite a leg up."

"How did you come to take the case?" asks Simon.

"My dear man, I was *handed* it. It was a hot potato. No one else wanted it. The firm took it pro bono – neither of the accused had any money, of course – and as I was the youngest, it ended up with me; and at the last minute, too, with scarcely a month to prepare. 'Well, my lad,' said old Bradley, 'here it is. Everyone knows you'll lose, because there's no doubt as to their guilt; but it will be the *style* in which you lose that will count. There is graceless losing, and there is elegant losing. Let us see you lose as elegantly as possible. We will all be cheering you on.' The old boy thought he was doing me a favour, and perhaps he was, at that."

"You acted for both of them, I believe," says Simon.

"Yes. That was wrong, in retrospect, as their interests proved to be in conflict. There were a lot of things about the trial that were wrong; but the practice of jurisprudence was much laxer then." MacKenzie frowns at his cigar, which has gone out. It strikes Simon that the poor fellow doesn't really enjoy smoking, but feels he ought to do it because it goes with the racehorse pictures.

"So you've met Our Lady of the Silences?" MacKenzie asks.

"Is that what you call her? Yes; I've been spending a good deal of time with her, trying to determine . . ."

"Whether she is innocent?"

"Whether she is insane. Or was, at the time of the murders. Which I suppose would be innocence of a kind."

"Good luck to you," says MacKenzie. "It was a thing I could never be satisfied about, myself."

"She purports to have no memory of the murders; or at least of the Montgomery woman's."

"My dear man," says MacKenzie, "you'd be amazed how common such lapses of memory are, amongst the criminal element. Very few of them can remember having done anything wrong at all. They will bash a man half to death, and cut him to ribbons, and then claim they only gave him a little tap with the end of a bottle. Forgetting, in such cases, is a good deal more convenient than remembering."

"Grace's amnesia seems genuine enough," says Simon, "or so I have come to believe, in the light of my previous clinical experience. On the other hand, although she can't seem to remember the murder, she has a minute recollection of the details surrounding it – every item of laundry she ever washed, for instance; and such things as the boat race that preceded her own flight across the Lake. She even remembers the names of the boats."

"How did you check her facts? In the newspapers, I suppose," says MacKenzie. "Has it occurred to you that she may have derived her corroborative details from the same source? Criminals will read about themselves endlessly, if given the chance. They are as vain in that way as authors. When McDermott asserted that Grace helped him in his strangling escapade, he may very well have got the idea from the Kingston *Chronicle and Gazette*, which proposed it as fact, even before there was an inquest. The knot around the dead woman's neck, they said, obviously required two persons to tie it. A piece of rubbish; you can't tell from such a knot whether it was tied by one person or two, or twenty, for that matter. Of course I made hash of this notion at the trial."

"Now you have turned around, and are pleading the other side of the case," says Simon.

"One must always keep both sides in one's head; it's the only way to anticipate the moves of one's opponent. Not that mine had a very hard job of work, in this case. But I did what I could; a man can but do his best, as Walter Scott has remarked somewhere. The court-room was crowded as Hell, and – despite the November weather – just as hot, and the air was foul. Nevertheless, I cross-examined some of the witnesses for over three hours. I must say it took stamina; but I was a younger man then."

"You began by disallowing the arrest itself, as I recall."

"Yes. Well, Marks and McDermott were seized on American soil, and without a warrant. I made a fine speech about the violation of international frontiers, and habeas corpus and the like; but Chief Justice Robinson was having none of it.

"I then attempted to show that Mr. Kinnear was something of a black sheep, and lax in his morals; which was undoubtedly true. He was a hypochondriac as well. Neither of these things had much to do with the fact that he'd been murdered, but I did my utmost, espe-cially with the morals; and it's a fact that those four people kept popping in and out of one another's beds like a French farce, so that it was hard to keep it straight who was sleeping where.

"I then proceeded to destroy the reputation of the unfortunate Montgomery woman. I didn't feel guilty about slandering her, as the poor creature was already well out of it. She'd had a child previously, you know – which died, I presume of midwives' mercy – and at the autopsy it was found she was pregnant. Undoubtedly the father was Kinnear, but I did my level best to produce a shadowy Romeo who'd strangled the poor woman out of jealousy. However, pull as I might, that rabbit refused to come out of the hat."

"Possibly because there was no rabbit," says Simon.

"Quite right. My next trick was an attempted sleight-of-hand with the shirts. Who was wearing which shirt, when, and why? McDermott had been caught in one of Kinnear's shirts – what then? I established the fact that Nancy had been in the habit of selling her employer's cast-off garments to the servants, with or without her master's permission; so McDermott could have come by his Shirt of Nessus honestly enough. Unfortunately, Kinnear's corpse had churlishly slipped on one of McDermott's shirts, which was a stumbling block indeed. I tried my best to avoid it, but the Prosecution hammered me with it, fair and square.

"I then pointed the finger of suspicion at the peddler to whom the bloody shirt thrown behind the door could be traced, as he had tried to palm off the same goods elsewhere. But that was no good either; there was testimony that the peddler had sold that very shirt to McDermott – a whole poker hand of shirts, in fact – and had then been unobliging enough to have vanished into thin air. For some reason he didn't wish to appear at the trial and run the risk of getting his own neck stretched."

"Cowardly fellow," says Simon.

"Just so," says MacKenzie, laughing. "And when it came to Grace, I must say I wasn't given much help. The foolish girl could not be dissuaded from dressing herself up in the murdered woman's finery, an act which was viewed with horror by the press and public; although if I'd had my wits about me, I would have advanced that very fact as evidence of an innocent and untroubled conscience, or, even better, of lunacy. But I didn't have the cunning to think of it at the time.

"In addition, Grace had muddied the trail considerably. She'd said at the time of her arrest that she hadn't known where Nancy was. Then, at the inquest, she said she suspected Nancy was dead and in the cellar, though she hadn't seen her put there. But, at the trial, and in her supposed Confession – that little item put out by the *Star*, and a tidy sum they made by it – she claimed to have seen McDermott dragging Nancy by the hair, and tossing her down the stairs. She never went so far as to admit to the strangling, however."

"But she did admit it to you, later," says Simon.

"Did she? I don't recall. . . ."

"In the Penitentiary," says Simon. "She told you she was haunted by Nancy's bloodshot eyes; or so Mrs. Moodie reported you as having said."

MacKenzie gives an uncomfortable wiggle, and looks down. "Grace was certainly in a troubled state of mind," he says. "Confused and melancholy."

"But the eyes?"

"Mrs. Moodie – for whom I have the greatest regard," says MacKenzie, "has a somewhat conventional imagination, and a tendency to exaggerate. She put some fine speeches into the mouths of her subjects, which it is highly unlikely they ever made, McDermott having been an unmitigated lout – even I, who was defending him, found it a stretch to scrape together a few good words for the man – and Grace a near child, and uneducated. As for the eyes, what is strongly anticipated by the mind is often supplied by it. You see it every day on the witness stand."

"So there were no eyes?"

MacKenzie wiggles again. "I couldn't swear to the eyes, on oath," he says. "Grace said nothing, exactly, that would stand up in court, as constituting a confession, although she did say she was sorry that Nancy was dead. But anyone might say that."

"Indeed," says Simon. He suspects now that the eyes did not originate with Mrs. Moodie, and wonders what other parts of her narrative were due to MacKenzie's own flamboyant tastes as a raconteur. "But we also have McDermott's statement, made just before he was hanged."

"Yes, yes; a scaffold pronouncement always makes it into the newspapers."

"Why did he wait so long, I wonder?"

"Until the very last, he hoped for a commutation, since Grace had been given one. He considered their guilt to be equal, and thought the sentences ought to be, as well; and he could not accuse her without knotting the noose very firmly around his own neck, as he'd need to admit to the axeplay and so forth."

"Whereas Grace could accuse him with relative impunity," says Simon.

"Just so," says MacKenzie. "Nor did she flinch from it when the moment came. *Sauve qui peut!* That woman has nerves like flint. She'd have made a good lawyer, if a man."

"But McDermott didn't get his reprieve," says Simon.

"Of course not! He was mad to expect it, but furious nonetheless. He considered that too to be Grace's fault – in his eyes, she'd cornered the clemency market – and as I read it, he then wanted to be revenged."

"Somewhat understandably," says Simon. "As I recall, he claimed that Grace came down into the cellar with him, and strangled Nancy with her own kerchief."

"Well, the kerchief was indeed found. But the rest of it is not hard evidence. The man had already told several different stories, and was a notorious liar into the bargain."

"Although," says Simon, "to turn Devil's advocate – just because a man is known to lie, it does not follow that he always does so."

"Precisely," says MacKenzie. "Well, I see the fascinating Grace has been leading you a merry chase."

"Not so merry," says Simon. "I must admit I've been baffled. What she says has the ring of truth; her manner is candid and sincere; and yet I can't shake the suspicion that, in some way I cannot put my finger on, she is lying to me."

"Lying," says MacKenzie. "A severe term, surely. Has she been lying to you, you ask? Let me put it this way – did Scheherazade lie? Not in her own eyes; indeed, the stories she told ought never to be subjected to the harsh categories of Truth and Falsehood. They belong in another realm altogether. Perhaps Grace Marks has merely been telling you what she needs to tell, in order to accomplish the desired end."

"Which is?" asks Simon.

"To keep the Sultan amused," says MacKenzie. "To keep the blow from falling. To forestall your departure, and make you stay in the room with her as long as possible."

"What on earth would be the point of that?" says Simon. "Amusing me won't get her out of prison."

"I don't suppose she really expects that," says MacKenzie. "But isn't it obvious? The poor creature has fallen in love with you. A single man, more or less young and not ill-favoured, appears to one who has long been sequestered, and deprived of masculine company. You are doubtless the object of her waking daydreams."

"Surely not," says Simon, flushing despite himself. If Grace is in love with him, she has preserved the secret extremely well.

"But I say, surely so! I had the very experience myself, or the twin of it; for I had to pass many hours with her, in her jail cell in Toronto, while she spun out her yarn for me to as great a length as it would go. She was besotted with me, and didn't wish to let me out of her sight. Such melting and languorous glances! A hand placed on hers, and she would have thrown herself into my arms."

Simon is disgusted. What a conceited little troll, with his natty vest and bulbous nose! "Indeed?" he says, trying not to let his anger show.

"Ah yes," says MacKenzie. "She thought she was going to be hanged, you know. Fear is a remarkable aphrodisiac; I advise you to try it some time. We lawyers are so often cast in the role of St. George, at least temporarily. Find a maiden chained to a rock and about to be devoured by a monster, rescue her, then have her yourself. It's the usual thing with maidens, wouldn't you agree? I won't say I wasn't tempted. She was very young and tender then; though no doubt prison life has hardened her."

Simon coughs, to hide his rage. How could he not have noticed that the man had a mouth like a depraved old lecher's? A provincial brothel-trotter. A calculating voluptuary. "There has never been any suggestion of that," he says. "In my case." He's considered the daydreams to be all on his side, but already he's beginning to doubt it. What has Grace really been thinking about him, as she sewed and recounted?

"I was very lucky," says MacKenzie, "and so of course was Grace herself, that the murder of Mr. Kinnear was tried before the other. It was obvious to everyone that she couldn't have helped to shoot Kinnear; and for Nancy's murder – indeed, for both of them – the evidence was circumstantial only. She was convicted not as a principal, but as an accessory, as all that could be proven against her was that she'd known of McDermott's murderous intentions in advance, and had failed to inform against him; and that she similarly neglected to broadcast the news of his completed achievement. Even the Chief Justice recommended clemency, and with the aid of several strong petitions in her favour I was able to save her life. By that time the death sentence had been pronounced against both of them and the trial had been closed, since it was thought unnecessary to go into the details of the second case; so Grace was never tried for the murder of Nancy Montgomery."

"And if she had been?" asks Simon.

"I couldn't have got her off. Public opinion would have been too strong for me. She would have been hanged."

"But in your opinion, she was innocent," says Simon.

"On the contrary," says MacKenzie. He sips at his sherry, wipes his lips daintily, smiles a smile of gentle reminiscence. "No. In my opinion, she was guilty as sin."

4 6 .

What is Dr. Jordan doing and when will he come back? Though what he is doing I think I have guessed. He is talking to people in Toronto, trying to find out if I am guilty; but he won't find it out that way. He doesn't understand yet that guilt comes to you not from the things you've done, but from the things that others have done to you.

His first name is Simon. I wonder why his mother named him that, or it may have been his father. My own father never bothered with the naming of us, it was up to Mother and Aunt Pauline. There is Simon Peter the Apostle, of course, who was made a fisher of men by our Lord. But there is also Simple Simon. Met a pie man, going to the fair. And said, Let me taste your ware, and had no penny. McDermott was like that, he thought he could take things without paying for them; and so does Dr. Jordan. Not that I don't feel sorry for him. He was always thin, and it's my impression that he is getting even thinner. I believe he is a prey to some gnawing sorrow.

As for what I was named after, it might have been the hymn. My mother never said so, but then there were many things she never said.

Amazing Grace! How sweet the sound
That saved a wretch like me!
I once was lost, but now I'm found,
Was blind but now I see.

I hope I was named after it. I would like to be found. I would like
to see. Or to be seen. I wonder if, in the eye of God, it amounts to
the same thing. As it says in the Bible, *For now we see through a glass,
darkly; but then face to face.*

If it is face to face, there must be two looking.

Today was Bath Day. There is some talk of making us bathe naked,
in groups, instead of by two's in our shifts; they say it will save time
and be more economical, as less water need be used, but I think it an
immodest idea and if they attempt it I shall complain to the authorities. Although perhaps I won't, as these things are sent to try us and
I should put up with it without complaint, as I do all the rest, for the
most part. The baths are unpleasant enough already, the stone of the
floor all slippery with dirty old soap, like a jelly, and there's always a
Matron watching; which may be just as well, as otherwise there
would be splashing. In winter you freeze to death, but now in the
heat of the summer with all the sweat and grime, which is twice as
much after working in the kitchens, I don't mind the cold water so
much, as it is refreshing.

After the baths had been got through I spent time at the plain
sewing. They are behindhand at the prison with the men's uniforms,
as more and more criminals keep being admitted, especially in the
dog days of summer when tempers are short and folks run to vindic-
tiveness; and so they must use my extra pair of hands. They have
their orders and their quotas to fill, just as in a factory.

Annie Little was sitting next to me on the bench, and she leant close and whispered to me, Grace, Grace, is he handsome, your young doctor? Will he get you out of prison? Are you in love with him, I suppose you are.

Don't be silly, I whispered to her, talking such rubbish, I've never been in love with any man and I don't plan to start now. I am condemned for life and there is no time for that sort of thing in here, and no space for it either when it comes to that.

Annie is thirty-five, she's older than I am, but besides being not always right in the head she has never grown up. That happens in the Penitentiary, some of them stay the same age all the time inside themselves; the same age as when first put in.

Get off your high horse, she said, and dug me with her elbow. You wouldn't mind a stiff piece in a tight corner, it never comes amiss; and you are so sly, she whispered, you'd find a time and a place for it if you wanted, Bertha Flood did it with a keeper in the tool shed, only she got caught and you'd never, you've got such a steady hand, you could murder your own grannie in her bed and never turn a hair. And she gave a snorting laugh.

I fear she has led a most disreputable life.

Silence there, said the Matron on duty, or I'll take down your names. They're becoming stricter again, as there is a new Head Matron; and if there are too many marks against you they cut off your hair.

After the noon meal I was sent over to the Governor's house. Dora was there again, as she has an arrangement with Dr. Jordan's landlady that she may come to us on the days of the great washing; and as usual she was full of gossip. She said if she told half she knew, it would take someone down a peg or two, and there was many a whited sepulchre wearing black silk and carrying lace handkerchiefs, and having sick headaches in the afternoons as if thoroughly respectable; and others could suit themselves, but she is not one to have the wool pulled over her eyes. She said that since Dr. Jordan went away, her mistress was spending hours in pacing the floor, and looking out the window, or sitting as if sunk into a stupor; which was no wonder, as she must be fearing he'll run off on her, as did the other one. And then who would pay for her whims and whams, and for all the running and fetching she required?

Clarrie for the most part ignores what Dora has to say. She is not interested in gossip about the better classes; she only smokes her pipe, and says, H'm. But today she said why should she care what the likes of those get up to, you might as well watch the hens and roosters scuffling in the barnyard, and God put such folks on this earth to dirty up the laundry as far as she could tell, because she couldn't for the life of her see any other use for them. And Dora said, Well, they are doing a fine job of that, I must say, they dirty it up as fast as I can get it clean, and the both of them are in the dirtying of it together if the truth was to come out.

At that a chill ran over my whole body, and I did not ask her to explain herself. I didn't want her saying anything bad about Dr. Jordan, as on the whole he has been very kind to me, and is also a considerable diversion in my life of monotony and toil.

When Dr. Jordan comes back, I am to be hypnotized. It has all been decided; Jeremiah, or I should think of him as Dr. DuPont because that is what I must now remember to call him, is to do the hypnotizing, and the others will watch and listen. The Governor's wife has explained it all, and said I need not be afraid, as I will be among friends who mean well, and all I will have to do is sit in a chair and go to sleep when Dr. DuPont tells me to. When I am asleep they will ask me questions. In this way they hope to bring back my memory.

I told her I was not at all sure I wanted to have it back, although of course I would do as they wished. And she said she was glad to find me in a co-operative state of mind, and she had the greatest faith in me and was sure I would be found innocent.

After the evening meal Matron gave us some knitting, to take into our cells and finish after hours, as they are behind on the stockings. In the summer it is light until quite late, and no candle grease need be wasted on us.

So now I am knitting. I am a quick knitter, I can do it without looking as long as it is only stockings and nothing fancy. And as I knit, I think: What would I put into my Keepsake Album, if I had one? A bit of fringe, from my mother's shawl. A ravelling of red wool, from the flowered mittens that Mary Whitney made for me. A scrap of silk, from Nancy's good shawl. A bone button, from Jeremiah. A daisy, from the daisy chain made for me by Jamie Walsh.

Nothing from McDermott, as I don't wish to remember him.

But what should a Keepsake Album be? Should it be only the good things in your life, or should it be all of the things? Many put in pictures of scenes and events they have never witnessed, such as Dukes and Niagara Falls, which to my mind is a sort of cheating. Would I do that? Or would I be truthful to my own life.

A piece of coarse cotton, from my Penitentiary nightdress. A square of bloodstained petticoat. A strip of kerchief, white with blue flowers. Love-in-a-mist.

4 7 .

The next morning, just after sunrise, Simon sets out for Richmond Hill, on a horse which he's hired at the livery stable behind his hotel. Like all horses accustomed to a succession of strange riders the beast is obstinate, with a hard mouth, and tries twice to scrape him against fences. After that it settles down, and plods along at a dogged canter, varied by a brisk, jolting walk. Although dusty and rutted in places the road is better than Simon has expected, and with several stops at wayside inns for rest and water he reaches Richmond Hill shortly after noon.

It's still not much of a town. There's a general store, a black-smith's, a straggle of houses. The inn must be the same one Grace remembers. He goes into it, orders roast beef and beer, and enquires about the location of Mr. Kinnear's former house. The landlord isn't surprised: Simon is by no means the first to ask such a question. In fact, they were fairly swarmed back then, he says, at the time of the murders, and ever since there's been a steady trickle of sightseers. The town is tired of being known only for that one thing: let the dead bury the dead, to his mind. But then, people want to gawk at tragedy; it's indecent. You'd think they'd leave trouble alone – but no, they want to partake of it. Some go so far as to carry things away with them – pebbles from the driveway, flowers from the flower beds. The gentleman who owns the house now is not so bothered, as fewer people have been coming. Still, he doesn't want idle curiosity.

Simon assures him that his own curiosity is far from idle: he's a doctor, and is making a study of Grace. It's a waste of time, says the landlord, because Grace was guilty. "She was a good-looking woman," he adds, with a kind of pride at having known her. "Butter wouldn't melt in her mouth. You'd never have guessed what she was plotting, under that smooth face."

"Only fifteen at the time, I believe," says Simon.

"But could have passed for eighteen. A shame, to have got so wicked, at her young age." He says Mr. Kinnear was a fine gentleman though loose, and most people had liked Nancy Montgomery, even though she'd been living in sin. He'd known McDermott too; a prime athlete, and would have done well in the end, except for Grace. "It was her led him on, and it was her put a noose around his neck for him too." He says the women always get off easy.

Simon asks about Jamie Walsh, but Jamie Walsh is gone. To the city, say some; to the States, say others. After Kinnear's place was sold off the Walshes had to shift. In fact there aren't many left in the neighbourhood who were here back then, as there's been a great deal of buying and selling and coming and going since; the grass being always greener on the other side of the fence.

Simon rides north, and has little difficulty in identifying the Kinnear property. He hasn't meant to go right up to the house – he's only been intending to look at it from a distance – but the orchard which was young in Grace's time has now grown up, partially obscuring the view. He finds himself halfway up the drive, and before he knows it he's hitched his horse to the fence beside the two kitchens, and is standing at the front door.

The house is smaller, and somehow dingier, than he has imagined it. The porch with its pillars is in need of a coat of paint, and the rose bushes have run wild, and show only a few infested blooms. What can be gained from looking, Simon asks himself; apart, that is, from a vulgar frisson, and the indulgence of morbid interest? It's like visiting the site of a battle: there is nothing to be seen except in the mind's eye. Such confrontations with the actual are always a disappointment.

Nevertheless he knocks at the front door, then knocks again. No one answers. He's turning to go away when the door is opened. A woman stands there, thin, sad-faced, not old but aging, soberly dressed in a dark print dress and apron. Simon has the sensation that this is what Nancy Montgomery would have turned into if she'd lived.

"You're here to see the house," she says. It isn't a question. "The master's not at home, but I have instructions to show you around."

Simon is taken aback: how did they know he was coming? Perhaps they have a lot of visitors, still, despite what the innkeeper told him? Has the place become a grisly museum?

The housekeeper – for that's what she must be – stands aside to allow Simon to pass into the front hall. "You'll want to know about the well, I suppose," she says. "They always do."

"The well?" asks Simon. He's heard nothing about a well. Perhaps his visit will be repaid, after all, with some fresh detail about the case, never before mentioned. "What about the well?"

The woman gives him an odd glance. "It's a covered well, Sir, with a new pump. Surely you would want to know about the well, when looking to buy a place."

"But I'm not looking to buy it," says Simon, flustered. "Is it for sale?"

"Why else would I be showing it to you? Of course it's for sale, and not for the first time neither. Those that live here never feel entirely comfortable. Not that there's anything, no ghosts or such, though you'd think there might be, and I never like to go down to the cellar. But it draws the idle gawkers."

She stares hard at him: if he's not a buyer, what is he doing here? Simon doesn't wish to be thought just another idle gawker. "I am a doctor," he says.

"Ah," she says, nodding shrewdly at him, as if this explains it. "So you want to see the *house*. We do get a lot of doctors who want to see it. More than the other sorts, even the lawyers. Well, now that you're here, you might just as well. In here is the parlour, where they kept the piano, I'm told, in Mr. Kinnear's time, that Miss Nancy Montgomery used to play at. She sang like a canary, so they say of her. Very musical, she was." She smiles at Simon, the first smile she's bestowed.

Simon's tour is thorough. He is shown the dining room, the library, the winter kitchen; the summer kitchen, the stable and loft, "where that scoundrel McDermott slept at night." The upstairs bed-rooms – "Lord only knows what went on up here" – and Grace's little room. The furniture is all different, of course. Poorer, shabbier. Simon tries to imagine what it must have looked like then, but fails.

With a fine showmanship, the housekeeper saves the cellar till the last. She lights a candle and descends first, cautioning him against slipping. The light is dim, the corners cobwebbed. There's a dank smell, of earth and stored vegetables. "He was found right here," says the housekeeper with relish, "and she was hid over by that wall. Though why they bothered to hide her, I don't know. Crime will out, and out it did. It's a pity they didn't hang that Grace, and I'm not alone in saying so."

"I am sure you aren't," says Simon. He's seen enough, he wants to be gone. At the front door he gives her a coin – it seems the right thing – and she nods and pockets it. "You can see the graves, too, in the churchyard in town," she tells him. "There's no names, but you can't miss them. They're the only ones with pickets round."

Simon thanks her. He feels he's sneaking away after some discreditable peepshow. What sort of a voyeur has he become? A thoroughgoing one, apparently, as he heads straight for the Presbyterian church; easy to find, since it's the only steeple in sight.

Behind it is the graveyard, neat and green, the dead kept under firm control. No rambling weeds here, no tattered wreaths, no jumble and confusion; nothing like the baroque efflorescences of Europe. No angels, no Calvaries, no nonsense. Heaven, for the Presbyterians, must resemble a banking establishment, with each soul tagged and docketed, and placed in the appropriate pigeonhole.

The graves he seeks are obvious. Each has a wooden picket fence around it, the only such fences in the graveyard: to keep the occupants penned in, no doubt, since the murdered have the reputation of walking. Even the Presbyterians, it appears, are not exempt from superstition.

Thomas Kinnear's picket fence is painted white, Nancy Montgomery's black, an indication perhaps of the town's judgment upon her: murder victim or not, she was no better than she should be. They hadn't been buried in the same grave – no need to endorse the scandal. Oddly, Nancy's grave has been placed at Kinnear's feet, and at right angles to him; the effect is of a sort of bed rug. There's a large rose bush filling almost the whole of Nancy's enclosure – the old broadsheet ballad, then, was prophetic – but no vine in Thomas Kinnear's. Simon picks a rose from Nancy's grave, with some half-formed notion of taking it back to Grace, but then thinks better of it.

He spends the night at an unprepossessing inn halfway back to Toronto. The windowpanes are so grimy he can scarcely see out of them, the blankets smell of mildew; directly below his room, a group of raucous drinkers carouses till well past midnight. These are the hazards of provincial travel. He places a chair against the door, to prevent unwelcome intrusion.

In the morning he arises early and inspects the various insect bites he's acquired during the night. He douses his head in the scant basin of lukewarm water brought by the chambermaid, who doubles as the scullery maid downstairs; the water smells of onions.

After breakfasting on a slice of antediluvian ham and an egg of uncertain age, he continues on his way. Few others are abroad; he passes a wagon, an axeman felling a dead tree in his field, a labourer pissing into the ditch. Wisps of mist float here and there above the fields, dissipating like dreams in the rising light. The air is hazy, the roadside weeds hung with dew; the horse snatches mouthfuls of them as it passes. Simon curbs it half-heartedly, then lets it amble. He feels idle, remote from all goals and effort.

Before taking his afternoon train, he has one more errand. He wants to visit the grave of Mary Whitney. He wants to make sure she really exists.

The Adelaide Street Methodist Church is the one Grace named; he's looked it up in his notes. In the graveyard, polished granite is replacing marble, and verses are becoming scarce: ostentation lies in size and solidity, not in ornamentation. The Methodists like their monuments monumental; block-like, unmistakable, like the thick black lines drawn under finalized accounts in his father's ledger book: *Paid In Full*.

He walks up and down the rows of graves, reading over the names – the Biggs and the Stewarts, the Flukes and the Chambers, the Cooks and the Randolphs and the Stalworthys. At last he finds it, over in a corner: a small grey stone, which looks older than the nineteen years that have passed. *Mary Whitney*; the name, nothing more. But Grace did say that the name was all she could afford.

Conviction leaps in him like a flame – her story is true, then – but it dies as quickly. What are such physical tokens worth? A magician produces a coin from a hat, and because it's a real coin and a real hat, the audience believes that the illusion too is real. But this stone is only that: a stone. For one thing, it has no dates on it, and the Mary Whitney buried beneath it may not have any connection with Grace Marks at all. She could be just a name, a name on a stone, seen here by Grace and used by her in the spinning of her story. She could be an old woman, a wife, a small infant, anyone at all.

Nothing has been proved. But nothing has been disproved, either.

Returning to Kingston, Simon travels first class. The train is almost full, and to avoid the crowding it's worth the expense. As he's carried eastward and Toronto recedes behind him, and Richmond Hill and its farms and meadows, he finds himself wondering what it would be like to live back there, in that lush and peaceful country-side; in, for instance, Thomas Kinnear's house, with Grace as his housekeeper. Not only his housekeeper: his locked and secret mis-tress. He'd keep her hidden, under a different name.

A lazy, indulgent life it would be, with its own slow delights. He pictures her sitting in a chair in the parlour, sewing, the lamplight falling on the side of her face. But why only mistress? It comes to him that Grace Marks is the only woman he's ever met that he would wish to marry. It's a sudden notion, but once he's had it he turns it over, considering it. He thinks, with a certain mordant irony, that she may also be the only one who would satisfy all of his mother's oft-hinted requirements, or almost all: Grace is not, for instance, rich. But she has beauty without frivolity, domesticity without dullness, and simplicity of manner, and prudence, and cir-cumspection. She is also an excellent needlewoman, and could doubtless crochet rings around Miss Faith Cartwright. His mother would have no complaints on that score.

Then there are his own requirements. There is passion in Grace somewhere, he's certain of it, although it would take some hunting for. And she'd be grateful to him, albeit reluctantly. Gratitude by itself does not enthral him, but he likes the idea of reluctance.

But then there's James McDermott. Has she been telling the truth in that respect? Did she really dislike and fear the man as much as she's claimed? He'd touched her, certainly; but how much, and with how much of her consent? Such episodes appear differently in retrospect than in the heat of the moment; nobody knows that better than he, and why should it be any different for a woman? One prevaricates, one makes excuses for oneself, one gets out of it the best way one can. But what if, some evening in the lamplit parlour, she were to reveal more than he would care to know?

But he does care to know.

Madness, of course; a perverse fantasy, to marry a suspected murderess. But what if he'd met her before the murders? He considers this, rejects it. Before the murders Grace would have been entirely different from the woman he now knows. A young girl, scarcely formed; tepid, bland, and tasteless. A flat landscape.

Murderess, murderess, he whispers to himself. It has an allure, a scent almost. Hothouse gardenias. Lurid, but also furtive. He imagines himself breathing it as he draws Grace towards him, pressing his mouth against her. *Murderess*. He applies it to her throat like a brand.

XIII.

PANDORA'S BOX

My husband had contrived a very ingenious sort of Spirit-oscope. . . . I had always refused to put my hands upon this board, which would move for people under the influence and spell out letter by letter messages and names. But being alone, I placed my hands upon the board, and asked, 'Was it a spirit that lifted my hand?' and the board rolled forward and spelt out 'Yes.' . . .

You, will perhaps think, as I too, have often thought, that the whole is an operation of my *own* mind, but my mind must be far cleverer than I, its owner have any idea of if it can spell letter by letter, whole pages of connected and often abstruse matter, without my knowing one word about it, for, it is not, until, Mr Moodie reads it over to me, after the communication is suspended that I know what it is about. My sister Mrs Traill, is a very powerful Medium for these communications, and gets them in foreign languages. Her spirits often abuse, and call her very ugly names. . . . Now, do not think me mad or possessed by evil spirits. I could wish you altogether possessed by such a glorious madness.

– Susanna Moodie,
Letter to Richard Bentley, 1858.

A shadow flits before me,
Not thou, but like to thee.
Ah, Christ, that it were possible
For one short hour to see
The souls we loved, that they might tell us
What and where they be!

– Alfred, Lord Tennyson,
Maud, 1855.

I felt a Cleaving in my Mind –
As if my Brain had split –
I tried to match it – Seam by Seam –
But could not make it fit.

– Emily Dickinson,
c. 1860.

4 8 .

They wait in the library of Mrs. Quennell's house, each in a straight-backed chair, each turned not too obviously towards the door, which is slightly open. The curtains, which are of maroon plush with black trim and tassels and remind Simon of Episcopalian funerals, have been drawn shut; a globe-shaded lamp has been lit. It stands in the centre of the table, which is oblong and made of oak; and they sit around it, silent, expectant, decorous and wary, like a jury before the trial.

Mrs. Quennell, however, is relaxed, her hands folded placidly in her lap; she anticipates wonders, but will evidently not be surprised by them, whatever they may be. She has the air of a professional guide for whom the ravishments of, say, Niagara Falls have become a commonplace, but who hopes to enjoy vicariously the raptures of visiting neophytes. The Governor's wife wears an expression of yearning piety, tempered with resignation, whereas Reverend Verringer manages to look both benign and disapproving; there's a glinting around his eyes as if he's wearing spectacles, although he is not. Lydia, who is seated to Simon's left, is dressed in some cloudy, shiny material, a light mauve shot through with white, cut low enough to reveal her charming collarbone; she exudes a moist aroma of lily of the valley. She's nervously twisting her handkerchief; but when her eyes meet Simon's, she smiles.

As for Simon, he senses that his face is set in a sceptical and not very pleasant sneer; but that's a false face, as underneath it he's eager as a schoolboy at a carnival. He believes in nothing, he expects trickery and longs to discover how it is worked, but at the same time he wishes to be astonished. He knows this is a dangerous state of mind: he must preserve his objectivity.

There's a knock at the door, which opens wider; and Dr. Jerome DuPont comes in, leading Grace by the hand. She isn't wearing a cap, and her coiled hair shines redly in the lamplight. She has on a white collar, which is something he's never seen her in; and she looks astonishingly young. She walks tentatively, as if blind, but her eyes are wide open, fixed upon DuPont with the timorousness, the tremulousness, the pale and silent appeal, which Simon – he now realizes – has been hoping for in vain.

"I see you are all assembled," says Dr. DuPont. "I am gratified by your interest, and, I hope I may say, by your trust. The lamp must be removed from the table. Mrs. Quennell, may I impose upon you? And turned down, please. And the door closed."

Mrs. Quennell rises and silently moves the lamp to a small desk in the corner. Reverend Verringer shuts the door firmly.

"Grace will sit here," says Dr. DuPont. He places her with her back to the curtains. "Are you quite comfortable? Good. Do not be afraid, no one here wishes to hurt you. I have explained to her that all she has to do is listen to me, and then go to sleep. Do you understand, Grace?"

Grace nods. She's sitting rigidly, her lips pressed together, the pupils of her eyes huge in the weak light. Her hands grip the arms of the chair. Simon has seen attitudes like this in the wards of hospitals – those in pain, or awaiting an operation. An animal fear.

"This is a fully scientific procedure," says Dr. DuPont. He is talking to the rest of them, rather than to Grace. "Please banish all thoughts of Mesmerism, and other such fraudulent procedures. The Braidian system is completely logical and sound, and has been proven by European experts beyond a shadow of a doubt. It involves the deliberate relaxation and realignment of the nerves, so that a neuro-hypnotic sleep is induced. The same thing may be observed in fish, when stroked along the dorsal fin, and even in cats; although in higher organisms the results are of course more complex. I do ask you to avoid sudden movements and loud noises, as these can be shocking, and perhaps even damaging, to the subject. I request that you remain completely silent until Grace is asleep, after which you may converse in low voices."

Grace stares at the closed door as if thinking of escape. She's so high-strung Simon can almost feel her vibrating, like a stretched rope. He's never seen her so terrified. What has DuPont said or done to her before bringing her here? It's almost as if he must have threatened her; but when he speaks to her she looks up at him trustingly. Whatever else, it isn't DuPont she's afraid of.

DuPont turns the lamp down lower. The air in the room seems to thicken with barely visible smoke. Grace's features are now in shadow, except for the vitreous gleam of her eyes.

DuPont begins his procedure. First he suggests heaviness, drowsiness; then he tells Grace that her limbs are floating, drifting, that she is sinking down, down, down, as if through water. His voice has a soothing monotony. Grace's eyelids droop; she is breathing deeply and evenly.

"Are you asleep, Grace?" DuPont asks her.

"Yes," she says, in a voice that is slow and languid, but clearly audible.

"You can hear me."

"Yes."

"You can hear only me? Good. When you wake, you will remember nothing of what is done here. Now, go deeper." He pauses. "Please lift your right arm."

Slowly the arm rises as if pulled by a string, until it is held out straight. "Your arm," says DuPont, "is an iron bar. No one can bend it." He looks around at them. "Would anyone care to try?" Simon is tempted, but decides not to risk it; at this point he wants neither to be convinced, nor to be disillusioned. "No?" says DuPont. "Then allow me." He places his two hands on Grace's outstretched arm, leans forward. "I am using all my force," he says. The arm does not bend. "Good. You may lower your arm."

"Her eyes are open," says Lydia, alarmed; and sure enough there are two half-moons of white showing between the lids.

"It is normal," says DuPont, "but of no import. In this condition the subject appears able to discern certain objects, even with the eyes closed. It is a peculiarity of the nervous organization which must involve some sensory organ not yet measurable by human agency. But let us proceed."

He bends over Grace as if listening to her heart. Then he takes from some hidden pocket a square of fabric – an ordinary woman's veil, light grey – and drops it gently over her head, where it billows and settles. Now there's only a head, with the merest contour of a face behind it. The suggestion of a shroud is unmistakable.

It's too theatrical, too tawdry, thinks Simon; it reeks of the small-town lecture halls of fifteen years ago, with their audiences of credulous store clerks and laconic farmers, and their drab wives, and the smooth-talking charlatans who used to dole out transcendental nonsense and quack medical advice to them as an excuse for picking their pockets. He's striving for derision; nevertheless, the back of his neck creeps.

"She looks so – so odd," whispers Lydia.

"'What hope of answer or redress? Behind the veil, behind the veil,'" says Reverend Verringer, in his quoting voice. Simon can't tell whether or not he intends to be jocular.

"Pardon?" says the Governor's wife. "Oh yes – dear Mr. Tennyson."

"It helps the concentration," says Dr. DuPont in a low voice. "The inner sight is keener when hidden from outward view. Now, Dr. Jordan, we may safely travel into the past. What is it you would wish me to ask her?"

Simon wonders where to begin. "Ask her about the Kinnear residence," he says.

"What part of it?" says DuPont. "One must be specific."

"The verandah," says Simon, who believes in starting gently.

"Grace," says DuPont, "you are on the verandah, at Mr. Kinnear's. What do you see there?"

"I see flowers," says Grace. Her voice is heavy, and somehow damp. "It's the sunset. I am so happy. I want to stay here."

"Ask her," says Simon, "to get up now, and walk into the house. Tell her to go towards the trapdoor in the front hall, the one leading to the cellar."

"Grace," says DuPont, "you must . . ."

Suddenly there's a loud single knock, almost like a small explosion. It has come from the table, or was it the door? Lydia gives a little shriek and clutches at Simon's hand; it would be churlish of him to pull away, so he does not, especially as she's shivering like a leaf.

"Hush!" says Mrs. Quennell in a piercing whisper. "We have a visitor!"

"William!" cries the Governor's wife softly. "I know it's my darling! My little one!"

"I beg you," says DuPont, with irritation. "This is not a séance!"

Under the veil, Grace stirs uneasily. The Governor's wife sniffles into her handkerchief. Simon glances over at Reverend Verringer. In the dimness it's hard to be sure of his expression; it seems to be a pained smile, like a baby with gas.

"I'm frightened," says Lydia. "Turn up the light!"

"Not yet," Simon whispers. He pats her hand.

There are three more sharp raps, as if someone is knocking at the door, imperiously demanding entry. "This is unconscionable," says DuPont. "Please request them to go away."

"I will try," says Mrs. Quennell. "But this is a Thursday. They're used to coming on Thursdays." She bows her head and clasps her hands. After a moment there's a series of little staccato pops, like a handful of pebbles rattling down a drainspout. "There," she says, "I think that's done it."

There must be a confederate, thinks Simon – some accomplice or apparatus, outside the door, under the table. This is, after all, Mrs. Quennell's house. Who knows how she may have rigged it up? But there's nothing under the table except their feet. How is it all worked? Just by sitting here he is rendered absurd, an ignorant pawn, a dupe. But he can't leave now.

"Thank you," says DuPont. "Doctor, please pardon the interruption. Let us proceed."

Simon is increasingly conscious of Lydia's hand in his. It's a small hand, and very warm. In fact the entire room is too close for comfort. He would like to detach himself, but Lydia is clutching him with a grip of iron. He hopes no one can see. His arm tingles; he crosses his legs. He has a sudden vision of Rachel Humphrey's legs, naked except for her stockings, and of his hands on them, holding her down while she struggles. Deliberately struggles, watching him through the lashes of her almost-closed eyes to see the effect she's having on him. Writhes like an artful eel. Begs like a captive. Slippery, a skin of sweat on her, hers or his, her dank hair across her face, across his mouth, every night. Imprisoned. Her skin where he's licked her shines like satin. It can't go on.

"Ask her," he says, "whether she ever had relations with James McDermott." He hasn't been intending to pose this question; certainly not at first, and never so directly. But isn't it – he sees it now – the one thing he most wants to know?

DuPont repeats the question to Grace in a level voice. There is a pause; then Grace laughs. Or someone laughs; it doesn't sound like Grace. "Relations, Doctor? What do you mean?" The voice is thin, wavering, watery; but fully present, fully alert. "Really, Doctor, you are such a hypocrite! You want to know if I kissed him, if I slept with him. If I was his paramour! Is that it?"

"Yes," says Simon. He's shaken, but must try not to show it. He was expecting a series of monosyllables, mere yes's and no's dragged out of her, out of her lethargy and stupor; a series of compelled and somnolent responses to his own firm demands. Not such crude mockery. This voice cannot be Grace's; yet in that case, whose voice is it?

"Whether I did what you'd like to do with that little slut who's got hold of your hand?" There is a dry chuckle.

Lydia gasps, and withdraws her hand as if burned. Grace laughs again. "You'd like to know that, so I'll tell you. Yes. I would meet him outside, in the yard, in my nightdress, in the moonlight. I'd press up against him, I'd let him kiss me, and touch me as well, all over, Doctor, the same places you'd like to touch me, because I can always tell, I know what you're thinking when you sit in that stuffy little sewing room with me. But that was all, Doctor. That was all I'd let him do. I had him on a string, and Mr. Kinnear as well. I had the two of them dancing to my tune!"

"Ask her why," says Simon. He can't understand what's happening, but this may be his last chance to understand. He must keep his head, and pursue a straight line of enquiry. His voice, to his own ears, is a hoarse croak.

"I would breathe like this," says Grace. She utters a high erotic moan. "I would twist and twine. After that, he'd say he'd do anything." She titters. "But why? Oh Doctor, you are always asking why. Poking your nose in, and not only your nose. You are such a curious man! Curiosity killed the cat, you know, Doctor. You should watch out for that little mouse beside you; and her little furry mousehole too!"

To Simon's astonishment, Reverend Verringer giggles; or perhaps he is coughing.

"This is an outrage," says the Governor's wife. "I won't sit here and listen to such filth! Lydia, come with me!" She half rises; her skirts rustle.

"Please," says DuPont. "Bear with me. Modesty must take second place to the interests of science."

For Simon this whole occasion is reeling out of control. He must seize the initiative, or at least try to seize it; he must keep Grace from reading his mind. He's been told of the clairvoyant powers of those under hypnosis, but he's never believed in them before. "Ask her," he says sternly, "if she was in the cellar of Mr. Kinnear's house, on Saturday, July 23rd, 1843."

"The cellar," says DuPont. "You must picture the cellar, Grace. Go back in time, descend in space. . . ."

"Yes," says Grace, in her new, thin voice. "Along the hallway, lift the trapdoor; go down the cellar stairs. The barrels, the whisky, the vegetables in the boxes full of sand. There on the floor. Yes, I was in the cellar."

"Ask her if she saw Nancy there."

"Oh yes, I saw her." A pause. "As I can see you, Doctor. From behind the veil. And I can hear you too."

DuPont looks surprised. "Irregular," he mutters, "but not unknown."

"Was she alive?" asks Simon. "Was she still alive, when you saw her?"

The voice sniggers. "She was partly alive. Or partly dead. She needed" – a high twittering – "to be put out of her misery."

There's a sharp intake of breath from Reverend Verringer. Simon can feel his own heart pounding. "Did you help to strangle her?" he says.

"It was my kerchief that strangled her." A fresh chirping, a giggling. "Such a pretty pattern it had on it!"

"Infamous," murmurs Verringer. He must be thinking of all the prayers he's expended on her, and all the ink and paper too. The letters, the petitions, the faith.

"It was a shame to lose that kerchief; I'd had it such a long time. It was my mother's. I should have taken it off Nancy's neck. But James wouldn't let me have it, nor her gold earrings neither. There was blood on it, but that would have washed out."

"You killed her," breathes Lydia. "I always thought so." She sounds, if anything, admiring.

"The kerchief killed her. Hands held it," says the voice. "She had to die. The wages of sin is death. And this time the gentleman died as well, for once. Share and share alike!"

"Oh Grace," moans the Governor's wife. "I thought better of you! All these years you have deceived us!"

The voice is gleeful. "Stop talking rubbish," she says. "You've deceived yourselves! I am not Grace! Grace knew nothing about it!"

No one in the room says anything. The voice is humming now, a high tiny music, like a bee. "'Rock of ages, cleft for me, Let me hide myself in thee! Let the water, and the blood . . .'"

"You are not Grace," says Simon. Despite the warmth of the room, he feels cold all over. "If you are not Grace, who are you?"

"'Cleft for me . . . Let me hide myself, in thee . . .'"

"You must answer," says DuPont. "I command it!"

There is another series of raps, heavy, rhythmical, like someone dancing on the table in clogs. Then a whisper: "You can't command. You must guess!"

"I know you are a spirit," says Mrs. Quennell. "They can speak through others, in the trance. They make use of our material organs. This one is speaking through Grace. But sometimes they lie, you know."

"I am not lying!" says the voice. "I am beyond lying! I no longer need to lie!"

"You can't always believe them," says Mrs. Quennell, as if talking about a child or a servant. "It may be James McDermott, come here to sully Grace's reputation. To accuse her. It was his last act in life, and those who die with vengeance in their hearts are often trapped on the earthly plane."

"Please, Mrs. Quennell," says Dr. DuPont. "It is no spirit. What we are witnessing here must be a natural phenomenon." He's sounding a little desperate.

"Not James," says the voice, "you old fraud!"

"Nancy, then," says Mrs. Quennell, who doesn't seem at all affected by the insult. "They are often rude," she says. "They call us names. Some are angry – those earthbound spirits who cannot tolerate being dead."

"Not Nancy, you stupid fool! Nancy can't say anything, she can't say a word, not with her neck like that. Such a pretty neck, once! But Nancy isn't angry any more, she doesn't mind, Nancy is my friend. She understands now, she wants to share things. Come, Doctor," says the voice, cajoling now. "You like riddles. You know the answer. I told you it was *my* kerchief, the one I left to Grace, when I, when I . . ." She begins to sing again: "'Oh no, 'twas the truth in her eye ever dawning, That made me love Mary . . .'"

"Not Mary," says Simon. "Not Mary Whitney."

There is a sharp clap, which appears to come from the ceiling. "I told James to do it. I urged him to. I was there all along!"

"There?" says DuPont.

"Here! With Grace, where I am now. It was so cold, lying on the floor, and I was all alone; I needed to keep warm. But Grace doesn't know, she's never known!" The voice is no longer teasing. "They almost hanged her, but that would have been wrong. She knew nothing! I only borrowed her clothing for a time."

"Her clothing?" says Simon.

"Her earthly shell. Her fleshly garment. She forgot to open the window, and so I couldn't get out! But I wouldn't want to hurt her. You mustn't tell her!" The little voice is pleading now.

"Why not?" asks Simon.

"You know why, Dr. Jordan. Do you want to see her back in the Asylum? I liked it there at first, I could talk out loud there. I could laugh. I could tell what happened. But no one listened to me." There is a small, thin sobbing. "I was not heard."

"Grace," says Simon. "Stop playing tricks!"

"I am not Grace," says the voice, more tentatively.

"Is that really you?" Simon asks it. "Are you telling the truth? Don't be afraid."

"You see?" wails the voice. "You're the same, you won't listen to me, you don't believe me, you want it your own way, you won't hear. . . ." It trails off, and there is silence.

"She's gone," says Mrs. Quennell. "You can always tell when they go back to their own realm. You can feel it in the air; it's the electricity."

For a long moment nobody says anything. Then Dr. DuPont moves. "Grace," he says, bending over her. "Grace Marks, can you hear me?" He lays his hand on her shoulder.

There's another long pause, during which they can hear Grace breathing, unevenly now, as if in troubled sleep. "Yes," she says at last. It's her usual voice.

"I am going to bring you up now," says DuPont. He lifts the veil gently from her head, lays it aside. Her face is stilled and smooth. "You are floating up, up. Up out of the depths. You will not recall what happened here. When I snap my fingers, you will awake." He goes to the lamp, turns it up, then comes back and places his hand close to Grace's head. His fingers snap.

Grace stirs, opens her eyes, looks around wonderingly, smiles at them. It's a calm smile, no longer tense and fearful. The smile of a dutiful child. "I must have been asleep," she says.

"Do you remember anything?" asks Dr. DuPont anxiously. "Anything of what has just passed?"

"No," says Grace. "I was asleep. But I must have been dreaming. I dreamt about my mother. She was floating in the sea. She was at peace."

Simon is relieved; DuPont too, from the look of him. He takes her hand, assists her from the chair. "You may feel a little dizzy," he tells her gently. "It is frequently the case. Mrs. Quennell, would you see that she is placed in a bedchamber where she may lie down?"

Mrs. Quennell leaves the room with Grace, holding her by the arm as if she's an invalid. But she walks lightly enough now, and seems almost happy.

4 9.

The men remain in the library. Simon is glad he's sitting down; he'd welcome nothing so much at the moment as a good stiff glass of brandy, to steady his nerves, but in present company there's not much hope of that. He feels light-headed, and wonders if his earlier fever is returning.

"Gentlemen," DuPont begins, "I am at a loss. I have never had an experience quite like this before. The results were most unexpected. As a rule, the subject remains under the control of the operator." He sounds quite shaken.

"Two hundred years ago, they would not have been at a loss," says Reverend Verringer. "It would have been a clear case of posession. Mary Whitney would have been found to have been inhabiting the body of Grace Marks, and thus to be responsible for inciting the crime, and for helping to strangle Nancy Montgomery. An exorcism would have been in order."

"But this is the nineteenth century," says Simon. "It may be a neurological condition." He would like to say *must be*, but he doesn't wish to contradict Verringer too bluntly. Also he is still quite unsettled, and unsure of his intellectual ground.

"There have been cases of this kind," DuPont says. "As early as 1816, there was Mary Reynolds, of New York, whose bizarre alternations were described by Dr. S. L. Mitchill of New York; are you familiar with the case, Dr. Jordan? No? Since then, Wakley of *The Lancet* has written extensively on the phenomenon; he calls it *double consciousness*, although he emphatically rejects the possibility of reaching the so-called secondary personality through Neuro-hypnotism, as there is too much chance of the subject's being influenced by the practitioner. He has always been a great foe of Mesmerism and related means, being a conservative in that respect."

"Puysegeur describes something of the sort, as I recall," says Simon. "It may be a case of what is known as *dédoublement* – the subject, when in a somnambulistic trance, displayed a completely different personality than when awake, the two halves having no knowledge of each other."

"Gentlemen, it's most difficult to credit," says Verringer. "But stranger things have happened."

"Nature sometimes produces two heads on one body," says DuPont. "Then why not two persons, as it were, in one brain? There may exist examples, not only of alternating *states* of consciousness, as claimed by Puysegeur, but of two distinct personalities, which may coexist in the same body and yet have different sets of memories altogether, and be, for all practical purposes, two separate individuals. If, that is, you'll accept – a debatable point – that we are what we remember."

"Perhaps," says Simon, "we are also – preponderantly – what we forget."

"If you are right," says Reverend Verringer, "what becomes of the soul? We cannot be mere patchworks! It is a horrifying thought, and one that, if true, would make a mockery of all notions of moral responsibility, and indeed of morality itself, as we currently define it."

"The other voice, whatever it was," says Simon, "was remarkable for its violence."

"But not without a certain logic," says Verringer dryly, "and an ability to see in the dark."

Simon remembers Lydia's warm hand, and finds himself flushing. At the moment he wishes Verringer at the bottom of the sea.

"If two persons, why not two souls?" DuPont continues. "That is, if the soul must be brought into it at all. Or three souls and persons, for that matter. Consider the Trinity."

"Dr. Jordan," says Reverend Verringer, ignoring this theological challenge, "what will you say about this, in your report? Surely the evening's proceedings are scarcely orthodox, from a medical point of view."

"I shall have to consider my position," says Simon, "very carefully. Although you do see that if Dr. DuPont's premise is accepted, Grace Marks is exonerated."

"To admit such a possibility would require a leap of faith," says Reverend Verringer. "One that I myself will pray for the strength to make, as I have always believed Grace to be innocent; or hoped, rather, although I must admit I have been somewhat shaken. But if what we have witnessed is a natural phenomenon, who are we to question it? The ground of all phenomena is God, and he must have his reasons, obscure though they may appear to mortal eyes."

Simon walks back to the house alone. The night is clear and warm, with a moon, almost full, enclosed in a nimbus of mist; the air smells of mown grass and horse manure, with an undertone of dog.

Throughout the evening he's maintained a plausible self-control, but now his brain feels like a roasting chestnut, or an animal on fire. Silent howls resound inside him; there's a confused and frenzied motion, a scrambling, a dashing to and fro. What happened in the library? Was Grace really in a trance, or was she play-acting, and laughing up her sleeve? He knows what he saw and heard, but he may have been shown an illusion, which he cannot prove to have been one.

If he describes what he witnessed in his report, and if his report finds its way into any petition submitted on Grace Marks' behalf, he knows it would immediately scotch all possible chances of success. It's Ministers of Justice and their kind who read such petitions; they are hard-headed, practical men, who require solid evidence. If the report were to become public, and a matter of record, and widely circulated, he would become an instant laughing-stock, especially among the established members of the medical profession. That would be the end of his plans for an Asylum, for who would subscribe to such an institution, knowing it to be run by some crack-brained believer in mystical voices?

There's no way he can write the report Verringer desires without perjuring himself. The safest thing would be to write nothing at all, but Verringer will hardly let him off the hook so easily. However, the fact is that he can't state anything with certainty and still tell the truth, because the truth eludes him. Or rather it's Grace herself who eludes him. She glides ahead of him, just out of his grasp, turning her head to see if he's still following.

Brusquely he dismisses her, and turns to thoughts of Rachel. She at least is something he can grapple with, take hold of. She will not slip through his fingers.

The house is in darkness; Rachel must be asleep. He doesn't wish to see her, he feels no desire for her this evening – quite the opposite; the thought of her, of her tense and bone-coloured body, her scent of camphor and withered violets, fills him with a faint disgust; but he knows all that will change as soon as he steps over the threshold. He'll begin to tiptoe up the stairs, intending to avoid her. Then he'll turn around, make his way to her room, shake her roughly awake. Tonight he'll hit her, as she's begged him to; he's never done that before, it's something new. He wants to punish her for his own addiction to her. He wants to make her cry; though not too loudly, or Dora will hear them, and trumpet scandal. It's a wonder she hasn't heard them before; they've become increasingly careless.

He knows he's reaching the end of the repertoire; the end of what Rachel can offer; the end of her. But what will come before the end? And the end itself – what shape will it take? There must be some conclusion, some finale. He can't think. Perhaps, tonight, he should abstain.

He unlocks the door with his key, opens it as quietly as he can. She's there, just inside; waiting for him in the hall, in the dark, in her ruffled peignoir, which gleams wanly in the moonlight. She winds her arms around him and draws him inward, pressing against him. Her body shakes. He has an urge to beat her away, as if she's a spiderweb across his face, or a skein of entangling jelly. Instead he kisses her. Her face is wet; she's been crying. She's crying now.

"Hush," he murmurs, stroking her hair. "Hush, Rachel." This is what he's wanted Grace to do – this trembling and clinging; he's pictured it often enough, though, he now sees, in a suspiciously theatrical way. Those scenes were always skilfully lit, the gestures – his included – languid and graceful, with a kind of luxurious quivering, as in the death scenes at the ballet. Melting anguish is a good deal less attractive now that he actually has to contend with it up close and in the flesh. Wiping the doe-like eyes is one thing, wiping the doe-like nose quite another. He rummages for his pocket-handkerchief.

"He's coming back," Rachel says in a piercing whisper. "I've had a letter from him." For an instant Simon has no idea who she means. But of course it's the Major. Simon has consigned him, in imagination, to some bottomless debauch or other, and then forgotten him.

"Oh, what will become of us?" she sighs. The melodrama of the expression does not diminish the emotion, at least not for her.

"When?" Simon whispers.

"He wrote me a letter," she sobs. "He says I must forgive him. He says he's reformed – he wishes to start a new life – it's what he always says. Now I must lose you – it's unbearable!" Her shoulders are shaking, her arms around him tighten convulsively.

"When is he coming?" Simon asks again. The scene he used to envisage, with a pleasurable prickling of fear – himself embedded in Rachel, the Major appearing in the doorway, all outrage and drawn sword – returns with new vividness.

"In two days," says Rachel in a choking voice. "The day after tomorrow, in the evening. On the train."

"Come," says Simon. He leads her along the hall to her bed-room. Now that he knows his own escape from her is not only pos-sible but necessary, he feels an intense desire for her. She's lit a candle; she knows his tastes. The hours remaining to them are few; discovery looms; panic and fear are said to quicken the heartbeat and heighten desire. He makes a mental note to himself – *it's true* – as for perhaps the last time he pushes her backwards onto the bed and falls heavily on top of her, rummaging through the layers of cloth.

"Don't leave me," she moans. "Don't leave me alone with him! You don't know what he'll do to me!" This time her agonized writhing is real. "I hate him! If only he were dead!"

"Hush," whispers Simon. "Dora may hear." He almost hopes she does; he feels, at this moment, in great need of an audience. Around the bed he ranges a shadowy assemblage of watchers: not only the Major, but the Reverend Verringer, and Jerome DuPont, and Lydia. Above all, Grace Marks. He wants her to be jealous.

Rachel stops moving. Her green eyes open, and look straight into Simon's. "He doesn't have to come back," she says. The irises of her eyes are huge, the pupils mere pinpricks; has she been taking laudanum again? "He might have an accident. If nobody sees him. He could have an accident, in the house; you could bury him in the garden." This isn't impromptu: she must have been making a plan. "We couldn't stay here, he might be found. We could cross to the States. On the railway train! We'd be together then. They'd never find us!"

Simon puts his mouth on hers, to silence her. She thinks this means he's consented. "Oh, Simon," she sighs. "I knew you would never leave me! I love you more than my life!" She kisses his face all over; her movements become epileptic.

It's another of her scenarios for inducing passion, in herself above all. Resting beside her shortly afterwards, Simon tries to picture what she must have been imagining. It's like some third-rate shocker, Ainsworth or Bulwer-Lytton at their most bloodthirsty and banal: the Major reeling drunkenly up the front steps, alone, in the dusk, then entering the front hall. Rachel is there: he strikes her, then clutches her cringing form with sottish lust. She shrieks and begs for mercy, he laughs like a fiend. But rescue is at hand: there's a sharp blow with the spade, on his head, from behind. He falls with a wooden thud and is dragged by the heels down the passageway to the kitchen, where Simon's leather satchel awaits. A quick incision to the jugular with a surgical knife; blood gurgles into a slop bucket; and all is over. A spate of digging in the moonlight, and into the cabbage patch he goes, with Rachel in a becoming shawl and clutching a dark lantern, and swearing she will be eternally his, after what he's dared for her sake.

But here is Dora, watching from the kitchen door. She cannot be allowed to escape; Simon chases her around the house, corners her in the scullery, and sticks her like a pig, with Rachel trembling and fainting, but then pulling herself together like a true heroine and coming to his aid. Dora requires more digging, a deeper hole, followed by an orgiastic scene on the kitchen floor.

So much for the midnight burlesque. Then what? Then he'll be a murderer, with Rachel as the only witness. He'll be wedded to her; chained to her; melded to her, which is what she wants. He will never be free. But here's the part she has surely failed to imagine: once they're in the States, she'll be incognito. She'll be without a name. She'll be an unknown woman, of the kind often found floating in canals or other bodies of water: *Unknown Woman Found Floating In Canal.* Who would suspect him?

What method will he use? In bed, at the moment of delirium, her own hair coiled around her neck, only a slight pressure. That has a definite frisson, and is worthy of the genre.

She'll have forgotten all about it, in the morning. He turns to her again, arranges her. He strokes her neck.

Sunlight wakens him; he's still beside her, in her bed. He forgot to return to his own room last night, and no wonder: he was exhausted. From the kitchen he can hear Dora, clattering and thumping. Rachel is lying on her side, propped on one arm, watching him; she's naked, but has twined herself in the sheet. There's a bruise on her upper arm, which he can't remember making.

He sits up. "I must go," he whispers. "Dora will hear."

"I don't care," she says.

"But your reputation . . ."

"It doesn't matter," she says. "We'll only be here for two more days." Her tone is practical; she regards it as settled, like a business arrangement. It occurs to him – and why for the first time only? – that she may be insane, or verging on it; or a moral degenerate, at the very least.

Simon creeps up the stairs, carrying his shoes and jacket, like a naughty undergraduate returning from a romp. He feels chilled. What he's viewed as merely a kind of acting, she's mistaken for reality. She truly thinks that he, Simon, is going to murder her husband, and out of love for her. What will she do when he refuses? There's a swirling in his head; the floor under his feet seems unreal, as if it's about to dissolve.

Before breakfast, he seeks her out. She's in the front parlour, on the sofa; she rises, greets him with a passionate kiss. Simon detaches himself, and tells her that he's ill; it's a recurrent malarial fever, which he contracted in Paris. If they are to fulfil their intentions – he puts it that way, to disarm her – he will have to have the proper medicine for it, at once, or he can't answer for the consequences.

She feels his forehead, which he's taken the precaution of dampening with his sponge, upstairs. She's suitably alarmed, yet there's an undertone of elation as well: she's getting ready to nurse him, to indulge herself in yet another role. He can see what's in her mind: she'll make beef tea and jellies, she'll pack him in blankets and mustard, she'll bandage any part of him that sticks out or looks likely. He will be weakened, he will be enfeebled and helpless, he will be firmly in her possession: that is her goal. He must save himself from her while there's still time.

He kisses the tips of her fingers. She must help him, he says tenderly. His life depends on her. Into her hand he presses a note, addressed to the Governor's wife: it requests the name of a doctor, as he knows no one locally. Once she has the name, she must hurry to the doctor and obtain the medicine. He's written down the prescription, in an illegible scribble; he gives her the money for it. Dora can't go, he says, as she can't be trusted to hurry. Time is of the essence: his treatment must begin immediately. She nods, she understands: she will do anything, she tells him fervently.

White-faced and trembling, but with lips set, she puts on her bonnet and hurries away. As soon as she's out of sight, Simon dries off his face and begins to pack. He sends Dora for a hired carriage, bribing her with a generous tip. While waiting for her return he composes a letter to Rachel, bidding her a polite farewell, pleading the health of his mother. He doesn't address her as Rachel. He includes several banknotes, but no terms of endearment. He's a man of the world, and won't be trapped that way, or blackmailed either: no Breach of Promise suit for him in case her husband dies. Perhaps she'll kill the Major herself; she's more than capable of it.

He thinks of writing a note to Lydia as well, but thinks better of it. It's a good thing he's never made a formal declaration.

The carriage arrives – it's more like a cart – and he hurls his two valises into it. "To the railway station," he says. Once he's safely away he will write to Verringer, promising some sort of report, stalling for time. He may after all be able to work up something; something that will not entirely discredit him. But above all he must put this disastrous interlude firmly behind him. After a quick visit to his mother, and a rearrangement of his economies, he will go to Europe. If his mother can manage on less – and she can – he can just barely afford it.

He doesn't begin to feel safe until he's in the railway carriage, with the doors firmly shut. The presence of a train conductor, in a uniform, is reassuring to him. Order of a sort is reasserting itself.

Once in Europe, he'll continue his researches. He will study the many prevailing schools of thought, but he will not add to them; not yet. He has gone to the threshold of the unconscious, and has looked across; or rather he has looked down. He could have fallen. He could have fallen in. He could have drowned.

Better, perhaps, to abandon theories, and concentrate on ways and means. When he returns to America he will bestir himself. He'll give lectures, he'll attract subscribers. He'll build a model Asylum, with well-tended grounds and the very best sanitation and drainage. What Americans prefer above all is the appearance of comfort, in any sort of institution at all. An Asylum with large comfortable rooms, facilities for hydrotherapy, and a good many mechanical devices, could do very well. There must be little wheels that go around with a whirring sound, there must be rubber suction cups. Wires to attach to the cranium. Apparatus for measuring. He will include the word "electrical" in his prospectus. The main thing must be to keep the patients clean and docile – drugs will be a help – and their relatives admiring and satisfied. As in schools for children, those who must be impressed are not the actual inmates, but those who pay the bills.

All of this will be a compromise. But he has now – very abruptly it seems – reached the right age for it.

The train moves out of the station. There's a cloud of black smoke, and then a long plaintive wail, which follows him like a baffled phantom along the track.

Not until he's halfway to Cornwall does he allow himself to consider Grace. Will she think he's deserted her? Lost faith in her, perhaps? If she is indeed ignorant of last evening's events, she will be justified in so thinking. She'll be bewildered by him, as he has been by her.

She can't know yet that he's left the city. He pictures her sitting in her accustomed chair, sewing at her quilt; singing, perhaps; waiting for his footfall at the door.

Outside it's begun to drizzle. After a time the motion of the train lulls him to sleep; he slumps against the wall. Now Grace is coming towards him across a wide lawn in sunshine, all in white, carrying an armful of red flowers: they are so clear he can see the dewdrops on them. Her hair is loose, her feet bare; she's smiling. Then he sees that what she walks on is not grass but water; and as he reaches to embrace her, she melts away like mist.

He wakes; he's still on the train, with the grey smoke blowing past the window. He presses his mouth to the glass.

XIV.

THE LETTER X

April 1, 1863. The convict Grace Marks has been guilty of a double or I may say (Bible) Murder. Her boldness does not show that she is a sensitive person and her want of gratitude is a convincing proof of her unfortunate disposition.

August 1, 1863. This unfortunate woman has become a dangerous creature, and I much fear that she will yet show us what she is capable of doing. Unfortunately, she has parties assisting her. She would not dare to lie as she does unless aided by parties near her.

– The Warden's Daybook,
Provincial Penitentiary,
Kingston, Canada West, 1863.

. . . her exemplary conduct during the whole of her thirty years incarceration in the penitentiary the later portion of which she spent as a trusted inmate of the home of the Governor, and that so large a number of influential Gentlemen in Kingston should think that she merited and deserved a pardon, all tend to show that there is room for grave doubts as to her having been the awful female demon incarnate, that McDermott tried to make the public believe that she was.

– William Harrison,
"Recollections of the Kinnear Tragedy,"
written for the *Newmarket Era*, 1908.

My letters! All dead paper, mute and white!
And yet they seem alive and quivering
Against my tremulous hands which loose the string. . . .

– Elizabeth Barrett Browning,
Sonnets from the Portuguese, 1850.

5 0 .

To Mrs. C. D. Humphrey; from Dr. Simon Jordan,
Kingston, Canada West.

August 15th, 1859.

Dear Mrs. Humphrey:

I write in haste, having been summoned home most
urgently by a family matter which it is imperative I respond
to at once. My dear Mother has suffered an unforeseen collapse in her always imperfect health, and is presently at
death's door. I only pray that I may be in time to attend her in
her last moments.

I am sorry I could not stay to bid you farewell in person,
and to thank you for your kind attentions to me whilst I was a
lodger at your house; but I am certain that with your woman's
heart and sensibility, you will quickly divine the necessity of

my instant departure. I do not know how long I may be away, or if indeed I shall ever be able to return to Kingston. Should my Mother pass away, I will be needed to tend to the family affairs; and should she be spared to us for a time, my place is by her side. One who has sacrificed so much for her son, must surely deserve some not inconsiderable sacrifice from him in return.

My return to your city in future is most unlikely; but I will always preserve the memories of my days in Kingston – memories of which you form an esteemed part. You know how I admire your courage in the face of adversity, and how I respect you; and I hope you will find it in your heart to feel the same, towards,

Your most sincere,

Simon Jordan.

P.S. In the attached envelope I have left you a sum which I assume will cover any little amounts which remain outstanding between us.
P.P.S. I trust that your husband will soon be happily restored to you.

– S.

❧

From Mrs. William P. Jordan, Laburnum House, Loomisville, Massachusetts, The United States of America; to Mrs. C. D. Humphrey, Lower Union Street, Kingston, Canada West.

September 29th, 1859.

Dear Mrs. Humphrey:

I take the liberty of returning to you the seven letters addressed by you to my dear Son, which have accumulated here in his absence; they were opened in mistake by the Servant, which will account for the presence of my own seal upon them, in place of yours.

My Son is at present making a tour of Private Mental Asylums and Clinics in Europe, an investigation very necessary to the work he is engaged upon – work of the utmost significance, which will alleviate human suffering, and which must not be interrupted for any lesser considerations, however pressing these may appear to others who do not understand the importance of his mission. As he is constantly travelling, I was unable to forward your letters to him; and I return them now, supposing that you would wish to know the reason for the lack of reply; although I beg to observe, that no reply is in itself a reply.

My Son had mentioned that you might make some attempt to re-establish your acquaintance with him; and although he very properly did not elaborate, I am not such an invalid, nor so cloistered from the world, that I was unable to read between the lines. If you will accept some frank but well-intentioned advice from an old woman, permit me to observe, that in permanent unions between the sexes, discrepancies in age and fortune must always be detrimental; but how much more so, are discrepancies in moral outlook. Rash and ill-advised conduct is understandable in a woman placed as you have been – I fully realize the unpleasantness of not knowing where one's husband may be located; but you must be aware, that in the event of the demise of such a husband, no man of principle would ever make his wife, a woman who had anticipated that position prematurely. Men, by nature and the decree of Providence, have a certain latitude allowed them; but fidelity to the marriage vow is surely the chief requirement in a woman.

In the early days of my widowhood, I found a daily reading of the Bible quite soothing to the mind; and some light needlework also helps to occupy one's thoughts. In addition to these remedies, perhaps you have a respectable female friend, who may comfort you in your distress without wishing to know the cause of it. What is believed in society, is not always the equivalent of what is true; but as regards a woman's reputation, it amounts to the same thing. It is as well to take all steps to preserve that reputation, by not spreading one's misery abroad where it may become the subject of malicious gossip; and to that end, it is wise to avoid the expression of one's feelings in letters, which must run the gauntlet of the public posts, and may fall into the hands of persons who may be tempted to read them unbeknownst to the sender.

Please accept, Mrs. Humphrey, the sentiments I have expressed, in the spirit of a genuine desire for your future well-being, in which they are offered, by,

Yours most sincerely,

(Mrs.) Constance Jordan.

❧

From Grace Marks, The Provincial Penitentiary, Kingston, Canada West; to Dr. Simon Jordan.

December 19th, 1859.

Dear Dr. Jordan:

I am writing to you with the help of Clarrie, who has always stood my friend, and got this paper for me, and will post it when the time comes in return for extra help with the laces and stains. The trouble is that I don't know where to send it, as I am ignorant of where you have gone. But if I find it out, then I will send this. I hope you can read my writing, as I am not much accustomed to it; and can only spend a short time at it each day.

When I heard you went off so quick, and without sending any word to me, I was very distressed, as I thought you must have been taken ill. I could not understand it, that you would go without a goodbye, after all the talking we had done together; and I fainted dead away in the upstairs hall, and the chambermaid went into a panic, and threw a vase of flowers over me, water, vase and all; which quickly brought me round, although the vase broke. She thought I was going off into fits, and would run mad again; but this was not the case, and I took very good control of myself, and it was just the shock of hearing about it in that sudden manner, and the palpitations of the heart which I have often been troubled from. I suffered a gash on my forehead from the vase. It is astonishing what a great quantity of blood may flow from a wound to the head, even if it is a shallow one.

I was unhappy that you left, as I was enjoying our talks; but also they said you were to write a letter to the Government on my behalf, to set me free, and I was afraid that now you would never do so. There is nothing so discouraging as hopes raised and then dashed again, it is almost worse than not having the hopes raised in the first place.

I do very much hope you will be able to write the letter in my favour, which I would be very thankful for, and hope you are keeping well,

From,

Grace Marks.

⚜

From Dr. Simon P. Jordan, care of Dr. Binswanger, Bellevue, Kreutzlinger, Switzerland; to Dr. Edward Murchie, Dorchester, Massachusetts, The United States of America.

January 12th, 1860.

My dear Ed:

Forgive me for having taken so long to write to you, and to acquaint you with my change of address. The fact is that things have been somewhat muddled, and it has taken me some time to straighten myself out. As Burns has remarked, "The best laid schemes o' mice and men gang aft a-gley," and I was forced to make a hasty escape from Kingston, as I found myself in complicated circumstances which could rapidly have become quite damaging, both to myself and to my future prospects. Someday over a glass of sherry I may tell you the whole story; although it seems to me at present less a story, than a troubled dream.

Among its elements is the fact that my study of Grace Marks took such an unsettling turn at the last, that I can scarcely determine whether I myself was awake or asleep. When I consider with what high hopes I commenced upon this undertaking – determined, you may be sure, on great revelations which would astonish the admiring world, I have cause almost for despair. Yet, were they indeed high hopes, and not mere self-seeking ambition? From this vantage point I am not altogether sure; but if only the latter, perhaps I have been well repaid, as in the whole affair, I may have been engaged on a wild goose chase, or a fruitless pursuit of shadows, and have come near to addling my own wits, in my assiduous attempts to unpick those of another. Like my namesake the apostle, I have cast my nets into deep waters; though unlike him, I may have drawn up a mermaid, neither fish nor flesh but both at once, and whose song is sweet but dangerous.

I do not know whether to view myself as an unwitting dupe, or, what is worse, a self-deluded fool; but even these doubts may be an illusion, and I may all along have been dealing with a woman so transparently innocent that in my over-subtlety I did not have the wit to recognize it. I must admit – but only to you – that I have come very close to nervous exhaustion over this matter. *Not to know* – to snatch at hints and portents, at intimations, at tantalizing whispers – it is as bad as being haunted. Sometimes at night her face floats before me in the darkness, like some lovely and enigmatic mirage –

But excuse my brain-sick ramblings. I have intimations of some vast discovery still, if I could only see my way clear; though as yet I wander in darkness, led only by marsh-lights.

To more positive matters: the Clinic here is run along very clean and efficient lines, and is exploring various lines of treatment, including water therapy; and might act as a model for my own project, should it ever come to fruition. Dr. Binswanger has been most hospitable, and has given me access to some of the more interesting cases here. Much to my relief, there are no celebrated murderesses among them, but only what the worthy Dr. Workman of Toronto terms "the innocent insane," as well as the usual sufferers from nervous complaints, and the inebriates and syphilitics; although of course one does not find the same afflictions among the well-to-do as among the poor.

I was overjoyed to hear that you may soon favour the world with a miniature copy of yourself, through the kind offices of your esteemed wife – to whom, please send my respectful regards. How calming it must be, to have a settled family life, with a trustworthy and dependable woman capable of providing it! Tranquillity is indeed much undervalued by men, except those who lack it. I envy you!

As for myself, I fear I am doomed to wander the face of the earth alone, like one of Byron's gloomier and more lugubrious outcasts; though I would be much heartened, my dear fellow, to be able to grasp once more your true friend's hand. This chance may soon come, as I understand that the prospects for a peaceful resolution of the current differences between North and South are not hopeful, and the Southern States talk seriously of secession. In the event of an outbreak of hostilities, my duty to my country will be clear. As Tennyson says in his overly botanical fashion, it is time to pluck "the blood-red blossom of war." Given my present tumultuous and morbid mental state, it will be a relief to have a duty of some kind set before me, no matter how deplorable the occasion for it.

> Your brain-sore and weary, but affectionate friend,
>
> Simon.

From Grace Marks, the Provincial Penitentiary, Kingston; to
Signor Geraldo Ponti, Master of Neuro-Hypnotism, Ventriloquist,
and Mind-Reader Extraordinaire; care of The Prince of Wales
Theatre, Queen Street, Toronto, Canada West.

September 25th, 1861.

Dear Jeremiah:

Your Show was on a poster, which Dora got hold of one of them, and pinned it to the laundry wall, to liven it up; and I knew at once it was you, even though you have another name and have grown your beard very wild. One of the gentlemen paying attentions to Miss Marianne saw the Show when it was at Kingston, and said the Future Told in Letters of Fire was a first-class item, and worth the price of admission, as two ladies fainted; and he said your beard was bright red. So I expect you have dyed it, unless it is a wig.

I did not attempt to contact you while in Kingston, as it might have resulted in difficulties if discovered. But I saw where the Show was next to be performed, and that is why I am sending this to the Theatre in Toronto, in hopes it will find you. It must be a new Theatre, as they had none of that name when I was last there; but that is twenty years ago now, although it seems a hundred.

How I would like to see you again, and to talk over old times, in the kitchen at Mrs. Alderman Parkinson's, when we would all have such fun, before Mary Whitney died and misfortune overtook me! But in order to pass muster here, you would have to disguise yourself more, as a red beard would not be enough at close quarters. And if they found you out, they would think you had tricked them, as what is done on a stage is not as acceptable, as the very same thing done in a library; and they would want to know why you are no longer Dr. Jerome DuPont. But I suppose the other pays better.

Since the Hypnotism, the people here seem to treat me better, and with more esteem, although perhaps it is only that they are more afraid of me; sometimes it is hard to tell the difference. They will not speak about what was said on that occasion, as they are of the opinion that it might unsettle my reason; which I doubt would be the case. But although I have the run of the house again, and tidy the rooms and serve the tea as formerly, it has not had any effect on my being set free.

I have often pondered about why Dr. Jordan left so suddenly, right after; but as you yourself left quite soon as well, I expect you do not know the answer. Miss Lydia was very taken aback at Dr. Jordan's departure, and would not come down to dinner for a week, but had it sent up on a tray; and she lay in bed as if ill, which made it very difficult to tidy her room, with her face all pale and dark circles under her eyes, and acted the tragedy queen. But young ladies are permitted to carry on in that way.

After that she took to going out to more parties with more young men than ever, and especially a certain Captain, which nothing came of him; and she got the name of a romp amongst the military men; and then there were rows with her mother, and when another month had gone by it was announced that she was engaged to be married to the Reverend Verringer; which was a surprise, as she always used to make fun of him behind his back, and say he looked like a frog.

The wedding date was set a great deal sooner than is usual, and I was kept very busy sewing from morning to night. Miss Lydia's travelling dress was of blue silk, with self-covered buttons and two layers to the skirt; and I thought I would go blind hemming it. They had their honeymoon at Niagara Falls, which they say is an experience not to be missed, I have only seen pictures of it; and when they came back she was a different person, very subdued and pale, with no high spirits any more. It is not a good plan to marry a man you do not love, but many do and get used to it in time. And others marry from love and repent at leisure, as they say.

I thought for a while that she had a liking for Dr. Jordan; but she would not have been happy with him, nor he with her, as she would not have understood his interest in lunatics, and his curiosities, and the strange questions about vegetables that he used to ask. So it was just as well.

As for the help Dr. Jordan promised me, I have heard nothing of it, and nothing of him, except that he has gone off to the Southern war, which news I had through Reverend Verringer; but whether he is alive or dead I do not know. In addition to which, there was a great many rumours going about, concerning him and his landlady, who was a widow of sorts; and after he left, she could be seen wandering in a dis-tracted manner by the lakeshore in a black dress and cloak and a black veil blowing in the wind, and some said she was intending to throw herself in. It was much talked about, espe-cially in the kitchen and laundry; and we got many an earful from Dora, who was once the servant there. What she had to tell, you would scarcely credit, of two such outwardly respectable people, with screams and groans and horrifying goings-on at night, as bad as a haunted house, and the bed linen a shambles every morning, and in such a state as made her blush to look at it. And Dora said it was a wonder he hadn't killed this lady and buried the body in the yard outside, as she'd seen the spade for it standing ready, and a grave already dug, which made her blood run cold; as he was the sort of man who would ruin one woman after another and then tire of them, and murder them just to get rid of them, and every time he looked at the widow lady it was with fearsome blazing eyes like a tiger's, as if ready to spring on her and sink his teeth into her. And it was the same with Dora herself, and who knew but that she might have been the next to fall victim to his ravenous frenzies? She had a willing audience in the kitchen, as there are many who like to listen to a shocking tale, and I must say she made a good story out of it. But I thought myself she got carried away.

At that same time the Governor's wife called me into the parlour, and asked me very earnestly if Dr. Jordan had ever made any improper advances to me; and I said that he had not, and that in any case the door to the sewing room had always been kept open. Then she said she had been deceived as to his character, and she had been harbouring a viper in the bosom of her family; and next she said that the poor lady in black had been interfered with by him, having been alone in her house with the servant gone, although I was not to speak of it, as to do so would cause more harm than good; and although this lady was a married lady, and her husband had been abominable to her, and thus it was not quite so bad as if she'd been a young girl, still Dr. Jordan had behaved most improperly, and it was a mercy things with Miss Lydia had never gone so far as an engagement.

Not that I think there was any idea of such, in Dr. Jordan's mind at all; nor do I believe everything that was being said against him, as I know what it is to have lies told about a person, and you not able to defend yourself. And widows are always up to tricks, until they get too old for it.

But that is all idle gossip. This is what I would especially like to ask you: Did you really see into the future, when you looked into my palm and said five for luck, which I took to mean all would come out well in the end? Or were you only trying to comfort me? I would very much like to know, as sometimes the time stretches out so long, I can scarcely endure it. I am afraid of falling into hopeless despair, over my wasted life, and I am still not sure how it happened. The Reverend Verringer often prays with me, or I should say he prays and I listen; but it is not much good, as it only makes me tired. He says he will get up another Petition, but I fear it will not be of any more use than the others have been, and he might as well not waste the paper.

The other thing I would like to know is, why did you want to help me? Was it as a challenge, and to outwit the others, as with the smuggling you used to do; or was it out of affection and fellow-feeling? You said once we were of the same sort, and I have often pondered over that.

I hope this will reach you, but if it does, I don't know how you will get word back to me, as any letter I might have they would be sure to open. However I think you did send me a message, as some months ago I received a bone button, addressed to me though with no signature, and the Matron said, Grace, why would anyone send you a single button? And I said I did not know. But as it was the same pattern as the button you gave to me in the kitchen at Mrs. Alderman Parkinson's, I felt it must be you, to let me know I was not altogether forgotten. Perhaps there was another message in it also, as a button is for keeping things closed up, or else for opening them; and you may have been telling me to keep silent, about certain things we both know of. Dr. Jordan believed that even common and unregarded objects can have a meaning, or else recall to memory a thing forgotten; and you may only have been reminding me of yourself, which indeed was not needed, as I have never forgotten you and your kindnesses to me, nor ever will.

I hope you are in good health, dear Jeremiah, and that your Magic Show is a great success,

From, your old friend,

Grace Marks.

❧

From Mrs. William P. Jordan, Laburnum House, Loomisville, Massachusetts, The United States of America; to Mrs. C. D. Humphrey, Lower Union Street, Kingston, Canada West.

May 15th, 1862.

Dear Mrs. Humphrey:

Your communication to my dear Son came to hand this morning. I open all his mail nowadays, for reasons I will shortly explain. But first permit me to remark, that I could have wished you to express yourself in a less extravagant manner. To threaten to do yourself an injury, by jumping off a bridge or other elevated location, might carry weight with an impressionable and tender-hearted young man, but it does not, with his more experienced Mother.

In any case, your hope of an interview with him must be disappointed. Upon the outbreak of our current lamentable war, my Son joined the Union army to fight for his country in the capacity of Military Surgeon, and was sent at once to a field hospital near the front. The postal services have been sadly disrupted, and the troops are moved about so quickly due to the railroads, and I had no word of him for some months, which was not like him as he has always been a most regular and faithful correspondent; and I feared the worst.

In the meantime I did what I could in my own limited sphere. This unfortunate War had already killed and wounded so many, and we saw the results daily, as yet more men and boys were brought in to our improvised Hospitals, mutilated and blinded, or out of their minds with infectious fevers; and every one of them a dearly loved Son. The ladies of our town were kept thoroughly occupied, in visiting them and arranging for them any little home-like comforts it was within our power to supply; and I myself aided them as best I could, despite my own indifferent state of health; as I could only hope that if my dear Son were lying ill and suffering elsewhere, some other Mother was doing the same for him.

At last, a convalescent soldier from this town reported hearing a rumour that my dear Son had been struck in the head by a piece of flying debris, and when last heard of had been lingering between this world and the next. Of course I was almost dead with worry, and moved Heaven and earth to discover his whereabouts; until much to my joy, he was returned to us, still alive but sadly weakened both in body and spirit. As a result of his wound he had lost a part of his memory; for although he recalled his loving Parent, and the events of his childhood, his more recent experiences had been completely erased from his mind, among them his interest in Lunatic Asylums, and the period of time he spent in the city of Kingston; including whatever relations of any kind he may or may not have had with yourself.

I tell you this that you may see things in a broader – and I may add, a less selfish perspective. One's own personal doings look small indeed, when faced with the momentous travails of History, which we can only trust are for the greater good.

Meanwhile, I must congratulate you on the fact that your husband has been at last located, although I must also commiserate with you on the unfortunate circumstances. To discover that one's spouse has passed away due to prolonged intoxication and the resulting delirium, cannot have been at all pleasant. I am happy to hear that he had not yet exhausted his entire means; and would suggest to you, as a practical matter, a dependable Annuity, or – what has served me quite well during my own trials – a modest investment in railway shares, if a solid company, or else in Sewing Machines, which are sure to make great progress in the future.

However, the course of action you propose to my Son is neither desirable nor feasible, even should he be in any condition to entertain it. My Son was under no engagement to you, nor is he under any obligation. What you yourself may have understood, does not constitute an understanding. It is also my duty to inform you, that before his departure my Son became as good as engaged to be married, to Miss Faith Cartwright, a young lady of fine family and impeccable moral character, the only obstacle remaining, being his own honour, which prevented him from requesting that Miss Cartwright bind herself to a man whose life was so soon to be imperilled; and despite his damaged and at times delirious state, she is resolved to respect the wishes of the two families, as well as those of her own heart, and is at present helping me to nurse him with loyal devotion.

He does not yet remember her in her proper person, but persists in believing that she is called Grace – an understandable confusion, as Faith is very close to it in concept; but we persevere in our efforts, and as we daily show him various little homely objects once dear to him, and lead him on walks through local spots of natural beauty, we have increasing hopes that his full memory will shortly return, or at least as much of it as is necessary, and that he will soon be well enough to fulfil his marital undertakings. It is the foremost concern of Miss Cartwright, as it should be for all those who love my Son disinterestedly, to pray for his restoration to health and the full use of his mental faculties.

In closing, let me add that I trust your future life will be more productive of happiness, than has been the recent past; and that the evening of your life will bring with it a serenity, which the vain and tempestuous passions of youth so often unfortunately, if not disastrously, preclude.

Yours most sincerely,

(Mrs.) Constance P. Jordan.

P.S. Any further communication from you, will be destroyed unread.

❧

From the Reverend Enoch Verringer, Chairman, The Committee to Pardon Grace Marks, Sydenham Street Methodist Church, Kingston, Ontario, The Dominion of Canada; to Dr. Samuel Bannerling, M.D., The Maples, Front Street, Toronto, Ontario, The Dominion of Canada.

Kingston, October 15th, 1867.

Dear Dr. Bannerling:

I presume to write to you, Sir, in connection with the Committee of which I am the Chairman, upon a worthy mission which cannot be unfamiliar to you. As the former medical attendant upon Grace Marks, when she was in the Toronto Lunatic Asylum almost fifteen years ago, I know you have been approached by the representatives of several previous committees charged with submitting petitions to the Government, on behalf of this unfortunate and unhappy, and to some minds, wrongly convicted woman, in hopes that you would append your name to the petitions in question – an addition which, as I am sure you are aware, would carry considerable weight with the Government authorities, as they have a tendency to be respectful of informed medical opinion such as your own.

Our Committee consists of a number of ladies, my own dear wife among them, and of several gentlemen of standing, and clergymen of three denominations, including the Prison Chaplain, whose names you will find appended. Such petitions have in the past been unsuccessful, but the Committee expects, as well as hopes, that with the recent political changes, most notably the advent of a fully representational Parliament under the leadership of John A. Macdonald, this one will receive a favourable reception denied to its predecessors.

In addition, we have the advantage of modern science, and the advances made in the study of the cerebral diseases and mental disorders – advances which must surely tell in favour of Grace Marks. Several years ago our Committee engaged a specialist in nervous ailments, Dr. Simon Jordan, who came very highly recommended. He passed a number of months in this city in making a detailed examination of Grace Marks, with particular attention to her gaps in recollection concerning the murders. In an attempt to recover her memory, he subjected her to Neuro-hypnosis, at the hands of a skilled practitioner of that science – a science which, after a long eclipse, appears to be coming back into favour, both as a diagnostic and as a curative method, although it has thus far gained more favour in France than in this hemisphere.

As a result of this session and the astonishing revelations it produced, Dr. Jordan gave it as his opinion that Grace Marks' loss of memory was genuine, not feigned – that on the fatal day she was suffering from the effects of an hysterical seizure brought on by fright, which resulted in a form of *auto-hypnotic somnambulism*, not much studied twenty-five years ago but well documented since; and that this fact explains her subsequent amnesia. In the course of the neuro-hypnotic trance, which several of our own Committee members witnessed, Grace Marks displayed not only a fully recovered memory of these past events, but also pronounced evidence of a somnambulistic *double consciousness*, with a distinct secondary personality, capable of acting without the knowledge of the first. It was Dr. Jordan's conclusion, in view of the evidence, that the woman known to us as "Grace Marks" was neither conscious at the time of the murder of Nancy Montgomery, nor responsible for her actions therein – the memories of these actions being retained only by her secondary and hidden self. Dr. Jordan was of the added opinion that this other self gave strong manifestations of its continued existence during her period of mental derangement in 1852, if the eyewitness reports of Mrs. Moodie and others are any indication.

I had hoped to have a written report to set before you, and our Committee has delayed the submission of its Petition from year to year, in expectation of it. Dr. Jordan had indeed fully intended to prepare such a report; but he was called away suddenly by a family illness, followed by urgent business on the Continent; after which the outbreak of the Civil War, in which he served in the capacity of a military surgeon, was a serious impediment to his efforts. I understand he was wounded in the course of the hostilities, and although providentially now making a recovery, has not yet regained sufficient strength to be able to complete his task. Otherwise I have no doubt that he would have added his earnest and heartfelt entreaties, to ours.

I myself was present at the neuro-hypnotic session referred to, as was the lady who has since consented to become my dear wife; and both of us were most profoundly affected by what we saw and heard. It moves me to tears to think how this poor woman has been wronged through lack of scientific understanding. The human soul is a profound and awe-inspiring mystery, the depths of which are only now beginning to be sounded. Well may St. Paul have said, "Now we see through a glass, darkly; but then face to face." One can only guess at the purposes of our Creator, in fashioning of Humanity such a complex and Gordian knot.

But whatever you may think of Dr. Jordan's professional opinion – and I am well aware that his conclusions may be difficult to credit, for one not familiar with the practice of Neuro-hypnosis, and who was not present at the events to which I allude – surely Grace Marks has been incarcerated for a great many years, more than sufficient to atone for her misdeeds. She has suffered untold mental agony, and agony of body as well; and she has bitterly repented whatever part she may have taken in this great crime, whether conscious of having taken it or not. She is by no means any longer a young woman, and is in but indifferent health. If she were at liberty, something might surely be done for her temporal, as well as her spiritual weal, and she might have an opportunity of meditating on the past, and of preparing for a future life.

Will you – can you, in the name of charity – still persist in refusing to join your name to the Petition for her release, and thereby perchance close the gates of Paradise to a repentant sinner? Surely not!

I invite you – I beg you once again – to aid us in this most praiseworthy endeavour.

Yours very truly,

Enoch Verringer, M.A., D. Div.

❧

From Dr. Samuel Bannerling, M.D., The Maples, Front Street, Toronto; to the Reverend Enoch Verringer, Sydenham Street Methodist Church, Kingston, Ontario.

November 1st, 1867.

Dear Sir:

I acknowledge receipt of your letter of the 15th of October, and its account of your puerile antics in regards to Grace Marks. I am disappointed in Dr. Jordan; I had some previous correspondence with him, in which I warned him explicitly against this cunning woman. They say there is no fool like an old fool, but I say there is no fool like a young one; and I am astonished that anyone with a medical degree would allow himself to be imposed upon by such a blatant piece of charlatanism and preposterous tomfoolery as a "Neuro-hypnotic trance," which is second in imbecility only to Spiritism, Universal Suffrage, and similar drivel. This rubbishy "Neuro-hypnotism," however beribboned with new terminologies, is only Mesmerism, or Animal Magnetism, re-writ; and that sickly nonsense was discredited long ago, as being merely a solemn-sounding blind, behind which men of questionable antecedents and salacious natures might obtain power over young women of the same, asking them impertinent and offensive questions and ordering them to perform immodest acts, without the latter appearing to consent to it.

So I fear that your Dr. Jordan is either credulous to an infantile degree, or himself a great scoundrel; and that, should he have composed his self-styled "report," it would not have been worth the paper it was written on. I suspect that the wound of which you speak, was incurred, not during the war, but before it; and that it consisted of a sharp blow to the head, which is the only thing that would account for such idiocy. If Dr. Jordan keeps on with this disorderly course of thought, he will soon belong in the private asylum for lunatics, which, if I recall aright, he was once so set upon establishing.

I have read the so-called "testimony" of Mrs. Moodie, as well as some of her other scribblings, which I consigned to the fire where they belong – and where they for once cast a little light, which they certainly would not have done otherwise. Like the rest of her ilk, Mrs. Moodie is prone to overwrought effusions, and to the concoction of convenient fairy tales; and for the purposes of truth, one might as well rely on the "eye-witness reports" of a goose.

As for the gates of Paradise to which you refer, I have no control whatever over them, and if Grace Marks is worthy to enter there she will doubtless be admitted without any interference on my part. But certainly the gates of the Penitentiary will never be opened to her through any act of mine. I have studied her carefully, and know her character and disposition better than you can possibly do. She is a creature devoid of moral faculties, and with the propensity to murder strongly developed. She is not safe to be entrusted with the ordinary privileges of society, and if her liberty were restored to her the chances are that sooner or later other lives would be sacrificed.

In closing, Sir, allow me to remark that it ill becomes you, as a man of the cloth, to pepper your screeds with allusions to "modern science." A little learning is a dangerous thing, as I believe Pope once observed. Busy yourself with the care of consciences, and with the delivery of edifying sermons for the improvement of public life and private morals, which God knows the country is in need of, and leave the brains of the degenerate to the authorities who specialize in them. Above all, in future, be pleased to desist from pestering with these importunate and ridiculous appeals,

Your most humble and obedient servant.

(Dr.) Samuel Bannerling, M.D.

XV.

THE TREE OF PARADISE

But persistence at last met with its reward. One petition after another went into the Government, and doubtless other influences were brought to bear. This almost unique malefactor received a pardon, and was conveyed to New York, where she changed her name, and soon afterwards married. For all the writer of these lines knows to the contrary, she is living still. Whether her appetite for murder has ever strongly asserted itself in the interval is not known, as she probably guards her identity by more than one alias.

– Author Unknown,
History of Toronto and the County of York,
Ontario, 1885.

Friday, August 2, 1872. I visited the City from 12 to 2 to see Minister of Justice about Grace Marks whose pardon I received this morning. It was Sir John's request that I and one of my daughters should accompany this woman to a home provided for her in New York.

Tuesday, August 7, 1872. Examined and discharged Grace Marks, pardoned after being imprisoned in this Penitentiary 28 years and ten months. Started with her and my daughter for New York at 1.00 P.M. by order of the Minister of Justice. . . .

– Notes from the Warden's Daily Journal,
Provincial Penitentiary, Kingston, Ontario,
The Dominion of Canada.

So with this Earthly Paradise it is,
If ye will read aright, and pardon me,
Who strive to build a shadowy isle of bliss
Midmost the beating of the steely sea,
Where tossed about all hearts of men must be. . . .

– William Morris,
The Earthly Paradise, 1868.

The imperfect is our paradise.

– Wallace Stevens,
"The Poems of Our Climate," 1938.

5 1 .

I have often thought of writing to you and informing you of my good fortune, and I've written many letters to you in my head; and when I've arrived at the right way of saying things I will set pen to paper, and thus you will have news of me, if you are still in the land of the living. And if you are not, you will have learnt about all of this anyway.

Perhaps you heard of my Pardon, but perhaps you did not. I didn't see it in any of the newspapers, which isn't strange, as by the time I was finally set free it was an old worn-out story, and nobody would have wanted to read about it. But no doubt that was just as well. When I learnt of it, I knew for certain that you must have sent the letter to the Government after all, because it got the results in the end, along with all the petitions; although I must say they took a good long time about it, and said nothing about your letter, but only that it was a general amnesty.

The first I heard of the Pardon was from the Warden's oldest daughter, whose name was Janet. This would not be a Warden you ever saw, Sir, as there were many changes since you went away, and a new Warden was one of them, and there had been two or three new Governors as well, and so many new guards and keepers and matrons I could scarcely keep track of them. I was sitting in the sewing room, where you and I used to have our afternoon talks, mending stockings – for I continued to serve in a household capacity under the new Governors, as I'd done before – when Janet came in. She had a kind manner and always gave me a smile, unlike some, and although never a beauty, she'd managed to become engaged to a respectable young farmer, for which she had my heartfelt good wishes. There are some men, especially of the simpler kind, that prefer their wives to be plain rather than handsome, as that sort buckles down to the work and complains less, and there is not a great chance of their running off with another man, as what other man would go to the bother of stealing them?

On this day Janet hurried into the room, and she seemed very excited. Grace, she said, I have the most astonishing news.

I did not even bother to stop sewing, as when people told me they had astonishing news it always concerned somebody else. I was ready to hear it of course, but not ready to miss a stitch over it, if you see what I mean, Sir. Oh? I said.

Your Pardon has come through, she said. From Sir John Macdonald, and the Minister of Justice, in Ottawa. Isn't that wonderful? She clasped her hands, and at that moment she looked like a child, although a large and ugly one, gazing at a beautiful gift. She was one of those who never did believe me to be guilty, being soft-hearted and of a sentimental nature.

At this news I put down my sewing. I felt very cold all at once, as if I was about to faint, which I hadn't done for a long time, ever since you left, Sir. Can it be true? I said. If it was another person I would have thought she might be playing a cruel joke on me, but Janet did not relish jokes of any kind.

Yes, she said, it is really true. You are pardoned! I am so happy for you!

I could see that she felt some tears were in order, and I shed several.

That night, and even though her father the Warden didn't have the paper actually in hand, but only a letter about it, nothing would do but that I had to be moved out of my prison cell and into the spare bedroom at the Warden's house. This was the doing of Janet, the good soul, but she had the assistance of her mother, as my Pardon was indeed an unusual event in the dull routine of the prison, and people like to have some contact with events of that sort, so they can talk about them to their friends afterwards; so I was made a fuss of.

After I'd blown out my candle I lay in the best bed, wearing one of Janet's cotton nightdresses instead of the coarse yellowy prison one, and looking up at the dark ceiling. I tossed and turned, and somehow I couldn't get comfortable, I guess comfort is what you're accustomed to, and by that time I was more accustomed to my narrow prison bed than to a spare bedroom with clean sheets. The room was so large it was almost frightening to me, and I pulled the sheet up over my head to make it darker; and then I felt as if my face was dissolving and turning into someone else's face, and I recalled my poor mother in her shroud, as they were sliding her into the sea, and how I thought that she had already changed inside the sheet, and was a different woman, and now the same thing was happening to me. Of course I wasn't dying, but it was in a way similar.

The next day at breakfast, the Warden's whole family sat beaming at me with moist eyes, as if I was some rare and cherished thing, like a baby snatched out of a river; and the Warden said we should give thanks for the one lost lamb that had been rescued, and they all said a fervent Amen.

That is it, I thought. I have been rescued, and now I must act like someone who has been rescued. And so I tried. It was very strange to realize that I would not be a celebrated murderess any more, but seen perhaps as an innocent woman wrongly accused and imprisoned unjustly, or at least for too long a time, and an object of pity rather than of horror and fear. It took me some days to get used to the idea; indeed, I am not quite used to it yet. It calls for a different arrangement of the face; but I suppose it will become easier in time.

Of course to those who do not know my story I will not be anybody in particular.

After breakfast on that day I was strangely dejected. Janet noticed it and asked me why, and I said, I've been in this prison now for almost twenty-nine years, I have no friends or family outside it, and where am I to go and what am I to do? I have no money, nor any means of earning any, and no proper clothing, and I am unlikely to obtain a situation anywhere in the vicinity, as my story is too well known – because despite the Pardon, which is all very well, a mistress in any right-thinking family would not want me in the house, as she would be afraid for the safety of her loved ones, it is only what I would do myself in their position.

I did not say to her, And I am also too old to go on the town, as I did not wish to shock her, she having been well brought up, and a Methodist. Though I must tell you, Sir, the thought did cross my mind. But what chance would I have, at my age and with so much competition, it would be a penny a time with the worst drunken sailors up an alley somewhere, and I'd be dead of disease within a year; and it made my heart fail even to consider it.

So now, instead of seeming my passport to liberty, the Pardon appeared to me as a death sentence. I was to be turned out into the streets, alone and friendless, to starve and freeze to death in a cold corner, with nothing but the clothes on my back, the ones I'd come into the prison with; and perhaps not even those, as I had no idea what might have become of them; for all I knew they had been sold or given away long ago.

Oh no, dear Grace, said Janet. All has been thought of. I did not want to tell you everything at once, as we feared the shock of such happiness coming after such misery might be too much for you, it sometimes has that effect. But a good home has been provided for you, it is in the United States, and once you have gone there you may leave the sad past behind you, as no one there need ever know about it. It will be a new life.

She did not use exactly these words, but that was the gist of it.

But what am I to wear? said I, still in despair. Perhaps I was indeed unsettled in my wits, as a person altogether in her right mind would have asked first about the good home that was being provided, and where it was, and what I was to do there. I thought later about the way she had put it, A good home provided, it is what you say of a dog or a horse that is too old to work any more, and that you don't wish to keep yourself or have put down.

I have thought of that too, said Janet. She was really a most helpful creature. I have looked in the storage rooms, and by some miracle the box you brought with you was still in there with your name on a label, I suppose it is because of all the petitions that were got up in your favour after the trial. They may have kept your things at first because they thought you were soon to be released, and then after that they must have forgotten all about it. I will have it brought up to your room and then we will open it, shall we?

I felt a little comforted, although I had some misgivings. And I was right to have them, for when we opened the box we found that the moths had been in and had eaten up the woollens, my mother's thick winter shawl among them, and some of the other things were much discoloured and musty-smelling from being shut up for so long in a dampish place; the threads in some were almost rotted through, and you could put your hand right through them. Any piece of cloth needs a good airing every once in a while, and these had been given none.

We took everything out and spread the things around the room, to see what could be saved. There were Nancy's dresses, so pretty when fresh, now for the most part ruined, and the things I'd had from Mary Whitney; I'd prized them so much at the time and now they looked shoddy and outmoded. There was the dress I'd made at Mrs. Alderman Parkinson's, with the bone buttons from Jeremiah, but nothing could be saved of it except the buttons. I found the piece of Mary's hair, tied with a thread and wrapped up in a handkerchief as I'd left it, but the moths had been into that too, they will eat hair if nothing better is left and it is not stored in cedar.

The emotions I experienced were strong and painful. The room seemed to darken and I could almost see Nancy and Mary beginning to take shape again inside their clothes, only it was not a pleasant notion, as by now they themselves would be in much the same dilapidated state. I felt quite faint, and had to sit down and ask for a glass of water, and for the window to be opened.

Janet herself was taken aback; she was too young to have realized what the effects of twenty-nine years shut up in a box might be, although she made the best of it according to her nature. She said that in any case the dresses were now sadly out of fashion and we could not have me going to my new life looking like a scarecrow, but that some of the things could yet be used, such as the red flannel petticoat and some of the white ones, which could be washed in vinegar to get rid of the smell of mildew and then bleached in the sun, and they would come out white as anything. This was not quite the case, as once we had done it they were indeed lighter in colour but not what you would call white.

As for the other things, she said, we would have to look about us. I would need a wardrobe, she said. I do not know how it was done – I suspect she begged a dress from her mother and went around among her acquaintance and collected up some other things, and I do believe the Governor contributed the money for the stockings and shoes – but at the end she'd gathered together a store of garments. I found the colours over bright, such as a green print, and a broadcloth with stripes in a magenta tone on a sky blue; it was the new chemical dyes that are now in use. These colours didn't exactly suit me; but beggars can't be choosers, as I've learnt on many occasions.

The two of us sat together and made the dresses over to fit. We were like a mother and daughter working on a trousseau, very friendly and cosy, and after a time I was quite cheered up. My only regret was the crinolines; they'd gone out of fashion and now it was all wire bustles and big bunches of cloth pulled to the back, with ruchings and fringes, more like a sofa to my mind; and so I never would have the chance to wear a crinoline. But we cannot have everything in this life.

Bonnets were gone, too. Now it was all hats, tied under the chin and quite flat and tilted forward, like a ship sailing on top of your head, with veils floating out behind them like the wake. Janet obtained one for me and I did feel queer the first time I put it on and looked in the mirror. It did not cover my streaks of grey hair, although Janet said I looked ten years younger than I really was, almost a girl in fact; and it's true that I'd kept my figure and most of my teeth. She said I looked a real lady, which is possible, as there is less difference in dress between maid and mistress now than there used to be, and the fashions are easily copied. We had a merry-enough time trimming the hat with silk flowers and bows, although several times I broke down in tears because I was overwrought. A change in fortune often has that effect, from bad to good as well as the other way around, as I am sure you have noticed in life, Sir.

As we were packing and folding, I snipped some pieces out of the various dresses I'd worn long ago, but which were now to be discarded; and I asked if I might have a prison nightdress of the sort I was accustomed to sleep in, as a keepsake. Janet said she thought it a strange keepsake, but she made the request for me and it was granted. I needed something of my own to take away with me, you see.

When all was ready I thanked Janet with deep gratitude. I was still fearful of what was to come, but at least I would look like an ordinary person and no one would stare, and that is worth a great deal. Janet gave me a pair of summer gloves, almost new, I don't know where she got them. And then she began to cry, and when I asked her why she was doing that, she said it was because I was to have a happy ending, and it was just like a book; and I wondered what books she'd been reading.

5 2 .

August the 7th of 1872 was the day of my departure, and I will never forget it as long as I live.

After breakfast with the Warden's family, at which I could scarcely eat anything I was so nervous, I put on the dress I was to travel in, the green one, with the straw hat trimmed to match and the gloves Janet had given me. My box was packed; it was not Nancy's box, as that one smelled too much of mildew, but another one provided by the Penitentiary, leather and not much worn. It probably belonged to some poor soul who had died there, but I was long past looking a gift horse in the mouth.

I was taken in to see the Warden, it was a formality and he did not have much to say except that he congratulated me upon my release; in any case he and Janet were to accompany me to the home provided, at the special request of Sir John Macdonald himself, as it was intended I should get there safely and they knew perfectly well I wasn't accustomed to modern modes of travel, having been so long shut away; and also there were many rough men about, discharged soldiers from the Civil War, some crippled and others with no means of support, and I might be in some danger from them. So I was very glad for the company.

I passed through the gates of the Penitentiary for the last time as the clock struck noon, and it went through my head like a thousand bells. Until that instant I couldn't quite trust my senses; while dressing for the journey I'd felt more numb than anything, and the objects around me appeared flat and lacking in colour, but now all sprang to life. The sun was shining and every stone of the wall seemed as clear as glass and lighted up like a lamp, it was like passing through the gates of Hell and into Paradise, I do believe the two are located closer together than most people think.

Outside the gates was a chestnut tree, and each leaf of it seemed rimmed by fire; and sitting in the tree there were three white pigeons, which shone like the angels of Pentecost, and at that moment I knew that I had truly been set free. At such times of more than ordinary brightness or darkness I used to faint, but on this day I asked Janet for her smelling salts and so remained upright, although leaning on her arm; and she said it would not have been in nature for me to have remained unmoved, on such a momentous occasion.

I wished to turn and look back, but I remembered Lot's wife and the pillar of salt, and refrained from doing so. To look back would also have meant that I regretted my departure and had a wish to return, and this was certainly not the case, as you may imagine, Sir; but you will be surprised to hear me say that I did indeed have a sort of regret. For although the Penitentiary was not exactly a homey place, yet it was the only home I'd known for almost thirty years; and that is a long time, longer than many people spend on this earth, and although it was forbidding and a place of sorrow and punishment, at least I knew its ways. To go from a familiar thing, however undesirable, into the unknown, is always a matter for apprehension, and I suppose that is why so many people are afraid to die.

After this moment I was back again in ordinary daylight, although light-headed. It was a hot and humid day, such as the climate beside the Lakes produces in August, but as there was a breeze coming off the water, the weather was not too oppressive; there were some clouds, but only the white kind that do not foretell rain or thunder. Janet had a parasol, which she held over both of us as we proceeded. A parasol was one item I lacked, as the silk of Nancy's pink one had all rotted away.

We went to the railway station in a light carriage driven by the Warden's servant. The train was not due to leave until one-thirty but I was anxious about being late, and once there could not sit quietly in the Ladies' Waiting Room but had to walk up and down the platform outside, as I was very agitated. Finally the train drew in, a large shining iron monster puffing smoke. I'd never seen a train so close up, and although Janet assured me it was not dangerous, I had to be assisted up the steps.

We took the train as far as Cornwall, but though it was a short enough journey I felt I should never survive it. The noise was so loud and the motion so rapid I thought I would go deaf, and there was a great deal of black smoke; and the blowing of the train whistle startled me nearly out of my wits, although I took hold of myself and did not scream.

I felt better when we descended at the Cornwall station and went from there to the docks in a pony trap, and took a ferry across the end of the Lake, as that form of travel was more familiar to me and I could get some fresh air. The motion of the sunlight on the waves was at first bewildering to me, but this effect ceased when I stopped looking at it. Refreshment was offered, which the Warden had brought with him in a basket, and I managed to eat a little cold chicken and drink some lukewarm tea. I occupied my mind with looking at the costumes of the ladies on board, which were varied and brightly coloured. Sitting down and standing up I had some trouble managing my bustle, as a thing like that takes practice, and I am afraid I wasn't overly graceful, it was like having another bum tied on top of your real one and the two of them following you around like a tin bucket tied to a pig, although of course I did not say anything so coarse to Janet.

On the other side of the Lake we passed through the Customs House of the United States, and the Warden said we had nothing to declare. Then we took another train, and I was glad the Warden had come, as otherwise I would not have known what to do about the porters and luggage. While we were sitting on this new train, which rattled less than the previous one, I asked Janet about my final destination. We were going to Ithaca, New York – that much I'd been told – but what would happen to me after that? What was the home provided to be like, and was I to be a servant in it; and if so, what had the household there been told about me? I didn't wish to be placed in a false position, you see, Sir, or expected to conceal the truth about my past.

Janet said that there was a surprise awaiting me, and as it was a secret she could not tell me what it was; but it was a good surprise, or so she hoped it would be. She went so far as to tell me it concerned a man, a gentleman she said; but as she was in the habit of using this term of anything in trousers above the station of a waiter, I was not any the wiser.

When I said what gentleman, she said she couldn't tell; but he was an old friend of mine, or so she'd been given to understand. She became very coy, and I couldn't get another word out of her.

I thought back over all the men it might be. I hadn't known very many of these, not having had the chance you might say; and the two I'd perhaps known the best, although by no means the longest, were dead, by which I mean Mr. Kinnear and James McDermott. There was Jeremiah the peddler, but I did not think he would be in the business of providing good homes, as he had never seemed the domestic type. There were also my former employers, such as Mr. Coates and Mr. Haraghy, but surely by now all were either dead themselves or very elderly. The only other one I could think of, Sir, was you yourself. I must admit that the idea did cross my mind.

And so it was with anxiety but also expectation that I descended at last onto the station platform at Ithaca. There was a crush of people meeting the train, and all talking at once; and the hustling of the porters, and the many trunks and boxes being carried and wheeled about on carts, made it hazardous to stand there. I held on tightly to Janet while the Warden arranged about the luggage, and then he conducted us to the other side of the station building, the side away from the trains, where he began to look about him. He frowned at not finding what he expected, and glanced at his watch, and at the station clock; and then he consulted a letter which he took from his pocket, and my heart began to sink. But he looked up and smiled, and said, Here's our man, and there was indeed a man hurrying towards us.

He was above the average height and bulky, but lanky at the same time, by which I mean that his arms and legs were long but he had a more solid and rounder middle part to him. He had red hair and a large red beard, and was wearing a black suit of the Sunday-best kind that most men have now if they are at all comfortable in worldly goods, with a white shirt and a dark stock, and a tall hat which he was carrying in his hands, held in front of him like a shield, by which I could tell that he too was apprehensive. He wasn't a man I'd ever seen before in my life, but as soon as he came up to us he gave me a searching glance and then flopped onto his knees at my feet. He seized my hand, glove and all, and said, Grace, Grace, can you ever forgive me? Indeed he almost shouted it, as if he'd been practising it for some time.

I struggled to pull my hand away, thinking he was a madman, but when I turned to Janet for help she was in a flood of sentimental tears, and the Warden was beaming away as if he had hoped for nothing better; and I saw that I was the only one who was completely at sea.

The man let go of my hand and stood up. She doesn't know me, he said sadly. Grace, don't you know me? I would have known you anywhere.

And I looked at him, and there was indeed something a little familiar about him, but still I could not place it. And then he said, It's Jamie Walsh. And I saw that it was.

We then repaired to a new hotel close to the railway station, where the Warden had arranged accommodations, and partook together of some refreshments. As you may imagine, Sir, a good deal of explanation was then required, for the last time I'd seen Jamie Walsh was at my own trial for murder, when it was his testimony that turned the minds of judge and jury so much against me for the wearing of a dead woman's clothes.

Mr. Walsh – for so I will now call him – proceeded to tell me that he'd thought at that time I was guilty, although he hadn't wished to think so, as he'd always had a liking for me, which was true enough; but as he'd grown older and had considered the matter, he'd come to be of the opposite persuasion, and had been overcome with guilt for the part he'd played in my conviction; though he was only a young lad at the time, and no match for the lawyers, who'd led him into saying things he did not see the results of until afterwards. And I was consoling to him, and said it was the sort of thing that could happen to anyone.

After Mr. Kinnear's death, he and his father were forced to leave the property, as the new owners had no use for them; and he took a position in Toronto, which he obtained due to his having made such a good impression as a bright and up-and-coming lad, at the trial, which was what they wrote about him in the newspapers. So you might say he'd got his start in life on account of me. And he saved up his money for several years, and then went to the States, as he was of the opinion that there was more opportunity for becoming a self-made man down there – you were what you had, not what you'd come from, and few questions asked. He worked on the railroads and also out West, saving all the while, and now owned his own farm and two horses all complete. He took care to mention the horses early on, as he knew how fond I once was of Charley.

He had married, but was now a widower, with no children; and he'd never ceased to be tormented by what had become of me through him, and had written several times to the Penitentiary to see how I was getting on; but he did not write direct to me, as he did not wish to upset me. And it was in this way that he heard of my Pardon, and arranged matters with the Warden.

The upshot was that he begged me to forgive him, which I did readily. I did not feel I could hold a grudge, and told him I would no doubt have been put in prison anyway, even if he hadn't mentioned Nancy's dresses. And when we had gone through all of that, he pressing my hand the whole time, he asked me to marry him. He said that although not a millionaire he could certainly offer me a good home, with all that might be required, as he had some money put by in the bank.

I made a show of hanging back, though the reality of it was that I did not have many other choices, and it would have been most ungrateful of me to have said no, as so much trouble had been taken. I said I did not want him to marry me out of mere duty and guiltiness, and he denied that such were his motives, and claimed that he'd always had very warm feelings towards me, and that I'd scarcely changed at all from the way I was as a young woman – I was still a fine looker, was how he put it. And I remembered the daisies in Mr. Kinnear's orchard with the stumps, and I knew he did think that.

The hardest thing for me was viewing him as a full-grown man, as I'd known him only as the gawky lad who'd played the flute the night before Nancy died, and was sitting on the fence the very first day I came to Mr. Kinnear's.

Finally I said yes. He had the ring all ready, in a box in his vest pocket, and he was so overcome with emotion that he dropped it twice onto the tablecloth before putting it on my finger; for which I had to remove my glove.

Matters for the wedding were arranged as quickly as possible, and we remained at the hotel meanwhile, with hot water brought to the room every morning, and Janet stayed with me as being more proper. All was paid by Mr. Walsh. And we had a simple ceremony with a Justice of the Peace, and I remembered Aunt Pauline saying so many years before that I would no doubt marry beneath me, and wondered what she would think now; and Janet stood bridesmaid, and cried.

Mr. Walsh's beard was very large and red, but I assured myself that it could be altered in time.

5 3 .

It is almost thirty years to the day, since when not yet sixteen years of age, I first went up the long driveway to Mr. Kinnear's. It was June then, as well. Now I am sitting on my own verandah in my own rocking chair; it is late afternoon, and the scene before me is so peaceful you would think it was a picture. The roses at the front of the house are in bloom – Lady Hamiltons they are and very fine, although subject to aphids. The best thing, they say, is to dust them with arsenic, but I do not like to have such a thing about the house.

The last of the peonies are flowering, a pink and white variety and very full of petals. I don't know the name, as I did not plant them; their scent reminds me of the soap that Mr. Kinnear used for shaving. The front of our house faces southwest and the sunlight is warm and golden, although I do not sit right in it, as it is bad for the complexion. On such days I think, This is like Heaven. Although Heaven was not a place I ever used to think of myself as going.

I have been married to Mr. Walsh for almost a year now, and although it is not what most girls imagine when young, that is perhaps for the better, as at least the two of us know what sort of a bargain we have got into. When people marry young they often change as they grow older, but as the two of us have already grown older there will not be as much disappointment in store. An older man has a character already formed and is not as likely to take to drink or other vices, because if he was going to do such a thing he would have done it by now; or that is my opinion, and I hope that time will prove me right. I have prevailed on Mr. Walsh to trim his beard somewhat and to indulge his pipe smoking only out of doors, and in time perhaps both of these things, the beard and the pipe too, will disappear altogether, but it's never a good idea to nag and push a man, as it only makes them the more obstinate. Mr. Walsh does not chew tobacco and spit, as some do, and as always I am thankful for small mercies.

Our house is an ordinary farmhouse, white in colour, and with shutters painted green, but commodious enough for us. It has a front hall with a row of hooks for the coats in winter, although mostly we use the kitchen door, and a staircase with a plain bannister. At the head of the stairs is a cedar chest for the storage of quilts and blankets. There are four upstairs rooms – a little one intended for a nursery, then the main bedchamber and another in case of guests, although we neither expect nor wish for any; and a fourth, which is empty at present. The two furnished bedchambers each have a washstand, and each has an oval braided rug, as I don't want heavy carpets; they are too difficult to drag down the stairs and beat in spring, which would be worse as I get older.

There is a cross-stitch picture over each bed which I did myself, flowers in a vase in the best room and fruit in a bowl in ours. The quilt in the best room is a Wheel of Mystery, the one in ours a Log Cabin; I bought them at a sale, from people who'd failed and were moving West; but I felt sorry for the woman, and so paid more than I should. There have been a great many things to be seen to, in order to make everything cosy, since Mr. Walsh had developed bachelor's habits after the death of his first wife, and some things had become none too savoury. I had a large array of cobwebs and hanks of slut's wool to sweep out from under the beds, and also a fair deal of scrubbing and scouring to do.

The summer curtains in both bedchambers are white. I like a white curtain myself.

Downstairs we have a front parlour with a stove, and a kitchen with pantry and scullery all complete, and the pump inside the house, which is a great advantage in winter. There is a dining room, but we don't have that sort of company very often. For the most part we eat at the kitchen table; we have two kerosene lamps, and it is very snug there. I use the dining-room table for sewing, which is especially handy when cutting out the patterns. I have a Sewing Machine now, which is worked by a handwheel and is just like magic, and I am certainly glad to have it as it saves a great deal of labour, especially for the plain sewing such as the making of curtains and the hemming of sheets. I still prefer to do the finer sewing by hand, although my eyes are not what they used to be.

In addition to what I have described, we have the usual – a kitchen garden, with herbs and cabbages and root vegetables, and peas in the spring; and hens and ducks, cow and barn, and a buggy and two horses, Charley and Nell, who are a great pleasure to me, and good company when Mr. Walsh is not here; but Charley is worked too hard, as he is the plough horse. They say there are machines coming in soon that will do all of that sort of work and if so, then poor Charley can be turned out to pasture. I would never let him be sold for glue and dog meat, as is the habit of some.

There is a hired man who helps on the farm, but he doesn't live on the premises. Mr. Walsh wanted to employ a girl as well, but I said I would prefer to do the work of the house myself. I wouldn't want to have a servant living in, as they pry too much, and listen at doors; and also it's much easier for me to do a task right myself the first time, than to have someone else do it wrong and then do it over.

Our cat is named Tabby; she is the colour you might expect and a good mouser, and our dog is named Rex, he is a setter and not bright, although well-meaning, and the most beautiful shade of reddish brown, like a polished chestnut. These are not very original names, but we don't wish to get a reputation in the neighbourhood for being too original. We attend the local Methodist church, and the preacher is a lively one and fond of a little Hell Fire on Sundays; however I do not think he has any notion of what Hell is really like, no more than the congregation; they are worthy souls, though narrow. But we have thought it best not to reveal too much of the past, to them or anyone, as it would only lead to curiosity and gossip, and thence to false rumours. We've given out that Mr. Walsh was my childhood sweetheart, and that I married another, but was lately widowed; and that since Mr. Walsh's wife died, we arranged to meet again, and to marry. That is a story easily accepted, and it has the advantage of being romantic, and of causing pain to no one.

Our little church is very local and old-fashioned; but in Ithaca itself they are more up to date, and have a good number of Spiritualists there, with celebrated mediums coming through and staying at the best homes. I don't go in for any of that, as you never know what might come out of it; and if I wish to commune with the dead I can do it well enough on my own; and besides, I fear there is a great deal of cheating and deception.

In April I saw one of the celebrated mediums advertised, a man, with a picture of him; and though the picture was printed very dark, I thought, That must be Jeremiah the peddler; and indeed it was, as Mr. Walsh and I had occasion to drive into town for some errands and shopping, and I passed him on the street. He was more elegantly dressed than ever, with his hair black again and his beard trimmed in the military fashion, which must inspire confidence, and his name is

Mr. Gerald Bridges now. He was doing a very good imitation of a man who is distinguished and at home in the world, but with his mind on the higher truth; and he saw me too, and recognized me, and gave a respectful tip of the hat, but very slight, so it wouldn't be remarked; and also a wink; and I waved my hand at him, just a little, in its glove, as I always wear gloves to town. Fortunately Mr. Walsh did not notice either of these things, as it would have alarmed him.

I would not wish any here to learn my true name; but I know my secrets are safe with Jeremiah, as his are safe with me. And I remembered the time I might have run away with him, and become a gypsy or a medical clairvoyant, as I was certainly tempted to do; and in that case my fate would have been very different. But only God knows whether it would have been better or worse; and I have now done all the running away I have time for in this life.

On the whole, Mr. Walsh and I agree, and things go on very well with us. But there is something that has troubled me, Sir; and as I have no close woman friend I can trust, I am telling you about it, and I know you will keep the confidence.

It is this. Every once in a while Mr. Walsh becomes very sad; he takes hold of my hand and gazes at me with the tears in his eyes, and he says, To think of the sufferings I have caused you.

I tell him he did not cause me any sufferings – it was others that caused them, and also having plain bad luck and bad judgment – but he likes to think it was him that was the author of all, and I believe he would claim the death of my poor mother too, if he could think of a way to do it. He likes to picture the sufferings as well, and nothing will do but that I have to tell him some story or other about being in the Penitentiary, or else the Lunatic Asylum in Toronto. The more watery I make the soup and the more rancid the cheese, and the worse I make the coarse talk and proddings of the keepers, the better he likes it. He listens to all of that like a child listening to a fairy tale, as if it is something wonderful, and then he begs me to tell him yet more. If I put in the chilblains and the shivering at night under the thin blanket, and the whipping if you complained, he is in raptures; and if I add the improper behaviour of Dr. Bannerling towards me, and the cold baths naked and wrapped in a sheet, and the strait-waistcoat in the darkened room, he is almost in ecstasies; but his favourite part of the story is when poor James McDermott was hauling me all around the house at Mr. Kinnear's, looking for a bed fit for his wicked purposes, with Nancy and Mr. Kinnear lying dead in the cellar, and me almost out of my wits with terror; and he blames himself that he wasn't there to rescue me.

I myself would as soon forget about that portion of my life, rather than dwelling on it in such a mournful way. It's true that I liked the time when you were at the Penitentiary, Sir, as it did make a break in my days, which were mostly the same then. Now that I come to think of it, you were as eager as Mr. Walsh is to hear about my sufferings and my hardships in life; and not only that, but you would write them down as well. I could tell when your interest was slacking, as your gaze would wander; but it gave me joy every time I managed to come up with something that would interest you. Your cheeks would flush and you would smile like the sun on the parlour clock, and if you'd had ears like a dog they would have been pricked forward, with your eyes shining and your tongue hanging out, as if you'd found a grouse in a bush. It did make me feel I was of some use in this world, although I never quite saw what you were aiming at in all of it.

As for Mr. Walsh, after I have told him a few stories of torment and misery he clasps me in his arms and strokes my hair, and begins to unbutton my nightgown, as these scenes often take place at night; and he says, Will you ever forgive me?

At first this annoyed me very much, although I did not say so. The truth is that very few understand the truth about forgiveness. It is not the culprits who need to be forgiven; rather it is the victims, because they are the ones who cause all the trouble. If they were only less weak and careless, and more foresightful, and if they would keep from blundering into difficulties, think of all the sorrow in the world that would be spared.

I had a rage in my heart for many years, against Mary Whitney, and especially against Nancy Montgomery; against the two of them both, for letting themselves be done to death in the way that they did, and for leaving me behind with the full weight of it. For a long time I could not find it in me to pardon them. It would be much better if Mr. Walsh would forgive me, rather than being so stubborn about it and wanting to have it the wrong way around; but perhaps in time he will come to see things in a truer light.

When he first began this, I said I had nothing to forgive him for, and he shouldn't worry his head about it; but that wasn't the answer he wanted. He insists on being forgiven, he can't seem to go on comfortably without it, and who am I to refuse him such a simple thing?

So now every time this happens, I say I forgive him. I put my hands on his head as if in a book, and I turn my eyes up and look solemn, and then kiss him and cry a little; and then after I've forgiven him, he is back to his usual self the next day, playing on his flute as if he's a boy again and I am fifteen, and we are out in the orchard making daisy chains at Mr. Kinnear's.

But I don't feel quite right about it, forgiving him like that, because I am aware that in doing so I am telling a lie. Though I suppose it isn't the first lie I've told; but as Mary Whitney used to say, a little white lie such as the angels tell is a small price to pay for peace and quiet.

I think of Mary Whitney frequently these days, and of the time we threw the apple peelings over our shoulders; and it has all come true after a fashion. Just as she said, I married a man whose name begins with a J; and as she also said, I first had to cross over water three times, since it was twice on the ferry to Lewiston, going and coming back, and then once again on the way here.

Sometimes I dream that I am again in my small bedchamber at Mr. Kinnear's, before all the horror and tragedy; and I feel so safe there, not knowing what is to come. And sometimes I dream that I am still in the Penitentiary; and that I will wake to find myself once more locked in my cell, shivering on the straw mattress on a cold winter morning, with the keepers laughing outside in the yard.

But I am really here, in my own house, in my own chair, sitting on the verandah. I open and shut my eyes and pinch myself, but it remains true.

Now here is another thing I have told no one.

I'd just had my forty-fifth birthday when I was let out of the Penitentiary, and in less than a month I will be forty-six, and I'd thought I was well past the time for child-bearing. But unless I am much mistaken, I am now three months gone; either that or it is the change of life. It is hard to believe, but there has been one miracle in my life already, so why should I be surprised if there is another one? Such things are told of in the Bible; and perhaps God has taken it into his mind to make up a little for all I was put through at a younger age. But then it might as easily be a tumour, such as killed my poor mother at last; for although there is a heaviness, I've had no sickness in the mornings. It is strange to know you carry within yourself either a life or a death, but not to know which one. Though all could be resolved by consulting a doctor, I am most reluctant to take such a step; so I suppose time alone must tell.

While I am sitting out on the verandah in the afternoons, I sew away at the quilt I am making. Although I've made many quilts in my day, this is the first one I have ever done for myself. It is a Tree of Paradise; but I am changing the pattern a little to suit my own ideas.

I've thought a good deal about you and your apple, Sir, and the riddle you once made, the very first time that we met. I didn't understand you then, but it must have been that you were trying to teach me something, and perhaps by now I have guessed it. The way I understand things, the Bible may have been thought out by God, but it was written down by men. And like everything men write down, such as the newspapers, they got the main story right but some of the details wrong.

The pattern of this quilt is called the Tree of Paradise, and whoever named that pattern said better than she knew, as the Bible does not say Tree. It says there were two different trees, the Tree of Life and the Tree of Knowledge; but I believe there was only the one, and that the Fruit of Life and the Fruit of Good and Evil were the same. And if you ate of it you would die, but if you didn't eat of it you would die also; although if you did eat of it, you would be less bone-ignorant by the time you got around to your death.

Such an arrangement would appear to be more the way life is.

I am telling this to no one but you, as I am aware it is not the approved reading.

On my Tree of Paradise, I intend to put a border of snakes entwined; they will look like vines or just a cable pattern to others, as I will make the eyes very small, but they will be snakes to me; as without a snake or two, the main part of the story would be missing. Some who use this pattern make several trees, four or more in a square or circle, but I am making just one large tree, on a background of white. The Tree itself is of triangles, in two colours, dark for the leaves and a lighter colour for the fruits; I am using purple for the leaves and red for the fruits. They have many bright colours now, with the chemical dyes that have come in, and I think it will turn out very pretty.

But three of the triangles in my Tree will be different. One will be white, from the petticoat I still have that was Mary Whitney's; one will be faded yellowish, from the prison nightdress I begged as a keepsake when I left there. And the third will be a pale cotton, a pink and white floral, cut from the dress of Nancy's that she had on the first day I was at Mr. Kinnear's, and that I wore on the ferry to Lewiston, when I was running away.

I will embroider around each one of them with red feather-stitching, to blend them in as a part of the pattern.

And so we will all be together.

Alias Grace is a work of fiction, although it is based on reality. Its central figure, Grace Marks, was one of the most notorious Canadian women of the 1840s, having been convicted of murder at the age of sixteen.

The Kinnear-Montgomery murders took place on July 23, 1843, and were extensively reported not only in Canadian newspapers but in those of the United States and Britain. The details were sensational: Grace Marks was uncommonly pretty and also extremely young; Kinnear's housekeeper, Nancy Montgomery, had previously given birth to an illegitimate child and was Thomas Kinnear's mistress; at her autopsy she was found to be pregnant. Grace and her fellow-servant James McDermott had run away to the United States together and were assumed by the press to be lovers. The combination of sex, violence, and the deplorable insubordination of the lower classes was most attractive to the journalists of the day.

The trial was held in early November. Only the Kinnear murder was tried: since both of the accused were condemned to death, a trial for the Montgomery murder was considered unnecessary. McDermott was hanged in front of a huge crowd on November 21; but opinion about Grace was divided from the start, and due to the efforts of her lawyer, Kenneth MacKenzie, and a group of respectable gentleman petitioners – who pleaded her youth, the weakness of her sex, and her supposed witlessness – her sentence was commuted to life, and she entered the Provincial Penitentiary in Kingston on November 19, 1843.

She continued to be written about over the course of the century, and she continued to polarize opinion. Attitudes towards her reflected contemporary ambiguity about the nature of women: was Grace a female fiend and temptress, the instigator of the crime and the real murderer of Nancy Montgomery, or was she an unwilling victim, forced to keep silent by McDermott's threats and by fear for her own life? It was no help that she herself gave three different versions of the Montgomery murder, while James McDermott gave two.

I first encountered the story of Grace Marks through Susanna Moodie's *Life in the Clearings* (1853). Moodie was already known as the author of *Roughing It in the Bush*, a discouraging account of pioneering life in what was then Upper Canada and is now Ontario. Its sequel, *Life in the Clearings*, was intended to show the more civilized side of "Canada West," as it had by then become, and included admiring descriptions of both the Provincial Penitentiary in Kingston and the Lunatic Asylum in Toronto. Such public institutions were visited like zoos, and, at both, Moodie asked to see the star attraction, Grace Marks.

Moodie's retelling of the murder is a third-hand account. In it she identifies Grace as the prime mover, driven by love for Thomas Kinnear and jealousy of Nancy, and using the promise of sexual favours to egg McDermott on. McDermott is portrayed as besotted by her and easily manipulated. Moodie can't resist the potential for literary melodrama, and the cutting of Nancy's body into four quarters is not only pure invention but pure Harrison Ainsworth. The influence of Dickens' *Oliver Twist* – a favourite of Moodie's – is evident in the tale of the bloodshot eyes that were said to be haunting Grace Marks.

Shortly after she saw Grace in the penitentiary, Susanna Moodie encountered her in the Lunatic Asylum in Toronto, where she was confined on the violent ward. Moodie's first-hand observations are generally trustworthy, so if she reports a shrieking, capering Grace, that is no doubt what she saw. However, soon after the publication of Moodie's book – and just after the appointment of the humane Joseph Workman as Medical Superintendent of the asylum – Grace was considered sane enough to be returned to the penitentiary; where, records show, she was suspected of having become pregnant during her absence. This was a false alarm, but who at the asylum could have been the supposed perpetrator? The wards of the asylum were segregated; the men with the easiest access to the female patients were the doctors.

Over the next two decades, Grace turns up in the penitentiary records from time to time. She was certainly literate, as the warden's journal depicts her as writing letters. She so impressed a good many respectable persons – clergymen among them – that they worked tirelessly on her behalf and submitted many petitions aimed at securing her release, seeking medical opinion to bolster their case. Two writers state that she was a trusted servant for many years in the home of the "Governor" – probably the governor of the penitentiary – although the admittedly incomplete prison records do not mention this. However, it was the custom of the time in North America to hire out prisoners for day-labour.

In 1872, Grace Marks was finally granted a pardon; records show that she went to New York State, accompanied by the warden and his daughter, to a "home provided." Later writers claim that she married there, although no proof for this exists; and, after this date, all trace of her vanishes. Whether she was indeed the co-murderer of Nancy Montgomery and the lover of James McDermott is far from clear; nor whether she was ever genuinely "insane," or only acting that way

– as many did – to secure better conditions for herself. The true character of the historical Grace Marks remains an enigma.

Thomas Kinnear appears to have come from a lowland Scots family from Kinloch, near Cupar, in Fife, and to have been the younger half-brother of the heir to the estate; although, strangely, a late-nineteenth-century edition of *Burke's Peerage* lists him as having died about the same time as he turned up in Canada West. The Kinnear house in Richmond Hill remained standing until late in the century and was a point of interest for sightseers. Simon Jordan's visit to it is based on an account by one of them. The graves of Thomas Kinnear and Nancy Montgomery are in the Presbyterian churchyard in Richmond Hill, although unmarked. William Harrison, writing in 1908, reports that the wooden pickets around them were taken down, at a time when all wooden markers were removed. Nancy's rose bush has similarly disappeared.

Some further notes: Details of prison and asylum life are drawn from available records. Most of the words in Dr. Workman's letter are his own. "Dr. Bannerling" expresses opinions that were attributed to Dr. Workman after his death, but which could not possibly have been his.

The design of the Parkinson residence has a great deal in common with that of Dundurn Castle, in Hamilton, Ontario. Lot Street in Toronto was formerly the name of a portion of Queen Street. The economic history of Loomisville, and its treatment of mill girls, loosely echoes that of Lowell, Massachusetts. The fate of Mary Whitney has a parallel in the medical records of Dr. Langstaff of Richmond Hill. The portraits of Grace Marks and James McDermott on page ten are from their Confessions, published by the Toronto *Star and Transcript*.

The Spiritualist craze in North America began in Upper New York State at the end of the 1840s with the "rappings" of the Fox sisters, who were originally from Belleville – where Susanna Moodie was by then resident, and where she became a convert to Spiritualism. Although it soon attracted a number of charlatans, the movement spread rapidly and was at its height in the late 1850s, being especially strong in upstate New York and in the Kingston-Belleville area. Spiritualism was the one quasi-religious activity of the times in which women were allowed a position of power – albeit a dubious one, as they themselves were assumed to be mere conduits of the spirit will.

Mesmerism was discredited as a reputable scientific procedure early in the century, but was widely practised by questionable showmen in the 1840s. As James Braid's "Neuro-hypnotism," which did away with the idea of a "magnetic fluid," mesmerism began a return to respectability, and by the 1850s had gained some following among European doctors, although not yet the wide acceptance as a psychiatric technique that it was to achieve in the last decades of the century.

The rapid generation of new theories of mental illness was a characteristic of the mid-nineteenth century, as was the creation of clinics and asylums, both public and private. There was intense curiosity and excitement about phenomena such as memory and amnesia, somnambulism, "hysteria," trance states, "nervous diseases," and the import of dreams, among scientists and writers alike. The medical interest in dreams was so widespread that even a country doctor such as Dr. James Langstaff was recording the dreams of his patients. "Dissociation of personality," or *dédoublement*, was described early in the century; it was being seriously debated in the 1840s, although it achieved a much greater vogue in the last three decades of the century. I have attempted to ground Dr. Simon Jordan's speculations in contemporary ideas that would have been available to him.

I have of course fictionalized historical events (as did many commentators on this case who claimed to be writing history). I have not

changed any known facts, although the written accounts are so contradictory that few facts emerge as unequivocally "known." Was
Grace milking the cow or gathering chives when Nancy was hit with
the axe? Why was Kinnear's corpse wearing McDermott's shirt, and
where did McDermott get that shirt – from a peddler, or from an
army friend? How did the blood-covered book or magazine get into
Nancy's bed? Which of several possible Kenneth MacKenzies was
the lawyer in question? When in doubt, I have tried to choose the
most likely possibility, while accommodating all possibilities wherever feasible. Where mere hints and outright gaps exist in the
records, I have felt free to invent.

ACKNOWLEDGMENTS

I would very much like to thank the following archivists and librarians, who helped to find some of the missing pieces, and without whose professional expertise this novel would not have been possible:

Dave St. Onge, Curator and Archivist, Correctional Service of Canada Museum, Kingston, Ontario; Mary Lloyd, Local History and Genealogy Librarian, Richmond Hill Public Library, Richmond Hill, Ontario; Karen Bergsteinsson, Reference Archivist, Archives of Ontario, Toronto; Heather J. Macmillan, Archivist, Government Archives Division, National Archives of Canada, Ottawa; Betty Jo Moore, Archivist, Archives on the History of Canadian Psychiatry and Mental Heath Services, Queen Street Mental Health Centre, Toronto; Ann-Marie Langlois and Gabrielle Earnshaw, Archivists, Law Society of Upper Canada Archives, Osgoode Hall, Toronto; Karen Teeple, Senior Archivist, and Glenda Williams, Reception, City of Toronto Archives; Ken Wilson, of the United Church Archives, Victoria University, Toronto; and Neil Semple, who is writing a history of Methodism in Canada.

I would also like to thank Aileen Christianson, of the University of Edinburgh, Scotland, and Ali Lumsden, who helped to track down Thomas Kinnear's origins.

In addition to materials in the archives cited above, I consulted the newspapers of the time, most especially the *Star and Transcript* (Toronto), the *Chronicle and Gazette* (Kingston), *The Caledonian Mercury* (Edinburgh, Scotland), *The Times* (London, England), the *British Colonist* (Toronto), *The Examiner* (Toronto), the *Toronto Mirror*, and *The Rochester Democrat*.

I found many books helpful, but most especially: Susanna Moodie, *Life in the Clearings* (1853, reprinted by Macmillan, 1959); and *Letters of a Lifetime*, edited by Ballstadt, Hopkins, and Peterman, University of Toronto Press, 1985; Chapter IV, Anonymous, in *History of Toronto and County of York, Ontario*, Volume 1, Toronto: C. Blackett Robinson, 1885; *Beeton's Book of Household Management*, 1859-61, reprinted by Chancellor Press in 1994; Jacalyn Duffin, *Langstaff: A Nineteenth-Century Medical Life*, University of Toronto Press, 1993; Ruth McKendry, *Quilts and Other Bed Coverings in the Canadian Tradition*, Key Porter Books, 1979; Mary Conway, *300 Years of Canadian Quilts*, Griffin House, 1976; Marilyn L. Walker, *Ontario's Heritage Quilts*, Stoddart, 1992; Osborne and Swainson, *Kingston: Building on the Past*, Butternut Press, 1988; K. B. Brett, *Women's Costume in Early Ontario*, Royal Ontario Museum/University of Toronto, 1966; *Essays in the History of Canadian Medicine*, edited by Mitchinson and McGinnis, McClelland & Stewart, 1988; Jeanne Minhinnick, *At Home in Upper Canada*, Clarke, Irwin, 1970; Marion Macrae and Anthony Adamson, *The Ancestral Roof*, Clarke, Irwin, 1963; *The City and the Asylum*, Museum of Mental Health Services, Toronto, 1993; Henri F. Ellenberger, *The Discovery of the Unconscious*, Harper Collins, 1970; Ian Hacking, *Rewriting the Soul*, Princeton University Press, 1995; Adam Crabtree, *From Mesmer to Freud: Magnetic Sleep and the Roots of Psychological Healing*, Yale University Press, 1993; and Ruth Brandon, *The Passion for the Occult in the Nineteenth and Twentieth Centuries*, Knopf, 1983.

The story of the Kinnear murders has been fictionalized twice before: as *A Master Killing*, by Ronald Hambleton (1978), which concerns itself mainly with the pursuit of the suspects; and by Margaret Atwood, in the CBC television play *The Servant Girl* (1974, directed by George Jonas), which relied exclusively on the Moodie version and cannot now be taken as definitive.

Finally, I would like to thank my chief researcher, Ruth Atwood, and Erica Heron, who copied the quilt patterns; my invaluable assistant, Sarah Cooper; Ramsay Cook, Eleanor Cook, and Rosalie Abella, who read the manuscript and made valuable suggestions; my agents, Phoebe Larmore and Vivienne Schuster, and my editors, Ellen Seligman, Nan A. Talese, and Liz Calder; Marly Rusoff, Becky Shaw, Jeanette Kong, Tania Charzewski, and Heather Sangster; Jay Macpherson and Jerome H. Buckley, who taught me an appreciation of nineteenth-century literature; Michael Bradley, Alison Parker, Arthur Gelgoot, Gene Goldberg, and Bob Clark; Dr. George Poulakakis, John and Christiane O'Keeffe, Joseph Wetmore, Black Creek Pioneer Village, and Annex Books; and Rose Tornato.

Margaret Atwood is the author of more than fifty books of fiction, poetry, and critical essays. Her latest book of short stories is *Stone Mattress: Nine Tales* (2014). Her most recent novel, *The Heart Goes Last*, was published in September 2015. Other recent works include the *MaddAddam* trilogy — the Giller and Booker prize–nominated *Oryx and Crake* (2003), *The Year of the Flood* (2009), and *MaddAddam* (2013). *The Door* is her latest volume of poetry (2007). Her most recent non-fiction books are *Payback: Debt and the Shadow Side of Wealth* (2008) and *In Other Worlds: SF and the Human Imagination* (2011). Her novels include *The Blind Assassin*, winner of the Booker Prize; *The Robber Bride*; *Cat's Eye*; *The Handmaid's Tale*—now a critically acclaimed television series—and *The Penelopiad*. In 2016, *Hag-Seed*, a novel visitation of Shakespeare's play *The Tempest*, and *Angel Catbird*—a graphic novel with co-creator Johnnie Christmas (Dark Horse)—were published. In 2017, Margaret was awarded with the Peace Prize, the Franz Kafka International Literary Prize, and the PEN Center USA Lifetime Achievement Award. Margaret Atwood lives in Toronto with writer Graeme Gibson.

www.margaretatwood.ca

NOW AVAILABLE